DATE			

TRIPLE CROSS

Brian Freemantle

THOMAS DUNNE BOOKS

ST. MARTIN'S PRESS

NEW YORK

THOMAS DUNNE BOOKS.
An imprint of St. Martin's Press.

TRIPLE CROSS. Copyright © 2004 by Brian Freemantle. All rights
reserved. Printed in the United States of America. No part of
this book may be used or reproduced in any manner whatsoever
without written permission except in the case of brief quotations
embodied in critical articles or reviews. For information, address
St. Martin's Press, 175 Fifth Avenue, New York, N.Y. 10010.

www.stmartins.com

Library of Congress Cataloging-in-Publication Data

Freemantle, Brian.
    Triple cross / Brian Freemantle.—1st ed.
        p. cm.
    ISBN 0-312-31551-1
    1. Cowley, William (Fictitious character)—Fiction. 2.
Danilov, Dimitri (Fictitious character)—Fiction. 3. Americans—Russia (Federation)—Fiction. 4. International cooperation—Fiction. 5. Government investigators—Fiction. 6.
Washington, (D.C.)—Fiction. 7. Moscow (Russia)—Fiction.
8. Organized crime—Fiction. 9. Rome (Italy)—Fiction.
I. Title.

PR6056.R43T75 2004
823'.914—dc22

                                                            2003065244

First Edition: March 2004

10 9 8 7 6 5 4 3 2 1

For Emma, whose turn it is this time. With love.

Detection is, or ought to be, an exact science, and should be treated in the same cold and unemotional manner. You have attempted to tinge it with romanticism, which produces much the same effect as if you worked a love story or an elopement into the fifth proposition of Euclid.

The Sign of Four
Sir Arthur Conan Doyle

TRIPLE CROSS

1

Each timber balk was fashioned into a perfect X, spread-eagling the man lashed to it at the wrist and ankle. Sacrificial nails had additionally been driven through the men's hands, and they were gagged by leather strips. Each was naked. As the frame of the next man was dragged from where the others were, he fouled himself. All their bladders had voided and two had vomited through the leather, smearing themselves. Everywhere stank.

Igor Gavrilovich Orlov stood patiently, oblivious to the smell, waiting for the new cross to be positioned in the stronger light in the center of the room, so that those to follow could see everything that was going to happen. He was wearing a long, chest-high butcher's apron, the green reinforced rubber red with gore. The already bloodstained boots, more red than green, were rubber, too, coming up beyond his knees. He was using a short-bladed knife razored on both edges but rounded where the pointed tip should have been, stained by the torture of the previous victim.

As Orlov approached, the trussed man threw himself violently left and right and tried to scream but couldn't. Orlov was careless cutting away the gag, gashing the man's face.

"No . . . please no . . . anything . . . no . . ." The voice was a scream, hysterical.

"There's no one to hear you. Only us, in here," said Orlov. His voice was quiet, conversational, his long angular face expressionless. "So let's talk."

"Anything . . . please . . ."

"Who actually did it?"

The man jerked his head sideways to the first victim, still strapped to the crossed spars. He had been emasculated and was eyeless. There were no ears and his teeth had been extracted, as had his tongue. He was dead.

"Nikita Yaklovich . . . it was him!"

"He said it was you." Orlov moved before the other man could jerk away, slicing open his left cheek for the teeth to show.

The man screamed again and yelled "*No*! Lied . . . not true . . ."

One of the other men, still gagged, was sick through the mouth restraint.

Orlov said, "Georgi was only a child."

"Not me," moaned the man. "Please . . . believe me, on my mother's life . . . It was Nikita Yaklovich Volodkin. He did it."

"But you were there. Snatched him from school."

"No!"

The knife flashed again, taking off the tip of the nose. "Georgi was ten. Just ten."

The man was crying, breath choking from him. He could only shake his head.

"He was buggered before he was killed. Before everything else was done to him."

"Volodkin," wailed the man. "You know what he was. I wasn't part of it."

Orlov turned to the woman standing in the shadows of the warehouse. "Do you want me to go on doing it, Irena?" It was a hopeful question.

She came into the light, a slim, sharp-featured, beautiful woman. "Do you have another apron?"

Orlov nodded. "And boots. You need boots with all this shit about."

The victim's head began to loll and his eyes rolled, hysteria edging into insanity. Orlov ignored the collapse, holding out the protective apron to help the woman. He said, "Mothers don't often get such a chance for revenge."

She didn't reply.

Orlov said, "There are more knives. A surgical saw. And clamps." He turned to his people. "Move the table closer, so that she has a choice."

Irena said, "Yes, I want something better than what you're using." She chose one with a blade at least fifteen inches long, more a short sword.

"You sure you're OK?"

"Georgi was my son."

"It's your right to do this," said Orlov. "It has to be you."

It took two hours, because Irena wanted it to, wanted it longer, even, but they died too quickly. She broke down, once crying bitterly in gulping sobs, which Orlov let her do. The second time it happened he once more hopefully offered to take over. She repeated, unnecessarily, "Georgi was my son."

Irena sagged with exhaustion when she finished, needing Orlov's physical support to take off the protective apron, more blood-congealed than his. He said, "Just leave it. They'll get rid of it. That's what they're for."

From the shadows Feliks Zhikin said, "In the river, like the others?"

Orlov said, "Don't forget the identities. Everyone has to know. And properly clean up all this shit."

"You know I won't forget anything." Feliks Romanovich Zhikin was Orlov's cousin, and as a proper family relation one of the few men in whom Orlov had any trust, although that was still limited.

Divested of his protective clothing, Orlov guided the woman from the warehouse into the adjoining premises, which was more an apartment suite than a business area. There was no stain on the clothes of either of them. He said, "What do you want to drink?"

"Brandy, I think. Yes, brandy."

Despite what he had just done, there was no tremor of tiredness or betrayal of emotion in Orlov's hand as he poured. He was a tall man, well over six feet, and had to bend forward to serve the diminutive woman. "Feel good?"

"Not particularly, not about what I did to them."

"I don't believe you."

"They didn't hurt enough! They couldn't hurt enough."

"You did as much as you could. They hurt a lot."

"I thought I'd cried enough: couldn't cry any more."

"You'll always cry for a child. But at least there's satisfaction now. Why wasn't Ivan here?"

"Your brother, the dedicated doctor!" she sneered, contemptuously. It was difficult for her to understand how she could have married someone she despised as much as she now despised Ivan. It was a mistake Irena was determined to rectify with Igor.

They were silent. They sipped their brandy. Orlov added, unresisted by the woman, to both their glasses. He said, "Give him my regards."

Irena said, "I want to fuck. Now."

Irena was a demanding woman, as spurred by the aphrodisiac of violence as he was. They came together, still half clothed on the couch upon which he had been sitting, and she screamed as she climaxed. She only had to put on her pants afterward, he to zip his fly.

"It was you Volodkin was after—wanted to hurt—wasn't it?" she accused, abruptly strident. "You he was trying to get at, through a ten-year-old boy!"

"And now Nikita Yaklovich Volodkin is dead. As well as everyone else who was with him when he did what he did. No one in our immediate family will ever be a target again, not after tonight."

"It doesn't bring Georgi back."

"I'll try to make up for it."

"Don't be a cunt!" There was no vehemence now, no emotion.

"I'm hungry," Orlov announced. "Do you want to come to dinner? Not our place. There's a new steakhouse. It would be a change."

"I'm too tired. I'll go home."

"To what?"

"My limp-dicked husband."

"Who couldn't punish the abusers and killers of his son."

"Or maybe he couldn't bring himself to confront you."

"He knew I had Volodkin. That there was a chance for vengeance."

She nodded. "And now he knows he is beholden, something he vowed never to be."

"I don't want anything from him, anymore than he does from me."

"Yet," she challenged, cynically. "He despises you so much—hates the resemblance even."

"There's nothing he can do about that."

"I despise you, too. I need you, but I despise you, like I despise myself."

"Go home, Irena. Go home to the man who wasn't brave enough to watch what happened to the men who did what they did to his son."

"I punished them, though," said the woman, as if reminding herself. "Now my tears are all gone."

————

General Dimitri Ivanovich Danilov, director of Moscow's Organized Crime Bureau, stopped just short of invoking the name of God, in whom he didn't believe, in expressing his disgust in front of his deputy, who was profoundly religious. Instead, he said, "The state of this lot is fucking unbelievable!"

The five crosses, rafted together, had snagged on some river debris on the island side of the Bol'soj Ustinkskij Bridge. They'd been dragged ashore and cut apart, to be laid out side by side.

Colonel Yuri Pavin, whose intelligence was equal to his towering stature, said, "It's impossible to imagine one human being doing this to another."

"Now you don't have to imagine anymore," said Danilov. The perpetual breeze from the Moskva ruffled the sparse blond hair, but he didn't bother to smooth it back. Danilov was a small, compact man of careful, considered movements. He was aware of the pathologist's quizzical examination and guessed the man was making the usual comparison between himself and his huge deputy.

Pavin said, "This brings the number up to eleven."

"All Mafia. All strapped—sacrificed—to crosses. All mutilated. All floated down the river," Danilov said.

"From four different brigades," Pavin added, using the Russian expression for an organized crime family. "We've got a turf war."

Danilov nodded toward the farthest body in the line laid out in front of them. "And this time we've got Nikita Yaklovich Volodkin, the brigadier himself."

"More mutilated—along with his lieutenants—than any previously," Pavin pointed out.

"You think that's important?" Danilov respected his deputy's instincts as much as he did the man's intelligence.

"I think it's a difference that should be flagged, until we understand it."

Danilov bent, flicking up a plastic envelope that had been taped to a victim's chest. "Why the easy identification?"

Pavin gestured, uncertainly. "Making it easy for us?"

Danilov shook his head. "Not for *us*. The other gangs they're trying to bring into line."

"Boss of bosses?" suggested Pavin.

"This fucking country is ruled by organized crime, not by the government," Danilov protested angrily. "A linkup—a carve-up—of the cake is a natural progression. I'm surprised it's taken so long."

To their left the medical examiner straightened from a corpse, although still bending sufficiently to read the taped identity. He called out. "This one, Nikita Volodkin, had his testicles and penis sewn into his mouth. He choked on them."

"What about the others?" Danilov called back.

The doctor straightened further, shrugging. "With this degree of mutilation, simple blood loss. Maybe with severe shock contributing."

"How long's it take to die from blood loss?" asked Pavin, as the man came nearer.

"Half an hour, forty minutes at the most," said the doctor. "It would have been most severe from the groin, where the genitalia were removed. There's an artery there, the femoral." He began stripping off his examination overalls. "They weren't in the water long— certainly less than twenty-four hours. Not enough time to wash the shit off the crosses or all the vomit from their bodies."

"What's the significance of that?" questioned Pavin.

"Could be they were made to watch what was being done to the one in front of them."

"Jesus!" said Danilov, momentarily forgetting his assistant.

Pavin didn't appear to notice. "What about fingerprints, from the plastic sheaths holding their IDs?"

The doctor gave another shrug. "Ask forensic. I'm a doctor. They'll need to be taken off the crosses before they can be transported to the mortuary for a proper post mortem."

"There might be something from those crosses," Pavin mused. "They're not just knocked together. They're well made, the work of a professional carpenter. Why go to all that trouble?"

"Another message we don't yet understand," suggested Danilov.

"There's a convoluted reasoning," said Pavin, answering his own earlier question. "Sacrificed as they are, they're reduced to total unimportance, just disposable totems—"

"To a superior being?" Danilov said.

Pavin shrugged. "What about the media?"

Danilov sniggered, humorlessly, gesturing toward the forensic examiners and the onlookers lining the river wall beyond them. "It's taking them a long time to get here. Surely there's a tipster or an informant among this lot."

"We stay with the line that it's a turf war?"

"That's what it is," said Danilov. He looked directly at Pavin. "Did we thoroughly check Volodkin for—"

"Yes. We couldn't find any connection between his brigade and Larissa's husband."

"Four different brigades," Danilov repeated hopefully. "We could get the breakthrough this time. There'll be a lot of stories on the streets."

"Let's hope we hear them," said Pavin, the only man who knew that every waking moment of Dimitri Ivanovich Danilov's life was motivated by the need to find the killer of his lover. A car bomb had killed her five years earlier.

"Let's use this war—and the media—if we can," urged Danilov. "Spread some panic among the brigades. Hear what the informers have to say."

"That won't be difficult," said Pavin, more objective than cynical. "Every brigade in Moscow has at least two well-paid sources in Ulitza Petrovka."

Dominating Ulitza Petrovka, the heavily corrupt Russian police building, was the Militia headquarters from which General Dimitri Danilov and Colonel Yuri Maksimovich Pavin led the supposed operation against organized crime in the Russian capital.

2

The windows of the Mercedes were darkened for anonymity, but the depth of the tint also cut the outside glare, and the air conditioning kept the inside pleasantly cool. Igor Gavrilovich Orlov was glad to be out of Moscow and even more glad to be out of Rome, but impatient with assurances that it shouldn't have been this hot until August, when everyone left for the coast. They were, in fact, driving along the Via del Mare toward Ostia, and Orlov wondered if the villa would be set beside the sea. It wouldn't be right to ask: any curiosity, no matter how inconsequential, might be construed as nervousness. Every impression had to be the one he intended. Orlov wasn't at all nervous, not as he knew the other two Russians traveling with him in the other car would be at not being armed. Vitali Mittel complained it was an unnecessary risk, and Fodor Lapinsh had argued it actually made them appear the supplicants, not unintimidated equals. Orlov acknowledged that, but was at the moment unsure how to rectify the impression.

"This is your first visit to Italy?" the Italian facing Orlov on the jump seat asked. The man was surprisingly young, studiously bespectacled, and intense. There had been no introductions in the hotel foyer. The man had approached them without hesitation, and Orlov concluded at once they had been under observation since their arrival, just as the Italians would be when they came to Moscow—if the negotiations were successful. That they were being constantly watched had been the immediate assumption of Mittel and Lapinsh, too, and increased their unease, because they hadn't spotted it and they were supposed to be Orlov's bodyguards, although increasingly—and too obviously—believing themselves to be in much more elevated roles.

"The first, perhaps, of many," said Orlov. They had found a conversational bridge with English, although the Italian had begun the encounter in excellent Russian. Orlov hoped Mittel and Lapinsh remembered his orders not to talk openly in Russian, misguidedly imagining they would not be understood. Having a Russian speaker in their car, too, would be an obvious precaution, as his would be to have an unsuspected Italian speaker at all times if Luigi Brigoli came to Moscow.

"I enjoyed Moscow when I studied there. But I preferred St. Petersburg. The Hermitage is magnificent."

Orlov had his hand through the support loop, looking out through the clouded glass, feeling himself—believing himself—totally in control. "Your history is older," he said. There were a few moments of silence. Orlov, acknowledging as a matter of fact that there would be listening devices in the car, wondered idly if the noise of the air conditioning would interfere with the reception.

The Italian said, "There are amazing archaeological remains in Ostia Antica itself, dating back to the fourth century before Christ. We could arrange a special tour for you."

Orlov finally understood the conversation and was disappointed at its obviousness. He said, "Stop the car!"

Silence again.

"I said stop the car!"

"I'm sorry . . . I do not understand . . ." the young man stumbled.

If he actually forced the car to halt, Mittel and Lapinsh would inevitably misunderstand and create a problem. "I am not here to admire history! I believed I had come to meet *il capo di tutti i capi*. I clearly haven't. Tell the driver to take us back to Rome! This is nonsense."

"There has been a misunderstanding . . . a bad one . . . my fault . . . I apologize most sincerely." The bespectacled man gabbled on. "Don Brigoli is most definitely *il capo di tutti i capi*, the boss of bosses. He is *the* man."

Which this unknown Italian secretary figure should not have volunteered to his mother, on her deathbed. A job-hunting former KGB officer had once, in a mistaken attempt at flattery, addressed Orlov as Don, until he had been made to stand with his trousers down while it was pointed out that in Russian slang the translation could mean that Orlov had a small penis, which physically he did, but which therefore he was murderously bent on preventing anyone suggesting. "He'll need to prove that to me now."

The Italian realized the entrapment. "My orders are to ensure your every comfort . . . liaise . . . because I speak—"

"Shut up!" Orlov commanded, in Russian this time. "I am not a sightseer interested in ancient history."

The car turned abruptly off the main highway, onto a country road, and from there almost at once onto an even smaller road that had originally been a macadamized blacktop but had long ago crumbled into disrepair. Despite its suspension the Mercedes bumped and lurched over potholes, throwing up a dust storm around them. Orlov acknowledged that their approach would be a warning from a long way off, from whatever or wherever they were approaching.

The young man said, "I'm sorry if I have offended—irritated—you." As if in explanation, which Orlov supposed it was, he added, "I speak Russian."

Orlov initially ignored him. In brief moments when there was less dust Orlov saw the track was lined with cypress and cork trees and that beyond there were the stunted shrubs of a vineyard and an olive grove. He hoped Mittel and Lapinsh weren't overreacting to the abrupt passage into a single-lane countryside. There wasn't, after all, going to be a view of the sea and an accompanying breeze. He still hoped there was air conditioning. Orlov said, "Become a translator."

The young man said, "Don Brigoli is my father."

Orlov said, "Even more reason to become a translator."

The car began to climb and the road became firmer, and men were visible in the fields and trees, although they clearly weren't farmworkers. They were mostly black suited, and twice Orlov saw, leaning against conveniently close trees, *lupera*, the wolf-hunting rifles of the traditional Mafia. Every head turned, unsmiling, at their progress. Orlov imagined Mittel and Lapinsh on the edge of their seats. The cypresses were tight together now, shading the avenue, and after an abrupt and final turn Orlov confronted the villa, at the very pinnacle of the hill. Orlov's perception was of an impregnable medieval castle atop a soldier-guarded escarpment, although the surrounding walls were not castellated. There must have been a signal from the driver—or perhaps from an observation point inside—because at their unslowed approach high metal gates swung inward.

The building was a square, predominantly two-story white building, but there were taller towers at its corners. The villa was sufficiently high to give a distant view of a sun-bejeweled sea. Orlov waited for the driver to open the door for him. The heat hit him like a blow, hotter than he expected, and Orlov felt the sweat at once prick out on his back and chest. There was no breeze whatsoever. From somewhere in the grounds Orlov heard the laughter and the noise of children playing and then the recognizable splash of water. The pool, he supposed, would be on the sea ward side of the villa.

The man who awaited Orlov by the metal-studded oak door was clean-shaven and hard-bodied and elegantly self-assured, despite Orlov physically dwarfing him. But for the thatch of totally white hair he would have looked at least ten years younger than the forty-six years Orlov knew Don Luigi Brigoli to be. There was a thin, single-strand gold necklace visible through the open white shirt uncreased into black slacks.

He said, in English, "Welcome to my home," and Orlov wondered how the man knew in advance that English was a common language between them. There was no unnecessary smile from the man, although the very white teeth were obviously sculpted by dentistry.

"It's good finally to meet," said Orlov, unsmiling, too. There was protective movement in the shrouded opening immediately behind Brigoli, but Orlov couldn't see how many men there were because of the glare of the sun. He was aware of Mittel and Lapinsh attentively to his right. Only Mittel had any English, and that not good. Orlov didn't look at either of them.

Brigoli said, "Come inside, out of the sun."

The handshake at the door was perfunctory, the briefest of formalities. There was air conditioning and Orlov was immediately chilled. He managed to avoid physically shivering or showing any scuffing uncertainty in the contrasting inner darkness against the outside dazzle, glad that his eyes adjusted quickly. The floors were all checkerboard marble, and most of the walls were marble too, although there was some rough-hewn stone and granite. One wall of the huge sunken lounge into which the Italian led him was entirely glass but soundproofed or maybe bulletproofed. Children and three women, two of them topless, were splashing or swimming in the main pool or the two adjoining shallow basins, a totally silent tableau. The men who had followed, including the two Russians, halted at a respectful distance on the raised surround, attendants to be seen but not heard. Brigoli's son was not among them.

The Italian said, "What will you take?" There was a smile at last. "There is Russian vodka."

"Water," said Orlov. He wondered if Brigoli was aware of the checks he'd had made upon the Italian, detailed enough to know that the man did not drink.

"*Acqua*," Brigoli demanded, without raising his voice or looking away from the other Mafia leader. He said, "It was good of you to come."

Lapinsh's remark about supplicant at once came to mind. Orlov said, "It was conveniently on my route. And it is, after all, my proposal to be explained in fuller detail."

Separate bottles of mineral water were placed on the glass-topped table between them by one of the attentive men, who returned immediately to the others. Brigoli remained impassive at Orlov's implied correction of precedence. He said, "I need it explained to me as fully as possible."

Orlov took his time breaking the seal and pouring his water. It was ice cold. He said, "Quite simply, I am proposing a business cooperation—cooperation but in no way a merger. Your most powerful families accept your leadership. Russia's most powerful brigades acknowledge my leadership. We each can speak for our respective countries."

"I can certainly speak for Italy," Brigoli agreed. "But those I represent are unsure of the advantages of your proposal. Maybe the practicality of it, too."

The other man doubted his authority. And his ability to deliver. Orlov said, "I would have hoped that was already obvious. I control Moscow's four airports, through which Asian heroin and Latin American cocaine can be brought in with impunity, for onward shipment here to be distributed throughout Europe. My brigades can sell as many luxury cars in Eastern Europe as can be stolen in the West. There are tens of thousands of women—boys, too—in the Russian Federation and Poland and Hungary and Slovakia and the Czech Republic with their legs and mouths open, a limitless supply for European brothels and the porn movie industries, of every description and taste. Just as limitless is the supply of art and antiques—genuine as well as fake—that can be shipped from Russia, to be moved on by you. The amount of fine art looted by the Nazis and in turn looted by the Red Army is incalculable. And available. No Russian government since the end of the Great Patriotic War has handed a bauble of it back to Germany or any other country claiming ownership. I'm prepared to compete with any Russian currency forger against any in the

West . . ." He hesitated. "There have been changes in Russia's intelligence organizations and its armed forces, displacing a large number of men with special destructive skills." There was another pause. "I have virtually a small army to guarantee enforcement and order, men who could be made available for such work anywhere in the West, on a contract basis."

"There have been stories . . . media accounts . . . of such enforcement," Brigoli broke in, sipping his water.

"Examples had to be made," said Orlov. First the arrogant bastard doubted his control in Moscow and now he was questioning how he enforced his authority!

"I believe publicity is best avoided."

"Unless it has its practical uses."

"Curious authorities can become an irritant."

Orlov smiled. "The situation in Russia is different from what I believe it to be here. I—and the people I represent—are not threatened by any civil authority."

"Let's specifically talk about the law."

"There is nothing specific to talk about. The law in Russia is a joke, to be treated as such." Orlov extended an open hand, then closed it, in a crushing gesture. "That is where the law is in Russia—in the palm of my hand."

"With who else have you had discussions?" asked Brigoli.

A moment for flattery, Orlov decided. "There would be no purpose in talking with anyone but yourself in Italy."

Brigoli gave another tight smile. "You spoke of this visit being conveniently on your route?"

"I have no further business anywhere in Europe."

"America?" Brigoli allowed the surprise to show.

"Would you have difficulty with a global association?"

"Of course not," said Brigoli, more annoyed with himself than with the other man. "You are meeting *il capo di tutti i capi* in the United States?"

"In Chicago, later this week."

"How would you see such an organization operating?"

"American families work under a ruling commission, with representatives from each," Orlov reminded him. "Ours would have a supreme, global commission."

"Who would be *il capo di tutti i capi*?" demanded the Italian at once.

"I would see the chairmanship alternating between us." Until I decide otherwise, though Orlov. He already had his chosen title and in Italian, too: *il rei dei rei*, the king of kings.

"Meeting where?"

"Alternating again, between Russia, Europe—East and West—and America."

"It's ambitious," Brigoli acknowledged.

Orlov recognized that the other man was impressed at last. Which put him in the superior position. "Unique. But eminently practical. And hugely rewarding."

"It deserves consideration."

"You need to consult with others?" patronized Orlov.

"We, too, have a commission. Courtesy has to be observed," said Brigoli.

"Why don't I return from America via Italy, for us to meet again? Can you get the views of others in that time?" further patronized Orlov. He became abruptly aware that there was no conversation between anyone on the higher-level surround of the sunken room and hoped they fully appreciated the confrontation being enacted before them.

"A week should be more than sufficient," said Brigoli, tightly.

"What if America takes longer than you expect?"

"We can reschedule by telephone, surely?"

"If it's necessary."

"I hope it won't be."

"So do I."

"Just as I hope this will prove to have been a successful first meeting."

"We shall see," said the Italian.

It was early evening before Brigoli's Russian-speaking son, whose name was Paolo, got back to the villa after the required courtesy of escorting the Russians to their hotel at the top of the Spanish Steps.

He said to his father, "Roberto and Joachim are watching them. And we'll know about any telephone calls, of course."

"Recorded?"

"Taps on all three phones."

"Good."

"I do not like the man."

Brigoli said, "I heard the recordings from the car, on your way here. He was rude to you. Arrogant. But liking or disliking doesn't come into it."

"Is the approach practicable?"

"Certainly worth exploring. The uncertainy is whether he can provide all he promises. He spoke as if we didn't already have connections in America."

"Perhaps he doesn't know that we have."

"I need to talk to New York, get the feeling there."

"Will you agree if America does?"

"It would be too big not to become part of. But I'd like to be surer of the man himself."

"Is he the *capo di tutti i capi*, able to talk as he did?"

"That's our weakness," admitted the older man. "Not having the sources in Moscow that we have through New York."

In the dining room of the Medici Hotel, Fodor Lapinsh said, "It wasn't correct, having whores flashing their tits."

Each was eating pasta. They were on their second bottle of Chianti.

Mittel said, "It was an impressive house."

Orlov nodded. "We need something prerevolutionary, in Moscow. An entire mansion for when they come. I'll call Feliks Romanovich: get it fixed."

"I'll find one!" Mitten volunteered eagerly.

Orlov hesitated, recognizing the jealous rivalry. "You think you could?"

"I know I could! Trust me."

Orlov smiled at the word with which he always had so much difficulty, objectively recognizing that it was a problem Luigi Brigoli was having, too. "Prove it to me then."

"There's the dacha, too," Lapinsh reminded him, equally anxious not to be left behind.

Now Orlov shook his head. "Not good enough. We need to find another when we get back." It was an oversight he should not have allowed. It irritated him. Orlov didn't like admitting oversights of any sort, not even to himself and even less to these two prostrating doormats.

"I'll find a better dacha, too," Mittel blurted out. "I'll get everything organized."

"We both will," Lapinsh said, determined not to be robbed of his part.

"OK," agreed Orlov, enjoying the fighting-dog performance. "See what you can do between you."

"We were too far away to hear," prompted Lapinsh, hopefully.

Orlov knew both men believed themselves part of an inner troika by having been included in this trip, the first outside Russia for either. It was a misunderstanding easily corrected when the time was right.

"He agreed?" further prompted the squat, square-bodied Mittel.

"Not yet."

"What if he doesn't."

Orlov concealed his irritation at Mittel's virtual interrogation. "He'll have to be replaced by someone who will." Replacing people was never a problem.

Pamela Darnley said, "That's your third."

"I'm OK."

"So how did it go?" On Tuesdays they normally lunched together, but as head of the FBI's Russian desk William Cowley had been all day at the triannual departmental conference at the Pennsylvania Avenue headquarters.

"Jim Burton didn't come out too good."

"For Christ's sake," the woman erupted, abruptly angry. "Since Nixon and before, no one on the Latin American desk has managed to conceive a strategy to stop cocaine getting here. Why's Jim suddenly getting shit?"

"Jed Parker's put forward a position paper."

Pamela sighed, theatrically. "It didn't take long, did it?" Jed Parker was the nephew of House Speaker George Warren, whose political influence had gained Jed a transfer from the Drug Enforcement Administration to the FBI's Planning Division. "He got Batman's private number?"

"The speaker's got the director's private number," said Cowley. "Jed doesn't need anything else."

"How did Terrorism come out?" asked the woman. Pamela was deputy head of the division.

"You didn't speak to Jack before you left?" Jack Custon was the section head.

"It's his kid's birthday. He went home direct from the conference."

"There were a lot of questions about Al Qaeda's infiltration," disclosed Cowley.

"The safest hobbyhorse being ridden up on the Hill by Mr. Speaker Warren," identified the woman, unnecessarily. "We're getting political interference here."

"We always did. And now Warren's got an inside track," Cowley reached for the whiskey bottle.

Pamela said, "You don't need another one."

Cowley stopped. "We're just living together. Only wives are allowed to nag."

"It's not a joke, darling," refused the woman, to whom Cowley had admitted the problem he'd had—and conquered—before they met.

"I said I'm OK."

"You don't need a fourth," she insisted.

"Then I won't have a fourth," he said capitulating. "Guess what I heard at the conference?"

"What?"

"Jed Parker's a fluent Russian speaker. Regards himself a Russian expert." The last thing I need, he thought, is the senator's nephew making a mess at my desk.

3

The ritual was virtually the same, but Igor Orlov discerned a subtle difference. From the moment of their arrival at Chicago's O'Hare Airport, the ambience was distinctly different, although at first Orlov could not identify how.

Initially, however, there were surprising similarities. The waiting escort in the smoked-glass limousine was bespectacled and comparatively young, but in contrast to Rome he was a successful, confident lawyer or banker. Sam Campinali identified himself by name but not by function. He did not refer to Joe Tinelli either in English or Italian as *il capo di tutti i capi* of the twenty-seven Mafia families in America. Nor did he use the respectful title of *don*. It was Mr. Tinelli. Knowing that Orlov and his companions had interrupted their journey in New York to recover from jet lag, they were going at once to Mr. Tinelli's home, Campinali announced. The second car would slightly detour to complete the hotel registration. There was no attempted sightseeing recital, not even when they skirted the sail-dotted Lake Michigan on their way to Evanston. There were periods of silence, although none was awkward. What the fuck was he missing, failing to recognize! Orlov asked himself.

They went abruptly inland from the lake, along flat, tree-lined roads. Just as abruptly there were fewer cars. Even fewer people walking. A lot of trees, much bigger and taller than those squashed by the heat of the Italian sun. The properties were walled or fenced, but none overprotectively. There was no positive barrier at all around the mansion they finally approached, although there was a twisting, alerting drive and Orlov guessed at sensors. There was a heavy thatch of trees, too, although no black-suited men nested in them. It only took imperceptible eye movement to search for security cameras. Orlov didn't see any but was sure there would be some. Only at the last moment were ground staff obvious but even more obvious—or rather conveyed—

was their appearance of being genuine gardeners. They wore gardening clothes and there were no stage-prop, single-barreled *lupera* wolf guns. Nor was there any swimming pool noise or anyone to greet him at the door.

It was a difficult house immediately to assimilate, broken between three to four stories. There were a lot of outside mock-Tudor wood beams and the chimneys were grouped together in Elizabethan clusters, unnecessary sentinels in the late spring sunshine, which was comfortably warm, not the stultifying heat of Rome. Campinali opened the car door and used a combination lock entry code to lead Orlov through echoing and empty paneled corridors into an even heavier wood-paneled library. The desk was directly in front of high leaded windows.

Tinelli would always have been a small man but was now wizened and appeared even older than what Orlov knew, from his preparation for this approach, to be his sixty-sixth year. There had been no indication in his preparation of ill health, which possibly made pointless, until a succession, his whole purpose in coming to Chicago.

An example very definitely needed to be made, Orlov determined. He'd spent a lot of time, effort, and money—none of which he ever wasted—setting up people within the concealment of the Russian émigré ghetto of Brooklyn's Brighton Beach. And they'd failed to provide a warning of Tinelli's infirmity. Or to advise him of the need to cultivate whoever the successor might be as the American Boss of Bosses. By coming here prematurely like this to the wrong, ailing man, he reduced the impact of an approach to whoever that successor might be. It was difficult, in those first realizing moments, for Orlov to suppress his fury.

There was, however, no frailty whatsoever—rather a robustness—in the way the American came around the desk to greet him. The handshake was very firm, as was the voice. "You've come a long way, which is courteous. I recognize and respect that. I hope this will finally be a successful encounter. You are sure you are OK with English?"

"Perfectly."

"That's good. I don't like working through intermediaries of any sort at our level and certainly not about what we have to discuss." He looked to Campinali. "Can you excuse us, Sam? We'll meet at lunch."

Without waiting for any acceptance from the younger American, Tinelli guided Orlov to deep leather armchairs around a dead hearth. On side tables there were family photographs, Tinelli with a gray-haired woman of about the same age as himself, both surrounded by what had to be two younger generations. Several appeared to have been taken at a family celebration. There were wine bottles and glasses on the table—some glasses raised in a toast—and the children wore party hats.

Tinelli was greeting him more as an equal, not like the greasy Italian. "I hope, too, that we are well met. And that we can take the proposal forward."

"You've already met Brigoli?"

Not Don Brigoli, Orlov noted. Who in Brighton Beach had been loose-tongued? If he had a name, there wouldn't be a tongue in the man's head for much longer. "Three days ago."

"What was his response?"

"Cautious," Orlov admitted honestly, aware that the information about his meeting Brigoli could have come directly from Rome. "I am returning through Italy, to hear how his commission reacted." Despite the appearance of ill health Tinelli had no physical indication at all of incapacity. He was totally impassive, as well, scarcely even blinking.

Tinelli said, "Tell me precisely what your proposal is."

It was not an imperious demand, just a direct invitation. Orlov repeated what he had outlined on the outskirts of Ostia, but immediately added, "For you here, in America, I think the male and female—and child—pornography should be made in Europe, to be shipped here for distribution. Neither do I think your legislation against transporting women across state lines for the purposes of prostitution makes it practical to bring whores here in sufficient number. But there is a proposal that could be more to your benefit than to a European business."

"What?"

"Russia is wide open. Too wide open, perhaps," said Orlov. "A lot of firms and companies are seeking joint-venture investments. Oil and gas exploration. Minerals. Pharmaceuticals. And construction, roads as well as buildings. More airports even. But a lot of investors and banks in the West have already been burned, putting money in but not getting any return. And there are certainly no civil law procedures that makes litigation worthwhile."

Tinelli allowed a bleak smile. "We invest from here and you, on the spot, ensure full and prompt return?"

"Better than that," Orlov promised. "Permanent, full, and prompt payment. A condition of your American investment would be to have our people on every board of directors of every company we initially finance. So they become our companies, operating quite legitimately."

"That's very good," Tinelli agreed. "We do it here. What about government permission, where necessary?"

The doubt that Brigoli had shown in Italy Orlov accepted: he had, ultimately, to prove himself to both *il capo di tutti i capi*. When he did, he'd make it spectacular, showing both who was *il rei dei rei*. "Buyable. Or enforceable. Not an obstructive difficulty, either way."

"The potential is enormous," accepted Tinelli.

"There is something more of particular benefit to you," Orlov continued, feeling very relaxed, sure of himself. "Cuba was once very important to your organization. And will be again, when Castro goes. Moscow has hugely scaled down its financial aid since 1991, but there's still a large Russian presence there, among them people I control. We could establish the same operations there, through paid and totally compliant Cuban fronts. Be in place, ready, when Cuba opens up. Within months the casinos and hotels and brothels—casinos and hotels and brothels we'd own—could be opened again, just like it was under Batista." Orlov paused, aware that he was holding the older man's total attention. "You might even consider establishing a ferry link between Havana and Miami. With casinos on board once they're beyond American territorial waters."

Tinelli's smile was wider this time. "You've put a great deal of thought into this. It's very impressive. You spoke of drugs?"

"In how many ports in America do you have influence?" Orlov asked in return.

"Those that matter on the West Coast. San Diego and San Francisco, certainly. Every one in Florida, both in the Gulf and on the Atlantic. Norfolk. New York and Boston. And here, obviously."

Orlov nodded, warmed by the awareness that the man to whose finger snap every family in America jumped was justifying himself to him! It wasn't a mistake to be dealing with Joe Tinelli, after all. A benefit, in fact. Whoever succeeded the man—and from the evidence over the past hour that succession was far from imminent—would be locked into any agreement he negotiated. Which, if he did get the agreement, meant the American successor would take office having to accede to his already being *il rei dei rei*. The reversal didn't in any way change the need for an example to be made in Brighton Beach.

"I have investment control of a freighter fleet operating out of Odessa, in the Black Sea. Which is conveniently close to the heroin production of Turkey and Pakistan and, increasingly, Afghanistan, in all of which I already have suppliers. Additionally, there's the Latin American cocaine that can be brought in through the Moscow airports, through which I can guarantee unrestricted and uninterrupted cargoes. I also have freighters operating out of Murmansk, although there is the winter problem. But I can also guarantee Gdansk, in Poland. I can load unimpeded at every port. All you have to guarantee is equally unimpeded delivery, through your ports here. And we're not just talking Turkish or Pakistan heroin. Just as easily Golden Triangle consignments can be channeled through Moscow airports. And as much Latin American marijuana as you can find customers for."

Tinelli became silent and sat completely motionless. It extended for so long that despite his reappraisal of the man's infirmity Orlov suddenly feared an infarct and realized that if Tinelli were to die—to become ill, even—in his sole presence, for whatever medically proven cause, he would probably not get out of the house alive, no matter how unguarded it appeared to be. Orlov shifted positively, to make the leather sound with his movement, but there was no reaction from the other man. He was about to move again when Tinelli said, "What do you propose if Brigoli is not interested?"

Orlov recognized at once that a wrong answer, a wrong implication, could destroy everything. He'd been accepted as an equal; he had to respond—be respected—as a Boss of Bosses in his own right. "There are obvious advantages to having a third partner in Western Europe. But it is not imperative."

"You have facilities there?"

"Berlin—in what used to be the east of the city—is available." It had taken him six months to create a brigade already for the largest single source of the stolen Mercedes and BMWs that reappeared in eastern Europe, some of the Mercedes looted direct and unused from the Frankfurt distribution center itself.

"There will be a loss of face if Brigoli rejects you."

"Which would be unfortunate," said Orlov, guardedly.

"Conflict is always best avoided," said the older man, in almost a parody of what Brigoli had said a few days earlier.

"Unless it is unavoidable," Orlov edged forward, still cautious, again practically a repetition of the Ostia conversation.

"How do you see the control?"

Another inch forward. "A ruling commission. Rotating chairmanship, rotating conference locations."

"Disputes?"

How long would it take him to understand this exchange? "I don't imagine any arising between the two of us. But there are no disputes that can't be negotiated between reasonable men. And I believe us to be reasonable men."

There was another silence, although not as prolonged as before. Orlov waited as uncertainly as before, although for different reasons. He didn't move to make the leather creak. Eventually Tinella said, "Your countrymen in Brighton Beach have become overambitious."

It had to be the information he'd demanded to be assembled upon the wizened figure opposite. He'd been positively separated from Mittel and Lapinsh. He could easily take this hunched old man, but as he'd already decided, he wouldn't get out of the house alive. Orlov said, "I regret that. How, precisely, too overambitious?"

"Brighton Beach is the agreed territory of my New York families. Concessions were allowed when you and I first made personal contact a year ago. Your outlet there was useful and very efficient for moving money. But the reciprocal right to operate"—Tinelli's pause, like his choice of word, was staged with an actor's precision—"*unimpeded* had limits. One was the right of businesses—even Russian businesses—to trade. There's been encroachment."

"I was not aware of that. And most definitely don't condone it."

"You would have hardly sought this meeting if you had been. I am not questioning your honor."

Orlov saw at once—and without offense, because they were discussing Russians—that he was being set a test, as he believed Brigoli
had set him a test to prove himself beyond Russian law. He said, "I
think this is a problem best resolved by me personally." As he always
liked solving problems, he'd make it as dramatic as possible. He'd
enjoy doing it himself.

"It would be appreciated. New York could, of course, resolve it for
themselves."

"That won't be necessary. I can delay my return by a day or two."

"Is that all it will take?"

"That is all it will take," Orlov assured him.

"Enough!" Tinelli abruptly declared. "We've talked sufficiently,
understand each other sufficiently. Now we should stop. Eat a little.
Reflect."

"Brigoli will expect an indication of how this meeting has gone,"
said Orlov.

"The commission will meet," promised Tinelli

Orlov was sure he already knew what the American's answer would
be. Sure, too, that he'd finally identified the difference between the
other two Boss of Bosses. Luigi Brigoli believed he occupied his position by uncertain agreement and needed the surroundings and trap-
pings of his role to reassure himself. Joe Tinelli was confident he
fulfilled his role by unalienable right. Which was, thought Orlov, how
kings occupied their thrones. He still needed ultimately to be recognized as untouchable as both of them. It was a natural progression to
his eventually establishing himself *il rei dei rei.*

There were three of them facing Orlov across the table. They were
young, the oldest probably no more than twenty-five. Twenty-eight at
the most. Orlov remembered his own thinking, his own confronta-
tions, at that age: I can do it . . . rise through the shit . . . be a big man.
The big man, the biggest. And he was getting closer by setting the sort
of personal examples he was going to set here, very soon. Some were
able. Some weren't. These three weren't. They just didn't know it yet.

To the three Orlov said, "There are agreements, understandings,
about enforcement."

The blond-haired man, whom Orlov knew only as Nick, the

adopted derivative of Nikolai, said, "What the fuck are we doing here!" He wore jeans and a sweatshirt proclaiming God to be black.

"You're here because I wanted you to be," Orlov said mildly. They were, in fact, in the reserved backroom of the nationalistically named Odessa Bar and Grill, actually on the Coney Island boardwalk of Brighton Beach, from which Orlov's group operated. They were all there, all eight of them, relaxed, smiling sycophantically at an already rehearsed performance. Maret Zubov, whom Orlov had appointed leader nine months earlier, was the most relaxed of all, knowing his part in the script. It had taken Zubov less than twenty-four hours to locate the three who were extracting additional tributes from the Russian émigré businesses. And in Orlov's opinion that was too quick for Zubov not to have already known. Which logically meant Zubov was taking a cut, exaggerating his own importance. And now, because of the preparation, he imagined himself unendangered.

"We're here because we were told we were going to be made an offer." The man known as Nick corrected him, spreading his hands expansively. "I think we're wasting our time." He looked to the two with him. "Let's stroll. It's late."

It was 3:30 A.M., the restaurant closed long ago, the staff dismissed.

"Do you know who I am?" Orlov asked.

"I was told someone important in Moscow," Nick answered. "You want to do business with me here in America, that's good. We'll do business."

"That is good," Orlov said. "That's what I want, to do business. Without the difficulties that have arisen."

He went to Zubov, who was grinning, one arm crooked over the back of his chair. Orlov held out his hand as planned. Alert for the gesture, Zubov slipped from his waistband the gun his jacket had been concealing, passing it across the table. It was in Orlov's hand before the three men were aware of it.

Nick said, "Now just a fucking minute!" and the man next to him snatched inside his own jacket. Orlov shot him, full in the face, sending him and his chair crashing backward. In the confined space the noise was deafening, and momentarily numbed everyone.

Using that moment, Orlov said, "Everyone stay as they are! No one move!"

No one did, among the men facing him, but Orlov was aware of Mittel and Lapinsh closing up protectively behind him.

There was no more bravado from Nick or his companion. Nick said, "OK, we made a mistake. I'm sorry. Very sorry. There won't be any more trouble—"

"I know there won't," Orlov agreed, and shot him, too, full in the face. The man took the chair with him as he went backward. Orlov looked directly at the third man. "No, please," he said.

"Be quiet," Orlov ordered, and obediently the man was.

Orlov said, "There's a reason—a reason for me—to let you live. You're a messenger, like everyone else here is a messenger. To spread the word about what happens to people who doubt my authority and step over a very positively drawn line. From now on, everyone does what they're allowed to do. Told to do. But no more than that, not even by an inch. You hear what I'm saying?"

The terrified man nodded, unable to speak.

"That's good. That's very important," said Orlov. He looked to Maret Zubov. "You hear what I'm saying?"

"Every word," said Zubov.

"There's been too many of those," said Orlov. "You listen to me, absolutely. All of you. And you say what I tell you to say. But you don't say more than that. And you have been saying more than you should, haven't you?"

Zubov, who had once more crooked his arm over the back of his chair, hurriedly straightened. "No! That's not true. That really isn't true."

"You were told to find out about someone, and you didn't do a good enough job. And he knew more than he should have about what I had been doing. That was wrong."

"I don't—"

Orlov shot him as he had shot the other two.

The terror in the reverberating room was now total, everyone petrified. Orlov looked around it, the one surviving outsider no longer outside. "That's how it's going to be from now on. Work properly, that's fine. Put a toe just an inch across the line, you're dead. Literally. So's anyone else with independent ideas. There's a new order—new rules—governing everything, everywhere. And everyone. You all understand that?"

No one replied positively. There were grunting sounds, nods.

Orlov said, "We're expanding into a new era. Too uncertain yet to anticipate. Your only purpose, all of you, is to do—*absolutely*—what you're told. Don't any of you, ever again, forget that."

The room remained silent, the puppets taut on their strings.

Orlov said, "Dump the bodies so they'll be immediately found, to make the message loud and clear." He smiled, caught by his own self-amusing thought. "And let's show up the law here as inefficient as it is in Russia. Let's show them up to be as stupid as they are." And show Joe Tinelli, too, he thought. Another was quick to come, a familiar reflection after a moment like this. Killing was better than sex.

He looked to the white-faced manager, in whose name the Odessa lease was registered. "You're in command here now. Your first test is to see how much of a runaround you can give the law."

"I'll see to it," promised the man, Veniamin Kirilovich Yasev.

"Then listen carefully to what I want you to do . . ."

William Cowley smiled when the recognizable voice came onto the line, not bothering to identify himself. "How you doing, Dimitri?" It was an excellent connection.

"It's been too long," replied Danilov, recognizing Cowley in return.

"You've got a turf war going on over there from what I've been reading?"

"Seems like it."

"You know who's winning?"

"Not yet." It was an irritating admission. In his impatience Danilov had expected by now to have got some street word, no matter how obscured the indications might have been from interfering lower-level militia corruption.

"Looks like we might have a situation over here, too. Three guys got whacked last night, up in Brighton Beach. Bodies were tossed on to the sand, in garbage bags."

"Russian?"

"That's what the IDs say."

"They were positively identified!" Danilov demanded, eager for patterns.

"Driving licenses. Credit cards."

"Where?" persisted Danilov.

Cowley hesitated. "You want to help me with that?"

"Where was the ID?"

"In their pockets."

"Not taped to the bodies?" Impossible though it would have been, Danilov had felt the familiar spurt of hope.

"They were fully clothed," said Cowley.

"Not nailed to crosses?"

Cowley, who was the only other man apart from Pavin to know about Larissa, took even longer to reply. "Still looking?"

"You know I always will."

"Garbage bags," repeated Cowley. "No crosses. Sorry."

"No connection, then?"

"Can't imagine it, can you?"

"Who knows? How can I help you, with your guys?"

"The names—the IDs—could be phony. I want to send them to you anyway. But with fingerprints. See if you've got any matches, under other names. See where that might take us."

"Pleased to help, as always," said Danilov, who had already successfully worked on three international investigations with William Cowley.

"Forensic lift any prints off the ID holders on any of your victims?"

"Totally clean, every one of them," said Danilov. "And we still don't fully understand the significance of the sacrificial crosses."

"Messages?"

"That's what Yuri thinks. How's Pamela?"

"Good. I'm a lucky guy."

"Everything else OK?" asked Danilov, who knew of Cowley's struggle with alcohol.

There was another pause at Cowley's end. "Not a problem."

"I'm glad. Let's keep in touch on this."

"As always."

"Give Pamela my love."

"And hers to you." Sometimes Cowley wondered what Danilov would do if he ever got a lead to Larissa's killer. Admiring—and liking—the man as much as he did, and knowing the obsession, he often worried it might be something stupid.

That night Danilov drove the roundabout route to Novodevisky Cemetery, a pilgrimage he'd stopped making because it had become maudlin. There were a lot of leaves and debris cluttering the grave. He had to clear them by hand because he hadn't set out that morning intending to stop off there and he didn't have a brush or a bucket. Unembarrassed— and unobserved—he talked as he worked. He said, "There's a lot happening, Larissa. Maybe this time there'll be something. I'll get it. Get whoever it was, no matter how long it takes."

4

William Cowley was a hands-on FBI division manager who didn't like supervising specialized investigations from behind a remote desk at headquarters. But on this opportunistic occasion there were additional reasons, personal as much as professional, behind his deciding to fly up to New York and take his own look—get his own take—at what had happened at Brighton Beach.

It would have been a wild exaggeration to think of uncertainties and atmospheres being created entirely by one individual, albeit a man championed by his House speaker uncle, but Cowley, who prided himself on internal political clairvoyance, was uncomfortably aware of a change within the J. Edgar Hoover Building since Jed Parker's arrival there. He didn't need a crystal ball to detect some of the attitude percolating down from above. The Bureau directorship was a political appointment, and it was no secret that after an initially ambivalent transition from the New York bench, upon which he had been senior judge, Leonard Ross now jealously protected his role. But Ross had made a serious miscalculation by opposing Parker's politically bulldozed appointment. And even more seriously, a powerful enemy in Congress, as well as one now deeply entrenched within his organization. By underestimating the bulldozer operator, Ross had been almost humiliatingly outmaneuvered.

The personal reasoning simply came down to his situation with

Pamela, which wasn't simple at all. He now deeply regretted sharing so openly and so soon everything about the long-ago collapse of his marriage, although he hadn't directly said booze had been its principal cause. Which it most definitely hadn't been. There were a lot of other, greater, influencing factors—his being at that stage of his FBI career so often away in the field being the most influencing of all—but Pamela had seized upon that above all others and twice isolated drink as the reason for their very infrequent disputes. Cowley knew the statistics and the arguments, from which he knew even more positively that by any judgmental standards his alcohol consumption wasn't excessive. Never had been, really. Just an occasional happy hour extending into a happy night. Certainly that hadn't happened since he and Pamela got together. Nor would it. But a quick trip to New York would be good for them both. Give them a break—a space—now that the first flush of their affair and her moving into his Arlington apartment was over. Not over, Cowley immediately corrected himself: settled down, as these situations always settled down. Two or three days apart would give them both time to realize how good things still were. Too good to be put at risk by bickering.

Cowley observed senior management protocol to the letter, memoing Ross in sufficient time for the trip to be countermanded and told Pamela he would only be away for a few days, passingly disappointed at her easy, unquestioning acceptance until reminding himself—another indication of how accustomed they had become to each other—that such personal participation would be completely understandable, expected even, to someone of Pamela Darnley's undiminished ambition. He was also careful to fax the FBI's Manhattan office of his impending arrival—even though his directorship of the Russian desk gave him unquestionable right and authority to become personally involved—and followed it up within an hour by calling the New York agent-in-charge, Hank Slowen. Cowley personally knew—and respected—the neat, precise man from a previous investigation at Brighton Beach, to which he'd then been accompanied by Dimitri Danilov himself. Slowen said he'd be glad to see Cowley. He needed all the input he could get. There seemed to be an impenetrable wall of silence around the Russian ghetto, and no one was raising a head above the parapets.

It was afternoon before Cowley got to Federal Plaza after stopping off on his way in from LaGuardia to register at the UN Plaza Hotel, which also held memories of his time there with Danilov. He made a point, for his own satisfaction, of spending fifteen minutes in the glass-reflecting bar and keeping to mineral water, telling himself on his eventual way downtown that abstaining hadn't been difficult at all, which he genuinely believed it hadn't.

Only Slowen and the secretarial staff were in the Manhattan field office, all the local agents being out at Brighton Beach. An incident room had been established, morgue photographs and crime-scene shots already on foamboard beside blank-eyed computers. It looked as empty and unproductive as it was.

"So what have we got?" Cowley asked. He was a big, crinkle-haired man, college football muscle melting into fat, although since his involvement with Pamela he'd tried to work out at least once a week, more if it were possible.

"Gang warfare's most likely," Slowen suggested.

Cowley picked up the doubt. "But what?"

"It doesn't feel right. Echo right."

"What do we know about the victims?"

"Nikolai Nyunin, know locally as Nicky Nunn, and Lev Gusev, who kept the surname but used Leo as the first, were that. Local. First-generation from Russian immigrant parents. Neighborhood hard guys, correctional institutes as minors, penny-ante theft, selling stolen driving licences and credit cards. The echo is that they were trying to set themselves up big time—protection, sharking, stuff like that."

"Third guy?"

"Different," said the New York supervisor. "Maret Zubov was older, forty-five maybe. Boasted locally of being a Muscovite. And of being connected. Immigration is running a check, but being Immigration, they're saying it's going to take weeks. No rap sheet, no social security number showing, so he could be an illegal. No proven local employment. Like I said on the phone, we're not being knocked over by the rush from any snitch to talk about him, either."

"The Genovese family have the Mafia license for Brighton Beach, right?"

"That's the first cracked echo. Nothing definite, but we're getting the vague word that the local Russian mobs have cut a deal: being allowed a little of the action."

"Why should the Genovese allow that?"

Slowen shrugged. "We're getting whispered words, since the killing, that this isn't Genovese irritation."

"Russian?" demanded Cowley. There seemed echos enough, he thought.

"Maybe. But wait until you see the bodies."

"You remember Dimitri Danilov?"

"Sure do." Slowen smiled.

"I'm sending him the names and the fingerprints, to see if there are any records there. Guess there won't be on the two younger guys, but Zubov might show."

"Not from what Dimitri told us last time about the state of Russian criminal records," Slowen recalled.

"There's always hope," Cowley said. It was good—stimulating—to be back in the field. He had every reason for making the trip to New York, but it would be even more justified if there was a definite Russian connection.

Their departure was delayed by two calls from agents working at Brighton Beach. Neither had any fresh information. The medical examiner was still at the city morgue, cleaning up after another autopsy, and clearly wasn't pleased at being held longer by their arrival. The name on his scrubs was Morrison.

Cowley said, "I'd appreciate your talking me through it."

"I've already given a preliminary report. I spoke to Hank," the medical examiner protested. He was a prematurely bald man who wore spectacles like a barrier.

"I'm liaising with Moscow," Cowley offered. "I need to know what I'm talking about, have all the answers."

The pathologist irritably yanked opened the three preserving drawers, momentarily misting the side room with the refrigeration. Briskly he said, "Not enough facial or cranial remains to be absolutely positive, but I'd say each was killed by a single frontal shot. Damage is too extensive to suggest a caliber for the weapon. According to forensics, no bullet was recovered from the garbage bags in which they were found. Again it's an estimate but I'd say the gun was fired from a few feet away:

there're no powder burns on the surviving tissue. There are marks on all three backs and buttocks from which I'd say they were sitting when they were shot and thrown back into their chairs by the impact.

Cowley interrupted. "What about restraint marks on their wrists or ankles?"

"None," said Morrison.

"Torture?"

"None," the man repeated.

"So three guys sit unrestrained in their chairs and wait to be shot, one by one, all the same way?" Cowley demanded.

"Like I said, it doesn't feel right," said Slowen, who was an instinctive operator.

"I'd say they were looking right at whoever shot them," the pathologist declared.

"And all the impact marks—bruising—is to their backs?" Cowley asked. "Not to any side, where they might have been turning away, trying to get away?"

"No," said Morrison, equally insistent.

"Why shoot them in the face, as if the killer was trying to conceal who they were, but then leave ID?" interjected Slowen, to Cowley.

"It wasn't identity concealment," decided Cowley.

"What then?"

"An example," said Cowley.

"To whom?"

"Others who were there. And others who weren't, maybe, but needed to understand through newspapers and television," said Cowley.

"What about there being three shooters, firing simultaneously?"

"That would explain the lack of avoidance," nodded Cowley. "They weren't shot on the beach?"

"At least not on the stretch where they were found," said Slowen. "Not even a footprint in the sand for forensic to take a cast."

Cowley went back to the medical examiner. "What about mess from this type of killing?"

"A lot of it, everywhere," said Morrison, openly looking at his watch.

"Let's stay with three shooters," speculated Cowley. "Three gunmen, three victims. Maybe people who had to watch, if it was example setting. Somewhere with a lot of room then?"

Slowen looked at Cowley in open doubt. "A warehouse, a garage, a factory, an office block, a storage facility?"

"Not on the beach, close to where they were dumped." Cowley stopped. "There you've got bars and restaurant, maybe a club or two. All places where these guys like to hang out."

Slowen's look was still doubtful. "The sort of places we're working our way through and so far getting jack shit."

"There's not that many, on the Strip itself," remembered Cowley. "They all come within public health regulations. Why don't we hit them with a health inspection, with us tagging along?"

"However much the mess, it will have been cleared away now!" Slowen said dismissively.

"Sure it will." Cowley smiled. "We're not looking for the mess. We're looking for a place which in the opinion of the inspectors is *too* clean. But wouldn't be, for forensics. We get a blood spot or a loose hair that matches any of these three, and we've got a place properly to start." It wasn't intentional mockery to look at his watch at the same time as Morrison once again looked at his. Cowley said to Slowen. "If you called right now, you'd probably find someone still in the public health department to set it up."

Which Slowen did. Afterward they stopped off at the UN Plaza for a drink that stretched into two in the glittering bar and parted in the foyer after arranging pickup times the following morning. Although he knew Pamela would not be home, Cowley called the Arlington apartment instead of Pennsylvania Avenue and left a message on the machine that he expected to be out, working, for most of the evening but would call if he got back at a civilized hour.

He had two—or maybe three—whiskies back in the bar before going out on to Second Avenue. He set off uptown on foot, barhopping until he got to Eamonn's, where he established himself in a corner seat at the bar for the tail end of happy hour. Slowen was right to be skeptical about the hygiene checks producing anything practical, but the activity might stir the Brighton Beach sand and unlock a tightly sealed mouth. He didn't break his journey on his way back to the hotel, but it was almost nine before he reached it. There was no message from Pamela. He decided against eating dinner in the restaurant, instead ordering a club sandwich from room service. He limited

himself to half a bottle of wine and while he ate and drank considered
making the promised call to Arlington, sure there would be no booze
sound in his voice. But then he wasn't sure. He could talk to her
tomorrow. It made much more sense waiting for tomorrow. There
might even be something positive to discuss this time tomorrow.

The mansion was on the curve of Ulitza Varvarka, with a better out-
look over the Kremlin than the river. It was a squarely built, ocher-
painted four-story property and unusual in the street for being
separated from adjoining buildings by narrow alleys on either side.
Fodor Lapinsh, who'd located it, was nervously acting as guide, leading Orlov from room to room and floor to floor. At the second level,
still arranged in the style of a main reception salon, Mittel anxiously
said, "What do you think?"

"I like it," said Orlov. "Feliks Romanovich won't have to bother."

Lapinsh matched Mittel's grateful smile, only just hiding his sigh
of relief. "A duke built it, around 1890. He was attached to the court,
obviously."

"The furniture looks old?" suggested Orlov.

"According to the man who was living here, a lot of it is original."

"Who is he, the man who had it?"

"A department head at the Interior Ministry. It's guest accommo-
dation for visiting foreign officials and ministers. He'd eased it off the
official register. He's been here for four or five years."

They reached the third floor, and the first of the bedrooms. There
were still clothes in the closets. "Was he a problem?"

Vitali Mittel shook his head, sniggering. "We said we wanted it and
he had to get out. He understood."

"Tell him I want the original furniture, too. And that he's got to get
all his other crap out by the end of the week." Orlov looked at Lapinsh. "It's very good. I'm pleased. Now I've seen enough."

"There's something more: something very special," smirked Mittel. "We kept it until last."

They had to descend two wide flights of steps to reach the cavernous basement, one entire wall of which was occupied by a partially
filled wine rack.

Orlov said, "I'll have the wine, obviously."

"That's not it," said Lapinsh, leading the way to a heavy oak door that he opened with a flourish, flicking on an inner light to a long corridor.

"What is it?" queried Orlov.

"It goes right under Rybnyj Lane, to the fourth house on the street. That's where the servants apparently lived and how they came to and from work."

"We got that house, too?" demanded Orlov.

Mittel nodded. "The Interior Ministry man kept everything intact: had a woman living there."

"Excellent," said Orlov.

"We thought you'd like it," said Lapinsh.

In the car Orlov said, "It'll make a good meeting place. Don't bother with the dacha. I'll keep what I've already got.'

"So we're accepting?" said Paolo Brigoli.

"Don Tinelli thinks it's a worthwhile proposition. The commission, too."

"I still don't like Orlov. Certainly don't trust him."

"He's replaceable, once everything's established." Brigoli smiled across at his son. "I certainly need someone I can trust. I want you to handle all the preliminary arrangements."

Paolo said, "Orlov won't like that."

"I know," said the father, the smile widening.

5

It was on the afternoon of the third day, by which time Cowley had already e-mailed the director—and soberly told Pamela—he was extending his hands-on time in Manhattan, that the FBI-attached health inspectors reached the Odessa Bar and Grill on the boardwalk. By that third day the inspectors had suspended the operating licenses of two restaurants and three unconnected bars for cockroach and vermin infestation and dutifully alerted their accompanying FBI agents to what was possibly blood at three different locations. Which, under more specialized, premises-closing forensic examination, turned out to be human. The recovery from the too-clean-to-be-true storage room of the Odessa was a blood-congealed three-strand clump of hair, two wisps of which still had follicle residue. There was no food preparation or serving proximity to justify closing the restaurant, although the original building plans listed the room not as a storage facility but a private dining room. Cowley sealed the en-tire restaurant, including restrooms and kitchens as potential crime scenes, as he additionally did the three previous premises. A bar and a lap-dancing club in which further hematological traces were found had been added to the closure list by the end of the fourth day, which was when they finally finished checking the boardwalk and beach. That was also the day when the first two blood specks were positively and separately matched to Nikolai Nyunin and Lev Gusev, which led to a premature celebration hosted by an ever-willing, excuse-seeking William Cowley in the FBI's local hang out just off Federal Plaza. The positive match justified the calling in of more forensic scientists even more thoroughly to examine the first confirmed restaurant and unattached bars, which meant there were sufficient crime technicians available when the correlation continued with all the other blood samples—two of them Maret Zubov's, along with the clotted hair and follicles from the Odessa.

The media coverage erupted on the second day and continued for the remainder of the week to occupy the front pages of all Manhattan newspapers. It was also reported daily on national as well as local television and radio. Cowley, who disdained personal publicity, gave one impromptu boardwalk interview—refusing to speculate upon a gangland war or utter the word "mafia," either American or Russian— and afterward referred all statement requests to FBI public affairs.

The FBI director personally recalled Cowley to Washington for a Thursday conference, and Cowley decided it was the logical time to hand back the day-to-day running of the investigation to Hank

Slowen. He did so with the insistence that there should be at least twice daily contact between them—obviously more if there was a positive development—and caught the first morning shuttle to give himself time to prepare in his own office. It also gave him the opportunity to stop off at the terrorist unit to see Pamela. She said he looked tired, and he asked what had she expected, glad he hadn't had a single drink the previous night. He was very self-satisfied that he'd been under control the entire time in Manhattan, apart from that first night and no one knew about that, which hadn't been bad anyway because he could remember every moment of it.

"Miss me?" Pamela demanded. She was a strong-featured, full-breasted woman, and exuded a confidence that some men, although not Cowley, found intimidating.

"Like hell. Miss me?"

"Like hell."

"Apart from you, what else have I missed?" The separation had most definitely been a good idea, personally as well as professionally.

"Word is that Brighton Beach has attracted the interest of Mr. Nosey Parker himself," Pamela announced, her voice lowered despite their being in her side office with the door securely closed.

Cowley frowned, both at the information and the way she uttered it. "What's it got to do with Planning?"

"Nothing," she said. "But everything to do with headlines."

"Let's not get paranoid." He wondered if Pamela was conscious of talking so quietly. She wasn't a woman given to theatrics or pretension, and this was verging absurdly upon both.

"Or complacent," she said. "Your decision to come back?"

"The director's. But it fitted: it was time."

"Nothing you couldn't have talked sufficiently about by telephone?"

"You *are* paranoid," he accused.

"It's contagious."

"Then we need to find a cure."

"I really am glad you're back," Pamela insisted.

For someone supposedly pleased at his return, Pamela was remarkably serious and still talking as if she didn't want to be overheard, which was very definitely absurd. "Why don't we stay in the city tonight: eat out somewhere?"

"You're not going back up to Manhattan?"

"Not without good reason, which I don't have at the moment."

"I'll book something in Georgetown."

Having supervised the investigation in the field, Cowley, in fact, had little to review, but he was disappointed nothing had come from Dimitri Danilov. During their second direct telephone conversation, from New York, Danilov had apologized in advance for the chaotic inadequacy of Moscow criminal archives but promised to do what he could, particularly to locate any possible information upon the Muscovite-claiming Maret Zubov.

Leonard Ross was a man of uncaring personal appearance whom Cowley thought to be wearing not just the same crumpled suit but the same shirt—creased even then—that he wore at the division director's meeting almost three weeks earlier. He waved Cowley to a seat at the side of a window-backed desk over which there was an unobstructed view of the Capitol and with the same gesture indicated the waiting coffee jug. He said, "Help yourself. I'm off even decaffeinated. Blood pressure."

Cowley poured himself a mug he didn't want because it was a required all-guys-together routine and asked himself what reason there was for criticizing Pamela for pretension and paranoia.

The permanently disheveled FBI director said, "Got yourself into a high-profile situation up in New York."

It sounded like an accusation, Cowley decided, surprised. "It was a logical way to expand an investigation. I couldn't anticipate it was going to turn out the way it did, bloodletting all the way along the Strip."

"So what's the story?"

"I don't have enough to tell one, not completely," Cowley at once admitted. "Hank Slowen says it doesn't sit right." The pause was perfectly timed. "And it doesn't."

"We've already had lawyers' letters from two bar owners and one of the restaurant chains, demanding the lifting of our closure orders."

Cowley didn't care if his brief astonishment was obvious at the tone—and the apparent direction—of the director's remark. Cowley said, "I've sealed under Bureau authority premises in which there is forensically identifiable links with a mass murder! Which is basic—

required—Bureau procedure. The public health restrictions are quite separate."

"I don't need help with the law or local regulations," said the former judge, stiffly. "And I've sat on enough murder trials. But not one where there are five different but positive scientific traces to a crime scene. You want to help me on that?"

"Like I already said, I can't. It's the biggest of our many problems that doesn't add up."

"So let's go through it. The early forensic reports talk of blood smears and blood spots. Which?"

"Both," said Cowley, discomfited. This was close to being a cross-examination rather than a review of the few known facts.

"Consistent with the murders having been committed in any one place?"

Cowley shook his head. "According to the medical examiner wherever they were killed would have looked—and been—like a slaughterhouse."

"So the killers are heavily bloodstained? It drips off them?" Ross suggested.

Cowley shook his head again, relieved that he had been at Brighton Beach and wasn't trying to answer from someone else's crime report. "For it to have dripped off, they would have been saturated. They couldn't have walked about like that without being seen and an alarm being raised."

"So how does the evidence get where it was found?"

"Planted," declared Cowley, who hadn't intended to offer the totally unsubstantiated opinion until the forensic examinations were completed, which they wouldn't be for at least two more days. "With one exception—a bar and restaurant called the Odessa—the blood spots and smears were all in publicly used parts of the establishments: bars, restrooms, dining areas. On the undersides of bar overhangs or stool seats or tabletops, places where they could be easily put. What was found at the Odessa was different: hair as well as blood for a positive DNA match to Maret Zubov. And not in such an obvious or apparently publicly used place. In a floorboard gap in a storage room—a remarkably neat, tidy, and clean storage room—described on the original building plans as a private dining room. Which, according to a liquor delivery man who's not certain enough to be a reliable witness, it was being used for as recently as three weeks ago when he was last there."

The indulgently fat director sighed, impatiently. "Who owns the Odessa? What do they say?"

"It's owned by a company registered in Canada, address in Toronto. We asked Toronto two days ago for a full company check, no reply yet. Manager is a now naturalized third-generation Ukrainian, Veniamin Yasev. Admits to knowing Zubov as a regular customer and that the storage area was a private room until five days ago. Not enough people used it, so they decided to close it and use it as a store. It's neat and tidy because it was a place where people ate, until recently. He says the lease was fixed through his lawyer, who confirms it. The rent is paid by monthly electronic bank transfer. We're trying to follow the money trail, obviously. Yasev says he never actually met the owners. It was all done through attorneys. The three regular waiters also say they knew Zubov, whom they called Marty. The cook and three kitchen staff deny knowing him." Cowley hesitated, realizing Ross would be listening and analyzing with a lawyer's mind. "Zubov was also a known and admitted customer in three of the other places where we found blood—one of the samples his— of the other two victims."

"If Zubov was a regular, they must know something about him," Ross insisted.

"No obvious job. He apparently talked a lot of playing the horses. We're checking bookmakers for a betting account. And of being a high roller at Atlantic City and Vegas. I've got people doing the rounds in Atlantic City, because it's conveniently close. Vegas would at this stage be a waste of manpower."

"Any suggestion of a family?"

"None. The Russians don't seem to be that properly organized up there. Small gangs, usually three or four, sometimes a little larger, but no more than eight to ten, according to Slowen."

"What about personal family?"

Cowley shook his head again, guessing he wasn't impressing the other man by how often he was having to admit ignorance. "None that we've located so far. Lived by himself in an apartment over a delicatessen, just back from the beach. We got a warrant, obviously. The only interesting thing was what we *didn't* find. No passport, no bank accounts, no driving documentation, no letters, no personal papers of any sort. And there's no traceable social security number and immigration can't find a visa approval. Some porn mags, three porn videos, one spare suit, and three shirts. All the clothes were souvenir American."

"What about the other two?"

"Both officially American citizens. Born here. Respectable immigrant families. Both Nikolai Nyunin's parents are dead. A sister living in Trenton, New Jersey, who hadn't seen him for three years, by mutual dislike and agreement. Says the last she heard he was setting up a gang, with Lev Guzev. Guzev's got a widowed mother, but didn't live at home. She says she doesn't consider she has a son anymore—that he's dead to her. Neither Nyunin nor Guzev's apartments produced anything. Neither married. Local hookers say they knew them both but strictly professionally, although we think they might have been pimping, but none of the girls will admit working for them."

"Small time wannabes who became a nuisance and had to be gotten rid of," concluded Ross. "Or maybe even smaller, a local falling-out at ghetto gutter level."

"We're looking away from the Beach now," said Cowley. "It's Genovese territory, like Atlantic City. Slowen thinks we might pick up more by asking around in Manhattan. And the people I've put into Atlantic City to check Zubov's supposed gambling have been told to do the same there."

"Anything from Moscow?"

"I spoke with Danilov a couple of days ago. Hope to do so again, later today. So far he hasn't come back with anything."

"Who else you talking to there?"

Cowley frowned at the continued cross-examination. "Only Danilov. If there was anything on Zubov, he'd be the person to know it." He introduced another hesitation. "He's the head of the Organized Crime Bureau."

"I'm aware of who he is! And if he knew anything, he should have come back with it by now, shouldn't he?"

"Moscow archives aren't organized like ours here. Which is their problem. There's scarcely any organization at all.

The director sighed. "I know you two have a cozy relationship that's worked well in the past, but I think you should bring in our guy at the embassy. That's what he's there for. And ask the CIA for assistance, too."

"I don't—" Cowley started but Leonard Ross overrode him.

"Small time wannabes getting three-inch headlines and prime-time television. If I'm asked questions, I want to have answers: certainly to be able to say we've done all the basic groundwork things like activating our own people on the spot in Moscow. How much longer do you intend keeping all the premises closed at Brighton Beach?"

This time Cowley let the astonishment show with a momentary silence. "They contain scene-of-crime evidence!"

"Which has been forensically established and lifted."

"At least three of the closures are also because of public health breaches."

"Which according to the lawyers' letters can't fully be complied with—which would get the public health closures removed—because we won't let our scenes be touched."

"Sir!" objected Cowley. "The longer we keep the places closed, the more desperate their owners and managers will become about the income they're losing. And the greater our chances of being told something to get us off their backs."

Now Ross was silent for several moments. "I don't want—won't have—the Bureau made to look stupid over this, with an unfair enforcement or harassment suit from some media-eager attorney. I'm talking to you now as a longtime lawyer and experienced judge. What we've got now—all we've got now, apart from three dead punks no one's going to mourn—is forensic evidence at six different places. You know what defense attorneys would do with that, if you brought anyone to court? Each would argue a blood spot or a hair wasn't proof of any crime having been committed upon their client's premises and file for dismissal. And sure as hell get it."

"We don't have anyone to bring to trial!" Cowley argued, exasperated. "The blood and the hair are just part of an eventual case! In two of the premises, the forensic examination hasn't even been completed!"

"How long?"

"Three, four days." Cowley exaggerated intentionally.

Ross shifted, uncomfortably. "Four days. If we haven't found anything more to incriminate any or all of the premises four days from now, we lift our crime scene closures. We've got the evidence. There are no legal grounds for us to keep them shut down. And liaise with our guy in Moscow and with the agency. Understood?"

"Yes, sir."

"I want this moved forward, Cowley. Moved forward and gotten rid of."

The last time they'd met, Cowley recollected, the director had called him Bill.

"If it wasn't you telling me, I wouldn't believe it," said Pamela.

"If it hadn't personally happened to me, I wouldn't believe it either," said Cowley.

They were in a new Italian restaurant they hadn't eaten in before, just off M Street on Wisconsin. Pamela's martini was still only half drunk. Cowley had finished his whiskey but held back from pouring for himself the Valpolicella that was already open on the table.

"A lot's happened while you were away," said Pamela. "The agent-in-charge in San Diego got suspended after a lawyer's complaint that his black client got beaten up. The confession was ruled inadmissible because of coercion and got us a whole load of bad publicity. And there's an emergency audit of the Finance Division here: someone in Planning leaked inflated budget estimates to Congress that didn't add up."

"*Someone?*" Cowley queried, heavily.

Pamela pulled a face. "George Warren didn't actually ask the question in the House: it was one of his jump-to-order caucus, the guy from Tennessee. Ross got called to the White House."

"He talked about blood pressure," Cowley remembered.

"I'm not surprised. He's being summoned before the Budget Committee."

"Why didn't you tell me this morning?" Their meal arrived—spaghetti for him, veal for Pamela—and Cowley at once tasted and accepted the wine.

"I thought you would have read something about it in New York. And you were accusing me of being paranoid, remember?"

"Do you know you were actually whispering?"

"Bullshit!"

"True."

"You *are* joking, aren't you?"

"No," he said, seriously.

"Jesus!"

"One man can't have this effect throughout the entire building. It's ridiculous!"

"If I'm whispering, it's certainly ridiculous!"

"If Jed Parker could be found to be the source of the budget leak, not even the Speaker could prevent his being fired."

"Which is why he's never going to be identified as the source," said Pamela. She shrugged again. "And let's be objective: perhaps he wasn't."

"You met him yet?"

Pamela shook her head. "Seen him around. Good-looking guy. The washroom gossip is that quite a few girls would like to trip him up and fall underneath him, but he isn't interested in mixing business with pleasure."

"Focused on his future," Cowley said. He added to his glass. Pamela shook her head in refusal.

"So what did Dimitri say?"

"Still nothing. It was probably too much to hope that there would be something. I called John Melton, our guy in Moscow, and briefed him. He said he'd talk to the CIA people there, but I e-mailed their Russian desk here, as back-up."

Pamela smiled. "Covering your ass in proper bureaucratic fashion!"

"From what you're telling me, it sounds wise to do so!"

The lovemaking that night was the best Cowley could remember and Pamela screamed aloud when she climaxed with him. Then she said, "I don't whisper all the time!"

Cowley said, "The times you shout are much better."

Igor Gavrilovich Orlov surveyed the brigade leaders assembled before him in the largest reception room of his newly acquired Ulitza Varvarka mansion, allowing himself the near sexual satisfaction at this moment of homage that defined him *il capo di tutti i capi* of Russian major-city organized crime. He said, "I appreciate your agreement to my heading what from this moment becomes the ruling, governing group of all our operations. Which means that from this moment there need no longer be any wasteful disputes between any of us. We are the commission that will resolve all disputes and complaints: resolve them by negotiation and compromise, until negotiation and compromise are no longer possible. On behalf of you and your brigades, I am establishing working business relationships with Italy and America. We are going to become part of a global conglomerate,"—Orlov paused, everything rehearsed—"the biggest international multinational in the world. When that formation is finalized, which it has yet to be, we will create a group—a committee—to meet and plan with their representatives, as multinationals do. Each of you, today, are on the threshold of more power and more wealth than you ever imagined, in your wildest dreams." He paused again, looking around the expressionless faces confronting him, knowing that every single man was already planning to succeed him at the first opportunity. "Is there anything else to be discussed?"

No one moved. No one spoke.

"We've every reason to celebrate," Orlov declared, gesturing through the double doors that opened on cue to the laid-out tables of champagne and vodka and caviar.

Orlov circulated with a glass of champagne but didn't drink, mentally isolating those who drank to excess or who were posturingly overanxious to dominate a conversation or situation or who remained soberly watchful, as he was, all and each of which was potentially dangerous. He made a point, though, of talking and listening to them all, either separately or in groups, knowing that Feliks Zhikin was doing the same on the other side of the room. It was late when the gathering finally broke up with handshakes and backslapping and sometimes bear hugs, which Orlov endured without once betraying his distaste. Zhikin was one of the first to leave.

Orlov was ready for the reaction from the increasingly confident Fodor Lapinsh when he announced there was a meeting that had to be kept, despite the lateness. "The bastards are already trying to ingratiate themselves, form alliances. I've agreed to a meeting."

Lapinsh smirked. "All trying to get close to the main man."

Mittel, who was driving the BMW to Orlov's backseat directions out toward Khoroshovo-Mnevniki, where the river bends most sharply, said sycophantically, "You've achieved everything, haven't you? You're on equal terms with Tinelli and Brigoli, and you've got all the major brigades to agree to your ultimate leadership. No one else has ever been able to achieve all that."

"Why did Feliks Romanovich leave so early?" asked Lapinsh

"He had something to do."

"You know you can rely on us," said Mittel.

Orlov frowned. "Don't you think I can rely on Feliks Romanovich?"

Mittel gave an awkward shrug, aware he'd overstepped himself. "He's family, real family.

"Who we meeting tonight?" asked Lapinsh, trying to help the other man.

"People who believe they have special importance," said Orlov, obscurely, hurriedly indicating a turn off the M25 and then, in quick succession, to two more side roads to bring them close to some darkened sheds and a small warehouse directly bordering the river.

"Something from tonight's meeting?" pressed Mittel, eager to move the discussion on.

"There!" demanded Orlov, pointing to an anonymous building shrouded in total darkness. "Stop there!"

Mittel braked obediently and turned the engine off. "Where are they? I don't see anyone here? It could be a setup."

Orlov eased the Makarov from beneath his coat with the movement of getting out of the car and, because he was half turned, shot Lapinsh first, in the back of the head, throwing him forward in the passenger seat. Mittel had no time to move before Orlov shot him the same way, the gun actually against the man's head. Orlov walked unhurriedly to the side of the shed farthest from where he'd made Mittel park, to where the gasoline was dutifully ready. He balanced a can on either hand walking back to the BMW, first splashing and finally upending both over the interior, leaving just a little to form a fuse to give him time to get clear, which was fortunate, because when the flickering rivulet reached the vehicle it exploded with a force that almost knocked him over.

Feliks Romanovich Zhikin was waiting at the rear of the building in his personal car, not one of the brigade fleet, from which he'd earlier unloaded the cans. The engine was idling, and Zhikin moved off, unhurriedly, as soon as Orlov got into the passenger seat. To regain the narrow road they had to go past the blazing car. Neither looked at it.

Zhikin said, "No trouble?"

"Of course not," dismissed Orlov. "Guess what Mittel hinted?"

"What?"

"That I couldn't rely on you, trust you." Orlov laughed, and Zhikin laughed with him, hoping the unease wasn't in his voice. He was convinced that Orlov was clinically insane, barely in control of himself. And that, irrespective of any family relationship, he was in personal danger.

Zhikin said, "They really saw themselves becoming second in command, didn't they?"

"It'll be a lesson to the rest of our people." He had that night been acknowledged Boss of Bosses. And by disposing of Mittel and Lapinsh he'd removed the only two men who could have provided a direct link to those with whom he'd negotiated the global conglomerate if he'd been overthrown. The Swiss lawyer knew a little about America, of course, but not enough to advise any successor. Orlov knew he was unchallengeable. It was a good feeling, knowing he hadn't made a single mistake.

He had, though. He had not gone back to check the BMW he believed by now would have been completely destroyed, along with its dead occupants.

6

Being a man of dedicated obedience, Mittel had taken every other aspect of the vehicles' maintenance seriously, even to ensuring that every gas tank of every vehicle was at all times filled to overflowing, as the BMW's had been. It was the thirty gallons of fuel that caused the car to explode so violently that it blew Mittel's already dead but now additionally fractured body a full fifteen yards from the inferno. The body was, of course, burning, but only superficially, and the ground bordering the river was sodden and the flames only burned away Mittel's outer clothing in places, mostly at the back, none at all to the corpse's front.

Which was how Mittel was lying when Dimitri Danilov and Yuri Pavin arrived at the scene in the early morning, alerted by Militia headquarters traffic control through Danilov's standing instructions that he be immediately notified of possible car bomb assassinations, which was how Larissa had died beside her corrupt Militia colonel husband.

Mist hung, like wet smoke, over the river and the swamp. It was impossible to see the far bank. Closer, the blackened, skeletally-reduced BMW smouldered from residual heat still hot enough to keep the Militia group at bay. A belly-sagging uniformed Militia major detached himself to stroll over to their car by the time Danilov got out. With obvious resentment the man said, "What brings Organized Crime here?"

"Curiosity," said Danilov curtly, at once recognizing the attitude.

"What makes you think this is organized crime?"

The hostile man believed his own payoff arrangements might be endangered if it did turn out to be a case, guessed Danilov. "Anything been touched?"

The man shook his head. "Our orders were to wait until you got here."

"What about forensic?"

"Our orders were to wait until you got here," the man repeated.

"You have a problem that we need to get out of the way?" challenged Danilov, impatiently.

"I don't think so."

"That's good," Danilov said with weary experience. "I don't want to interfere with your part of the investigation and I don't want to have to suspend you from my particular interest in it."

"Which is what?" demanded the major.

"I don't know, not yet," said Danilov. And I certainly wouldn't tell you if I did, he thought. "What have you done so far?"

"We were told—" began the man.

"To wait until we got here," Danilov finished for him. "Let's not fuck around, Major. You've no need to know what I'm looking for beyond being told that we're not enquiring into how you conduct your investigations."

"Unless we have to," picked up Pavin. "And if we have to, that could become extremely upsetting and tiresome for all of us, so let me ask you this, without wanting you to answer: If there is an inconvenience or a misunderstanding between a general and a colonel and a major, who do you think stands to be the biggest loser?"

The uniformed major didn't speak.

Danilov said, "So, has anything been touched?"

"No."

"You haven't searched the body?"

"No."

"I have your assurance of that?"

"Yes."

"Who found him?"

The man nodded over his shoulder, toward the fire-scarred building in front of which heat still wisped from the BMW. "The cleaner. It's a draftsman's office."

"You sure she didn't touch anything?" demanded Pavin.

"It's a man. He said he telephoned us immediately. Was too frightened to go near anything."

"Where is he now?" asked Pavin, looking around the deserted, early morning forecourt.

"He asked to go home. Said he felt sick. He was definitely shaking."

Danilov sighed. Flatly, resigned, he said to Pavin, "He stole something."

"Not from here he didn't," insisted the uniformed officer, jerking his head once more in the direction of the burned-out shell. "There's another one in the car. Reduced to a skeleton. Can't even tell if it's a man or a woman."

"Get forensic here," ordered Danilov. As the surly uniformed man squelched back toward his group Danilov said: "Everything stinks of gasoline."

Pavin, who had gone down to an awkward crouch beside Mittel's body, said, "He's soaked in it. I don't understand why he didn't burn more. His hands have virtually gone, though. And a lot of his face, although he's still recognizable."

"Shot, then incinerated," suggested Danilov. Now he indicated the fire-scorched walls of the building close to the blackened wreck. "But there was an explosion that blew this one clear."

"From the way he's lying, both legs look as if they're broken," agreed Pavin. Because they were the most convenient, he eased his hand first into Mittel's trouser pockets. "They're empty. Not even coin."

"So the cleaner stole the money," accepted Danilov, in fresh resignation.

"And a watch, too," said the hunched Pavin, gesturing toward the outline of a watch on the empty but burned left wrist of the body. He got his own left hand beneath the body, slightly raising it with his right. "I'm going to stink of gas now."

The traffic division officer came back from his own group. "Forensic are on their way."

Danilov saw the man was smoking a cigarette. "Put that out, for fuck's sake!"

"Sorry," said the man. "I didn't think . . ."

"I believe you," said Danilov, heavily. "And send someone to pick up the cleaner. Take him direct to Petrovka."

"What's he done?"

"Just do it!" demanded Danilov.

"Got something," announced Pavin, as the major stomped off for the second time. "American cigarettes, Kent"—he enumerated, as he began retrieving the contents of Mittel's inside jacket pockets—"two pens. I haven't got there yet but it feels like a gun, so it looks definitely like something for us . . . a wallet . . . ah, and look at this!'

Danilov accepted the proffered passport, turning immediately to its identification page. "Vitali Petrovich Mittel," Danilov read aloud, flicking through the pages. "And here's an interesting entry!"

"What?" asked Pavin, straightening gratefully from beside the body.

"An entry visa for America, as recently as last month. And a European Union stamp for Italy, a week before that, and again, immediately after America."

"He wouldn't have been allowed in if they knew he normally carried this," said Pavin, holding up a 9-mm Makarov by its trigger guard to avoid overlaying any fingerprints on the butt.

"The name mean anything to you?" asked Danilov. Pavin's encyclopedic memory was frequently more useful than official records.

Pavin shook his head. "But we've got a complete face, from the passport—" The man abruptly stopped, staring down at the wallet from which he had just extracted a folded sheet of paper.

"Important?" demanded Danilov, seeing the expression on Pavin's face.

"An address at Brighton Beach, New York. And a telephone number . . . against the name of Maret Afanasevich Zubov!"

"You're right," said Danilov. "It's very definitely something for us."

They stayed at the scene for a further two hours, until Mittel's body was removed for autopsy, their satisfaction at the intriguing connection with William Cowley's overdue request tempered by the forensic technicians' insistence that there was little that would be recovered from the vehicle shell apart from its make and that so many people had milled around the vehicle and the spot where Mittel's body had been found that any worthwhile footprints would have been destroyed.

Upon Danilov's telephoned instructions, the cleaner, Oleg Osipof, had been locked into a cell, although he was allowed to keep all his property, which Danilov thought a better guarantee of its remaining intact than being placed in porous Militia safekeeping. When Danilov finally entered the unheated, concrete-walled, concrete-bedded cubicle the sharp-boned man was shivering, although not from cold. At Danilov's entry, he jumped to his feet into a loose, uncoordinated attention. Danilov at once accepted that he was going to have to become the sort of man he didn't like to be but balanced the awareness by the reassurance that it was necessary. Quite apart from whatever connection there was with Cowley's American enquiry, there was, additionally, the all-important personal fact that it was a car-bomb killing.

Sharply, bullyingly, which was how Osipof would have been treated every day of his miserable life, and to which he would respond, Danilov said, "Sit down! Take your shoes off."

The man collapsed at once on to the jutted ledge and snatched off cardboard-composite shoes, which were sufficiently mud-splattered for Danilov's bluffing intention. They stank of constant, sweated wear. Both socks were holed at the toes, in several places. Danilov returned at once to the still-ajar door and passed them through, without any conversation, to the waiting, rehearsed warder. Still standing at the door Danilov said, in a loud voice, "What did you steal from the body away from the car?"

"Nothing!" The voice was cracked, sniveling.

"I don't have time to waste!"

"I didn't go near the body!"

"Your shoes are being measured now, against casts of footprints found around the body," lied Danilov. "We both know they'll match. Go on lying to me and I will charge you with obstruction or even complicity and see that you are jailed for hampering an important investigation. Stand up!"

As if on strings, Osipof jerked to his feet.

"Turn out your pockets, on to the bed space."

The shaking worsened as the frail man emptied his pocket contents onto the thin, single blanket. Danilov saw it at once, and the physical twitch of pity was stronger than the renewed but unexpected satisfaction. Danilov said, "Where's the money?"

"I don't—"

"Get out of the way, over there!" demanded Danilov, flicking his hands toward the now closed door. The man scurried away from the bunk. Danilov didn't have to disturb the man's belongings to search through the single threadbare fold of the blanket, locating the abandoned dollars beneath the stained pillow roll. He turned to Osipof and said, "Don't go on lying to me!"

"I'm sorry . . . I didn't mean any harm . . . didn't . . . I'm sorry . . ."

Danilov believed he already had enough, but he was a detective who always believed in squeezing out the last pip. "You're looking at five years. Go on lying and I'll guarantee ten. What else did you take to hide or sell, before you were brought here?"

"Nothing . . . please believe me . . . nothing . . ."

"What about these?" demanded Danilov, carefully sliding his pen beneath the cover flap of the book of matches imprinted with the name Odessa, in Roman type, along with an address in Brighton Beach.

"Oh, yes. I'm sorry . . . so sorry. I forget . . . didn't think."

"From the dead man?"

"Yes. The money was kind of wrapped around it."

Danilov had more—far more—than he could have hoped, although at that moment he had no idea of what any of it meant. He tilted his pen, to drop the matches into the evidence bag he took from his pocket, and beckoned the man back toward his other belongings. "There were cigarettes on the body. Why didn't you take the cigarettes, too?"

"I don't smoke."

Who had he wanted to impress with such a pitiful foreign souvenir, wondered Danilov. "Sit down," he ordered again.

Osipof slumped down, his strings cut.

"Tell me, from the beginning!"

"I got there about six. It's an early bus. I have to walk the last mile," said the man. "There was a smell, before I got there. Burning. And gasoline. I saw the car first and the funny shape, of someone near the passenger seat, all burned and black. Then I saw the other body. There was smoke coming from it. There was hardly any head . . ."

He began to shake.

Quickly Danilov said, "What about anyone else around the body? Or the car?"

"No," insisted the man.

"Tell me exactly what you saw. I know you stole things, so tell me all about that, too."

"Just the car. Smoke coming from it and from the body there, as if it was alight. . . . I'm sorry . . . I took the money and the matches. That's all . . . nothing else. I've got a wife . . ."

Danilov decided the man was probably telling the truth. "You telephoned the Militia?"

"From the office, inside the building."

"Did you phone before or after you stole the money and the matches?"

"After."

"So if the first bus is around six and you had to walk and then go through the man's pockets it would be more like six-thirty. Later even."

"I suppose so."

"Don't you know?"

"I don't understand . . ." stumbled the man.

"There was a watch missing from the body."

"No! I didn't take a watch . . . Believe me."

Once more Danilov did believe him. "You didn't see a watch on his wrist?"

"No! I got frightened . . . thought I heard something . . . Didn't look . . ."

"What was it you heard?"

"A sound, like somebody moving."

"Was there anyone?"

"I ran into the office: locked the door behind me, and didn't unlock it until the Militia arrived."

"Didn't you look out of the windows?"

Osipof hesitated. "Yes."

"Who did you see?"

"I'm not sure it was anyone. It was still half-dark. A shadow, perhaps."

"How close to when the Militia arrived?"

"Almost at the same time."

Danilov rifled through the tiny bundle of dollars, a currency more readily acceptable in Russia than rubles. There was $35, in singles and tens. There had been a time, when he had been a uniformed colonel in charge of a Moscow divisional suburb, when he would have confiscated the money for his own benefit, but that time was now very long ago, like so much else. He tossed the tiny roll into Osipof's lap and said, "Enjoy it."

The man looked at him narrow-eyed, suspicious. "What's happening?"

"I'm giving you back the money."

"Why?"

"Because it's the only time in your sad life you'll ever know what it's like to be rich."

"You're letting me go!"

"Don't rob dead bodies again."

Yuri Pavin was slumped in the large, sagging, out-of-keeping arm-chair that Danilov had specially installed for the comfort of his enormous deputy in his top-floor office, the onion domes of Red Square distantly in view. He knew at once from the satisfied expression on Pavin's face that there was a quick development.

"Tell me!"

"Four years ago Maret Afanasevich Zubov, with two others, gave Vasili Mittel an alibi that got him off an armed robbery charge involving a German tourist. Mittel was working the gypsy cab scam from Sheremet'yevo Airport, robbing and dumping the unsuspecting victim halfway into the city."

"We got the names of the other two?"

"Both dead."

"How?"

Pavin hesitated, knowing the importance of his answer to the other man. "Car bomb. It was one we looked into, after Larissa's death. We didn't get anywhere."

"Why didn't we get Zubov before now?"

"He was a witness, not a defendant. There's no computerized cross-reference."

"I've got a feeling about this!" declared Danilov.

Always the too-quick reaction, always with Larissa in mind, thought Pavin. Cautioningly, he said, "We've had feelings before, Dimitri Ivanovich."

"This is a good one. What about a brigade?"

Pavin shook his head. "Not yet. What's the cleaner say?"

Danilov took the plastic envelope from his pocket, dangling it for the other man to read the contents, and explained its recovery and admitted dollar theft.

"The Odessa again," recognized Pavin. "We've got something to tell Bill Cowley after all."

"This could be another joint case." Danilov was excited at the possibility of working in America again, as he had in the past.

"You believe that's all Osipof took?"

"Osipof told me he didn't take the watch, and I believe him."

"It could have been destroyed."

Danilov shook his head. "He wasn't burned badly enough for that."

"Someone from the Militia then?"

"Most likely," agreed Danilov. "My worry is that something else that might have been useful was also taken."

"We'll never know," accepted Pavin, with professional resignation. "Do you think this is anything to do with the turf killings?"

Danilov gave a doubtful head shake. "The wrong pattern. All the rest were sacrificed and floated down the river to be found and identified. It's only a fluke that Mittel's body survived."

"A different brigade, fighting back?" suggested Pavin.

"Maybe. Certainly why we've got to find out who Mittel's people were. We got an address for him?"

"Way out in Jasenevo—an apartment building. I thought you'd want to come out with me."

Danilov looked at his own watch, calculating the time difference with Washington, D.C. "Now that we've finally got something to tell him, I want to talk to Bill first." Danilov smiled eagerly across the room at his deputy. "This one has got a feel about it. I know it has!"

Danilov had convinced himself already, Pavin realized. Which was the wrong way for any objective investigation to begin.

William Cowley let Danilov talk himself out, his hope—excitement even—rising in parallel to that of the Russian's at the other end of the line. Then Cowley said, "I think you're right. We've got a combined one again. And it might finally turn out to answer your other questions." He hoped his uncertainty at Danilov finding Larissa's killer wasn't going to be answered at last.

"It's going to be good working together again."

Cowley was momentarily silent. "You heard from John Melton: he's our man in Moscow?"

"No," said Danilov. "What do you want me to do when there's contact?"

"Stall," replied Cowley. "What you've given me turns everything around. I think we're back on track together."

"I hope so," said Danilov.

"So do I," said Cowley. He abruptly decided there was every indication of this turning out to be a case of international proportions and Cowley wanted his to be the name on the front of the dossier.

7

Cowley protectively put everything in place before submitting a full report to Leonard Ross, along with the request for another meeting, confident that he had once again proved the benefit of the continued and unique association with Dimitri Danilov in Moscow. With the Odessa Bar and Grill now their obvious focus, Cowley positively set out, however, to obscure that interest as much as possible. He very specifically told Hank Slowen to put the Odessa, and its leaseholder Veniamin Yasev, under twenty-four-hour physical, filmed, and deep-probe observation. He also couriered to New York the Moscow-wired copies of Vasili Petrovich Mittel's criminal records to be shown at every repeated questioning swoop on every forensically identified Brighton Beach premises to confuse the concentration upon the Odessa. Also knowing from the passport visa that Mittel had entered through Kennedy Airport, Cowley spoke personally to the New York immigration supervisor as well as to the department's deputy director in Washington, D.C., to emphasize ("my director personally contacting yours, if that's what it takes") the importance of discovering Mittel's signed application—upon which an American address needed to be given—and with that visa's dates and an Alitalia flight numbers now to work from extended the search to any other Russians on the same Rome flight on the same day, more hopeful than expectant to find their hotel the same as Mittel's. Determined against any oversight or misunderstanding, Cowley followed up each conversation with e-mails repeating every detail he had relayed by phone. Cowley continued the same procedure of personal telephone contact with the Carabinieri's anti-organized crime director in Rome before e-mailing everything, as well as wiring Mittel's photograph, of the man's visa-proved visits to Italy. Additionally, he asked for the passenger list of the known Alitalia flight from Rome to New York, as well as the names of the complete flight crew whom bureau agents could question during their subsequent stopovers in New York. Cowley maintained the personal-before-officially-documented link with Toronto to pursue the ownership trail to the Odessa and was promised a response within twenty-four hours.

Cowley didn't expect the quickness of the director's summons, within an hour of his report being delivered. Leonard Ross was again alone in his top-floor office. The crumpled suit was the same, even more crumpled, but at least the shirt was fresh.

Ross tapped the dossier and said, "This is impressive."

"Thank you."

"And worrying."

"I agree," said Cowley. The other man's attitude was more relaxed than before but still short of the amiability there had once been.

"You think it could be some kind of international association—a linkup—we don't know about: worldwide Mafia?"

Cowley frowned at the suggestion. "That could possibly be the ultimate scenario."

"This all come from John Melton?"

Cowley hesitated. "Danilov returned my call."

"You did brief Melton?" asked Ross, suspiciously.

"Completely. And told him to liaise with the agency people there and backed it up by messaging Langley here."

Ross nodded, although cocking his head doubtfully. "This could be too important for cozy internal coteries."

"I don't conduct any investigation with cozy internal coteries," defended Cowley, careless of the forcefulness offending the other man.

"I'm determined that you won't," Ross came back. "I think a special task force should be established."

"With respect, sir, I believe that would be premature," cautioned Cowley. "I agree yours could be one conclusion—an extreme conclusion—from what we've got. And if it proves to be the case, then most certainly a special task force will be necessary, coordinating, even, with other bureaus from Italy and Russia. But I don't think there's sufficient evidence yet to justify that."

"I want the Bureau leading, not following others on this," stated the director.

Ross didn't mean the Bureau, Cowley decided: he wanted himself politically to be seen in the forefront. It was a moment—a useful opportunity—to show his own political savvy. The difficulty was going to be how he phrased it. "It would need to be a combined operation, including Moscow and Rome. Which would diplomatically require discussions here with the State Department, for their liaison with Moscow and Rome. And at least with the chief of staff at the White House. A wrongly timed move on our part wouldn't reflect well upon the Bureau or its judgment." Cowley would have liked to have expressed it better and hoped Ross correctly interpreted the implied warning against personally looking foolish by crying wolf too soon.

The director was silent for several moments, staring down unseeingly at Cowley's dossier. Finally he said, "I want there to be some preliminary planning, so that we can respond"—he snapped his fingers—"the moment we get something—anything—that takes us the smallest step forward. Ensure Melton establishes a proper working relationship with Danilov. Alert whoever our man is at the Rome embassy. Put him on standby. Come back to me by tomorrow with suggestions for what else we might prepare for. What are you going to do about Brighton Beach?"

"Wait until tomorrow—which brings us to the deadline we agreed—to see if Mittel's photograph produces anything," said Cowley, confident he'd anticipated everything. "If it doesn't, lift all the scene-of-crime closures, including that on the Odessa. Spread the word that we're stymied, to create a false confidence. Within those twenty-four hours we'll have a judge's order for a wiretap on the Odessa phone and on Veniamin Yasev's apartment, which we've traced to Thirty-first Street. We're also going to try to get a wire in Yasev's car as well as fitting a tracker, to know where he goes and where he is at all times if our observation loses him, which I hope it doesn't."

"I don't want this to go wrong," Leonard Ross suddenly announced.

"Neither do I, sir."

"It's important."

The man wasn't talking only of an international crime amalgamation. "I know," Cowley said, trying to intrude a tone in his voice to indicate that he genuinely did.

"You've got open-door access, day or night. I want to know anything ten seconds—five even—after you do."

"You will," Cowley promised, with nothing else to say. He couldn't, after all, tell the FBI director he knew the man was determined to have his name in bigger type on the dossier than Cowley's own.

It was Yuri Pavin who labeled Vitali Mittel's apartment a magpie's nest of haphazardly unconnected, hoarded bric-a-brac. The apartment itself was mid story in one of the 1960s blocks that hedge Moscow's suburbs in decaying, jerry-built clusters. The leg-aching climb up ten flights of graffiti-emblazoned, piss-soaked stairs was agonizing beyond six landings but still preferable to making the same ascent engulfed by an even worse stench of urine and excreta from within the elevator that was fortunately broken.

The wearily experienced Pavin already had a selection of variously shaped picklocks in his left hand when he rang the bell with his right, using the wait for a reply to recover his breath after the climb, which Danilov was also doing. Danilov was still breathing heavily when he said, "Open it up."

Pavin did so within seconds, with his third choice of tumbler-turning probe. Inside was a bachelor's mess. A padded winter coat remained on the floor on to which it had fallen from a broken hook, only partially covering discarded shoes, in the immediate hallway. More clothes, mostly dirty and none of them ironed, littered the bedroom floor, chair, and even the bottom of the single closet of mostly ignored hangers and hooks and drawers. The only exception was a carefully hung and obviously new blue suit with an American label—Gant—and two carefully folded shirts, also American. The stained, unmade bed was a rumpled confusion of rarely changed gray sheets and gray blankets and gray pillows. The sink and bath were strataed with scum lines, and the lavatory was black from excreta-clinging lime scale, the only new and comparatively clean icons the shaving soap, razor, toothpaste dispenser, and cologne, all American. There was an undisturbed rodent scuffling somewhere within the overflowing rubbish bin beside the kitchen sink in which some of the lowest crockery in the pile had already developed a green mold, as had two of the food congealed plates uncleared from the table upon which there was an empty vodka bottle, a match for the three on the dirt-grimed floor. By comparison, which Pavin suggested came from everything disposable having already been dumped elsewhere, the living room was unexpectedly tidy, littered only by a solitary pair of shoes and an inside-out sweater and by discarded although new magazines, all of them American porn. Everywhere was pervaded by the stale smell of bad air and sweat and dirt.

As he stacked the magazines more neatly on the solitary table, Pavin said, "Why do villains only look at pornography?"

"It's their culture," suggested Danilov.

"Who could live like this?" asked Pavin, rhetorically.

He virtually had lived in the neglectful squalor in which his wife, Olga, had kept their apartment, Danilov remembered. Maybe even more so, until he'd got a grip upon himself, after Larissa's murder and Olga's death from aborting another man's baby when he'd finally, too late, announced their marriage to be over. Danilov said, "We could be lucky. This *is* a magpie's nest. We could find a lot here."

"Or become infected," said Pavin, who was a fastidiously clean man.

They worked side by side, a perfectly coordinated team, starting with the living room. In a bureau drawer they found a half-empty carton of Kent cigarettes, six separate books of matches—one from the Odessa again—from American bars and restaurants.

Pavin said, "Odd things to collect."

"Not really," contradicted Danilov. "They're very much the sort of souvenirs people keep from foreign trips." He was talking and examining the tiny hoard, stopping at the fourth. "Not just New York. These last two are from Chicago."

"Addresses?"

"On both. Could be useful to Bill."

The only letters in the bureau were payment demands for utilities and threats of disconnection. In the very bottom drawer Pavin found a cheap spiral notebook that Mittel had clearly improvised into a telephone book but without any names, the numbers listed against only initials and in no alphabetical order. Danilov went cursorily through it, trying to identify dialing codes, and said abruptly, "Here's America!" He turned to the table, where the American mementos lay and said, "It's the Odessa number. Against the letter Y."

"Which doesn't fit the spelling of Maret or Zubov," said Pavin, unnecessarily. "Anything for Italy?"

Danilov continued on through the book, finally shaking his head. "Nothing."

"Chicago?"

"No. We're going to have to trace every identity backward, through the numbers."

"The telephone people always say it's impossible."

"And somehow you always make it possible. I know you'll do it again. And try to get as many telephone records as you can, from Mittel's number here."

In the bedroom they found another sealed carton of Kent cigarettes and two further books of matches, both from the Hotel Medici in Rome. In a bedside cabinet there was another Makarov handgun, with three additional clips of ammunition, a round-tipped knife honed to razor sharpness on both edges, and a knuckle-duster. Danilov and Pavin both agreed there was what appeared to be blood on both and carefully bagged them for forensic examination. They left the stinking kitchen until last. Pavin kicked the waste bin until the rat ran. Danilov, waiting at the doorway with a rarely used broom, shooed it further into the flat. Pavin used the handle of the broom to stir through the bin, but there was only rotting food and food containers and another empty vodka bottle.

Pavin said, "We might have helped Bill, but there's not much here for us."

Danilov said, "What about the blood on the knife and knuckle-duster?"

"What are the possible alternatives?" demanded Pamela. She was frightened that the man she loved—but sometimes couldn't trust not to sink into the bottom of a shot glass—wasn't taking as seriously as he should the internal political intrigue.

"Not the Doomsday scenario of a full-scale global, family-to-family amalgamation: a much simpler—and by comparison smaller—Russian arms selling operation," proposed Cowley. "We know there is a trade with America. Italy is as good a marketplace as any."

"That brings it into terrorism, which is my backyard," said Pamela.

"Which is why I'm telling you I put it on my risk list to Ross."

"What else did you put?"

"Drugs, with the same limited explanation. We know there's a lot of heroin being shipped through Russia from Pakistan and Iran and Afghanistan. Cocaine from Latin America, too."

"Still organized crime on a global scale," insisted Pamela.

Cowley rose with her to clear the dinner table. Pamela firmly corked the remaining half of the wine bottle. He said, "Ross is worried that it's a major linkup. If we've stumbled upon the sort of gang-to-gang stuff we already know to be going on, it's something we can hopefully break without overreacting with war-sized task force."

"If he turns out to be right—which makes you wrong—you're the guy who made the bad call."

"And if I'm right—which makes him wrong—I've saved the Bureau, and Judge Leonard Ross, from looking stupid by firing all sorts of emergency flares when there isn't an emergency. Besides which, we're initiating provisional planning in the event of Ross being right, so it isn't a win-or-lose contest."

"Just you doing the planning?" pressed Pamela.

"Sure. Who else?"

"Jed Parker's in Planning," reminded Pamela. "And you told me he considers himself a Russian expert."

"What input could Parker have?"

"You tell me. And after you've told me tell a lot of other paranoids in the J. Edgar Hoover building, starting with the director himself."

"Why the hell didn't you check!" demanded Orlov, the man who could not make mistakes.

"I'm sorry," apologized Zhikin, knowing he was expected to take the blame.

"Why didn't we know at once?"

"It was the way it happened, through traffic. There's some arrangement with the Organized Crime Bureau about car bombings."

"Don't we have a source inside Petrovka?" demanded Orlov.

"Of course. A sergeant, Alexandr Ognev."

"What's he say?"

Zhikin shifted, knowing Orlov was not going to like what he heard. "The investigation is being handled by the commanding general himself, Danilov."

"The straight one?"

"And his deputy," nodded Zhikin. It would inevitably come out, so there was no point in holding back. "Apparently there's been some contact with America."

It was several moments before Orlov could speak through his tight-lipped fury. "How closely can Ognev monitor things?"

"He's not sure, not yet. He does know Danilov searched Mittel's apartment, out at Jasenevo."

"What did he find?"

"Ognev doesn't know."

"There won't be anything," insisted Orlov, for his own reassurance.

"I doubt it," agreed Zhikin, obediently.

"Tell Ognev it's important. That there will be bonuses. A lot of money."

"I already have."

"Tell him again."

8

All William Cowley's new leads were initiated from Moscow or Rome, which gave the impression of positive developments, which indeed they were, although on later, more balanced examination, that information turned out to be chips rather than picture tiles in the mosaic. And which, contravening the director's edict to Cowley, made the FBI appear to be following rather than leading, which was an unfair—even illogical—assessment.

As is invariably the case in complicated investigations, those first chips were thrown up by the most basic of police procedures. With a positive entry date from Vitali Mittel's passport, it took Italian police, protectively involving the U.S. embassy-based FBI agent to cover themselves in the event of mistakes, less than half a day to recover from their immigration records the names of I. Orlov, V. Mittel, and F. Lapinsh, not from the direct Aeroflot flight from Moscow, which was their first search, but from an Alitalia flight from Geneva. Further needles were just as quickly picked out of that potential haystack that very same afternoon when the visa-recorded names of I. G. Orlov and F. A. Lapinsh appeared immediately adjacent to that of Mittel in the register of the matchbook-identified Hotel Medici, on Rome's Via Sistina. Orlov's name was first, indicating an order of precedence, as it was on the visa-indicated Alitalia departure flight to New York four days later. And again upon the return of all three, ten days after their first visit, along with their second reservation at the same hotel at the top of the Spanish Steps. The canceled exit visa for all three was on the same day that Aeroflot Flight 322 left Fumincino Airport for a nonstop flight to Moscow's Sheremet'yevo Airport.

With names and arrival dates to work from, the INS at John F. Kennedy finally located American visa entries for the three, each giving the Grand Hyatt Hotel on Manhattan's Forty-second Street as their New York addresses, which corresponded with three of the matchbook souvenirs found by Danilov in Mittel's Jasenevo apartment. Guided once more by the matchbook mementos, Chicago's FBI field office easily located the Russian's two-day stay at the Hyatt Regency, on East Wacker Drive.

There were no rental car bookings from either Hyatt. Nor had there been any during the group's two stays at Rome's Medici Hotel. In both Italy and America the hotel systems wiped outgoing telephone call numbers from their automatically recording computers when bills were presented and paid, which they had been in every case in cash, leaving no credit card trail.

Cowley got the promised return call from Toronto within an hour of ordering Hank Slowen officially to lift the scene-of-crime order against the Brighton Beach premises. The Odessa Bar and Grill on Riegelmann boardwalk was owned by Pet-a-Pick Supplies, a pet-shop food company that had gone bankrupt four years earlier, leaving only its dormant name on the companies register. It had been bought "off the shelf" by a Toronto civil law firm—two of whose attorneys comprised its fiduciary-operating directors—upon instructions from Heidlecker and Boyer, a law firm at 15, Rue de la Servette, Geneva, Switzerland. In the Canadian companies register Pet-a-Pick Supplies was listed as a wholly-owned subsidiary of PF Holdings, registered at the same Geneva address as the law firm. The Toronto lawyers were acting legally within Canadian financial law and had cooperated fully. The audited and up-to-date records of the Odessa's business trading showed an after-tax profit of $200,000 on the first year, rising to $2,000,000 in the last complete year's accounts. Those accounts—and those that preceded them—showed the leaseholder, Veniamin Kirilovich Yasev, had throughout his tenancy paid his rent promptly upon every due date. Cowley thanked the Canadians for their offer but said he'd take over the inquiry in Switzerland. America had a disclosure agreement if Swiss-held bank accounts could be proved to be the proceeds of crime.

It only took the afternoon and early evening of that same day for the photograph of Vitali Mittel to be shown in all the premises along the boardwalk, including those in which the blood of the victims had been found. None admitted recognition in any of them. At the Odessa, Veniamin Yasev himself disclaimed any recognition of the man. The two carefully rehearsed FBI men complained in front of Yasev of the investigation getting nowhere and of its being scaled down.

None of the Alitalia crews remembered Mittel as a passenger. Unless there was an incident out of the ordinary, passengers to them were faceless, anonymous occupants of seats. Nor did any of the staff at the New York Grand Hyatt recall him or his two fellow Russians as guests. But the doorman at Chicago's Hyatt Regency did, from the Russians' cardinal error of not tipping, despite being arrogantly demanding, actually snapping their fingers several times to gain his attention. They'd made an odd trio, Mittel's remarkable shortness exaggerated by the height of the man whose name the doorman didn't know but to whom Mittel and the other unknown middle-height Russian very obviously deferred. It was from the FBI's Chicago field office that the unnecessary reminder came that in their suburb of Evanston lived the FBI's acknowledged *capo di tutti i capi* of America's Mafia, Joseph "Slow Joe" Tinelli.

Throughout Cowley had complied with Leonard Ross's instructions constantly to be updated. It was the passed-on reminder of Tinelli's position in America's organized crime that brought the personal summons to the seventh floor of the J. Edgar Hoover Building.

"I'm right!" Ross insisted. There was a food stain on his tie that seemed to match that on the lapel of the creased suit.

"We've got closed-circuit TV cameras, supposed to be speed monitors, on the approaches to Tinelli's house," said Cowley. "There's been no vehicle sighting of Mittel."

"You get every occupant of every car?" demanded the director.

"No," admitted Cowley.

"We've got dates," persisted Ross. "We identify every occupant of every car going in and out of Tinelli's property while the Russians were in Chicago!"

"No," said Cowley.

"I'm right," repeated Ross. "The Russians came here to set up a partnership with our Mafia."

"Three of them," qualified Cowley. "One of whom we certainly know to be dead. One of the others—either Lapinsh or Orlov—is most likely dead as well. If it was a partnership, it didn't last very long."

"Tell me where we're at," said Ross.

He already had, thought Cowley at least twice. "I've filed the request, through State, for us to be granted treaty-agreed access to the accounts and shareholders' identity in PF Holdings in Geneva. And spoken to our guy at the Basel embassy to follow up the formal approach. I've gone back to Moscow, both directly and through John Melton with the names of Lapinsh and Orlov. If they're in records, we can get photographs to check out here, particularly with the doorman at the Hyatt Regency in Chicago. We've got the authorized tap on the Odessa telephone and a twenty-four hour blanket over Yasev himself, although we haven't yet been able to get a wire into his car. We hope to, in a day or two. We've increased manual surveillance on Tinelli and started working our way through snitches in New York itself, to pick up any ripples from the families there. Immigration has put a computer tag on the names of Orlov and Lapinsh—"

"What about our records on those names," pounced the director.

"Checked. Negative," said Cowley. He'd deserve a drink, after this inquisition. And would have one. It was Pamela's night out with her reading circle group: they were doing Steinbeck's *Travels with Charlie*.

"Everything's too spread out. It's not centralized," protested Ross.

"It is centralized! Here!" insisted Cowley, in equal protest. "Everyone's been briefed and knows what to do. It's all coming to me, on the Russian desk. And from me, it's coming to you. We've got the full handle."

"Moscow's the lead," insisted Ross.

"Where we couldn't be in better shape, with Danilov."

"My understanding—from your briefing papers—is that law in Russia is a joke!"

"Dimitri's a straight arrow. So's his deputy."

"Two men!" rejected Ross, contemptuously. "Come on, please!"

It was an argument open to ridicule, Cowley conceded. "Two men who've proved themselves more than adequate on every cooperating occasion in the past."

"The past is the past," the director said. "My concern is the present and what it might bring about in the future."

"What more would you have me do?" demanded Cowley, in direct challenge.

"We'll talk tomorrow," said Ross.

Cowley drove home over the Fourteenth Street Bridge and kept himself to two drinks in a bar quite close to the Arlington apartment in which there was no chance of his encountering anyone else from the Bureau. He was home an hour before Pamela, which was more than sufficient to clean his teeth, rinse with Listerine, and afterward munch on several crackers to take away the distinctive odor of the mouthwash. Why, wondered Cowley as he set the table for dinner, had Leonard Ross's remark about their meeting the following day sounded like a threat?

Dimitri Danilov chose to meet the two Americans at the same time and included Yuri Pavin in the Petrovka introduction. John Melton was a quiet-talking, precise man who wore rimless spectacles and had all three buttons of his Ivy League suit secured. The CIA officer, Al

Needham, was black, with a football quarterback's build that made him almost as big as Pavin. The two Americans arrived together, in the same car. Danilov had thermosed tea as well as vodka ready. Melton declined either. So did Pavin, who was teetotal. Needham accepted the vodka in a Southern drawl that seemed to start low in his stomach. Danilov joined him.

Melton said at once, "You have any records on these two guys, Orlov or Lapinsh?"

Danilov sighed, confronting the familiar embarrassment with an overseas force, particularly knowing as he did the archival resources of the FBI, glad that an hour earlier he'd exchanged everything he had to offer with Cowley, who wouldn't be critical. He said, "No records as such. There's a limited file on Orlov, though. Until five or six years ago he was thought to have been a bull, an enforcer, for a brigade operating in the north of Moscow, around Mytishchi. The suggestion is that he took it over, but we haven't any confirmation of that. You know what we've got on Mittel. Nothing at all on Lapinsh."

"Is there a picture of Orlov?" asked Melton.

"No," said Danilov. He and Pavin had decided against mentioning their suspicion that the Orlov file had been tampered with.

"So that's it?" rumbled Needham.

"That's it," admitted Danilov. "But there is something else."

"What?" demanded Melton.

"Forensic managed to lift enough blood for a DNA comparison from an odd-shaped knife we found in Mittel's flat out in Jasenevo. It matched that of Nikita Yaklovich Volodkin, one of the last cross-sacrificed bodies in the river." Danilov decided he'd waited just long enough for the announcement: it had deflected the American's impending criticism.

There was a momentary silence, neither American wanting to commit himself. Then, professionally, Melton said, "The patterns don't fit. You got what, eleven, twelve gang guys, on sacrificial crosses floating down the Moskva. Classic turf war stuff, clearer messages than Western Union could have provided. In Brighton Beach it's slam-bam-fuck-you execution. As it was here, with whatever happened to Vitali Mittel and his as yet positively unidentified companion. No pattern."

"What about Brighton Beach, which is why you're here and we're having this conversation?" demanded Danilov, anxious to recover from the factual emptiness of what he'd been able to offer. "And their known visit to Chicago, where Tinelli lives? And to Rome?"

"You think it's a worldwide mob partnership?" demanded Melton, in return.

Instead of directly answering, Needham said, "Two pattern breaks. Triple deaths in Brighton Beach, car bombing here. Without Chicago and Rome, turf war, pure and simple."

"But they did go to Chicago and Rome," persisted Danilov, relentlessly. "So it isn't pure and simple. We've got to know why and where it fits. Without knowing which, you're right: it's a broken pattern. So where's your guide from Chicago?"

Both Americans shifted, uncomfortably.

"On what there is, I am not going with International Crime Incorporated," said Needham.

"On what there is, we haven't sufficient even to make a guess," said Melton.

"And we need more from America to reach that judgment," insisted Danilov, at once.

"We need more from everywhere," said Pavin, supportively.

When more came, within hours, it added to the confusion as much as edging the inquiry forward. The first, that night, was a call from the tapped telephone at the Odessa Bar and Grill to the prerevolutionary mansion on Ulitza Varvarka. The second was another telephone call within five minutes of William Cowley arriving at his office in the J. Edgar Hoover building.

John Melton said, "Who's Jed Parker?"

"Why?" asked Cowley, feeling the first stir of unease.

"Guy's just called me direct, from Washington, wanting to be filled in on everything that's happening here."

"What did you tell him?"

"That you're my boss and that he should ask you."

"That's what you should have told him," said Cowley. Today's meeting with Leonard Ross was going to be more important than he'd anticipated.

9

Because their previous encounters on this specific case had been one to one, Cowley expected only Leonard Ross to be waiting in the seventh-floor executive suite. The third, unexpected man was short—five-foot five inches on tiptoe—and slight, tightly dark-haired, saturnine, and soberly dressed in a muddy blue suit, maybe deep gray: the guy in the back corner of the elevator whom no one notices, not even when they step on his unprotesting foot because he's so insignificant.

"Jed Parker," the director said. Another surprise was how relaxed Leonard Ross appeared.

Cowley hesitated, momentarily disoriented. Parker took the same hesitant time to half rise to offer his hand, sitting just as quickly. Cowley had never tried—thought even—of deeply involving himself in internal headquarters intriguing: there was a vague, until-now unacknowledged conceit that he was above such crap, not needing—nor prepared to offer—the butt-sucking sycophancy and backslapping or backstabbing, even more conceitedly content to be judged by his investigatory record. Which he knew, racheting up the self-confidence, to be way above and beyond every other division director in the building. Which is how he intended to go on. He didn't give a damn about who Jed Parker's uncle was or how influential the man was. His only concern was the current inquiry and preventing it going offtrack.

He said, "I was going to look you up today."

"How's that?" said Parker.

"I head the Russian desk."

"I know."

"And we're in the middle of an investigation."

"I know that, too. Although from what I've been told you're hardly in the middle of it yet. More like just beginning."

Cowley refused to rise to the jibe. "There's an operational rule that you may not know of, having only just arrived here. Inquiries from other divisions into an ongoing case are always channeled through the case supervisor, to avoid duplication and confusion and giving field agents the wrong steer. Screwing things up, in fact."

Parker looked sideways to the director, as if in invitation. When Ross did not speak, Parker said, "The director felt you might benefit from some overall planning input."

"I didn't get a memorandum to that effect," said Cowley. "Any approach to Moscow should still have been made through me."

"It was my oversight, not advising you of Jed's involvement," said Ross, entering the conversation at last.

Jed, noted Cowley. "What, precisely, is the overall planning input going to be?"

"That's what we're here to discuss," said Ross. "You have anything to bring us up to date with?"

Cowley hesitated again, offering the already translated transcript across the desk to the director. To Parker he said, "I've only got one copy. The tap on the Odessa picked up a conversation between Yasev and Orlov. It was an outgoing call, from Brighton Beach. Audio managed to get the tonal register from the dialing, to give us the Moscow number. I'm passing it on to Danilov, through Melton. They should get Orlov's address from it sometime today."

"Perhaps you'd take me through the conversation," smiled Parker. He added, "In the closest possible detail."

Like a schoolboy being asked to perform for the teacher, thought Cowley, feeling a fresh burn of irritation. "Yasev starts by asking how we got Mittel's identity. Orlov says Mittel and Lapinsh had to be gotten rid of—which establishes the identity of the second body in the burned-out car—but that it went wrong. He says it's not a problem—nothing they can't handle there—and that nothing's off course. Yasev says there's nothing they can't handle at this end, either, that the Bureau doesn't have anything and that they are scaling down. Orlov asks if everyone learned the lesson, and Yasev says he's sure they have: no one is going to make that mistake again. Orlov says he doesn't know when he's coming here again but that the next meeting will be somewhere 'closer to home' . . ." Cowley paused. " 'Closer to home' is a direct quote. Orlov tells Yasev to keep in touch and not to upset part-

ners—that's another direct quote, 'Don't upset our business partners'—and Yasev replies that he understands and sends his regards to
Feliks Romanovich."

Cowley was glad to stop, his feeling of delivering a chosen piece
heightened by Parker's vague head nodding, as if in approval.

At once, looking down at his transcript, Leonard Ross quoted,
"'You know we've got Petrovka in our pocket?'"

Cowley said, "My paraphrase was that there's nothing to worry
about: that there's nothing they can't handle."

"Petrovka," isolated Parker. "Headquarters of the Organized
Crime Bureau, headed by your friend, General Dimitri Danilov."

"Who's in nobody's pocket," Cowley came back, at once. "Let's
not go over well-trodden ground about Russian militia corruption."

"Let's not ignore, either, the very direct boast from a gang leader
who's got a source inside the very organization with which we are supposedly cooperating on an investigation."

"I haven't," said Cowley. "Neither has Danilov. Doesn't it occur to
you that our knowing it gives us a potential advantage?"

"If we knew who Orlov's source was," agreed Parker. "Do we?"

Fuck, thought Cowley. Caught out. "Danilov is on to it."

Parker's silence was sufficient ridicule to Cowley's weak promise.
The man let it stretch just sufficiently before saying, "Who's Feliks
Romanovich?"

"That hasn't been established yet."

"But Danilov is working on it," mocked Parker.

"Yes," said Cowley, tightly. Properly, he hoped. Not with any
secret, self-avenging agenda.

"Orlov flew into Italy from Switzerland," reminded Parker. "The
Odessa is own by a Geneva holding company. In the four years of its
ownership, according to audited Toronto records, the Odessa has
shown a profit of over $5,000,000. That's impossible through trading.
It's a money-laundering operation."

"A point very fully and clearly made in my application to the Swiss
authorities for access to PF Holdings," said Cowley. He realized that
Parker must have read every report he'd submitted to the director.

"That's good to hear," said Parker. "What else is there to read from
the actual, word-for-word translation?"

Before Cowley could answer, Ross quoted, " 'No one is going to make that mistake again.' What mistake isn't going to be repeated?"

Cowley still didn't get the opportunity to speak. Parker said, "Brighton Beach was an example. Nyunin, Guzev, and Zubov somehow got out of line and had to be slapped back. Literally. It fits with not upsetting business partners."

"Bill?" questioned the director.

He was back on Christian-name terms, Cowley recognized. He said, "It's the most obvious interpretation. I'm not comfortable putting all three in the same bag. Nyunin and Guzev were local punks. Zubov wasn't. In my book there's a difference there somewhere."

"Which isn't the most important part of the conversation," Parker interrupted, impatiently. "It's definitely an organized crime partnership."

"My judgment from the start," said Leonard Ross. "You still arguing against me, Bill?"

"I didn't argue against you, Mr. Director," corrected Cowley. "I said it was one of the possibilities, but that there were others."

"But a global tie-up heads the list," persisted Parker. "You asked for a planning assessment, Mr. Director. In my opinion, this investigation requires a specific task force."

"Also my feeling from the beginning," said Ross.

It was as if the director were proving himself to the other man, thought Cowley. He said, "For which everything is already in place. Brighton Beach is well established. So is Chicago. I've agents on standby to supplement Rome and Geneva. I can drop them off— spend a day in detailed briefing, if I think it's necessary—on my way to Moscow."

"No," said Ross.

"Sir?" frowned Cowley.

Leonard Ross theatrically splayed a hand, dropping each finger as he counted. "Brighton Beach . . . Chicago . . . Moscow . . . Geneva . . . Rome. Five points of investigation in four different countries, worldwide. The task force needs an overall supervisor, and you're it, Bill. But you can't be it in Moscow. I want you here, on top of everything."

"Who's going to Moscow?" questioned Cowley, expectantly.

"Jed," announced the director.

It had all been rehearsed, Cowley accepted. Directly, uncaringly, he said to Parker, "You confident you have sufficient field experience?"

Parker smiled. "Two years in Bolivia and Colombia. Two and a half in Moscow. The director seems happy enough with the CV."

He'd made himself look stupid, Cowley acknowledged. "I'll see you get the contingency planning, for the task force: all the names."

"And I'd like the telephone intercept from the Odessa in the original Russian, so I can listen to the inflexions and anything I might interpret as innuendo."

"Of course," said Cowley, with indignant fury.

"And let's be clear about how this is to run," said the director. "Bill is the investigation supervisor, Jed. He's the link through which you liaise in the command chain."

For the first time there was a visible dip in the other man's complacency, a quickly dispelled frown. Then he said, "Of course."

"That's good," said Ross, enthusiastically. "Now let's get to work: sort this whole goddamned business out. Double quick."

"This is the Odessa Bar and Grill." Veniamin Yasev's voice, warm, inviting.

"It's me." Igor Orlov, flat but with a question in the identification.

"Oh? Is anything wrong?"

"You tell me."

"I don't know what you're saying?"

"I just had a call from Switzerland."

"What?"

"The FBI. An official government inquiry, about PF Holdings, under some fucking legal agreement about the proceeds of crime!"

"Shit!"

"It's OK. Wolfgang argued there was insufficient proof for disclosure and won. We're going sideways into another company. Everything will be handled direct, lawyer to lawyer. But you told me everything was scaling down?"

"That's what the fuckers said. Two of them."

"They still around?"

"Not for a day or two."

"You sure everything's secure there?"

"Positive."

"I don't want anyone forgetting."

"No one will. How did the bastards discover Switzerland?"

"A company register search, according to Wolfgang. We're moving on from PF Holings. Wolfgang says it's not a problem."

"There are never problems for someone like Wolfgang, bubble-wrapped in Switzerland."

"He's right!" Orlov's voice was strident, angry. *"They're not going to get anywhere in Switzerland. If they try again, they'll find PF Holdings disappears into another company. But be careful there. They're still sniffing: nothings been scaled down. Don't use this landline anymore. You got the cell phone?"*

"Of course."

"That's how we'll talk, from now on. And change the phones every week. New number. Let the phones get lost: stolen, left around."

"I'll need to tell everyone about this line."

"Do it. Today. That's why I'm calling."

"Do you think . . . ?" started Yasev but stopped.

"What?"

"Nothing."

"What!" insisted Orlov, strident again.

"What about our friends?"

"No need to worry them unnecessarily. You just handle things at your level."

There was a pause. Then Yasev asked, *"Anything else I should do?"*

"Just everything I tell you. Exactly as I tell you."

"What about you, in Moscow?"

"We're taking all the precautions." There was a snigger. *"I'm going to enjoy myself. Find out how clever these bastards really are."*

Dimitri Danilov said, "I expected it to be you."

Cowley said, "I expected it to be me, too."

"Have you got a problem?"

Cowley hesitated, his integrity stretched. "Jed Parker is politically well connected."

"I can't hold back on cooperation. That wouldn't be right."

"That offends me, Dimitri!"

"I'm sorry . . . I didn't mean . . ."

"It's unthinkable that you wouldn't fully cooperate."

"We could still talk, though. Direct."

Cowley hesitated. "I don't want to deal behind a colleague's back."

"From what you've implied, he's dealt behind yours."

"Does that mean I've got to sink to his level?"

"Yes," said Danilov at once. "If we're talking about survival, that's exactly what you've got to do."

"It's not the way I've operated professionally." No backslapping, no backstabbing, he thought.

"You're talking in the past tense," said Danilov. "Welcome to the present. Welcome to the real world."

"You realize what the bastard's done!" demanded Pamela, jagged-voiced. "Leonard Ross has screwed you: fucked you back, front, and center! He's put you at war with Parker. You're the official overall supervisor. You get the shit for anything and everything that goes wrong. Which Jed Fucking Parker—whose superior you've very definitely and again officially been appointed—will ensure you do, because no stain will ever dirty Jed Parker's pure white suit. The only thing he's going to get covered in is approval, and you're not going to get any of that, despite the bullshit about links in chains. Disaster, it's yours. Success, it's Parker's. And Leonard Ross is out of danger, in every which way it falls!" Pamela stopped, breathless.

Cowley, who'd had the afternoon to reflect and analyze, said, "I already worked all that out."

"Bastard!" repeated the woman, left with nothing but anger.

"I do have the overview."

"If Jed Parker allows you."

Cowley was glad he hadn't told Pamela about his conversation with Danilov. From the vehemence of this outburst she would have approved—he was surprised she hadn't already suggested it—but there was a feeling he couldn't identify, embarrassment maybe, at degenerating into back-channel deviousness. "I'll be OK."

Pamela remained for several moments, legs astride and with her hands on her hips, looking skeptically at him. "I think, my darling, that you should have a drink."

"That was something I never expected you to say."

"There are times. We just got to one."

Pamela got to the telephone on the second ring. Handing it to Cowley she said, "It's the Watch Room."

The night duty officer at the J. Edgar Hoover Building said, "Manhattan just picked up something they thought you should hear immediately."

Cowley listened without interruption. As he put the phone down he said to Pamela, "We just got another time. And I certainly need that drink now."

10

Yuri Pavin's finding the Ulitza Varvarka mansion of Igor Gavrilovich Orlov was the most positive success of his telephone number trawl. He failed, though, to find an official land or ownership registration. With the Odessa Bar and Grill listing in Vitali Mittel's makeshift telephone book immediately identified by comparison with the man's matchbook souvenir, the only other potentially useful address was a newly opened American theme restaurant, called in English the Brooklyn Bite, on Skornjaznyj Lane. The other numbers were divided between prostitutes, garages, and car repair shops. An ownership registration search for the restaurant found Feliks Romanovich Zhikin to be a joint partner with Orlov, which identified the person to whom Yasev sent his regards on the first FBI-eavesdropped telephone conversation. There was no criminal record on a man named Feliks Romanovich Zhikin.

It was Danilov's suggestion that he and Pavin personally take their discoveries to the American embassy, to get them away from the informer-ridden Ulitza Petrovka, and Danilov who immediately conceded his operational problem the moment they were seated in John Melton's office. There was coffee percolating, but no alcohol.

"We don't know who Orlov's source is within our headquarters. Until we do, it's best we meet here. When we do identify him, we can turn it back, feeding whoever it is what we want Orlov to be told." It was a suggestion that Cowley had unnecessarily repeated during their hurried overnight telephone conversation.

Al Needham looked up from what Danilov had just given him. "So how do you find out who it is?"

"We're installing taps of our own, on the house and the restaurant," said Pavin.

Melton shook his head, passing Danilov a single sheet of paper. "We picked up a conversation between Orlov and Yasev, at the Odessa. In a nutshell the Swiss refused our access request and the lawyers told Orlov. He knows we're on to him, says he's taking precautions. And he's insisting now that he and Yasev use cell phones."

"What's the legal opinion on the calls so far?" asked Pavin.

"They don't constitute evidence of criminal intent."

It only took Danilov minutes to read the whole transcript, already aware of its substance from Cowley's call. He said, "The precaution is only for conversations with America. That's where his information—and his caution—is coming from. We've got to hope he doesn't suspect we've got his house or his restaurant: certainly not that we're listening to both."

"When will the taps be in place?" asked Needham.

"An hour," promised Pavin.

"We'll selectively leak things—bullshit things that look and sound like they're important—around Petrovka and wait for it to be relayed back."

"Could take a while," complained Needham.

"It's what's got to be done," insisted Pavin.

"But the problems in between are obvious," said Danilov. "We can't risk Orlov learning we know about his Varvarka house or the Brooklyn Bite. The only people who do know are Yuri and me. And Yuri is personally going to handle the tapes."

"But there needs to be some physical surveillance," anticipated Melton.

"Most important to get some idea of what the son of a bitch actually looks like—a mugshot so we know who the target is," said Needham.

"OK," accepted Melton. "So the surveillance is on us."

"We haven't gone near, just literally driven by," warned Pavin, practicably. "There's certainly an alley either side of the mansion, separating it from the adjacent buildings. There'll be a linking alley at the rear, too. It's very obviously prerevolutionary, so there'll be servant exits and entrances: probably quite a lot. There's clearly a delivery alley at the rear of the restaurant, too."

"We'll manage," mocked Melton, lightly.

"Just pointing out what I saw on the drive-by," Pavin smiled back, accepting that it was camaraderie, not ridicule.

"A task force has been set up in Washington," announced Melton. "We're getting a bunch of guys drafted in. Man in charge is named Parker. I'm to tell you he wants a meeting as soon as he gets here."

It sounded peremptory, thought Danilov. He had been curious if the Americans would disclose the formation of the special squad. "As soon as he likes."

"No reason for us to hold back casing the house and the restaurant," said Needham.

"The message was to wait until he gets here before initiating anything," cautioned Melton.

"He's your boss, not mine," said Needham, pointedly.

"He said he was talking to Langley," said Melton.

"Langley ain't talked to me, and they're the people I take orders from."

Danilov had wondered how long it would take for interagency rivalry to emerge. He supposed it was inevitable. How difficult would it be to make a three-cornered arrangement work?

"How could you have let it to happen!" Leonard Ross's face was mottled with genuine anger, the second FBI transcript on the desk separating him from William Cowley, who was sweating from even greater anger, recognizing at once that the Swiss failure would officially be recorded as his personal responsibility.

Determinedly, he said, "You saw the formal legal application to Basel, before it was sent. It was jointly prepared, by our legal department here working with the attorneys at State. Each—separately and together—considered there was sufficient proof of suspicion to get the Swiss to agree. I spoke with counsel before coming here this morning. They say we can appeal the rejection. Or resubmit when we get more."

"It's too *late!*" insisted the exasperated Ross, lifting and then letting drop, disgustedly, the intercept and the formal Swiss refusal for information on the Geneva company. "Orlov knows we're on his back. He's already juggling Swiss holding companies and we can't ask for access to what we don't have the names of. You've heard—read—what he said. PF Holdings will by now be a post office, the fine mesh filter through which everything goes before disappearing. And he's obviously unsure of the landline, so that's closed off against us, too. This is not good, Bill. In fact, it's disastrous."

"I've already got our technical people sending digital scanners up to New York. And Parker's taking enough with him to Moscow to monitor every cell phone in the city."

"Orlov ordered the cell phones changed every week," reminded Ross, tapping the papers in front of him.

"Technical says they can handle that. And we've got the wire on Yasev's apartment, too."

"What about his car?"

"Not yet."

"Bill, come on!"

"We spook him, we're in an even worse mess."

"If that's possible," said the director.

Cowley indicated the early morning cable that he'd personally delivered with everything else on his first meeting of the day with the older man. "Danilov's getting Orlov's home and a restaurant wired in Moscow . . ." He looked unnecessarily at his watch. "Should even be in place by now."

"Thank God Jed's getting there today. Pity we can't divert him to Basel. You told Moscow about this fiasco?"

"Overnight," said Cowley. "It'll be waiting for Jed when he gets there."

"Jed has to know what he's got to get out from under," said Ross. "We shouldn't have lost Switzerland."

Cowley accepted that irrespective of the legal presentation having been prepared and made by lawyers—irrespective, even, of that application having been approved in advance by Leonard Ross—he was stuck with the responsibility for what Ross called a disastrous fiasco. Disrespectful in his anger, Cowley said, "Look at the end of the transcript!"

"What!" demanded Ross.

"Orlov thinks we have lost. He thinks he's better than us."

"So far he's proving to be."

"So far he's proving to be nothing of the sort." Cowley refused to go along. "We've had a setback. Nothing more than that. Like our knowing Orlov's got a source within Petrovka—a conduit we can use when Danilov discovers who it is—we can use this, too. He's not worried, panicking . . ." Cowley snatched up his own copy of the transcript. " 'I'm going to enjoy myself. Find out how clever these bastards really are,' " he quoted. "He's sure as hell going to find out who's the cleverer!"

"This isn't the goddamned gunfight at the OK Corral!"

"That's what I think it is," insisted Cowley. How many guns was he facing, he wondered. And from how many different directions?

Jed Parker convened the conference from the embassy car phone on the way into Moscow from Sheremet'yevo Airport to Novinskij Bul'var, telling the agents with him they had just one hour to settle into the Savoy Hotel. Parker filled that hour reading all the new Washington material and hearing from John Melton of that morning's encounter with Dimitri Danilov. He also demanded to know from Al Needham why the CIA man had carried out a preliminary survey of Igor Orlov's mansion on Ulitza Varvarka and the American-style restaurant.

"I hadn't then been told by Langley that I had been seconded to your task force," said Needham smoothly. At Parker's insistence he was in the front row of the seats being filled up by the newly arriving Americans.

"But now you have?" said Parker.

"Yes," acknowledged the man, still smooth.

"So from now on there won't be any misunderstandings," insisted

Parker, moving on to address the fully assembled room. "I'm running the tightest ship any of you've ever sailed in. No one thinks, blinks, or speaks without my knowing about it." In the hour since his arrival—and less since his reading the overnight information from Washington—Parker had had the Swiss rejection enlarged on a projector now illuminating a screen behind him. Jerking his hand toward it, he said, "That's the sort of thing I mean and won't—and listen up, all of you, by won't I very definitely mean won't—have on my watch. What you're reading is a major screwup we can't begin yet to evaluate. Anyone in this task force screws up, your ass will be out of here, to total oblivion, in the time it takes for the car to get you to the airport. Everyone hearing me loud and clear?"

There were shuffles and movements and occasional grunts.

"We've got a further, inbuilt problem with the Russians," continued Parker. "Their whole system is as rotten as hell. We know, for a fact, that the guy we want has got eyes and ears in the very headquarters building of the agency we're supposed to be cooperating with. So we're not going to. All the dealings with the Russians are through me: I get what they have; they get what I choose to tell them. Understood?"

There were more agreeing shifts and sounds.

"Any questions?"

No one moved or spoke in reply, but Needham bent slightly sideways toward Melton and murmured, "Fuck me!"

Parker said, "I didn't catch that!"

"I remarked that this was going to be one hell of an investigation," said Needham, blank-faced.

"You just better believe it!" said Parker.

Yuri Maksimovich Pavin considered he had some idea of the effect the disclosure would have upon Dimitri Danilov, but he wasn't altogether sure after so many self-promises and so many dedicated, graveside vows and so much self-imagined vengeance. Pavin actually remained for more than thirty minutes in his locked and secure office before venturing farther along the corridor, unsure what to say or how to say it.

Danilov frowned at the expression on his deputy's face and said, "What is it?"

"We got a perfect intercept: Feliks Zhikin using the private line at the restaurant to talk to Orlov at the Varvarka house."

"What about?" demanded Danilov.

"His source here is not getting anything worthwhile to pass on."

"Because we haven't baited the trap yet," said Danilov. "Why are you looking like that?"

"The last thing Orlov says is 'maybe we should have kept Yevgennie Andreevich instead of getting rid of him like we did. As a colonel he would have had better access.' "

It was beside Yevgennie Andreevich Kosov, the gang-cheating Militia colonel husband she planned to divorce to marry Danilov, that Larissa had been sitting when the car bomb exploded, annihilating her.

11

So long had the obsession to find Larissa's killers consumed Dimitri Danilov and so often and so variously had he imagined the retribution he would exact that in the first immediate seconds Danilov's mind totally blanked, a sensation he had never before known. He had never ever fainted, either, but supposed his recovering disorientation to be a similar feeling, an unreal sense of numbed weightlessness. Not trusting himself to speak—at least not coherently—he wordlessly held out his hand for the tape, fumbling to fit it into the replay machine, which he was still awkwardly doing after Pavin locked the door and slid the 'in conference' sign into its outward facing panel. Pavin also had time to turn down the volume to prevent it being audible in the outer corridor before the exchange began.

"It's Feliks Romanovich. You coming down?"

"I'm not sure. Maybe."

"Some of the guys are here."

"Any visitors, from other brigades?"

"Not so far."

"Call me if any of them do arrive. I'll definitely come down if any do."

"You want me to come over there?"

"No. Someone's here?"

"You heard from our new partners?"

"I don't expect to. It was left to me to convene the meeting after they had sufficient time to consider and discuss it with their people."

"What about Switzerland?"

"All fixed."

"Pity it happened."

"All out of the way now. We'll call Veniamin Kirilovich tomorrow."

"We need to know what's happening there."

"You spoken to our Petrovka friend?"

"This afternoon. He says Danilov and the big bastard who's always holding his dick don't seem to be doing much."

"You tell him how grateful we'll be?"

"Of course. He said he hopes to get something soon."

"Maybe we should have kept Yevgennie Andreevich instead of getting rid of him like we did. As a colonel he would have had better access."

"I'll call if we get any visitors."

The line went dead without any farewells.

"I said I had a feeling about this," reminded Danilov, finding words at last. "I've got him! At last I've got him!"

Pavin shifted in his deep easy chair, confronting the moment he had always feared would one day come. Warningly he said, "You're a policeman, Dimitri Ivanovich: a proper policeman who tries to observe and follow the law, not take it into his own hands."

"I don't need—won't have—a lecture."

"I wasn't giving you one."

"I haven't decided how I'm going to do it," said Danilov. In all his fantasized vengeance there had been featureless men at his mercy, paradoxically with his inflicting upon them the sort of merciless torture to which the sacrificed victims in the Moskva River had been subjected

"Do what?" persisted Pavin.

Danilov looked directly and steadily at the man he respected probably more, even, than William Cowley. "Fit the punishment to the crime."

"There is only one way punishment can be exacted to fit a crime—by law, using law."

"Which requires indisputable evidence, to bring before a court. This isn't it, is it?"

Pavin shifted again. "No."

"But do you have any doubt, from what we've just heard, that Igor Gavrilovich Orlov was responsible—either committing it or ordering it—for Larissa's killing?" demanded Danilov.

"It incriminates Orlov in the murder of Yevgennie Andreevich Kosov. There is nothing to show he knew Larissa would be in the car when the bomb went off."

"That's pedantic shit and you know it," dismissed Danilov, completely in control of himself and his emotions, confusion replaced by ice-cold clarity. "Of course he didn't know that Larissa or anybody else would be in the car when the bomb went off. And he wouldn't have given a fuck if he had. He was prepared to destroy everyone in that car. And he did."

"Don't let yourself be destroyed, too."

"I am not going to be the one destroyed." Danilov realized how tightly he was gripping the tape, a man holding a never-to-be-surrendered grail.

"Are you going to tell the Americans?"

Danilov considered the question. "How many transcripts are there, in full?"

"This is the fourth, the nighttime intercept."

"What's on the others?"

"Nothing identifiably from either Orlov or Zhikin," said Pavin. "The mansion has been quiet ever since we got the intercept in place. All there is on the previous three from the restaurant is connected with it: table booking, food and wine ordering, stuff like that."

Danilov paused again. Raising the tape between them, he said, "This doesn't contribute anything to the current investigation."

"That tape you're holding indicates another international meeting," challenged Pavin.

"Which we already knew would be coming."

"Orlov also says Switzerland has been fixed."

"We knew that, too. We'll let the Americans have the other three."

"Which don't contribute anything either."

"It's proof we've got listening devices in place."

"Are you going to tell Bill?"

"No," decided Danilov at once. "It would compromise him." He smiled across at the other man. "And I won't compromise you, either, with whatever happens in the future."

"It's your compromise that concerns me."

"I want to confront him," said Danilov, making another decision although this time to himself. "I want to confront Igor Orlov and tell him that I know, that the punishment is more for killing Larissa than for what he's done—or is doing—now."

Danilov's immediate awareness was of how completely Jed Parker had taken over the local FBI man's office. It had been cleared of everything he remembered from his previous visit to John Melton's room, the silver-framed family photographs on the desk, three professional qualification diplomas that had hung on one wall, even two spiky cacti plants on top of the filing cabinet. It had also very obviously been cleaned, so thoroughly the ambience was sterile.

Parker came smiling from behind the pristine desk, hand outstretched. "Good of you to come right away, Dimitri. Appreciate it; appreciate it a lot."

"No reason for any delay, although I thought you might have needed some sleep." The other man showed no sign of having traveled what had to be at least five thousand miles over however many time zones. The suit was uncreased, the shirt fresh, and he was obviously freshly shaved: a sterile man in a sterile office.

"Constitution of an ox," boasted Parker, waving Danilov toward a desk-fronting chair as he retreated back behind it. There was a tensed urgency about his movements. Matching it verbally, Parker said, "So let's get this thing up and running right away!"

"This thing?" queried Danilov. He had an unsettling impression that this wasn't going to be an easy encounter.

Parker made another waving motion. "This investigation." He finished the wave by extending two fingers, side by side. "That's how I see us working together. Tight."

His impression had been right, Danilov decided. "So let's agree on that. And decide how we're going to achieve it."

"Jurisdiction is going to be tricky," suggested Parker.

"The target's here, in Moscow, for a crime committed in America," accepted Danilov. "That's a problem for lawyers, surely?"

"I was thinking more operationally," said the American.

I know you were, thought Danilov. "How's that?"

"John's filled me in on your headquarters' difficulties."

"Which can be handled—used—because we know there's an inside source," said Danilov, well rehearsed. "We just don't have an identity yet."

Parker shook his head. "Use it to a degree, sure. But that use is strictly limited. We can't guarantee against a leak of something we don't want to get out if we try to work from two different places. I think it's better we coordinate everything from here."

"We'll *cooperate* in everything with you here," qualified Danilov.

"Cooperate, coordinate!" dismissed the American, with another wave. "Same thing."

"It's not," refused Danilov, in further qualification. He offered the three tapes across the desk to the other man. "And here's the start: the intercepts so far from the restaurant on Skornjaznyj Lane to Orlov's mansion. Nothing worthwhile on any of them."

"What about *from* Orlov's place at Ulitza Varvarka?" seized Parker.

"No pickup yet on any outward calls."

"So we don't know if the equipment works!"

"Of course it works!" said Danilov, grabbing the chance to puncture the other man's arrogance. "What have you got, from your on-street surveillance?"

Parker shuffled the cassettes to vent his irritation. "It's not an easy target: no good concealment in such a busy road and the alleys are too narrow to avoid anyone being seen from inside the house."

"So what have you got?" persisted Danilov.

"Certainly movement inside."

"Identifying photographs?"

"Couldn't be taken unobtrusively. We're not fully set up yet."

"What about the Brooklyn Bite?"

"We're in far better shape there. The American theme is a bonus. We can go in as tourists, looking for a taste of home."

"You had anyone in yet?"

"Needham's having dinner there," said Parker, impatiently. "But let's go on talking about the telephone intercept."

Danilov decided he was better able to play bat and ball than Parker, at once recognizing his own arrogance. "We already have. They've been in place for the past seven hours. What I've given you is the results so far. And as I've already told you, there's nothing on them. Only myself and my deputy are involved. There's no risk whatsoever of a leak."

"What about telephone-exchange technicians?"

"What about telephone-exchange technicians?" My volley to your weak lob, thought Danilov.

"The leak could come from them?"

Flight fatigue had to be clouding Parker's reasoning. The mental limitations of an ox matched the physical resilience of a muscle-bound beast, although there was little in the stature of the increasingly fidgeting, slightly built man to hint at muscularity, either. "To whom? To where?"

The cassette cases shuffled around the limited space directly in front of Parker, like a find-the-pea, backstreet shell game. "I don't want our cooperation to begin badly."

"Neither do I. Nor do I see why it should. Even before you arrived to lead your part of the investigation, it was going well. You're working the physical surveillance; we're handling the eavesdropping. It's the perfectly equal, operational divide." Not according to the other man's inept admission, thought a satisfied Danilov: his was the more likely route to produce the way forward. His personal way forward, which was now the primary—the only—consideration, despite Yuri Pavin's denied but very definite lecture on professional integrity

"You know how close this investigation is already to being blown: certainly compromised?" demanded Parker.

"No?" said Danilov, apparently ingenuous.

"I'm talking about the total screwup in Switzerland," said the other man.

"I thought it was a refusal of the Swiss to allow you access?"

"Which Orlov knows about: knows he's the focus!"

"Which doesn't endanger our operation," insisted Danilov. "The Swiss decision just makes our job more difficult."

"I—" started Parker, abruptly stopping to correct himself. "We won't be responsible for letting anything like that happen from here."

"I hope you're right," said Danilov. It would bruise Jed Parker's overwhelming conceit not to have maneuvered himself into a position of superiority.

"You're a friend of Bill Cowley's?" demanded Parker.

"We've worked together on previous cases: I respect his ability," said Danilov, cautiously.

"I'm the case officer of this task force,"

Danilov shrugged. "That's already been made clear to me."

"I want it to be very clear indeed," said Parker. "Everything goes through me."

Danilov was sure he perfectly timed the indignant pause. "That inference is close to being offensive. It is offensive!"

"I'm not trying to be offensive. I just don't want any misunderstandings between us," said the American.

Only subjugation, which you're not going to get, thought Danilov. "Then let's not create situations in which any can arise."

"I'll certainly not allow any," lied Parker.

"Nor will I," lied Danilov.

"Where does Ivan think you are?" asked Orlov.

"Putting flowers on Georgi's grave," said Irena.

"Didn't he want to go with you?"

"His way of grieving is to close his mind to ever having had a son."

"What's yours?"

"Not forgetting for a moment that I had a son."

"What would he do if he discovered we were fucking each other?"

"Nothing. Cry maybe."

"If you despise him so much, why don't you leave him?"

"Would you take me in?" It was a forever hopeful question.

"No," said Orlov at once.

"So it's convenient to stay and go on like this," she said, disappointed. The sex had been good, as it always was, although loveless, as it always was. Irena shifted, looking more fully toward him across the bed. "Just as it's convenient for you, because I'm not any sort of threat."

Orlov returned her look. "Is that what you think?"

"I think you don't trust anyone." Irena held up her hand, her forefinger narrowed fractionally against her thumb. "But I think you allow yourself just this much for family."

"Maybe you're right." It was an unsettling insight. He hoped she wasn't going to become a nuisance. But there again she owed him a debt for his having caught Georgi's killers for her to help execute. And she and Ivan could well have other uses if he decided upon the idea formulating in his mind to prove to Joseph Tinelli and Luigi Brigoli just how legally untouchable he was.

"I know I am."

"Do you want to come to the restaurant?"

Irena considered the invitation. "Why not?"

"Do you want to call Ivan?"

"I won't bother."

As they went through the basement passage into the adjoining house on Rybnyj Lane, Irena said, "What was this for originally?"

"Servants' access, from where they lived," said Orlov. "But maybe the duke who built it had a mistress next door. Or perhaps he wanted a way to go in and out without being seen, as I do."

"I thought your war was over?"

"One is," said Orlov.

Feliks Romanovich Zhikin emerged from the rear of the restaurant, alerted by the doorman of the arrival of Orlov's car, and said at once: "I think we've got uninvited company."

"You sure?" demanded Orlov at once.

"I'm sure enough to put it to the test."

"Let's do that! Enjoy ourselves!"

"You want to eat in the back or out here?"

"We'll eat out here. But decide what we're going to do in the back, afterward."

The prepared setting to which Zhikin led them was surrounded by tables occupied by Orlov's brigade. Zhikin said: "There's no one from any other brigade."

"They're adjusting to a new order of things," decided Orlov. "They'll pay homage soon enough. They've got to."

"I haven't seen a black man here before," said Irena, looking out into the restaurant.

"American," identified Zhikin.

"I knew the theme would work, like McDonald's did," said Orlov.

12

The BMW drew up outside Ulitza Varvarka precisely at eleven A.M. pointing in the direction of the river-skirting Moskvoreckaja Nabereznaja. The driver kept the engine running but got out courteously to open the door for the emerging man, who was very short and so fat he waddled when he walked and who was closely escorted by two others. The car went briefly parallel with the river before swinging up into the city, finally stopping at the Arbat. There it halted beneath a No Parking sign for the passenger to whom the other three were deferring to window shopping undecidedly for some time before entering a jeweler's to purchase a silver pendant.

Two men and a woman were already waiting in the bar of the Metropole, the champagne chilling in an ice bucket, when the BMW passengers entered. There were handshakes and a kiss on the cheek for the woman. Again there was deference. The attentive escorts occupied an adjoining table. The group stayed drinking for an hour before moving into the grill. The escorts again sat at the next table. After a leisurely lunch the man, his bodyguards, and the woman reentered the waiting BMW. It went to the Radisson Slavjanskaya Hotel, where the man and the woman had a sauna and a massage at the health club. One escort went into the sauna, the other remained outside. From the hotel the BMW went to the Muzhskaya Moda, where it again parked under a No Standing sign. In the shop the closely guarded man bought three imported Italian silk ties. The car was back outside the mansion on Ulitza Varvarka just before five P.M. There was a brief pavement conversation with the driver before the man, the woman, and his two companions went inside.

Jed Parker flustered into the embassy's FBI office and said, "I'm sorry I had to put you off until now, Al. I've been coordinating an operation."

"What?" asked the CIA man.

"Got a sighting of Orlov at last! And I was ready. Everywhere he went, we went. We've got the lot. Photographs, scanner chat, everything!"

"That's good," said Needham. Prick, he thought.

"That's how it's going to be, all the way! So, tell me about last night?"

"It's a good place," Needham began. "Great ribs. Seats maybe fifty, and there's obviously a back-office arrangement. And there's a kind of automatic separation in the restaurant itself. There was a bunch of guys who looked dirty, all together toward the back. I was seated on the other side and more toward the front. Nothing much happened, just eating and drinking until around eight. A tall guy and a woman came in. Got a lot of attention from a guy who came from the back, from all the guys in a huddle together, in fact. The couple was seated right in the middle of that group. We're talking total protection. I stayed as long as I thought I could without becoming obvious and hung around outside. Which wasn't a load of fun because the guy and the gal didn't come out until after midnight. They had a chauffeured limo, a Mercedes, with escorts, another Mercedes and a BMW, front and back. I lost them at lights on Prosvin Pereulok so I headed straight for Varvarka but they didn't show. There were lights from inside, though."

"How tall's tall?"

"Six-four, maybe a bit more. I'd say between one-sixty-five and one-eighty pounds."

"The bellman at the Hyatt Regency in Chicago said one of the three was very tall."

"I remember."

"Could you make them again?"

"No problem with the tall guy and the woman. Nor with quite a few of the others, either," promised Needham, confidently. "Identification was what I was there for."

Parker made a show of looking at his watch. "Let's go see how good that identification is. All today's photographs will be printed up by now."

The embassy's requisitioned conference room was wallpapered with enlarged photographs of the Varvarka group and of those with whom they had lunched at the Metropole. There was also a variety of street shots, at the Arbat, outside the Metropole and Radisson Slavjanskaya Hotels, the Muzhskaya Moda, and finally back at Varvarka.

Al Needham was provided with his own complete personal set, over which he pored for more than thirty intense, occasionally grunting minutes. Every so often he marked a face. Five times, upon reexamination, he erased the initial identification. At last he said, "Those I've marked I recognize."

"The tall guy with the woman?" demanded Parker.

"I don't see him. Last night's guy wasn't the one who left Varvarka to lunch at the Metropole."

"You sure?"

"Course I'm sure."

"Look again."

Needham did, although not for thirty minutes this time. "He's definitely not here."

"What about that woman?" demanded Parker, jabbing his finger at the image of the female leaving the Metropole after that day's lunch.

"I already told you, she's not the one from last night, either," insisted Needham. "And you don't have to ask me any more if I'm sure. I am."

"No doubt about those you have marked?"

"They were all there last night, part of the separate, dirty group I told you about."

"It's still good."

Needham didn't say anything.

"It's been a good day," insisted Parker.

"You said it," remarked Needham.

Jed Parker had mentally composed the self-congratulatory cable to Washington, so it did not take him long to write it. While he wrote, he had all the photographs wired to America. He described them as the first record of members of the Orlov Brigade, although so far Orlov himself had not been definitely identified. He would be, very shortly, hopefully within days. They had established the inner layout of the restaurant—which was clearly the gang's meeting place—and hoped the Russians would be more successful locating official records and drawings of the Skornjaznyj Lane restaurant than they had been of Orlov's home. There they were severely limited—to the extent of being obstructed—by the Russians' inability to find any officially recorded or listed plans, description, or architectural history of the mansion, upon which there was as complete an observation as was possible within the constraints of operating from limited concealment on a main, too-well-lighted highway.

Parker impatiently allowed an hour to pass after his final transmission before telephoning William Cowley.

"You got everything?" Parker demanded at once.

"Of course." More than he wanted, thought Cowley, who had just hung up the telephone from a worrisome conversation with Yuri Pavin.

"I marked it for the director's attention."

"I saw that," Cowley assured him.

"Has it gone!"

"I'm still reading it. There're a lot of photographs to look through as well."

"All of which are important."

"I read that, too. Pity we didn't positively pick up Orlov."

"We got more in around twenty-four hours, tops, than was achieved in the previous week!" retorted Parker, defensively.

"You've done very well."

"When's your next meeting with the director?"

"There isn't one scheduled."

"I think this is important enough to make one."

"I'll decide when I've gone through it all."

"What else is happening?"

"We finally got a wire into Yasev's car. And a digital cell phone scan around the Odessa and Yasev's apartment. It's not perfect: intermittent. But it's sufficiently understandable from what we have heard to be fairly sure we haven't missed anything."

"Fairly sure?" echoed Parker.

The son of a bitch was recording their conversation, independent of the automatic FBI sound loop, guessed Cowley. "It's going through enhancement."

"What have we got so far?"

"Nothing," admitted Cowley. "You met Dimitri yet?"

"Yesterday."

"How'd it go?"

"So–so."

"So–so what?"

Parker paused. "I suggested we coordinate everything from here to get rid of the Petrovka risk. He says he can handle it." There was another pause. "That's our weak spot. We've started well here. Couldn't be better. If there's a fuckup, it'll come from the Russians."

If all Parker's protective flags came down at the same time, they could make up the man's funeral shroud, thought Cowley. Or somebody else's, came the afterthought. Which brought his mind back to his conversation with Pavin.

"You told Dimitri about all you've done?"

"Too busy until now. Keeping things in priority."

"But you will now?"

"Sure."

"With the photographs, there could be criminal files."

"Are you joking!"

"Just keeping things on track."

"They'll get them."

"Anything else?"

There was a silence. "Better luck at your end."

"That's what we need." Cowley let the anger seep away, giving himself time to think about the conversation, not needing the reply. He signed off the disc and took it from the machine, sealing it by time and date, as the regulations required. Then he called Leonard Ross's personal assistant. After that he direct-dialed Moscow, which meant the call bypassed the automatic recording procedure.

"Sounds as if they've done well," praised Danilov.

"I want to make sure you get all the photographs, for comparison against records." And for you to tell me yourself about what you learned from the interpreted tape, he thought.

"What if he withholds them?"

"It wouldn't make sense for him to do that. He's overambitious, not stupid."

"It'll be a slow process without names." Danilov wondered how he would feel actually looking at the face of the man who had murdered Larissa.

"With luck, you or Yuri might recognize someone, get a lead from that."

Danilov frowned at the desperation in the remark. "Slow or not, it'll be done." Personally if necessary, no matter how long it took. Danilov had the sudden urge to tell Cowley about his Orlov discovery but just as quickly subdued it. The time for explanations and apologies was a long way off.

"I'll call tomorrow to make sure you've got the prints," promised Cowley, before he hung up. A rift, a separation, had arisen between them, accepted Cowley. Pavin had told him of Danilov's promise not to compromise either of them. The conversation he'd just had with Danilov made him fearful that Danilov was, indeed, intending something stupid.

His personal line rang almost at once. Hank Slowen said, "We got a scanner intercept, between Orlov and Yasev. It's intermittent, but there's enough for it to be understood. And you're not going to like it one little bit."

Neither was Leonard Ross, decided Cowley, as he put the telephone down five minutes later.

13

"No possible doubt?" demanded the director.

"Absolutely none," insisted Cowley. "There are reception gaps, but it's quite comprehensible. And Yasev was in his car, so we've got a fuller duplicate of his half of the conversation, from the wire we've got into it."

"You told Parker?"

Parker, not Jed, immediately isolated Cowley. "I've sent the verbatim transcript and put the scanner intercept, in Russian, on his voice mail, as well as the backup car wire. Parker has got everything we've got." Cowley knew that professionally he should be thinking things like disaster and blown operations and humiliation. But Ross hadn't used them yet, and they weren't in the forefront of his mind, either. This was the up-shit-creek, where's-the-paddle analysis moment. Cowley didn't have a paddle, or know in which direction to row by hand.

The older man stared down at Cowley's update folder and said, head still bowed. "Let's have it."

"Orlov set us up in Moscow—totally set us up and blew us out in bubbles," declared Cowley, although carefully not naming the man who less than three hours earlier had demanded his then imagined coup be rushed to the director. "I guess that's what he meant when he talked on the previous intercepts of taking precautions. He picked up the surveillance—"

"Whose surveillance!" broke in Ross, instantly. "Ours? Or the Russians?"

"Ours," replied Cowley, just as quickly. "We weren't following, not for a moment! Orlov was leading us— by the nose—to find out if he *was* under surveillance. And proved it, every which way. He had his guys ready and waiting at every place he took us to. Yasev's on the tape laughing himself silly as Orlov says he's got photographs of our guys taking photographs of what they thought was him and his guys."

"I don't think I need to hear any more," Ross interjected. "I can read and hear the rest for myself."

"That's about it, anyway."

"It's totally disastrous."

A long time getting to the familiar word, but there it was, Cowley recognized. "Totally," he agreed.

"You really think they've photographed our guys?"

"We've got to assume they have."

"How many?"

"Along with everything else, I've asked Jed for numbers. They'll all have to be replaced, of course." To bring with them—and then spread—a full account of the debacle, reflected Cowley.

"Of course."

"I'm not clear yet whether Jed was personally involved. I've asked him that, too."

"He'll be compromised if he was," said Ross, pointlessly.

"Do you want him withdrawn with the others?" A relative of the House speaker, no matter how determinedly macho, shouldn't be put to any physical risk.

"I want a detailed account of what went wrong! And why," Ross announced. "Earlier today I was being told that in Moscow we'd had the first success in the entire investigation"—there was a confessional pause—"and I told the White House chief of staff."

You weren't told it was a success by me, thought Cowley. And was at once irritated with himself. OK, he had for the first time, perhaps surprisingly, been caught up in office politics, which he'd always disdained. Been initially beaten, even, in such an unfamiliar contest. But thinking as he had been doing during this encounter—and before—was ridiculous. It was juvenile and paranoid and all the other attitudes for which he'd so recently derided others. Where *was* the professionalism that until now had been his watchword, whatever the setback? He said, "OK, so we haven't got Orlov yet. But the photographs have to be of people connected to him. Al Needham identified a bunch from the restaurant, from the previous evening. They could lead us to Orlov. And although Orlov suspects it, he doesn't know how well we're still hearing him. And the arrogance has got to be to our advantage if we can work it."

Leonard Ross looked unimpressed. But for the first in a very long time unworried. "Let's get Jed Parker's explanation, OK?"

"A detailed account?" echoed Jed Parker.

"That's what the director's asked for," said Cowley.

"What else did he say?"

"Nothing. Only that he told the White House what he thought you'd got before knowing what really happened."

Parker's voice was subdued—not whispered, humbled, but there was uncertainty, close to tilting over into unthinkable subservience. "It happens."

"No," denied Cowley. "It *happened*. Now we're into recovery—reversal." This wasn't an accusation, implied or otherwise. Nor, neither, for the telephone recording that was automatic on such an ongoing operation. This was strictly, unarguably, professional. Which he'd always been. And was determined to remain, from now on.

"There had to have been a leak," insisted Parker.

"From where?" demanded Cowley.

There was a moment's hesitation. "Petrovka's an open book."

Jed Parker was flaky, Cowley decided, surprised. The even greater surprise was that the man was allowing it so openly to show from five thousand miles away. "You didn't tell Petrovka—neither Danilov nor Pavin—in advance what you were doing or when you were doing it, did you?" *That* was for the official record: he wasn't having the shit dumped on Danilov.

"That was the coordination," insisted the other American. "We were to establish the physical surveillance, under extremely difficult circumstance. Which your two special friends knew, from the beginning."

"They didn't know in advance when—or what—you were doing," persisted Cowley. "Neither did I. You got suckered, plain and simple, Jed. Very plain and very simple. How many of our guys got burned?"

"We can't be sure, just from Orlov's remark, that any got burned."

"How many of our guys were involved in the operation, from the moment of the surveillance group leaving Ulitza Varvarka until the time they got back there?" insisted Cowley, relentlessly.

"Sixteen." The admission was low voiced, strained.

"Send them back. They'll be replaced."

"We don't know they're identified!" repeated Parker.

"They're being replaced," said Cowley. "What about you?"

"What about me?"

"Were you on the street, physically part of it?"

"No!" said Parker at once.

Cowley extended the pause. "We're talking operational here. If you got caught, anywhere, on any camera, you're out of there with everyone else who's compromised. Otherwise, everyone else who may be able to work there—which in itself is uncertain at this stage—is compromised, endangered, if they're seen with you."

"This conversation is recorded, right?"

"You know it is. That's operational procedure, too." Revolving tapes everywhere, thought Cowley, all picking up the wrong messages.

"So on the record I am telling you I was no part of the physical surveillance and therefore there is no possibility of my having been photographed or of being identified in any way whatsoever. I was in the incident room here at the embassy, coordinating everything by radio and telephone, OK!"

"That's what I am trying to ensure, Jed. That whatever's left is OK."

"I just told you, it is."

"Good!" said Cowley. "So let's start thinking—operating—professionally. You just told me you were coordinating, *listening* to telephones, right?"

"Yes?" The agreement was reluctant, suspicious.

"As well as all the radios and all the telephones in the car. Were our guys using the digital cell phone scanners?"

Another pause and then a further questioning answer. "Yes?"

"You have them on Varvarka, when all this was going on?"

"Yes."

"*All* the time it was going on?"

"Yes."

"And on that goddamned ridiculously named restaurant?"

"Yes."

"Then how come you didn't get from your end the same intercept we got in Brighton Beach thousands of miles away?"

The hesitation now was even longer. "I'd have gotten round to it," Parker declared, defensively.

"We're not talking theory of relativity—we're talking logic. Did you have the mansion's street and alleys covered, even after who we thought was Orlov left and got back after his day out?"

"Of course: it's a twenty-four-hour operation." The admission now was resigned.

"Anyone leave or enter while we were being given the tourist guide to Moscow?"

"Not according to the log." Parker's voice was flat, beaten.

"From that log—and the time difference between New York and Moscow—we know to the second that Orlov talked to Yasev thirty-five minutes after the bullshit return to Ulitza Varvarka. From which, again according to your log, no one left or returned while the scam was carried out. Yet we know, from Danilov's wire, that Orlov is definitely—but only *sometimes*—there. How's he doing it?"

"Danilov can't produce any structural plans of the house."

"Flag it," instructed Cowley. "Your sixteen replacements will be there in forty-eight hours. Get your guys out immediately. And don't forget the director wants a full account, right away."

"Is it likely that I would forget!" stopped Parker, in weak fight back.

"Filed through me," completed Cowley. That was procedure, not protective.

Danilov said, "Parker's call came thirty minutes after we got the photographs, asking for me to call the moment we got an identification. Now I know why."

"Have you identified anyone?" demanded Cowley, at once. There was definitely a distancing between them, he recognized sadly.

"I told you before of the problem, without names," said the Russian. "But we're trying a shortcut. Pavin's running the visual check through the entire squad. We could get names against photographs at the same time as picking up Orlov's source telling him he's got nothing to worry about because neither he—nor anyone else–has made an identification, even if there has been a recognition."

"That's good," agreed Cowley. "That could work."

"Something needs to," said Danilov, depressed. "Things couldn't get much worse."

But they could. And they did.

14

Cowley got drunk.

He didn't consciously set out to do so—he never did—but that night it was even more genuinely unintended. With Pamela again at her literary group, there was time to stop at the anonymous Arlington tavern, although he didn't establish himself at the bar but in a booth, nursing the initial drink, closing himself off to everything around him, just to think and analyze: to think and analyze professionally, removing all the ridiculous personal paranoia from every equation.

It certainly wasn't the first time a target had discovered himself to be precisely that, a target: every *capo* of every Mafia family in America was aware he was the subject of permanent FBI inquiry, with open case files constantly updated. Joseph (Slow Joe) Tinelli knew he was on the Most Wanted List in the J. Edgar Hoover Building as the *capo di tutti i capi*. The FBI's problem was of their own head-up-their-ass creation. Believing themselves, either rightly or wrongly, under political scrutiny, they—or, more objectively, the director—were compounding every difficulty on an exaggerated Richter scale, elevating tremors into earthquakes. Allowing themselves, even, to be made fools of.

Cowley nodded to the waitress's invitation to another whiskey.

He'd never before been involved in such a widespread or complex operation, so there wasn't a criterion by which to reach such a judgment.

A fresh glass replaced the empty one in front of him, but there was still another hour at least before Pamela got home, so that was OK.

They knew the name if not the face of a Russian *capo* maintaining contacts in Italy and America. And as Orlov had been to Chicago, the known fiefdom of Joe Tinelli, it was a further reasonable, working assumption that Orlov's trip was of major international criminal importance. A task force was up and running, with teams established everywhere they should be, with him at the top of the pyramid coordinating everything. Orlov's known American conduit was identified, by name as well as by photographs wired in every conceivable way and under permanent observation, as was Orlov's outlet premises in Brighton Beach. And Dimitri Danilov had telephone taps on the Ulitza Varvarka mansion and the restaurant on Skornjaznyj Lane—which were also being covered by cell phone scanners—and it was again reasonable to assume that although Orlov was guarding against mobile telephone intercept he didn't positively suspect his Moscow landlines were bugged.

Cowley held up his empty glass to the passing waitress.

The most obvious minus was the refused Swiss company register disclosure and Orlov's easy discovery of American surveillance. It was embarrassing having to replace so many agents in Moscow, but at least it was an in-house embarrassment. They should by now have had positively identifying photographs of Igor Gavrilovich Orlov. And known the connection between an apparent turf war in Moscow and a triple slaying in Brighton Beach. And . . . Cowley was sure there was another minus but at that moment he couldn't call it to mind. Didn't matter: he'd remember it later, if it was important.

He shook his head against a refill, gesturing for his tab, and was surprised at the amount, more than he had on him in cash, so there was a further delay while he settled by American Express. He was glad he'd stopped off, given himself the time calmly to run it all through his mind.

It seemed brighter outside than Cowley had remembered, and he had to squint, momentarily unable to pick out his car. There were other cars tight around him, and it took a lot of shunting back and forth to get out of his space. He thought he might have touched a couple of other cars, fender to fender, but didn't bother to check. That's what fenders were for, to fend off. There was more room in the apartment's parking lot and Cowley was glad he didn't have to maneuver into a space because the glare was making his head ache.

He sensed Pamela's presence before seeing her as he crossed the threshold, and it was the surprise at her already being home that made him drop his keys. It was instinctive, nothing more than that, to support himself against the wall to pick them up. When he straightened, he saw she was standing, looking at him from the main room.

"Hi."

"Where have you been?"

"Working."

"I called the office. You weren't there and your cell phone's off."

"I stopped off on the way. Needed to think things through. There's been a hell of a screwup in Moscow." She was angry but wouldn't be when he told her how Jed Parker had been suckered. He did so hurriedly, although having to stop to get the account in sequence, not letting her interrupt. "Ross called it a total disaster."

Pamela said: "You're drunk."

"I had a drink."

"You had a lot of drinks. You're slurring, stumbling. If you'd been stopped in the car you'd be in jail now."

"I didn't. And I'm not. And I'm not drunk, either."

"You thought things through."

"Yeah." Cowley hadn't intended the belligerence.

"Know where you're going from here?"

"Kind of."

"So tell me—kind of—what your way forward is?"

"You know what I mean."

"No, Bill, I don't know what you mean. Nor would anyone else, listening to you. You're almost incomprehensible."

"I'm OK."

"You're stumbling drunk, hardly able to string two intelligible words together. You're also the overall commander of an internationally emplaced FBI task force who turned off his cell phone and disappeared into the bottom of a shot glass for close to three hours and who, if called upon to do so at this moment, couldn't be trusted to make a decision that wouldn't physically endanger four times as many agents as Parker exposed in Moscow." Pamela was tight with anger, rigidly white faced, arms hard against her sides.

"I told you I'm OK!" Cowley was careless now of the belligerence, sufficiently sobered to acknowledge the accusations Pamela was making, but determined not to admit any of them.

"Don't put me to a test, Bill."

"What the hell does that mean?"

"It means I think I love a super guy who's terrific at what he does—

at *everything* he does—and whom I'm beginning to think I want to spend the rest of my life with. It means that he isn't the guy to whom booze is more important than the possible physical safety of his colleagues and a multinational criminal investigation. And it means that if I seriously believed there was the possibility of such a danger, I might feel it a professional responsibility to give an official warning, to ensure it didn't happen."

Totally sober now, Cowley remained for several moments wordless in the center of the room, facing the woman. Finally he said, "You don't mean that."

"Don't put me to a test," threatened Pamela Darnley.

The dacha of Igor Gavrilovich Orlov, stilted to lift it above the winter snows, was among the farthermost hills surrounding Moscow, toward Zagorsk, where the pine and fir forests completely concealed one country house from another. The nearest was protectively that of Feliks Zhikin, who at that moment sat opposite Orlov on the open-sided veranda that skirted the mostly wooden framed, shingle-roofed building. On the low table between them were glasses and a bottle of the imported scotch that Zhikin preferred to the vodka Orlov was drinking. There was also the unwanted remains of the blinis and Beluga caviar they couldn't finish.

Orlov said, "I think I'll come down to the restaurant tonight. And stay at the house. I'm bored here." He'd been at the dacha for two days. The cell phone reception was good from that elevation.

"Maybe we could go on to a club somewhere afterward?" suggested Zhikin.

"The Night Flight," agreed Orlov. "I'll call Irena."

Zhikin sniggered. "I don't imagine all those supposed supercops enjoyed their night flight back to Washington."

Orlov laughed more openly. "They'd have been even more pissed off if they'd known I was at Sheremet'yevo, waving them goodbye."

Zhikin looked over the bordering rail, to where six or seven men loitered around three cars specifically parked in a protective semicircle. Nodding toward the group, he said, "The Americans have pictures of Arkadi Alekseevich. And Valeri Dorofevich. And the others from that day."

Orlov nodded, understanding the remark. "Fix it."

Zhikin decided the other man was sufficiently relaxed by the vodka and the memory of the departing Americans not to erupt into one of his unpredictable rages at being questioned. "We need to set up the decisive meeting with America and Italy," he began, cautiously.

Orlov nodded again, adding to both their glasses but saying nothing.

Zhikin was unsettled by the silence. "I'm not trying to exceed my authority."

"Good."

Asshole, thought Zhikin, which was what he almost invariably thought these days. "The Americans—Petrovka, too, although that's not a problem—are on the edge of this."

"So?"

Zhikin's stomach turned, a literally uneasy physical sensation. Orlov was settled back, nursing the vodka glass into which he was looking. Waiting. Zhikin said, "They could get in the way. Make difficulties."

Orlov nodded once more. "I know. I've been playing. Now the playing's got to stop. I've really got to teach a lot of people a lot of lessons." The plan was virtually complete in his mind now, and when he put it into operation would erase any doubt Brigoli or Tinelli might have about him and his invulnerability. He'd make it truly spectacular, proving himself not just to the brigades he controlled in Russia but those of Italy and America as well.

Zhikin continued cautiously against any outburst. "Do you think it's safe any more to hold the first meeting here, in Moscow?"

There was another reflective, glass-examining pause. "No."

He'd done it right, Zhikin decided. "Where?"

"We're established in Berlin. We'll have it there. Low-key: nothing ostentatious. Cars, protection, safe houses obviously. But we're not trying to impress. We don't have to: it's our deal. You fix everything, OK?"

"OK," accepted Zhikin. When the fuck was this brain-blocked, beanstick motherfucker going to do anything more than get his rocks off torturing people into subservience and then boasting about it?

"You call Irena: tell her what we're doing tonight," ordered Orlov. "I'm going to need her. And Ivan."

"Ivan?" queried Zhikin, who knew the antipathy between the brothers.

"They owe me. It's payback time. And call the club. I'll have my usual place, in the balcony."

"Tell him it's Aleksandr Mikhailovich."

There was the sound on the tape of receding footsteps, a door opening and closing, then opening again. Approaching footsteps, the phone being picked up.

"What is it?" Zhikin's voice, without any greeting.

"Danilov's running a check throughout the building on some photographs. Arkadi Alekseevich Novikov is on them. And the Chobotov brothers."

"What's he want?"

"Identities."

"Did he get any?"

"Not from the people on my shift. I haven't heard that anyone else did either. But I can't be sure."

"What about records?"

"A lot, on the brothers."

"Any mention of Igor Gavrilovich? Or me?"

"Already removed, on both of you." A self-satisfied laugh.

"You're done well, Aleksandr Mikhailovich."

"Other people at Petrovka might recognize someone."

"We're shifting them to the Berlin brigade. There's shortly going to be a need for them there."

"You're happy with what I've given you then?" The voice was wheedling.

"Very. Come by here tomorrow for your money. Maybe Igor Gavrilovich will want to thank you himself." The line went dead, as usual without farewells.

"What?" demanded Orlov, when Zhikin went back into the restaurant.

"Our Petrovka investment has come through," said Zhikin. "He's resolved what could have been a problem for us. And I've decided what to do about those we can't keep here anymore. I'll take them to Berlin with me. From now on they can work from there."

"That's good," accepted Orlov.

"Ognev is coming by tomorrow, to be paid. I thought you'd like to tell him personally that he's done well. He'll have to deal direct with you while I'm in Berlin."

The logic took away the offense of an arrangement being made without his previous agreement, but Orlov still frowned. "All right." He gestured at Irena's arrival. "What about our balcony place at the Night Flight?"

"It's ours, of course," said Zhikin. Asshole, he thought.

"Then it's been a good day," Orlov decided.

At Petrovka Danilov straightened from the playback of the Brooklyn Bite intercept, smiling expectantly across at Pavin.

The big man smiled back and said, "Aleksandr Mikhailovich. . . . There's only one. Alexandr Mikhailovich Ognev. He's a sergeant."

"And now he's ours, not theirs," said Danilov. "And how I'm going to use him." Closer, he thought. I'm getting closer.

15

They had practically a day to prepare, and throughout it Jed Parker liaised with everyone, his needs firmly established, some moves already made, others in his mind in strict order of priority. He had a lot—too much—to recover from before he could again risk solo initiatives. Added—or perhaps compounded—to which there were unsettling similarities between this second possibility and the first. His personal recovery motivated everything but was planned behind protective, bunkerlike firewalls to ensure his involvement was invisible.

Dimitri Danilov—included with Pavin in the preparation—provided the Petrovka personnel photographs and details of the corrupt sergeant Ognev to be copied and distributed as the Orlov-isolating marker for everyone involved in the surveillance, particularly the two Russian-speaking agents—one a woman—chosen from the Washington replacement agents that night to play romantically vacationing Americans inside the restaurant. Largely for their benefit, and in the outside hope of their overhearing a comment or remark, every recording believed to have Orlov's voice was played, which practically amounted to their only recognizable feature of the faceless man, apart from the general description of his being noticeably tall and thin.

"That's all we've got," declared Parker, when the last recording came to an end. "Now it's input time. Anyone with a contribution, make it as the idea comes. Don't hold back worrying about it being incomplete." Parker caught the sour look that passed between the intended restaurant customers, a fresh-faced Harvard graduate seconded from the Washington field office named Peter Jepson and Mary Dowling, an equally young, blond, and milk-fed Midwesterner. Feigning humility, Parker said, "I know. We're coming from behind—from far, too far behind." It was the only admission—most certainty the only humility, feigned or otherwise—they were going to get. And was, anyway, a remark easily apportioned elsewhere in the far distant analysis of the operation.

Such was Jed Parker's determination to recover that he'd invited Danilov to share the slightly raised dais in the embassy conference room—shared command, shared responsibility—and Danilov only just prevented his surprise at the total change in Parker's demeanor—becoming obvious to the people arrayed before him. In the front row, facing him, Pavin also remained impassive, but Danilov guessed it had been as difficult for his deputy as it was for him.

Peter Jepson said, "You want us to try for photographs if we see Ognev with a tall, thin guy? Us vacationers take pictures all the time, don't we?"

"Too obvious, after last time," refused Parker.

"What about a hidden Minox?" queried Mary Dowling.

Parker looked sideways to Danilov, who in turn looked around the room to locate Al Needham. "You've been inside the place. You think a hidden camera's feasible?"

Needham considered the question. "With difficulty. It's quite brightly lighted. Mary might just get away with it pretending it's a compact to fix her makeup, something like that. But I don't think it would be easy, all the more so—again—because of last time."

"What if we don't get away with it?" Parker asked. "We get seen and we're blown again. But worse than before. This time they'll guess we've tracked them by having a wire on the place."

"We're stumbling around in the dark, getting nowhere. We need a face," insisted John Melton. The Moscow-based FBI agent had escaped Washington recall because of Parker's insistence that he remain in the embassy's radio-supervising incident room immediately to recognize the street maneuvers of Orlov's then unsuspected sting. Melton was unsure whether that was his good or bad luck.

"That and a lot more," said Parker, cynically, to move the discussion on.

"Surely it's a decision—and a judgment—that can only be made at the time, according to circumstance," suggested another newly arrived agent, from the middle of the room. "Mary and Pete go in prepared. If the chance is there, they take it. If not, they don't."

Perfect, decided Parker. "Not if there's the slightest *element* of risk. Only if it's a totally safe opportunity. Either of you have any doubt, you forget it."

Resigned—but pointedly—Jepson said: "OK, so it's down to us."

An agent in the front row, a woman, raised the Russian-provided file on Aleksandr Ognev and said: "I know from the transcript it sounds like he's coming to the restaurant to get his kickback, but what if everything gets changed and we don't know about it and sit in and around the place for nothing?" She gestured with the file again. "We got his home address and he works at Petrovka. Shouldn't we cover him from both, keep the leash tight?"

"We can't possibly restrict ourselves to the restaurant," said Danilov, swiveling to Parker. "Ognev's got desk duties until six. Yuri and I will be back there long before then. *And* we'll have checked the intercept on the restaurant on our way. We can be ready and waiting when Ognev leaves, for Yuri or me to give the signal to the outside surveillance."

Balancing his entry, Parker said, "Of course I'm not proposing we just stake out the restaurant. We'll pick him up at Petrovka, with emergency backup if his apartment needs to be covered." He looked around the room and said briskly, "Any more thoughts for tonight?"

Danilov watched the room just as intently and when no one spoke said, "Not about tonight. But there's more to consider from last night's recording. We haven't known until now that Orlov's got a Berlin brigade—"

"Which there's soon going to be a need to build up," came in Pavin, virtually quoting from the transcript. "What's the need?"

The Russians had rehearsed well, conceded Parker. But couldn't have anticipated how much would be to his benefit. He said, "It's covered. Before we began today I spent some time talking to Washington and sent them a full transcript. We're expanding the task force to Berlin. There'll be a supervisor, obviously, but it'll be under my overall command. It's an obvious adjunct to the operation here."

"It's got to *start* from here," said Danilov. "We've got the faces of those who are being moved to Germany. We can stake out the Tempelhof flights from Sheremet'yevo and catch the same plane—or planes—as they do, to lead us to where they are in Berlin. It's a reasonable inference that they'll all go together. And soon."

"That's what I suggested to Washington," said Parker, welcoming the Russian's intervention. He looked out into the room, toward the locally based FBI man. "That's for you, John. Form up a squad and move out to the airport. Our guys should be arriving in Berlin by tonight. I've already had the photographs wired to our embassy there. Your guys go out to Sheremet'yevo packed to travel. But if you can't, you'll have plenty of time to give Berlin flight numbers and times, so our guys can be ready and waiting to pick up the pursuit when Orlov's crew arrives. Even if there are seats, someone stays behind to alert Berlin. Pursuit cars, communications, and manpower, everything, will be set up by the time you touch down." He looked sideways to Danilov. "Anything that hasn't been covered?"

"I don't think so," said Danilov.

Parker looked out into the room again. "Anyone?"

There was no response.

"Then we're all set," said the American. "And this time it's going to go our way." I hope, he thought.

Which was among Danilov's thoughts as they drove back to Petrovka, along with a lot of others. All the reflections, in varying degrees, resulted from frustration. Having promised in no way to compromise

Yuri Pavin with his private agenda—and having excluded William Cowley for the same reason—there was no one with whom Danilov was able to talk, no one off whom, even, he could bounce an idea or an impression or a suspicion. No one to offer half thoughts that didn't stand up to objective examination and by so doing clear his head of preconceptions and obsessional cul-de-sacs to get Igor Gavrilovich Orlov into the inescapable cage—either literally or figuratively—in which to incarcerate him like the animal he was. And where the man would be entirely at his mercy, without the distraction of proper justice or human dignity or right and wrong, because none of those considerations featured in his thinking about Igor Orlov. The only objective was finally and properly to avenge Larissa.

Which created the greatest frustration of all. To get to Orlov he was too dependent upon others: too dependent upon others not to make another mistake—as they had before and would do again, because there were always mistakes—that might allow Orlov to escape once more.

But he wouldn't escape. Couldn't escape. Ever. Dimitri Danilov finally, honestly, confronted his turmoil, the first acknowledgment being that frustration had nothing whatsoever to do with it. His only reliance upon others was in their achieving a physical identification of Igor Orlov. Which could be within hours. After which it was simply a matter of personal retribution, which he'd refused to discuss with Pavin but which he was forcing himself to contemplate now.

Could he kill, coldly murder, another man? Danilov demanded of himself: inflict the torture of his fantasies, wanting to hear Orlov scream for the mercy that wouldn't be given? Yes, Danilov answered himself. Even arguing it was the only path to follow, Pavin had agreed there was no way the man could ever be legally arraigned for Larissa's killing, so it had to be natural justice, and Danilov was sure—totally convinced—that he could without hesitation pull the trigger or plunge the knife. All he needed was the identification. He'd make his own opportunity.

Beside Danilov in the car, Pavin said, "There's more this time. But Orlov and his people will still be looking for surveillance."

Danilov said, "There hasn't been a voiceprint identifiable as Orlov's from inside Varvarka for more than two days. The house stands apart, so he has to be getting in and out underground. A sewer maybe. It would be appropriate."

"You think the city engineers might have something, plans even, that the land registry doesn't?"

"I certainly think it's worth an inquiry."

"I'll make it, of course. But I doubt there were recorded sewer plans over a hundred years ago."

Danilov remained silent for several moments. "I'm worried about Germany."

"Worried?" Pavin frowned across the car.

"We've no operational jurisdiction there."

Thank God, thought Pavin, who rarely called upon the Deity in whom he devoutly believed but considered it justified if the prayer saved a man he admired and regarded as a friend from destroying his professionalism and integrity—possibly even himself, physically—attempting to exact his own justice. Pointedly he said, "If Germany is where the opportunity comes to prevent whatever it is Orlov is setting up, then it will have to be left to the Germans and the Americans, won't it?"

"I don't want that," admitted Danilov, flatly.

"Dimitri!" protested Pavin.

Danilov ignored the other man, totally absorbed by his overwhelming determination. "It's got to be Ognev. That's how I'll get to him. Through Ognev. It'll be a sting like no other."

He'd prevent it, decided Pavin. Whatever—however—he'd stop Danilov betraying himself.

William Cowley couldn't define the feeling because it wasn't a single emotion. There was anger and frustration and disappointment and guilt and—forcing the honesty—he admitted to himself that there was also fear, which surprised and disappointed him even more.

Because they'd never before had a serious argument—no passing disagreement had ever grown into anything like an argument—he'd been totally shocked by the strength of Pamela's fury. Strength wasn't the right word: strength would have been shouted, yelling anger—hysteria and tears perhaps—but there hadn't been shouts or tears.

The complete reverse. She'd been furious, certainly, but it had been a cold, calculating fury. And it was her icy refusal to allow any excuse or explanation—difficult though it was in his befuddled state to bring either comprehensibly to mind—that disturbed him most of all.

After last night's argument he was sure Pamela would carry out her threat, sure that if she thought he was endangering an operation—this operation—she'd report him to personnel or perhaps even the director himself. He had tried—and believed he'd succeeded—in arguing the personal disaster of that: inevitable demotion, possibly even dismissal from the Bureau. My destruction, he'd declared. To which she'd replied that it was he, not she, who risked destroying not just his career but himself, physically. She wouldn't listen to anything about logic or love ("It's because I love you—which is the first time I've told you that—that I won't let you do it. And it's because I respect and take seriously the job I do and the Bureau I serve that I won't let you endanger an operation or colleagues who'd stand up for you: who *have* stood up for you.") and virtually dismissed in unconcealed disbelief his promise that it would never, ever, happen again.

Which wasn't being pussy-whipped into a blame-groveling joke. The guilt came from his accepting—honestly again—that Pamela was unarguably right about the professional irresponsibility of disappearing for three hours during an investigation of this magnitude. OK, he'd gotten away with it, but only by the grace of a God to whom he didn't bend a knee. If last night there'd been this second chance of identification in Moscow for which he'd been summoned into the J. Edgar Hoover Building before seven that morning, everything would have imploded in upon him. Luck, which he couldn't expect to get again.

Leonard Ross's direct line rang stridently on his desk. "Well?"

"Everything—everyone—is in place. You've seen it all. I'm waiting to hear."

"So am I. And I want to, immediately."

"You told me," said Cowley.

At that moment, in the Brooklyn Bite on Moscow's Skornjaznyj Lane, Peter Jepson was sitting awkwardly with both caressing hands stretched across the table lovingly cupped over those of Mary Dowl-

ing, who was looking and hand-caressing back at him with equal ado-
ration, the miniature camera hidden between them.

He said, "We could probably get better at this if you really do sleep
with me tonight."

She said, "I'm sure I've got three good exposures."

"How about that fourth, later?"

"I was always told Kansas girls saved it until their wedding night."

"OK, marry me."

"I'm from Oklahoma. I was just telling you what I've always heard
about Kansas girls."

In Washington Cowley picked up the phone expecting it to be
Moscow, but it was Jimmy Pearce, the Chicago head of station. Pearce
said, "We got a snatch not worth a bag of beans from the scanner on
Tinelli's house, but you said you wanted anything."

"What's intelligible?"

"Hardly anything, but Germany's mentioned. That mean anything?"

"What have you done with it?"

"Already on its way to you by courier, for enhancement."

"It could be worth a hell of a lot more than a bag of beans."

16

The Brooklyn Bite photographs were hailed as the hoped-for breakthrough, which they strictly weren't, but so slowly—and mostly
badly —had the investigation gone until now that no one challenged
the exaggeration, and Cowley, who recognized it as such, actually
thought the encouragement was good for the general morale if not
necessarily for his own. Jed Parker, predictably, was the self-appointed
cheerleader.

There were, in fact, four images—five if the last, most indistinct, was included—of the man they identified as Igor Gavrilovich Orlov. But snatched as they had been from beneath light-obscuring, finger-blocking cowled hands, none was complete or sufficiently sharp to be definitive, despite every later attempt at scientific enhancement. What those scientific efforts and analyses confirmed was a man provably six feet, five inches tall whose thinness established his weight at approximately 161 lbs, allowing for a variation of no more than one pound. The criminal profiling interpretation was of a man inherently suffering embarrassment at his height from the way every photograph showed him stoop-shouldered to reduce his stature, diminishing himself instead of standing fully upright, which a confident man would have done. The hair was black, quite long and comparatively thick, although receding slightly from the front, and in every limited photograph the man was not once shown with his hands or arms in the same position, confirming the independent verbal description from both the photographing agents that Orlov talked a lot with his hands. The psychologists flagged that up as a further indication of inherent inferiority, from which they concluded that outwardly the man was most likely an aggressive, even violent bully. As well as confirming their limited interpretation from the static imagery, those verbal descriptions greatly added to the scientific analyses. The strongest recollection of both Peter Jepson and Mary Dowling was of the almost abject deference toward the man, the most obvious from the corrupt Petrovka sergeant. The impression of both FBI agents was that no one initiated a conversation, but waited for Orlov's lead, and obediently stopped at his first interruption. Laughter was immediate and loud at any remark inferred to be amusing, but no one appeared to joke back. At no time were they near enough actually to hear the man's voice for comparison against their tapes. They thought Orlov was accompanied by a sharp-featured, heavy-busted woman whose image was even more indistinct upon the only two photographs on which she featured, but Mary Dowling was sure she would recognize the woman again.

Long before the end of that first day the photographs had been wired to Washington and before complete enhancement were rewired to Chicago, along with the verbal description. Jimmy Pearce personally reinterviewed the Hyatt Regency doorman, who said the person in the photographs, fuzzy though they were, sure as hell looked like the guy they were inquiring about. He also, positively, reconfirmed his identification of Vitali Mittel. Pearce obviously refused to give any specific details of the investigation but agreed that if it ever developed into a court case, there was a good chance of the doorman being called as a witness and for the man's name to appear in the newspapers and maybe even to be seen on TV.

Cowley also took unenhanced photographic originals to his first-of-the-day meetings with Leonard Ross, as well as transcripts of the scientific attempts upon the Chicago scanned intercept of Joseph Tinelli.

"We making progress at last?" demanded the FBI director, wanting to hear rather than read.

"Some," qualified Cowley, refusing the exaggeration of his conversations with Jed Parker, although he'd dutifully included in the latest dossier all Parker's written claims from Moscow.

"What's the most important?"

Cowley hesitated, conscious that he'd be conceding he had most definitely been wrong in his initial reservations about how the investigation should be conducted. "It's the first sheet, on today's file. Chicago has a transcript from Tinelli's phone, but it's scarcely enough. Science has done their best—I spoke to the audio people before coming here—but they can't do any more to improve it: it was a cell phone, from both ends, and Tinelli was moving about the house and there was a lot of drown-out noise, like he was in a boiler room or a garage or something that they couldn't clean up . . . maybe even a baffler . . ."

"What *did* we get?" broke in Ross, customarily impatient.

"A voiceprint that we're taking to be Orlov's. Science is prepared to put it as a match against what we got earlier from Moscow. We don't have a positive voiceprint of Tinelli. We've only been able to lift six unmistakable words, from the whole scan. But one of them is 'Joe,' in Orlov's voice."

"What are the others?" persisted Ross.

Cowley sighed. " 'Berlin,' he quoted. "One of the words audio can't be sure about could be 'German' or 'Germany.' 'OK' comes up twice, but there's no context to infer who or what is OK. 'Rest,' which audio are reading to be *the* rest, as in 'others.' And 'told' but again there's insufficient context or inflexion to suggest an interpretation."

"It fits," decided Ross. "And it's what I always said it was, right from the start, a global confederation."

"And the way the investigation has been mounted, right from the start," said Cowley and waited to be challenged upon his early reservations, but Ross was looking away from him, tapping the dossier.

Ross's determination to justify himself was unnerving. The director said, "I think it's a reasonable assumption that the rest—the others—are Italian."

"So do I," agreed Cowley, glad the moment for criticism had passed. "I've already had a preliminary conversation with our guys in Rome. As soon as the photographs are enhanced, I'm going to courier everything over to the embassy there. If Orlov is talking direct with Tinelli, then it's another reasonable assumption that he's dealing with Italy's *capo di tutti i capi*. Who should be known to their Anti-Mafia Commission. That should give us a name and hopefully a photograph. I'm going to talk direct with them today, too."

Ross turned to the snatched pictures in his folder. "They're not good, are they? That's not a criticism, just as observation. What's the chances of their being improved beyond this?"

"Not good," admitted Cowley, at once. "They were working with a miniature camera with everything technically against them. Guys on the second floor are frightened the images will break up altogether under any greater enlargement. And there's little they're confident of sharpening."

"They still did good," insisted Ross. "Tell them that."

"I've already have."

"Tell them again, from me. What *about* Germany . . . Berlin?"

"You know everything I've put in place so far. The additional task force personnel are already on station, and there's an airport watch at Sheremet'yevo and at Tempelhof. We know who we're looking for from the sting: photographs crystal sharp."

"What about someone on the inside at Sheremet'yevo, to warn us in advance of reservations?"

Where's your legally trained assimilation of facts, thought Cowley.

"We've only got photographs, sir. No names. It's got to be a visual identification. And there's no way we could get our own asset into place in time, nor guarantee that our trying to do so wouldn't leak out and warn the other side." Cowley enjoyed the older man's momentary embarrassed silence.

Hurriedly recovering, the director said, "What's in place in Germany?"

"The new team were operational as of ten this morning. The German authorities were of course advised, initially as a matter of courtesy as well as for agreement. Because of the Chicago intercept, inadequate though it is, I am personally speaking to the Organized Crime Bureau director of the Bundeskriminalamt later this morning, after we've hopefully got better photographic enhancement that I can include in the material when we ask for operational and jurisdictional cooperation."

"Do we know whether the Germans are aware of Orlov's brigade?"

"They didn't when we originally spoke. They might have more before the end of the day."

Ross lapsed into another silence, the sound of his drumming finger against the manila folder like the dripping of a tap. Abruptly he declared, "We should establish a twenty-four-hour watch on O'Hare Airport."

"It's already in place," announced Cowley, deciding it was time for more personal precaution. "If we're guessing right, Tinelli certainly needs to fly out from some airport, although not necessarily direct from Chicago. He could go by road to fly to Europe from any one of a dozen major, convenient airports. And he doesn't have to fly directly into Berlin, either. Again, if he's cautious—and again, if we're guessing right, they've every reason to be because Orlov knows we're on to him—Tinelli could arrive anywhere in Europe and finish the journey by road or rail. Likewise Orlov and whoever it might be from Italy. We can't monitor every land route."

"You've made the point," accepted the other man. "Maintain the watch upon O'Hare."

"I always intended to."

"We've got our breakthrough, Bill," insisted Leonard Ross.

Cowley didn't think they had, but he supposed there should be some satisfaction at being back on Christian-name terms. He wondered how long it would last.

Dimitri Danilov didn't wait for the photographs to be enhanced but started at once upon the hazy originals. He covered the specific comparisons he intended by withdrawing from Records what was available on six acknowledged and identified brigades, interested only in what little existed on Zubov and Mittel and the Mytishchi Brigade in which Orlov was once believed to have been an enforcer. There were only five Militia file photographs to compare against those taken at the restaurant the previous night, but he also included in the check those that had been taken during Orlov's FBI-identifying sting. In none was there anyone vaguely resembling the blurred pictures or verbal description of Igor Orlov. Danilov did not concentrate solely on attempting a comparison with Orlov but tried to extend the examination, under the strongest magnifying glass he had available, between the sting photographs and those figures in the background of the restaurant images, once more unable to decide upon any similarity. He fruitlessly repeated the entire search when the scientifically improved version was couriered from the American embassy, and he was working his way through photographs in the cover files when Yuri Pavin entered the room.

Recognizing at once that the dossier at that moment open in front of Danilov had no connection with their investigation, Pavin asked, "Something come up?"

Danilov shook his head, closing the file. "Got them out to disguise the checks I was really making. Thought I might as well look through them, while I was waiting for you."

"No identification then?"

"Not that I can make. Parker says it's all going through spectrum microscopes and trained Bureau photoanalysts in Washington but that's scarcely helping me, is it?"

"It could help the investigation." Pavin decided he was totally justified in doing what he intended, personally and professionally repugnant though it was. It was his night for stopping for worship on his way home. It would be an unusual experience, praying for himself instead of for others. It was not something he could—or would—share with his priest, either.

"It's not the same thing," insisted Danilov. "How did you get on?"

Now Pavin shook his head. "It was too much to hope that there'd be any sewer plans for a place as old as the Varvarka mansion."

"It was worth a try," said Danilov, gathering up the photographs. "Like this was worth a try. Pity neither worked."

Yuri Pavin's search *had* worked, although not from an original building source. When the mansion had been refurbished in 1986 as guest accommodations for visiting foreign diplomats, the sewers had been found to have collapsed and all needed either replacement or repair. Unusually, considering the shoddiness of Russian workmanship, the architect had made a thoroughly comprehensible map of the work, even clearly marking as quite separate from the sewer system the different site line and direction of what he'd described as a servants' corridor into the fifth house on Rybnyj Lane. It was the first time in his incorruptible and honorable life that Yuri Maksimovich Pavin had ever consciously withheld information or impeded an investigation, and he accepted that it would forever remain a burden upon his conscience. But he hadn't needed to see Danilov scrabbling pointlessly through unconnected archival material—clearly prepared to compare every criminal picture in Petrovka's inadequate records—in his desperate determination to find and personally destroy Igor Orlov. Which Pavin did not have the slightest doubt Danilov would attempt to do if he learned how the man was obviously getting unseen in and out of Ulitza Varvarka. Whatever he did—and however he achieved it—Pavin knew he had to keep Danilov away from the man responsible for Larissa's death until he was safely in American custody and literally beyond Danilov's reach. And if that involved his doing again what he was doing now, then he would without question impose further burden upon his already weighted conscience.

Jed Parker handed each his own copy of Cowley's congratulatory cable and said, "That'll translate into a commendation, on both your personnel records. And that doesn't happen this early in an agent's career.

Your names have got stars against them." And so, by association and inference has mine, mentally added Parker, contentedly.

Peter Jepson looked sideways to Mary Dowling, with whom he had slept the previous night, and said, "Something else to celebrate."

"I'm sure as hell glad I come from Oklahoma and not Kansas," said the girl.

"We're doing good, after a lot of bum starts," said Parker, who hadn't understood the exchange between the two. "You were in the restaurant last night, right in front of them. I can't risk using either of you in direct surveillance again. I'm putting you out at the airport. Which isn't in any way your being sidelined. That's where this whole thing is going to move on to, Germany. You're both still at the pointy end."

"That's where we want to be," said Jepson, speaking proprietorially for both of them. "What have the scientists got from the photographs?"

Parker said, "It doesn't take away from what you two guys achieved, but what we've got is what we can see. There's no technological trick that can bring anyone into better, more easily identifiable focus."

"So we're scoring five out of ten," said Mary Dowling.

"Give yourself eight: the rest of us are."

That wouldn't have been the score if there'd been a sharper image in two of the misted restaurant photographs of a burly, balding man who was sitting close behind Igor Orlov and who had also featured in the sting operation for a very specific reason. The man had served in the KGB's surveillance division, trained in recognition.

"You're meeting as equals," instructed Brigoli. "Don't infer subservience in anything you say or do."

"I understand," assured his son. "I won't."

"The Russians are being very cautious in their planning."

"A good thing, surely?" suggested Paolo.

"How do you feel about being 'Signore Craxi'?"

Paolo grinned. "Maybe they are taking it a little far, with false names!"

"Bettino Craxi got caught, was driven from the premiership in disgrace, and spent the rest of his life in exile. Don't follow his example."

"I won't get caught," promised Paolo.

"And take care the Russians don't try to form an alliance with Tinelli's people."

"What if Tinelli's consigliere tried an alliance with us?"

"Go along with it. But leave any possible commitment to me."

17

"It's the same whore," announced the observer, stirring in the seat in which he'd uncomfortably slumped and sometimes slept, despite his supposed open-eyed purpose, with eroding weariness and boredom over every unproductive period of every unproductive day during which concentrated surveillance had been maintained upon Veniamin Yasev. So unproductively demoralizing had this specific segment of the now-global investigation become that, whatever the period in the twenty-four hours, it was referred to, even by station head Hank Slowen, as the Dog Day watch. "How about it being true love, like in those movies your mother liked?"

"How about her being the latest hooker he's trying out to make sure she knows all the tricks before pimping her?" suggested the driver, whose name was Dave Herskey and who had difficulty fitting his bulging stomach behind the steering wheel.

The girl at that moment emerging with Yasev from his apartment on Brighton Beach's Thirty-first Street was not one of the hookers on the FBI's initial interview list. To have approached her now would have blown the FBI's continuing interest in the Odessa and its true function, although increasingly the disillusioned Dog Day mutts feared their supposedly clandestine operation was an open secret on the boardwalk. Radios blared constantly throughout Yasev's apartment and in the car, defeating the wires, and there had been nothing incriminating discussed over the bugged apartment or restaurant landlines. Twice Yasev had been followed to a junkyard and was seen personally throwing his constantly changed and renumbered cell phone into a crusher and staying to watch while it was pulverized.

"Nice tits," admired Herskey.

"Tools of the trade," said the observer, Jack Budden. He was contrastingly thin compared to his partner and completely bald. "Come on, Veni, pat her fanny goodbye."

Yasev did, as if on cue, and Herskey said, "Must be odd, humping a chick knowing that four or five or six guys have already been there before you that night."

"You're just an old romantic," said Budden. "Hello! We're going for a ride."

As Yasev got into his car, a '90 Ford, Budden used his cell phone to alert the electronics monitoring van parked in readiness three blocks away, traced a thin finger of his other hand across the map spread open on his lap, and told the technicians on their permanently open channel, "He's going along Thirty-fourth Street. You'll pick him up at the intersection."

Herskey let two cars get in between their vehicle and Yasev's and said, self-mocking: "He'll never guess he's got a tail."

"We've got to hope to Christ he doesn't," said Budden, seriously.

The voice of the electronics observer in the van came clearly on to their receiver. "Got him visually . . . scanning as we talk . . ." Then: "Jesus! Almost blew my goddamned head off. Guy's going to make himself deaf, playing his shit music that loud. And me with him. I'm putting it on to record, for the audio guys to try to find something."

The lights worked conveniently, and the eavesdropping van, unmarked white, windowless at the sides and rear, and with what appeared to be a normal radio aerial, swung out directly behind Yasev.

Budden said, "That was about as subtle as putting a Smart Bomb up his ass."

Dismissively Herskey said, "What the fuck!"

The Russian took the spur and the first signs appeared toward the parkway. Budden straightened in his seat and said, "He's always gone into Manhattan before."

"I've been with you, remember?"

Budden said, "You thinking what I'm thinking?"

"It could be the airport," agreed Herskey.

"We got the choice of two," reminded the observer, already on his cell phone to the Manhattan field office on Broadway.

Hank Slowen said they conveniently had three easily switched men already at JFK, waiting for an incoming Alitalia flight from Rome to complete the photocomparison of Igor Orlov and that he would helicopter in more from Manhattan's Thirty-fourth Street heliport. He'd also run a schedule search—and passenger manifest check if possible—on any flights from Moscow or Rome into either JFK or LaGuardia.

Herskey said, "We're going to look fucking stupid we've rung alarm bells and he stops at K-Mart for a change of underwear after what he and the hooker were up to."

"We're going to look even more fucking stupid we don't ring bells and he meets Igor Orlov with a bunch of flowers and kisses on both cheeks, the way these guys do." Budden gestured to his right. "And that's Jamaica Bay and those birds flying all over it don't have feathers."

"You're going for a prize, right?"

"Every other son of a bitch has got one. Why should we be left out?"

Herskey said, "He's taking the Belt Parkway!"

The monitoring van, which was keeping to within two car lengths of Yasev, blurted abruptly into the car again. "I don't know how the bastard can do it! He's playing rap with the volume off the register and talking on a cell phone at the same time."

"Your guys going to be able to clean it off, hear what he says?" asked Budden, depressing the talk-back key.

"I think he's running something like a white noise as well. We're getting words that don't make sense."

"Like this whole fucking investigation doesn't make sense."

"Where do you think we're going?"

"Either airport," said Budden. "I've warned Manhattan, who've got a couple of guys at JFK already and are helicoptering in more."

"About time we got a bit of the action," complained the other observer. Then, abruptly, "He's taking the JFK exit!"

Herskey began to indicate. "We got about a million guys, all over the world. When the possible break comes, there's seven of us   two of them technical—no backup, no preparation, no idea what the hell we're sticking our dicks into."

"That's how you get to be a star."

"That's how you get syphilis."

Budden was already on the cell phone again to Manhattan, positively identifying the airport destination, sighing at Slowen's predictable response that it would be at least another thirty minutes—most likely longer—before there was any chance of the already airborne support group linking up with them. The three agents already there would make contact direct. Budden disconnected with one hand, depressing the communications button to the van in front with the other, and said: "You guys got mobile monitoring stuff?"

There was a theatrical sigh from the other end. "And our morse code set and semaphore kit and we can do it by flags, on a rope, as well."

"Heads up, guys," insisted Budden, abruptly taking control, the microphone close to his mouth. "We're not in good shape. We've got no proper advance preparation, just three guys wanting to know what to do, and we don't have enough people anyway to stop anyone stealing pennies from a blind man's cup. You got cameras?"

"Still and movie," came the subdued assurance from the other vehicle.

"Take everything you got, but don't make yourselves obvious. You move quite separately from us," ordered Budden. "We need as much photographic cover of whatever he does: most obviously of anyone he meets. The plates of any vehicles he goes to or in. It's a giveaway, I know, which is why you've got to do it right, but one of you keep an earpiece in. We lose contact, get split up in any way, use your own judgment. If he goes for a plane, catch it with him . . ." The cell phone rang on vibrate in Budden's other hand. "Wait," he said, into his radio mike. "I've got New York," and released the talk button briefly to put the mobile telephone to his ear. He was back to the van in less than a minute. "Like the wise man said, life ain't easy. New York's checked the schedules. In the next hour we've got one incoming flight direct from Moscow, one outgoing. Three in from Rome, two out. Another two out to Geneva. We lose Yasev for a minute, we lose him forever."

"Neither of us could follow him on an international flight," admitted the other observer. "We don't have passports."

Heskey said, "How the hell did we ever get anyone on the moon!"

Budden's telephone went again and a voice said, "Paul Peters. We're here waiting for you, Jack. What do you want us to do?"

Budden hesitated. "You've all got identity mugshots of Yasev. Stake out the Moscow and Rome arrivals." Sweat made the phone slippery in his hands.

"What voice band you going to be operating your body mike?"

"Three," said Budden at once. "Everyone copy that. We're talking on three."

The electronics observer suddenly announced, "He's going into the short-term lot."

"I see him," said Herskey. "Not flying off anywhere then."

"We hope not," said Budden, on the phone to Manhattan again to warn the incoming agents and those already there to rent cars if Yasev and anyone he'd come to collect had to be followed. To Herskey he said, "Anything we haven't thought of?"

"I don't think so," said Herskey.

"Think again, harder!"

"Easy, Jack," cautioned Herskey. "No, we got it covered."

The two technicians were already moving separately from their white van, parked three rows behind Yasev, before they had even halted farther back. Budden had his earpiece in place and the microphone clipped to his shirt, beneath his tie. As he got out of their car he said: "You hearing me?"

"Loud and clear," said the other observer. He didn't look in their direction in acknowledgment.

"I got you, too," came Peters's voice.

Yasev was moving unhurriedly toward the exit, although at the top of the ramp he checked his watch. One of the technicians, the driver, was close behind Yasev when he turned out of view and at once Herskey and Budden sprinted as best they could between the parked vehicle. Neither technician—nor Yasev—was among people grouped around the elevator bank when they rounded the corner.

"Where are you?" Budden asked, head low over his microphone.

There was no response from the technicians, but Peters said. "I just told you!"

"I'm calling technical," said Budden. Then, to Herskey: "Too much concrete. No signal."

"Arrivals?" suggested Herskey, pushing the designated floor number when they filed into the elevator.

It was two floors, and as they emerged on to the milling concourse there was a crackle of static and inaudible words in Budden's ear. He said, "See anything?"

Herskey shook his head. "Let's split. I'll try departures."

Budden stood briefly beneath the indicator screen, relief flooding through him at already having at least one man in place for the arrivals from Moscow and the first of the incoming Italian flights within half an hour of each other at separate piers in separate terminal wings. He chose to back up the Moscow plane, moving as quickly as he believed possible without attracting attention into the arrival concourse of the screen-identified D section, straining around him for sight of Yasev or either of the FBI technicians and not detecting any of them. Sweat was rivering his back, and he mopped a handkerchief over his face, using its cover to say into his microphone: "Anyone hearing me? I'm checking the Moscow flight, on D section. I repeat, D for Delta. The Rome plane is on E. Anyone hearing me, try E."

At once another voice announced: "Ed Murray. I'm coming up behind you, on D. There's four of us, spreading out. Two more rental cars. I'm seeing you, Jack. I'll catch you at the barrier."

Budden didn't slow or turn. Neither did Paul Peters, a rawboned Texan, when Budden moved alongside him. Murray was minutes behind.

Peters said, "There's two guys covering E."

Murray said, "You see Yasev here? I don't."

"No," said Budden.

"Lot of people," complained Peters.

"Too many," agreed Budden, jerking his head toward the melee of arrivals filing out. "There're some Moscow Customs markings. Let's back off a little, spread out to give ourselves the wider view." He'd assumed the supervisor's role and no one had challenged him, Budden realized.

Murray moved unquestioningly to the right, Peters to the far side directly in front of the exit from the arrivals hall. Budden went to the

left, putting his back against a pillar, giving them a combined view of
the whole area. After a few minutes Murray said into his mouthpiece:
"We're wasting our time. This isn't it."

"It's a blank on E, too," came in Herskey's voice.

He'd made a mistake, Budden abruptly—sickeningly—realized. It
had seemed obvious for the technicians, as well as for him and
Herskey, to follow Yasev into the terminal, initially pursuing only one
target. But with three agents already inside, someone should have
stayed with Yasev's car, their only marker, as insurance against their
losing him, which it seemed they had done. Urgently he said, "Anyone
close to the garage second level, get there. Yasev's car's in the first lane,
at B: black '90 registered Ford, New York plates you've all got the
numbers of. If he's slipped us, he could be leaving with someone.
Whoever's with the cars, heads up. Liaise. Let's not lose him." Like
we already have, Budden thought.

"Ellison," identified a voice, over the system. "On the level above,
already on my way down. Got all the car recognition."

Almost at once there was another burst of static into Budden's earpiece, then a jumble of inaudible words. He waited for Murray and
Peters to reach him. Peter said, "I don't want to think what I'm
thinking."

"Neither do I," said Budden. It had been his call; it was no excuse
that Herskey or the guys already at JFK hadn't thought of staking out
the Ford.

"Where to?" asked Murray, content to leave the responsibility-
laden team leadership to Budden.

"Next floor up, where the reception's better," decided Budden. "I
want to be able to talk to everyone, get a schedule going. So we need
somewhere central, from where it's easy to move." There was another
unintelligible gurgle of static.

Head hunched down against his chest Budden said, "I'm not getting all the transmissions. Someone like to relay for me?"

Too many people tried, creating a worse discordant babble. There
was total blankness enclosed in the ascending elevator, but there was
sudden, jarring clarity the moment they emerged on to the upper
floor.

Impatiently Ellison said, "You copying me!"

"I've got you," said Budden, urgently.

"But we ain't got Yasev," announced the agent. "His car's gone and him with it."

The alert from New York that Veniamin Yasev was possibly on the move to either John F. Kennedy or LaGuardia was the good news of the morning, the message from Switzerland the predictably bad.

William Cowley believed in delegation and trusted Hank Slowen sufficiently to hope that, hastily arranged though it was, the surveillance would be well organized. He decided against giving an early warning to the director and was glad when the call came from Basel, recognizing he needed a success to balance the continuing failure of the Swiss company search, which had very definitely been personally logged against him. He wanted to talk to somebody about it, though, and Pamela was free for lunch, which he'd hoped she would be. Since the confrontation, there had been an underlying uncertainty that was slow in going. Which he decided the familiar menu and surroundings of the J. Edgar Hoover commissary would do nothing to relieve but which the sunshine—but no wine—at one of the pavement cafes on Pennsylvania Avenue might. He chose the one with green umbrellas opposite the old Post Office.

"You sure you can be away from your desk?" she said.

"I'm sure. Science is on my side." He put his pager beside his water glass.

They both ordered tuna on rye, with a side pickle. Pamela remained convincingly studying the menu, but Cowley knew she was alert to his ordering iced tea to accompany her mineral water.

"You want the good or the bad first?" he asked.

"Good."

"Something could be moving in New York. Yasev's at JFK. We're playing catch-up but Hank's on top of it."

"We shouldn't have come out of the building," Pamela said at once.

"I can be back in five minutes, tops. It's three minutes to my office from the commissary."

"What's the bad?"

Cowley shook his head. "Orlov's an arrogant son of a bitch."

"What?"

"We got into PF Holdings on the second application. There was a change three weeks ago in its charter. It's been reregistered as a charitable holding company." He grimaced across the table. "Would you believe $2,000 goes automatically on the ninth of every month to the International Red Cross!"

"Yes," agreed Pamela. "He *is* an arrogant son of a bitch. So who or what's the new parent company of PF Holdings? And who or what now owns the Odessa?"

"It's a fiduciary structure, registered in the name of Wolfgang Becker, one of the two Swiss lawyers in the firm that acted in the original establishment of PF Holdings."

"Where's that leave us?" frowned Pamela.

"On the outside not able to look in, unless we have positive proof the fiduciary company is crime financed. Which we don't. And we've been made to look stupid pressing for access to PF Holdings."

Pamela nibbled her sandwich in silence for several moments before saying, "Orlov's arrogance is his weakness."

He always seemed to forget that Pamela's major was psychology. Cowley said, "He's doing a hell of a job hiding it at the moment."

She shook her head. "The more he thinks he's beating us, the more arrogant—and careless—he'll get. It's classic bullyboy textbook, unchallengable gang boss convinced he can make fools of the law."

"I'm sure what you're telling me *is* textbook," said Cowley. "But so far that's exactly what he is doing."

"Stop thinking in movie plots," Pamela said. "Reality is that ninety-nine out of every hundred investigations foul up and run off track somewhere along the line. And another reality is that a proportion of those ninety-nine never get solved or result in any sort of prosecution."

"But not many of those ninety-nine involve a potential international conglomerate of American, Italian, and Russian Mafia families."

"You trying to frighten yourself into fucking up?" she demanded.

"Of course not! That's ridiculous!" He was surer of himself with this confrontation than he had been with the one before.

"Good," she smiled, immediately retreating. "I like my men to be winners, not losers. Let's get back, see what you've won in New York."

The feeling was getting easier between them, decided Cowley, guardedly.

"Main concourse," ordered Budden. "Everyone back to the main concourse. I'm close to Information." There was a hell of an irony there, he thought, Murray and Peters uncomfortably beside him. The one thing he didn't have was information, about anything. He'd take the heat. The eavesdropping technicians were exactly that, technicians, not field operatives. Peters and his team had obeyed his orders, like the guys flown in from Manhattan. And he'd be an asshole, trying to offload on Herskey. As the thought came to him, he saw his partner coming toward him with Ellison, the bespectacled black agent who'd announced the disappearance of Yasev's car.

At once Herskey said, "What about the technical guys?"

"I haven't heard," said Herskey.

"Neither have I," said Ellison.

"If they lost him, we're screwed," said Herskey.

"Tell me something I don't already know." The first thing to do was warn New York and get more people to Brighton Beach to pick Yasev up again.

Other Manhattan agents approached from opposite directions but arrived at the same time, and over the head of one Budden recognized the driver of the electronics van. The observer was even further behind but hurrying to catch up but hadn't done so by the time the driver got to the waiting group.

The man said, "Signals are crap here. Too much metal, concrete, and conflicting electronics. Couldn't get you once."

"Did you stay with him?" demanded Budden, forcing a calm self-control.

"Sure. He met a guy, and they went out on the observation deck. Planes taking off and landing made a mess of any remote mike pickup but we tried."

"You monitored their conversation?" In his relief Budden's words were spaced, monotone.

"Tried. Don't know what we've got."

The observer arrived in time to hear his partner's remark. "And I've got three shots of the guy Yasev met."

"Where's he now."

"Took off in a private jet, which is why I'm not with him. But I def-initely got two pictures of it, so we can trace it through its registration markings."

"What about Yasev?"

"I tried to stay with him after they split," said the driver. "He pushed himself into an already packed elevator. It would have been too obvious if I'd tried to force my way in as well."

"You think he made you?" demanded Murray.

"I don't think so."

Not a disaster after all, Budden realized, maybe even a success. To the technicians he said, "I think you guys just saved our lives." *My* life, he qualified, mentally.

The driver said, "You guys do this all the time? It was great!"

"You get it right, it's great," agreed Herskey. "You get it wrong, it's wanna-die shit. You got the good bit."

18

The airport material was incomplete, but there was sufficient for some interpretations, and that night a practically intact scan of a cell phone conversation between Igor Orlov in Moscow and Veniamin Yasev in the Odessa at Brighton Beach filled in virtually all the gaps. And before that, in midafternoon, the Anti-Mafia Commission in Rome identified Luigi Brigoli as *il capo di tutti i capi* of the Italian families. By evening three photographs of Brigoli—one a full-face criminal records picture taken fifteen years earlier—had been wired through the U.S. embassy in Rome and recirculated, again by wire, to the FBI teams in Moscow and Berlin. By then, too, the computer search of the FBI's cross-referenced criminal record photographs had named the man whom Yasev met at John F. Kennedy Airport as Samuel George Campinali, a lawyer who had in the past successfully represented three known members of the Tinelli family. Campinali's photograph,

as well as the three he had earlier represented, were also wired to
Moscow and Berlin.

The quick-breaking developments infused Cowley's division with
an expectation that spread down from Leonard Ross and kept Cowley
shuttling back and forth between his office and the director's suite,
and when Ross demanded a final assessment, Cowley called Pamela
and told her to eat dinner without him.

"Will you be late?"

She was worried about his stopping on the way home. "I shouldn't
be. Ross is playing commander in chief, which is a pain in the ass."

"I'll wait. I'm still stuffed from the sandwich."

She was definitely trying to impose a time schedule. "See you when
I get there."

Leonard Ross was standing at the window of his office, gazing up
Pennsylvania Avenue to the Capitol. The suit was so baggy Cowley
thought the director looked like an animal in the process of shedding
its skin.

"I'm pleased," declared the older man, waving Cowley toward a
chair and sitting himself. "I've just brought the White House up to
speed."

Before this demanded final analysis, Cowley thought at once. So
what was the need for him to be there—the need for the pretence? He
felt a sweep of disappointment about a man whom until now he'd
respected and admired. Perhaps he could get this over in time still to
stop on the way to Arlington. Cautiously he said, "It's been a good
day, a day we needed—"

"So let's not lose it," Ross broke in.

"I don't intend to," stopped Cowley, in return. "We got everything
covered."

"Tell me."

Cowley believed he already had. "Whatever's planned—the international formation of a ruling and operational Mafia commission is
the strongest possibility—is scheduled in Berlin on the sixteenth. The
date's registered twice on the intermittent JFK tape, and is clearly
audible"—the pause was heavily intentional—"on the transcript I've
already given you of the Moscow intercept between Orlov and Yasev

two hours ago, which is night Moscow time." Why the fuck was he having to do this, perform like a puppet on Ross's lap!

"Tell me about the Germans."

That, at least, had not been discussed. "Total cooperation. It has to be their legal jurisdiction, obviously. I've provided the entire case overview—virtually everything we've got, in fact. They're establishing a Task Force, to match ours—"

"Parker—?"

"Is moving to Berlin to head up our people already in place," said Cowley again, impatiently. "John Melton, our resident in Moscow, is taking over as supervisor there."

"Which might be unnecessary," said Ross, carelessly.

Cowley was surprised at the lapse from a former judge. He let another pause into the exchange before saying, "I've spent a long time on the telephone to Berlin today, and with our legal counsel here. It *is* German legal jurisdiction. There is no outstanding international arrest warrant against Joseph Tinelli, Luigi Brigoli, or Igor Orlov—no legal cause or reason whatsoever for official German inquiry, investigation, and certainly not for arrest."

Leonard Ross remained silent for several moments. Then he said, "Shit!"

Cowley said, "What we—the Germans—have under their legal statute is *cause* for inquiry, based upon the information we've made available to them. Which means we and the Germans can keep the three of them—and whoever else we can connect with them—under every sort of surveillance if we locate them in Berlin. But unless they contravene or in any way infringe German law, they can't be questioned, detained, or in any other way put into custody." Cowley, enjoying himself now, waited for Ross's intervention, which didn't come. "We're the only country with a Racketeer Influenced and Corrupt Organizations Act, which doesn't apply there."

Recovering, Ross said, "Sometimes the law gets in the way of the law."

"That's a philosophical argument I'm not qualified to debate," said Cowley. "From where I'm looking, it more often protects it. Except this time."

"The Germans got a fix on Orlov's setup in Berlin?"

Cowley reckoned he'd answered that same question at least three times before. Again he said, "No. But because of what we've told them, it's now a major investigation. And from the intercepts we know we've got the faces of those we photographed on their sting now being shifted from Moscow to Berlin."

"I'm not happy that that's a good-enough lead," complained the director.

Neither was Cowley. He said, "The Berlin flights from Moscow go out of Sheremet'yevo. Jed's covered every departure, since it's become a factor."

"It's our weak point," Ross insisted.

"One of several," agreed Cowley. "The Germans have been supplied with the photographs, and I was told today they've already been issued to Immigration."

"When's Jed get there?"

"Tomorrow."

"How many agents have we got there?"

"Ten, eleven including Jed."

"That going to be enough?"

"Jed and I are going to discuss manpower after he's met with the Germans. Theirs has to be the lead."

"What about technical support?"

"I think the Germans are well up there with us on criminal science."

"Tell Jed to offer, just the same. What about Italy?"

"Airport watch, combined with the Italians. Brigoli's picture has been given to the Germans, for the same arrivals watch."

"Any indictments outstanding against Brigoli upon which the Italians could get an international warrant?"

Cowley shook his head. "I asked, obviously."

"I'll talk to counsel here. See if we could get something under the RICO statute."

"I already have," reminded Cowley. "They said no."

"I'll ask again," insisted Ross. "And think about it overnight. There has to be something."

As he drove over the fourteenth Street Bridge, Cowley decided there was time to fit in just one quick drink, and he slowed at the turn into the tavern. But then he changed his mind and carried on to the apartment, pleased at the decision when he got there because Pamela tried—but failed—to detect booze on his breath when she kissed him.

Dimitri Danilov's mind cut within minutes through the excited, competitive—too often unconsidered—babble, deciding he had more reason than any of them for self-congratulation for having arranged the meeting he had to follow this. Murder was an extraditable offense, with the addition of bribery and corruption as a follow-up accusation, and Danilov was careless of any exaggeration that might be necessary to persuade the federal prosecutor there was a case to make the application after Orlov's arrest in Berlin. Orlov was not, after all, going to live to be brought before a court; he would live only as long as it took for the man to be handed over into his custody for repatriation, told he was going to die for killing Larissa and then shot, while trying to escape.

Aware of the exchanges around him flagging and choosing his moment, Danilov said, "So your legal guidance from Washington is that there's no reason why the intended Boss of Bosses of the Mafias of Russian, Italy, and America cannot gather in Germany, talk about whatever they want to talk about, and go back to their respective countries and homes, presumably to set up their global corporation? While we, who know it's happening, sit and watch and can do nothing about it?"

"We've got time enough," Parker insisted, confidently. "More than a week for our lawyers and German lawyers to go through every statute book that's ever been enshrined to find a detainable offense."

"You seem to have overlooked Russian law," said Danilov. "Here's where the gang wars began, remember?"

Parker, surfing on the current of Washington's euphoria, physically colored, the reaction a combination of irritation at his not having considered the possibility of a Russian charge and of the oversight being made obvious in front of the task force. "You think there's an indictment!"

"It's being considered by the federal prosecutor," overstated Danilov

"That would be the answer to a lot of prayers," said Parker.

But only one that matters, thought Danilov: mine. "I might even get a decision today. I have an appointment."

"You'll let me know the moment there's a decision?" urged Parker. If there was evidence of Joseph Tinelli consorting in Berlin with a Russian gangster arraigned on a criminal charge in Moscow there'd be sufficient under the RICO statute to arrest the American *capo di tutti i capi*. Which would be sensational.

"Sometime this afternoon," Danilov promised.

As they drove away from the American embassy on Novinskij Bul'-var, Yuri Pavin said, "You didn't tell me you were meeting the federal prosecutor?"

"It's a logical formality," said Danilov. "You can drop me off on the way."

"I'm not a qualified lawyer," said Pavin. "But I can't see we've any evidence whatsoever involving our gang war upon which to apply for a warrant that would be valid in Germany."

"There's Mittel's murder. And we know Alexandr Mikhailovich Ognev, an officer in the Organized Crime Bureau, is on Orlov's pay-roll. That's bribery and corruption of a police officer."

"I don't see there's sufficient legal proof of Orlov's involvement in Mittel's killing," argued Pavin. "And I don't see police corruption enough for an international arrest warrant."

"It's a matter for lawyers," said Danilov. He straightened, as Pavin pulled up outside the Justice Ministry. "I'll see you back at Petrovka."

"I'll be waiting," said Pavin. Which he was, when Danilov entered the building two hours later. He said, "Well?"

"Very well," smiled Danilov, picking up the other man's word. "There's enough for an application to Berlin the moment Orlov's seized. I'll obviously go with Parker. You stay here, as backstop."

"Don't do this, Dimitri Ivanovich," directly challenged Pavin. "Don't even think of doing what I know you're intending to do."

"All I'm intending to do is to find a reason to detain Igor Gavrilovich Orlov and break up whatever they're trying to establish," Danilov lied.

He had to do something more to prevent Dimitri Ivanovich destroying himself, Pavin decided. But what?

The traffic out of Moscow the following morning was heavier than he expected and Stefan Sergeevich Cherny, the balding, heavyset American-identified Russian from the humiliating FBI sting, bustled anxiously into Sheremet'yevo Airport, close to being late for his Berlin relocating flight. It was not until thirty minutes later, when he got to the already emptying embarkation lounge, that the former KGB surveillance specialist fully remembered—and only then when they hurriedly arrived behind him for the same flight—the couple who'd looked vaguely familiar near the check-in desk as the two obvious Americans who'd been unable to leave each other alone three nights earlier at the Brooklyn Bite, on Skornjaznyj Lane.

They weren't as attentive to each other now as they had been then. They appeared far more attentive to him, and Cherny decided it was fortunate he had been selected to travel ahead of the main FBI-exposed group to link up in Germany with Feliks Zhikin, who was already installed at the Grand Hotel, on what had formerly been the East Berlin side of the Friedrichstrasse, to arrange the formation conference with the consigliere of Joseph Tinelli and Luigi Brigoli.

The schedule had been for Cherny to join Zhikin at the same hotel. Instead the man took a taxi to the Am Zoo Hotel, on the faraway Kurfürstendamm in former West Berlin. From there he telephoned Zhikin to announce, "The fucking Americans are staking out Sheremet'yevo."

"You sure?" demanded the other Russian.

"The two lovers the other night, at the restaurant? They followed me on the same plane. I didn't want to lead them—or anyone else—to you."

Two hours and several cell phone conversations later Feliks Romanovich Zhikin caught the midday plane from Berlin to Moscow. There Igor Orlov was also on the move. So was Jed Parker, going in the opposite direction with Dimitri Danilov beside him in an embassy car.

19

There was a single track along which to approach the protectively secluded hillside dachas of Orlov and Zhikin, and two Mercedes were parked across its turn-off spur from the larger forest lane, rendering it impassable. A third Mercedes sat behind the barrier, every seat occupied by Orlov's bodyguards, some of whom clasped automatic weapons in their laps, others with their guns beside them, in easy reach. Other guards, also openly armed, leaned against the vehicles or the surrounding, tightly packed firs. Two carried walkie-talkies.

It was the guards on foot who came forward to check Zhikin, even going through the trunk although he knew every one by their given names, as they knew him. As one gestured for the blocking cars to be moved, to allow Zhikin's to pass, Zhikin said, "When's the war start?"

The man shrugged. "Orders. There's others all around in the woods. And spotters, back along the main road . . ." He waved a hand toward one of the men with a walkie-talkie. "We knew you were on your way fifteen minutes ago."

"But you still had to check me out?"

"Orders," repeated the man, who had been at the warehouse slaughter of Nikita Volodkin and his crew.

Zhikin was unsettled that he hadn't identified the early-warning guards. There was another car, a BMW, parked about fifty yards deeper along the track as well as a foot patrol and men with communication equipment. He slowed at the hand-stopping insistence of men he also knew, to be examined again, although this time they didn't bother with the trunk. Outside Orlov's villa the cars were in a shielding nose-to-tail semicircle. Zhikin guessed there were about twenty armed men in and around them.

He called out, "It's going to be hell in the winter."

No one smiled or acknowledged him.

The dacha door was opened by one protector with another standing about five yards behind, Makarov in hand. Igor Gavrilovich Orlov was standing impatiently in the main room and said at once, "I expected you before now. Where have you been?"

"The plane was delayed," said Zhikin. Paranoia in nervous motion, he thought.

"You weren't followed?"

"No."

"You're positive?"

"Yes," said Zhikin. He hadn't seen the main road spotters, he reminded himself.

Orlov gestured toward arranged easy chairs. There was scotch and vodka and glasses already set out. Zhikin poured, automatically adopting his role.

Orlov said, "Could Stefan Sergeevich have been mistaken?"

"He's a trained observer. That's why we took him on," Zhikov pointed out. "I recollect the couple, too. We laughed about them crawling all over each other, remember?"

Orlov shook his head in reply. "What have you told him to do?"

"Make no contact whatsoever with our brigade already there. Do all the tourist things, to see how close they stay with him. And to keep in touch with me."

"What about the others ready to go to Berlin?"

"I've stopped them, until we decide what to do."

"And the Berlin brigade?"

"To lie low. Avoid any regular places."

"Stefan Sergeevich did well, identifying them."

"I've told him it won't be forgotten."

Orlov was briefly silent. "So they know about the restaurant, as well as Varvarka. And we've got to assume they're listening to our telephone conversations so they'll know Berlin's the meeting place. And the planned date."

"Cell phones should still be safe enough," suggested Zhikin. "That's how I called you from Germany and I wasn't followed here." I hope, he thought.

Orlov shook his head again. "The Americans might be able to bug cell phones. That's why I'm up here. No one can get close enough to me to overhear."

You're up here because you're scared shitless, thought Zhikin. "I'll spread the word to avoid landlines."

"You think there could be an informer among our people?" demanded Orlov.

If there were, it would reflect directly upon him, Zhikin accepted. "I don't think so. If that's how the Americans found out about the restaurant, the information is far more likely to have come from one of the other brigades we've brought into line. That could be why we haven't seen any other family paying their respects."

"Find out," ordered Orlov. "If it's one of ours, we'll make an example. If it's another brigade, we'll totally destroy it, like we destroyed Volodkin."

How was he expected to find out, set up a confessional box! "I'll try to pick up rumors, if there are any."

"Get on to Ognev, at Petrovka. Tell the bastard he's got to work harder for his money."

Zhikin decided there was no point arguing that Petrovka was the headquarters of the Russian Organized Crime Bureau, not of the American. "He might have heard something."

"He's not doing enough," Orlov insisted. "Tell him we're not satisfied." He held out his glass for more vodka.

As he poured again, leaving himself out, Zhikin said: "What about the conference? Berlin?"

Orlov smiled for the first time. "I've been thinking about a safeguard before all this.'

Zhikin didn't speak, knowing it would be wrong to prompt although he wanted to. It was several moments before Orlov said, "How ready are you in Berlin?"

"Everything's more or less set up. There's a choice of villas, at Wannsee. The one I prefer is right on the lake. It's big enough but not ostentatious. And easily guarded."

"That sounds good."

"I'm due to meet the Americans and the Italians at the weekend, to check the villa out with them. We'd better warn them off."

"You got names?"

"Sam Campinali from Chicago. Paolo Brigoli from Rome."

A confusing frown came with Orlov's nodded approval. "I'm glad it's Campinali. He's next to Tinelli. It shows they're taking us seriously, according the proper respect."

"But?" asked Zhikin, detecting the reservation.

"Paolo Brigoli's the son. He's a smart-ass."

"Surely sending his son shows Brigoli is taking everything seriously?"

"Watch him. He'll try to be clever."

"But what about warning them?" Zhikin risked repeating.

Instead of answering, Orlov said again, "If they're listening to our conversations, they know it's the sixteenth?"

"That's why I'm suggesting we warn them," said Zhikin, barely keeping the irritation from his voice.

"Maybe the Americans will draft extra people in. Italy, too."

"Maybe."

"Do our people in Berlin have any German police on the payroll?"

Zhikin shook his head. "Not that I'm aware. Things aren't as easy there as they are here."

"How could we find out if groups of Americans or Italians—Russians, even, although we should have heard about that—have suddenly arrived?"

Zhikin added to his own glass, to give himself time to think. "We're well established with taxi drivers who tout for our whores. Taxi drivers are always around hotels, hear what's going on inside."

"Good!" enthused Orlov. "Organize the checks at all the most likely hotels."

"You want me to go back to Berlin?" Zhikin frowned, openly surprised.

"Of course," said Orlov, as if there had never been any doubt. "Keep the arrangement with Campinali. And with Rome. Look at the villas, as if we're going to use them. Which is what I want them to think until we tell them otherwise. It's all got to be done very cleverly, keeping the sequence absolutely right."

"What has?" asked Zhikin, bewildered.

"Proving to the Americans and the Italians how completely in control we are of everything, not just here in Russia. And how untouchable we are." Orlov laughed, overloudly. "And we'll watch the watchers becoming the watched again."

Zhikin shook his head, although preventing the gesture betraying total exasperation. "I don't understand!"

"Listen," ordered Orlov. "Listen carefully because it all has to be got right the first time."

Even though Parker, from abruptly presented necessity, had to tell him in advance of every Berlin arrival arrangement, Dimitri Danilov still duplicated most of the arrangements and approaches in his own right before leaving Moscow, maneuvering the telephone conversation for the suggestion of his sharing their introductory encounter in Berlin to come from Chief Superintendent Horst Mann, head of the Bundeskriminalamt's Organized Crime Bureau. Danilov also booked into the Hilton Hotel and shared Jed Parker's cab from the airport. He was actually glad briefly to escape the American's cloying presence when Parker announced a get-together meeting at the U.S. embassy with the already established task force.

It had, of course, been a required courtesy for Danilov to advise his own legation of his presence, but Danilov wasn't in a hurry to make personal contact until there was a more positive reason—and benefit—for his doing so. From past operating experience outside Russia, Danilov knew there would be predictable lectures about avoiding diplomatic embarrassments and determined attempts by the Sluzhba Vneshney Razvedki, the KGB's foreign intelligence successor, to take over the investigation, which almost inevitably would get in his way. He couldn't, of course, avoid them too long. Unlikely though Danilov anticipated it to be—and accustomed as he was to the backstreet, bribe-backhanding reality of Moscow—it might just be possible that the SVR would know something about Russian brigades in the German capital that would alert him to Igor Gavrilovich Orlov's arrival in Berlin ahead of any American telephone intercept. But Danilov decided that the Bundeskriminalamt—and what he might infer if not positively learn—had priority over diplomatic correctness and doubtful Russian intelligence competence.

Danilov arrived early, but Parker was earlier from his embassy conference, although still standing and handshaking and therefore clearly not having managed any private conversation, which Danilov had hoped to achieve himself. It was a functional although small conference room, an annex to Mann's larger office, bare except for its oval table and chairs and single sideboard upon which there was mineral water but no evidence of alcohol. Danilov guessed, unconcerned, that the room was equipped with recording apparatus.

Horst Mann was a person whose short-statured smallness strangely appeared to make him more, rather than less, formidable. He had a mat of blond hair and blue, unwavering eyes when he spoke. There were few hand gestures, and apart from occasional, flinty smiles, few facial expressions, either. Mann's chair, in the middle of the oval, with Danilov and Parker directly opposite, was clearly set to establish the German's intended dominance.

Expressionlessly Mann began, "We're facing a lot of uncertainty."

"Facing it as one and with a common aim," quickly came in Danilov. "For my part, personally and quite separate from my government at a higher level, I appreciate this cooperation."

"As do I and my government," picked up Parker. Obedient to the relayed instructions of the FBI director, he went on, "And I wish to offer, on behalf of my Bureau, any technical assistance that might contribute to the investigation."

Danilov was not sure that it was physically possible, but it seemed that Mann's impassive face tightened and became more impassively masklike. The impression was heightened by the pause the German allowed before replying.

Quietly, Mann said, "We are very confident as well as proud here in Germany of our forensic technology and our expertise in using it."

Parker visibly colored. "I expressed myself wrongly. We *are* confronting uncertainties. Although a lot of intelligent guesses have been possible, we scarcely know what's involved or what we are likely to encounter. What I meant to convey was America's intention fully to cooperate at every level." He *was* uncertain, although not as yet by anything in this hardly begun meeting. Takeover surveillance had been in place at Templehot airport the previous day and arrival photographs positively confirmed the unnamed Russian as being one of those who had tricked them in Moscow. But the man had led them nowhere except around the tourist spots of the city. He'd eaten alone and not been seen by the tightest possible observation to meet anyone.

Mann's tight smile didn't reveal his teeth. "Of course I understood that."

"I see our status here to be that of observers in an entirely German-led and -controlled investigation, unless called upon to be anything otherwise," lured Danilov. He decided Parker was where he was, although spluttering out of his depth, through his uncle's political influence, certainly not from any ability or aptitude to perform the function for which he had been so wrongly elevated. Indeed, it might have been that failure which led to his transfer from the Drugs Enforcement Administration. Which was a professional judgment, not a cynically dismissive one. Whatever, it made the man a hindrance, about which Danilov didn't have any problem, providing it got into other people's way, not his.

"Myself as well," hurriedly came in the American.

"I'm glad that's agreed," said Mann. "I want us to set out on this investigation with no misunderstandings or misconceptions."

"Which I'm already sure there won't be," said Danilov, anxious to move on from foreplay. He nodded sideways to Parker. "There's been the fullest cooperation between Jed and myself in Moscow, from which I know everything we have uncovered, both in Russia and America, has been passed on to you?"

"Yes?" agreed Mann, questioningly.

"Has—" Parker started, but Danilov took over the question. "Have you any information on an Orlov gang? Association, even, with organized crime here in Berlin?"

Mann's physical shift in his chair toward someone he recognized to be the person with whom he had to deal was perceptible. "No. Berlin's become the crime crossroads between East and West. But Orlov—the name or the man—hasn't emerged so far. Which makes me curious."

"About what?" asked Parker, with a safe question.

"According to what you've given me, he's not a recorded gang leader in Moscow," said the German. "There's no record in America, which I accept is not surprising. But now you're suggesting he's organizing a global confederation. How can an unknown achieve that degree of acceptance in the United States and Italy?"

"I don't know," Danilov admitted at once, recognizing the question as a challenge directed specifically at him. "As you say, it is not surprising Orlov is unknown to the FBI, until now. I am ashamed to admit that organized crime investigation in Russia since—and even before 1991 leaves much to be desired. Too much."

Mann nodded, for the first time lowering his direct stare. "I admire your honesty."

It had been a test, and he'd passed, Danilov decided. "I'm sure I'm not telling you anything you don't already know."

"It's the admission I admire."

Parker recognized that it had become a two-man conversation. Was there any benefit in his any longer keeping to himself the arrival in Berlin of a known and proven associate of Igor Orlov? He said, "There are known Russian gangs operating in the city?"

"There have been arrests and criminal prosecutions of Russian nationals," allowed Mann, guardedly. "Only once has a prosecution uncovered what could be regarded as an established gang."

Danilov abruptly guessed that Mann had received guidance—instructions even—from a government determined that Germany not be seen as a haven for foreign criminals, from which it logically followed there would be even more determination that Berlin not be the city in which a global Mafia was established. Which, if he were right, could be manipulated to his particular and very personal advantage. Danilov said nothing, briefly content for Parker to stumble on, which he did.

"Is there a concentration of Russians, anywhere in the city? A ghetto?"

It was Danilov who winced at the word and its wartime connotation. Mann said, "Berlin was until relatively recently a divided city. We've found that Russians who do choose to settle here do so in what was formerly the Communist-controlled eastern suburbs."

He was right about government guidance, Danilov decided.

Parker said, "Aren't there any rumors—hints—from the known areas?"

"About what?" demanded the German.

"Something big, about to happen."

"I thought I'd made it clear that we've got no information about what you believe to be an organized crime gathering? Or, specifically, about a group linked to anyone named Igor Gavrilovich Orlov."

It was time he reentered the discussion, to establish his growing impressions, decided Danilov. Intentionally, content for the German to underestimate him because he needed to guide the already officially guided policeman in an already chosen direction, Danilov said, "Is there anything in German law making illegal a meeting here between an Italian, an American, and a Russian, providing there is no outstanding arrest warrant against any of them in their own countries?"

Mann turned very positively back to face Danilov before saying: "Absolutely not."

"So where's the offense, even if we locate them and discover where they are meeting and install surveillance?"

Mann was too astute to take that as an ill-considered question. "What's your point?"

"Extradition," announced Danilov, simply.

"Explain that?" demanded Mann.

"There is legal, provable evidence that two men, Vitali Mittel and Fodor Lapinsh, traveled to America with Igor Orlov," said Danilov. "Mittel was murdered afterward. It has so far been impossible positively to identify the second victim as Lapinsh. We still hope to do so. We also have evidence, sufficient for arrest and interrogation, that Orlov bribed a corrupt police officer within the headquarters of Moscow's Organized Crime Bureau."

"But there is no official charge on file?" pressed Mann.

"Not at this precise moment," skirted Danilov.

"But if we were to discover Igor Orlov's whereabouts, Moscow would demand his arrest, prior to extradition?" seized Mann, light flickering upon a distant horizon.

"I believe murder qualifies for extradition under existing legal treaties between our two countries," said Danilov. "The bribery allegation would obviously be secondary." It sounded much better here, more legally convincing, than it had during his discussion with the federal prosecutor. But how much muted pressure—and acceptance—could be imposed upon the German judiciary from a government eager to rid itself of an unwanted and unacceptable problem?

"Could an official request be lodged from Moscow to seize and detain Igor Orlov were he discovered to be in this country?" demanded Mann.

"I have the federal prosecutor's assurance," said Danilov.

"There's a lot more to be considered here," tried Parker.

"I think there's a very definite and positive way forward," said Mann. This time there were teeth in the smile, the two most obvious surprisingly misshapen and crossed.

"So do I," said Parker. He could restore his credibility, although not today, by disclosing the presence of the sightseeing Russian at the Am Zoo Hotel.

"I'd like this conversation officially confirmed as soon as possible," said Mann, directly addressing Danilov.

"I expect us to be in daily contact," said Danilov.

"All three of us," Parker hurriedly added.

"I've been remiss in not offering hospitality," apologized Mann, turning to the sideboard and opening one of its sliding doors. "This is a really excellent Rhine wine, the effervescence close to champagne. It might be premature but if we can only find the bastards, the three of us will have every good reason to celebrate."

"Every good reason indeed," agreed Danilov.

"What's happening?" demanded Cowley, recognizing the voice on the telephone before Pavin identified himself.

"It's all going wrong," warned Pavin. "I thought the danger was avoided with everything switching to Berlin, but Dimitri thinks he's found a way around it."

"Shit!" said Cowley.

"He's going to kill him, Bill. I'm sure of it. And I don't know how to prevent it."

20

What the devout Yuri Pavin had described in their first telephone contact as his Judas approach had now grown into an unsuspected complication to Jed Parker's request earlier that day for the Justice Department and the attorney general's office and any other available legal authority to rule upon the possibility of a grand jury hearing, under the RICO statute, into Joseph Tinelli's organized crime association with Igor Orlov, after any successful extradition of the Russian from Berlin to Moscow.

And it put William Cowley, who until now believed he'd been there too many times before, between the sort of rock and a hard place in which he'd never imagined being so tightly squeezed.

Cowley knew of Danilov's devastation at Larissa's death. He'd stood beside the emptied Russian in Moscow's Novodevisky Cemetery and heard the vow uttered aloud against her murderer. And now, after Pavin's call, Cowley had no doubt whatsoever that Danilov intended his own murderous revenge. From doing which—attempting which—Danilov had to be stopped at all costs and in any way. But how? Attempting persuasion would be pointless, quite irrespective of his making such a direct approach destroying the unique relationship not just between Danilov and his deputy but with Cowley himself. To warn Jed Parker was as unthinkable as it was trying to calculate the repercussions of doing so, ranging from endangering an international investigation, ruining Danilov's career—albeit one Danilov himself seemed prepared to sacrifice—and his own when it became known, as Parker would ensure it inevitably did, because he had ignored the FBI director's explicit order against maintaining Russian back-channel contacts.

Cowley wished his luck at finding Parker still at the Berlin embassy had been matched by his having even the slightest idea how the call could solve his problem. At its best, the conversation might just give him a feel for what was happening in Berlin, although he was thousands of miles away. The barrenness of the words echoing in his head, Cowley said, "So how did it go with the Germans?"

"Haven't you got my report?"

The demand stopped short of truculence, thought Cowley. But only just. "What about your impressions? How do you think it's likely to go?"

"We were just getting to know each other, really."

Cowley thought the other man sounded disoriented, as if Parker were having as much trouble with words as he was. "What's this about RICO and Russian extradition? I'd like more of a steer on that."

"Covering bases is all," said Parker. It was a bitch having to channel everything through Cowley, although he couldn't be denied—or be made to share—the credit if everything worked. Even *getting* a grand jury convened to examine the activities of the American Mafia Boss of Bosses would guarantee a future career in glittering lights, irrespective of whether an indictment was returned.

"I don't understand?" pressed Cowley.

"You have filed today's legal requests?" Parker demanded, suspiciously.

"Of course I have," said Cowley. "I'm asking the basis for your suggesting it?"

"Danilov thinks there's an extraditable murder charge if we get Orlov in custody."

"Mittel," identified Cowley. "I wouldn't have thought there's enough from what I've read to support an extradition application."

"I'm just telling you what happened at today's meeting. Maybe more's come up that the Russians haven't told us. It's their turf war, not ours."

There wasn't, Cowley knew. He'd specifically checked, during his conversation with Pavin. But maybe the remark indicated some tension in Berlin. "How are things between you and Danilov?"

Sufficiently apart from the rest of the task force in the FBI section of the embassy, Parker smiled at what he saw as an undermining opportunity, remembering the friendship between Cowley and the Russian. "Could be better."

"How?"

Unaware of how it fitted the reason for Cowley's call, Parker said, "I think he's holding back."

At once Cowley imagined an opening. "On what?"

"Maybe whatever the extradition material is, additional to what he's already told us."

Could there be something that Danilov hadn't even told Pavin, in his determination to get to Orlov? There was certainly ground upon which snares could be laid before he ensnared himself. "I don't like the sound of that."

"You asked for impressions. I'm giving one to you. It could be wrong," said Parker, covering his back.

Cowley thought he saw another opening. It wasn't perfect—scarcely a chink—but snares really were all he could hope to put in Danilov's way, absurd though it seemed to think of obstructing the man. "How are things personally between you?"

"OK," begrudged Parker, cautiously.

"You working together all the time?"

"Well enough."

Cowley didn't believe it was. But how could he manipulate it from afar? "You're right about Tinelli being our target."

My target, thought Parker. "What are you telling me?"

"Orlov is Danilov's. He's got to be ours, too. We need Orlov to get Tinelli. And if we get Tinelli, we hurt American organized crime as badly as it's ever been hurt before."

"That's the point of what I've asked Justice!" protested Parker, genuinely confused.

"You've got to be with Danilov all the time. No side deals, between Danilov and the Germans." The idea came to Cowley as he talked, and he decided to run with it as far as he could. "I'm going to talk to the State Department—suggest the director does, that is—if the legal opinion is that we've got a route through the Racketeer Influenced and Corrupt Organization law. Get State officially to talk to Moscow, to register our interest, so that if Orlov's extradited, we're even part of any escort back to Moscow." The idea grew. "Maybe we should approach Berlin diplomatically, too? It's already been accepted as a multinational investigation."

Parker abruptly realized that the impetus, the whole idea, was being taken away from him. "Shouldn't we wait to see what the legal opinion is? No reason to set off bells if the fire truck doesn't have anywhere to go."

"Leonard Ross is a judge," Cowley reminded him. "He's best to decide the route."

"Has the director got all I sent today?" repeated Parker, anxiously.

"You were in on the arrangements. You know how the director wants everything to work," said Cowley.

"What's coming out of Moscow?"

"Not enough," said Cowley. Or was it, he asked himself, too much?

"Found you!" greeted Cowley.

"I didn't expect you to call me here," said Danilov, soberly. He hoped Cowley didn't intend a long conversation. The belated appointment at the Russian embassy was in less than an hour and he'd realized a very essential reason for making contact.

He shouldn't have contacted Danilov in Berlin, Cowley accepted. The Hilton's telephone register would record the incoming Washington call—and its traceable number—to the Russian. "Surprised you didn't tell me you were going. Every reason to be there if there's a chance of extradition, though."

"How'd you know I was here?" It had definitely been a mistake, not to have told Cowley. And that was a stupid question.

"Jed," said Cowley, lying to protect Yuri Pavin. There had been three references to Danilov in Parker's embassy cables.

"Nothing from Yuri Maksimovich?" He'd forbidden the man to say anything about Larissa to Cowley if there was any contact, and Pavin did not disregard orders.

"Or from our guys in Moscow. Seems to have gone quiet." Danilov's attitude was unquestionably different from their normal exchanges. How? Aloof, Cowley decided. There was a distancing in Danilov's voice, as if he intended to keep everything between them strictly professional, with none of the instinctive friendship and trust that had grown between them.

"What about Brighton Beach?"

"Nothing from there, either. Could be Berlin's the place it'll move."

"Why do you think that?" seized Danilov.

Too quickly suspicious, Cowley decided. "We know something's going down, on the sixteenth."

"But not where or precisely what," warned Danilov.

"How's it going with the Germans?"

"What's Parker said?"

It wasn't like Danilov to avoid giving an opinion by answering a question with a question. "That they seem to have put all the obvious checks into place. Is that what you think?"

Considering his earlier assessment of Parker's ability, Danilov wasn't surprised at the American's failure to infer the German reluctance at being the center of a global Mafia summit. "They seem pretty thorough. Nothing left out from what we might have done, but they can't control all the rail or road links. I think the lead's still got to come from how we've got it so far." And Danilov felt isolated from it, despite Berlin being the only place it was possible for him to be.

"How's Parker shaping up?" openly demanded Cowley.

Danilov hesitated, acknowledging how much more difficult his intentions would have been if Cowley had been with him in Berlin. He was abruptly swept by the desire to tell the American about Orlov's link to Larissa—although obviously not the revenge he planned—but just as quickly rejected the urge. Apart from compromising the American it was impossible to predict Cowley's reaction. Knowing Cowley—and his professional expertise—as well as he did, Danilov thought it more than likely Cowley would guess at personally imposed justice. Bringing himself back to the American's question, Danilov said cautiously, "Probably a better desk man than field operator."

Cowley was surprised at Danilov's slip, interpreting it at once. Danilov believed he could manipulate the investigation whichever way he chose. "How's the liaison?"

"Fine." With no need for any change or improvement, until he had Igor Gavrilovich Orlov at the point of a gun, Danilov thought.

"What about the Bundeskriminalamt guy who's leading the investigation?"

"Good," Danilov said at once.

"This chance of extradition back to Moscow? It's the Mittel murder, right?"

"And Lapinsh," replied Danilov, guardedly. "That's obviously who the second body was."

"I've gone through everything you've sent. You think there's sufficient evidence?"

"That's a legal judgment." Danilov tried to duck.

"What's yours?"

"Reasonable suspicion." The embassy appointment was in forty-five minutes.

Cowley said, "You got anything extra to what I've already seen?"

"It's a matter of presentation and interpretation." He'd gone as far as intimating to the federal prosecutor that there was a forensically established voiceprint linking Igor Orlov to the burned-out car and an American-domiciled Russian émigré as a potential witness to the actual planning of the murder.

"Maybe I'll give you another call, in a day or two?" Cowley suggested.

"Do that," said Danilov. And perhaps the next time he'd be able to discern a better reason for the conversation than he had on this occasion.

In his Washington office Cowley decided it was the first instance he'd ever suspected Danilov of lying to him. It could only be something to do with the supposed extradition evidence—evidence American lawyers might just be given access to if RICO provided a way to move against Joseph Tinelli.

Irena maneuvered her tour of the dacha to bring them out again on to the encircling veranda, with its view of the tightly surrounding forest. "So this was the surprise?"

Orlov was uncertain at what little time, a few days, he'd had to prepare her. "Part of it."

Nodding down toward the barricading cars, she said, "Why all the men and guns?"

"You didn't mind them when we were hunting Volodkin."

"I don't mind them now. I'm just asking why I thought you'd gained control?"

She knew too much. It worried him that he still needed her. "I have. Just being careful, that's all."

Irena led the way back into the dacha. "I like it here. Why haven't you brought me before?" Imagine being the lady of the house, she thought, wistfully.

Orlov shrugged. "No reason. The occasion never came up before." He knew she'd enjoyed the audience of the guards, in and around the cars.

"Now it has?"

"Now it has," he agreed. She was irritating him.

"Why now?" she asked, presciently.

He didn't have time for any further preparation. "I told you I wanted you and Ivan to do something for me, remember?"

"Me *and* Ivan!" she echoed.

"I caught the man who killed Georgi. Gave him to you."

The sharp-featured woman turned fully to face Orlov, anxious to learn at last what he'd been leading up to these last few days.

There was no anger in her voice, he noted. "I'm not making any demands. I'm asking a favor. I just want you to take a little trip. Everything will be arranged. Airfare and hotel paid for, restaurants and theaters arranged. Money."

"What do we have to do?" She wished Ivan hadn't needed to be involved.

"Just enjoy yourselves on a little vacation."

Irena remained looking at him for several moments, unsure whether she could risk it. There wouldn't again be a chance like this. "We're two of a kind, you and I."

"You've told me before. Quite a few times."

"I want to tell you again."

"You have." What deal was she working toward?

"I don't want to be with Ivan any more. Haven't done so, for years."

Now it was Orlov's turn to stay briefly silent. "You've told me that before, as well."

"I wanted to tell you that again, too."

"What?"

She'd committed herself. No going back now. "I want to know everything. And why. I'll make it my idea, not tell Ivan it's anything to do with you, because if I do, he won't even listen. But I want you to take me in, afterward. I want to leave Ivan and be with you, all the time."

Orlov allowed another pause. "You know what you're asking?"

"I won't mind about other women. Just as long as I'm first."

Orlov hesitated before finally saying, "All right."

"You mean it?"

"I said all right. But you and Ivan have to do exactly what I want."

"And I said I could do it. Now tell me why."

Orlov was letting the dacha grow finally dark around him, not bothering yet with the lights, letting his irritation with the woman burn off. But she was right, he conceded. They were two of a kind, the perfect immoral and amoral pairing. If he'd needed a partner of any sort, which he didn't, Irena would have been the only—the natural—choice. It could, for as long as he wanted, be an amusing diversion after he'd amused himself with all the more immediate diversions. Orlov snapped on the light before answering the cell phone, saying nothing.

Zhikin said, "Found them. The Hilton."

"How many?"

"Fifteen, definitely. Could be one or two more. And Dimitri Ivanovich Danilov is with them."

Orlov laughed at the identification of the man named by their Petrovka source as the person leading the hunt for him. "Now wouldn't that be something if we got him as well! What about vehicles?"

"Rental cars, to supplement embassy vehicles."

"You identified them all."

Zhikin allowed himself a sigh. "Numbers, make, colors, the lot."

"No change in Campinalli and Brigoli's arrival?"

"Everything on schedule. Everything arranged. What about you?"

"On schedule."

"She agreed?"

"Of course she agreed."

"So I go ahead and make all their arrangements?"

"Everything I told you to do."

Danilov was unconcerned at the obvious irritation at the homegoing delay his late arrival caused at the Russian embassy, correctly guessing it would minimize the length of the ritual lecture against diplomatic offense and the already predicted efforts of the SVR station chief— who was unable to offer anything upon organized Russian crime in the German capital—to involve himself in the operation. Both, however, still took more time than Danilov judged necessary, particularly as—to the intelligence officer's increasing annoyance—Danilov insisted on using the embassy's secure communication facilities to ask the federal prosecutor formally to file an extradition intention to the German Justice Ministry if Igor Gavrilovich Orlov were successfully detained.

It was past eight in the evening of a long day before Danilov finally emerged from the communication room to the resigned SVR officer waiting patiently outside. The man said, "I will, of course, have to file a report to Moscow about your presence. And the reason for it."

Danilov said, "Lubyanka has already been officially notified, but you must do what you think necessary."

"I must also ask for guidance about my involvement."

"If you feel you must." He'd been particularly careful that the federal prosecutor had endorsed his formal advice to SVR headquarters that the Berlin inquiry was entirely criminal, with nothing to involve intelligence participation.

"Is there anything else we need to discuss tonight," sighed the man.

"Yes," said Danilov at once, coming to the real purpose of his being there and welcoming the invitation coming from the other man. "I obviously couldn't travel into the West with a weapon. I need a handgun. And several clips of ammunition."

"Of course," accepted the intelligence officer, without question.

21

It hadn't been planned for Sam Campinali's rail journey from Frankfurt, where his delayed plane from Toronto landed, to take longer than Paolo Brigoli's, who'd evasively zigzagged from Italy by flying from Milan to Cologne, but it gave the waiting Feliks Zhikin the opportunity to judge separately the other two consiglieri. It was important to both to have been booked—under their Russian-designated assumed names—into the Bristol Kempinski, further along Berlin's Kurfürstendamm from the Am Zoo, in which Orlov's former KGB surveillance specialist was himself being kept under twenty-four-hour FBI watch easily identifiable by the former critically unimpressed professional.

Briefed upon the father's abstinence, Zhikin didn't expect the son to order alcohol, which he did, although only beer, in the hotel's expansive bar in which Zhikin experimentally let the younger, bespectacled man select their table, acknowledging the apparently casual choice—which was anything but casual—beyond any possibility of their being overheard. Zhikin ordered beer as well.

As they touched glasses, Brigoli said: "They took extreme precautions to get me here. And the name Craxi has unfortunate connotations in my country. He was a politician on our side who got found out."

If you only knew half of how you're now being manipulated, thought Zhikin, as he'd increasingly reflected since arriving in Berlin, all the more so after shuttling back and forth to Moscow: his was the name and the face that would be held perhaps even more responsible than Orlov himself. And he again who had to ensure Orlov's convoluted scheme worked with clockwork precision. Zhikin said, "As our association hopefully progresses, you'll come to realize we don't put anything or anyone at risk, particularly no one involved in something as important *as* that association."

"It might also be inferred as uncertainty," said the Italian, ineptly.

"Caution is not uncertainty. It is important, essential, that no one forgets what we are trying to establish here. We get it right, we virtually rule the world."

"We do that now," declared Brigoli, bombastically.

Zhikin shook his head, although keeping the gesture short of being dismissive, which was how he genuinely considered it. "Until now we've just nibbled at the edges. If this is done properly, we get the whole cake, with all the cherries."

"We expected the formation meeting to be in Moscow," announced Brigoli.

"Why?" demanded Zhikin, flatly.

"Don Orlov initially came to us. His respect should have been reciprocal."

Was it a test or an oversight? wondered Zhikin. "I believed you to understand Russian?"

Brigoli frowned. "We're talking in Russian now!"

"But not colloquially," said Zhikin, who believed he could understand why this man had irritated Orlov. "Colloquially in Russian 'Don' is not a term of respect. It indicates someone sexually ill equipped. Maybe you should tell your people, to avoid a mistake in the future?"

Brigoli visibly flushed. Sincerely he said, "Thank you." Then, at once, "We were discussing why the meeting will not be in Moscow?"

"Berlin is conveniently central but at the same time neutral," said Zhikin, rehearsed as he believed himself to be prepared for every question and eventuality. "This is the formation gathering, no one given—or seeking—the impression of superiority from the venue."

Brigoli smiled. "That shows great consideration."

"Everything that's being suggested has been put in place with the greatest consideration." Except what Orlov was improvising now, Zhikin thought.

The Italian continued smiling. "My father will be pleased with that reassurance."

"Did you have doubt!" Orlov had obviously been overbearing.

"Perhaps some misunderstandings were allowed to arise."

"Then I am glad they've been reconciled."

"As I am," said Brigoli. "Do you imagine much of the liaison being between the two of us, as far as Italy and Russia are concerned?" It was an important question to help another speculation that was hardening in his mind.

"I would expect so."

"And I would welcome that."

Brigoli's reply told Zhikin that the Italian Mafia had committed themselves to an association that one day—in how many days or weeks or months?—this man would inherit from his father. Zhikin believed what Orlov intended to do here in Berlin—to oppose which would quite literally cost him his life—to be ridiculous, nothing more than unnecessary macho posturing to achieve or prove nothing. Igor Gavrilovich Orlov was a homicidal paranoiac whose reign would inevitably end—in how many days or weeks or months? he wondered again—at the barrel of a gun or the searing blast of an explosion. Which logically would put him in line to inherit the kingdom—its place in this impending conglomerate—created already at the cost of so much blood. Zhikin answered the Italian's smile and raised his glass, conscious as he did so that although ordering it, Brigoli had drunk none of his beer. "Here's to a successful, and long, personal relationship."

At last the Italian took a token sip, holding his glass back to examine it quizzically. "So much to be toasted in beer!"

"Champagne can—and will—follow," promised Zhikin. I hope, he thought. He would need to be extremely careful: a misplaced word—a wrong look—could get him nailed alive to a cross and floated down a drowning river. But at that moment he positively made the decision somehow to succeed Igor Gavrilovich Orlov to bring some sanity into what they were trying to create.

The need for the most absolute care was a doubly warning thought when the already rewarded bellman came into the bar to tell him of Campinali's arrival, bringing Zhikin back to the current machination he was dangerously orchestrating. The urbane American—using the Russian-suggested pseudonym of Harrison—came showered and changed into the bar just fifteen minutes later, ordered Macallan scotch as he sat from an immediately attentive waiter, and said, "What do I need to catch up on?"

"We've just been talking generally, waiting for you," said Zhikin. There *was* a difference between the two men, quite apart from age. By himself Paolo Brigoli appeared self-confidently mature. But against the American's instinctive authority there was the marked dissimilarity upon which Orlov himself had remarked. Objectively—but unconcerned—Zhikin knew Campinali would be subjecting him to the same scrutinizing comparison.

Campinali said, "It was quite a runaround to get here."

"We were talking about that, too," said Brigoli.

"It's not the sort of journey Mr. Tinelli would consider undertaking," cautioned the American.

"Something to put on our agenda," suggested Zhikin. "At this stage my consideration is security, to enable us to get everything arranged and in place for those we represent. We're here to fine-tune everything."

"You have a place?" asked the American.

"Subject to both your approval."

"There are alternatives, if we don't approve?" demanded Brigoli.

Zhikin judged the Italian just slightly too anxious to contribute and wondered how often he had acted for his father—and with his father's authority—in the past. "Of course. Two."

"What about accommodations?" asked Campinali.

"Another reason for our meeting in advance like this," said the Russian, going into English with Campinali's arrival. "The two alternatives are both villas, with extensive living accommodations and staff facilities. As is my first choice. I'd imagine they would be preferable to hotel accommodations, although that obviously could be arranged in a moment."

"Mr. Tinelli will want a villa, with his own staff," insisted the American.

"As will Don Brigoli," said the Italian.

Which meant he would have to go through the pretense of selecting one for Orlov, Zhikin accepted. "We can view them all and make decisions tomorrow."

"You've scheduled appointments beyond our seeing the villa of your first choice?" demanded Brigoli.

Zhikin allowed the censorious hesitation. "Obviously I've arranged for us to see all three. My first choice might very well *not* be yours. Or Sam's."

The tour of the villa bordering Wannsee took over an hour next morning because the two other consiglieri insisted upon inspecting every room—even the basement—and, after that, thoroughly examining the garden, checking particularly for buildings from which it might be observed, which it wasn't. Zhikin had already assured himself of that—and of the other two—and already asked virtually every question posed by the American and the Italian. As they reentered the mansion, the agent, Otto Müller, remarked that from the attention to detail it was obviously an important conference, and with the clearly inferred prospect of future and substantial business to come, Sam Campinali replied that it was also an extremely sensitive commercial project the privacy of which was paramount and had to be protected at all times, to which Müller hurriedly assured the three of them that he understood.

The surveys of the two other properties—also at Wannsee, although smaller and deeper in the forest—were conducted just as painstakingly, and Zhikin felt a flicker of uncertainty toward the end of their tour of the third. If the other two consiglieri approved—Campinali's acceptance being more important than that of the younger Italian—it would not just be his choice that was confirmed. More essentially, for what was to follow, his security judgment also had to be respected.

It was Zhikin who insisted they return to the villa on the lake to finalize the renting of all three mansions, to the delighted surprise of Müller, who until that moment imagined himself only offering a choice. Sensibly, however, he did have contracts for all three properties in his briefcase. He agreed immediately that it was immaterial that the renting in each case was in the name of a Swiss-registered company when Zhikin handed over, in advance and in dollars, fully and unquestioningly, the three fees, insurance coverage, and full inventory deposits.

"Our Swiss company is not required to exchange tax information with Germany," said Zhikin.

"I understand," smiled the agent, who most definitely did.

"I hope you also understand our need for privacy," repeated Campinali.

"You have my absolute guarantee of discretion," the man assured him. "Which brings us to the question of staffing."

"It does not," Zhikin objected, only just ahead of Campinali. "We will staff all three villas ourselves."

"But cleaners . . . food . . . wine . . . ?" stumbled the man.

"We will cater entirely for our own needs," insisted Campinali. "We require nothing more than the villas we have hired from you today and for which we would appreciate having the keys right now. They will be returned to you at the end of the rental period."

The agent shook his head in bewilderment. "There must be something—"

"Nothing," came in Brigoli. "Our business is done. Thank you."

The meal the previous night at the Kempinski had been an excellent recommendation for their eating there again. As soon as they'd ordered Campinali said, "The houses are secure. Good choices. Now they need to be assigned."

Pecking-order peccadillo, Zhikin recognized: another charade that had to be played out. "We regard ourselves as the hosts. You are our guests. Yours has to be the choice."

Brigoli knew the premier villa beside the lake, where the commission was to be created, was where his father would expect to be. He smiled uncertainly. "We could draw straws?"

"We don't *play* games of chance. We profit from people who do," reminded Campinali, heavily.

Zhikin said, "The commission is going to be the bringing together of equals who meet as equals. But speaking for Igor Gavrilock Orlov, I believe—as he would believe—that the conference villa should be allocated to Mr. Tinelli. It is he who has the farthest to travel and—again speaking solely for Moscow—the man whose age and authority should be respected." Zhikin knew he wasn't speaking at all for Orlov, who would have wanted the first choice, but no conflict was going to arise.

"Paolo?" invited Campinali.

"I agree," capitulated the Italian, without argument. Trying to show some determination, he added, "We will take the second house."

"And we the third," accepted Zhikin.

"There is still much to discuss but I think this has been a good beginning," said Campinali.

So do I, thought Zhikin. He'd impressed these two men and he would impress their *capo di tutti i capi* when he overthrew Orlov.

Despite the promise of an open door Cowley's meeting with the FBI director had been delayed because of Leonard Ross's appearance before critically inquiring congressional budget committees. Even before Cowley was seated in the seventh-floor office, the crumpled man said, "George Warren buttonholed me, to talk privately about his nephew. Wanted to know how things were going."

Why was Ross telling him? Cowley wondered. As an unneeded reminder of Jed Parker's influence? Or had Parker perhaps talked directly to his uncle? There'd been two calls earlier that morning from Parker in Berlin, demanding to know why there hadn't been any response to his RICO inquiries. And one from Moscow, from Yuri Pavin. Cowley said, "What did you tell Warren?"

"That Parker was involved in a complicated, ongoing investigation that I didn't feel I was able to discuss in detail."

Had Ross really been that forthright? thought Cowley. "And he accepted that?"

"He wants to be kept in touch, when I feel able to tell him something."

Cowley decided Ross was passing on the political pressure, which he didn't need added to all the other pressure. Pavin's call had been to tell him the indication from the federal prosecutor's office was of some exploratory legal contact being made with Berlin. "You had time to look at Jed's legal proposal?"

Ross said, "In this country there'd be a prima facie RICO case against Tinelli and Brigoli, both on criminal charges, consorting with a gang leader against whom an indictment could be returned."

"I know that, sir. So does Parker. That's why he's put forward the idea. But we're not in this country."

"You spoken to State?"

"And to Justice. They say they need time to go through the legal steps of treaties between Germany and Russia and Russia and our-selves."

"We don't have time," dismissed Ross.

"From my conversations with State and Justice it also seems that because Russia has, comparatively, so recently emerged from Communism such treaties don't exist." It was the State Department that had given the reassurance Cowley still had to pass on to Pavin.

"What about between Germany and us?"

"I thought we'd established there's nothing illegal under German law in the three of them meeting."

"It could be a matter of diplomacy." Ross smiled.

Could this at last be why Ross had talked about private conversations with one of the most powerful—arguably *the* most powerful—politician in Congress, backdoor, country-to-country diplomacy to get into custody the most powerful crime figure in the United States of America? And at the same time cover with glory Jed Parker, the instigator of the enterprise? It fitted, if cynically, better than any other guess he'd so far made because Cowley knew such arrangements had been made in the past. About which, at that moment, he didn't give a damn. His only concern was that Orlov wasn't surrendered into Dimitri Danilov's murderous custody. How far could he take the conversation? Cowley asked himself, posing another question more directly. "Diplomacy between whom?"

"Interested parties," said Ross.

Fuck it, thought Cowley. "Sir, I am trying to supervise the American contribution to an international criminal investigation. I make decisions on the basis of *all* of what I know, hopefully coming from *every* available source. For me not to know something could easily result in my making a wrong decision, one that might jeopardize—wreck even—what we're trying to achieve."

"Quite a lecture," said the director, no longer smiling.

Cowley acknowledged the outspokenness hadn't done him a lot of good. But then he wasn't trying to do himself a favor. "I felt—and feel—it is a point that I professionally had to make."

Ross nodded, not immediately responding. Then he said, "I will talk to State. And to Justice. You will be informed of everything relevant to what you are doing."

Which was the remark Cowley quoted verbatim to Pamela at their pavement cafe lunch opposite the Old Post Office Building. To which she immediately replied, "What about anything he considers *not* to be relevant?"

Cowley sipped his root beer, hating it. "I'm the donkey turning the revolving wheel, keeping everything grinding along."

Pamela frowned at the self-pity. "You sound like a donkey!"

"Maybe I deserve that."

" 'Maybe' doesn't come into it!"

"Point well and truly made." He felt better, having told Pamela everything.

She said, "So let's go back to the beginning. I'm not for a moment trying to shit on your friend, but if Dimitri wants to play out a Russian novel and commit suicide, professional or otherwise, avenging the woman he loved, that's Dimitri's choice. The romance of it all is terrific. But from what you've just told me, you didn't exactly endear yourself to the director this morning. Don't endanger your own career trying to do any more than you've already done to stop Dimitri." The woman halted, to emphasize what was to come. "And whatever you do, don't intentionally screw up the investigation to keep Orlov away from Dimitri. It happens, it happens. I don't want you trapped in the crossfire."

Pamela *would* have turned him in to FBI personnel or to the director—still would, in fact—if she believed his drinking risked an internal inquiry, Cowley decided, confronting her subjective ruthlessness. "You really think I'd throw a case like this!"

"I think you'd be tempted. You're too nice a guy."

"You're wrong."

"Good."

"This whole goddamned thing might be academic. We haven't yet got any of them in the bag: got any proper idea where the hell they're going to be on the sixteenth."

"Berlin isn't that big."

"It's big enough," insisted Cowley

Which was what Jed Parker was thinking, tensed forward in Horst Mann's office in the Bundeskriminalamt building to which he'd been hurriedly summoned, together with Dimitri Danilov, an hour earlier.

Parker said, "The visa was very definitely issued to Samuel George Campinali?"

"Unquestionably," agreed the German policeman, reluctantly.

"But that was the name we gave you!" protested Parker, outraged. "You told us you'd put a watch on it!"

"It was circulated to other airports, but the expectation was that he would come in direct, through Tempelhof. That's where the name was flagged. And why it took so long to percolate through the system."

"What?" began the American, furiously, but Danilov intervened, impatiently determined against Parker exacerbating the inquest into more of an open argument.

"Which means he's been here two days. It was a direct flight. How many other American passengers disembarked in Frankfurt?"

Mann shifted, further discomfited. "We're still checking from the airline manifest."

The check either hadn't started or, worse, hadn't been initiated, Danilov decided. "Campinali is a consigliere, a legally trained fixer. He could be leading an advance crew. So we have to assume there are Italians and Russians here, too."

"We've put an alert against the name Brigoli, but Italy is in the European Union. There's no visa requirement." He shook his head, a gesture of defeat. "I don't think there's much chance of his being identified as being here from a visual immigration check, unless he came in through Tempelhof. The only Russian name we have is Igor Gavrillovich Orlov. No one with a visa in that name has passed through any German airport in the last three days."

Parker decided he finally had to disclose that the Americans had identified Stefan Cherny, a disclosure that would threaten other admissions. Trying to minimize them, he said, "A Russian Orlov used as a decoy to establish he was under our surveillance—and whom our agents later saw with Orlov in the Moscow restaurant he uses virtually as his headquarters—is here, in Berlin. He's registered at the Am Zoo Hotel, under the name of Stefan Cherny."

Horst Mann's office froze into a chilling silence, the German and Dimitri Danilov held by different furies. Eventually, his voice an over-controlled whisper, Mann said, "How do you know this?"

Haltingly, worsening his discomfort by trying to limit what he said, Parker admitted to the departure watch at Sheremet'yevo and the placement on the same plane of the two FBI agents who had watched the brigade-surrounded Orlov in the Skornjaznyj Lane restaurant.

"When?" demanded Mann, in a still unnaturally quiet voice.

"Three days ago," the American conceded. "Throughout that time he has been under permanent surveillance. He's met no one, nor been approached by anyone."

"What *has* he done?" demanded Danilov.

"Just looked at the sites, like he's on vacation." Parker's voice was hoarse, a croak.

"He's identified you," declared Danilov, flatly.

"I don't believe he has," said Parker, desperately.

"You know he has!" said Danilov.

"Mr. Parker," began Mann, formally, louder now. "Germany agreed to join in your investigation on the understanding of full, open, and totally reciprocal cooperation. You, clearly, have no intention of keeping to that agreement. There is no further purpose in our continuing this conversation or this meeting. Whether there will be any further meetings—any further liaison between us at all—is a decision for my superiors here at the Bundeskriminalamt and at the Justice Ministry. Immediately you leave, which I am now asking you to do at once, I am going to ask them to make that decision."

"Wait!" burst in Parker. "This is a misunderstanding. Of course, I—"

"Mr. Parker," the German stopped him. "Don't go on treating me like the fool you clearly take me to be! I've asked you to leave. Please do so, now!"

"I knew nothing of this!" insisted Danilov, urgently. "I was in no way part of any deception. There is no reason whatsoever for our cooperation to be ended!"

Horst Mann hesitated and then said, unconvincingly, "I will make that point."

Dimitri Danilov held his anger as they emerged from the police headquarters, wheeling upon Parker the moment they cleared the building. Danilov said, "If you've ruined it—wrecked everything—

I'll ensure an official Russian protest is made both to your government and to the Bureau. And I'll also make sure that everyone in America and Italian law enforcement and counterintelligence knows what an incompetent fucking amateur you are! I'll make you the laughingstock that you really are, a fool who shouldn't be allowed out without a minder!"

"Fuck you!" said Parker.

"If this goes wrong you're going to be the one who's fucked! Trust me!"

"Sounds good." Orlov was in a wicker rocking chair, on the veranda of the dacha, vodka glass in hand.

"Just the button left to be pressed," assured Zhikin, who'd rehearsed the remark.

Orlov laughed. "You sure you got enough stuff?"

"If Hitler had this much in 1945, he could have resisted our troops for another month at least," said Zhikin.

"What about Irena and Ivan?" asked Orlov.

"Keeping strictly to their itinerary, which means I can't go into the Kempinski any more, which is unfortunate. The food's good. According to our people watching them, they don't talk to each other."

"They don't do anything to each other any more," said Orlov. "You sure there's nothing more left to do?"

"Positive."

"So it really is button time?"

Zhikin grimaced. "In a day or two."

"Tomorrow I'll send in those the Americans can identify from their photographs, to meet up with Cherny. I'll need to hear that the Americans have picked them up."

"I know," said Zhikin.

"I'll go back to Varvarka immediately. Ring me there, so that the call will be picked up. I'll go out through Sheremet'yevo tomorrow, too."

"So we move Campinali and Brigoli?"

"Yours has to be the timing. You think they trust you?"

Zhikin hesitated. It would be a mistake to indicate any close relationship. "They'll go, the moment I tell them an investigation is concentrated here in Berlin."

Orlov said, "It's got to be my finger on the button."

Which is what I'd hoped, thought Zhikin, his own plans formulating in his mind.

22

Dimitri Danilov was totally ostracized at the Berlin Hilton and was happy to be so, sure that after the previous day's debacle at the Bundeskriminalamt the Americans would be under permanent German observation and determined against any incriminating association, although he stopped short of actually moving to another hotel because he wanted to watch them as much and as effectively as he could. He wanted to go to the Am Zoo to identify Stefan Cherny from the sting photographs he had seen, but he didn't do that, either, again because of the risk of association with Americans already in place there. An added danger was Cherny isolating him in return, as Danilov was sure the Russian had identified his pursuing Americans with ease.

Danilov's surprise wasn't at the quickness with which Yuri Pavin answered his direct line at Petrovka but at the tone of his deputy's voice, oddly sharp for a man whose speech was normally—and confusingly to those who misjudged it as slowness—measured and reflective. Danilov said at once, "Is there something!"

"What? No. Didn't recognize your voice." stumbled Pavin badly, who rarely stumbled verbally *because* he always measured his replies.

"I didn't speak, *for* you to recognize my voice. What's up?"

The minimal exchange gave the quick-thinking Pavin the moment to recover, although he still allowed himself more time. "We don't know. Which is the trouble."

"Yuri, what the hell are you talking about! Or, rather, not talking about?"

"There's been nothing picked up for days by the telephone taps— or the scanners—from either the Varvarka mansion or the restaurant."

"You sure Melton's cooperating with the scanners?"

The sideways question confused Pavin. "Now I don't understand what you're saying?"

The relief flooded through Pavin as Danilov explained, and when he stopped, Pavin said: "You think Germany will withdraw cooperation!"

"They're looking for an excuse. Parker's given it to them. The bastard!"

"You spoken to Bill about it?" Who could have imagined Danilov being saved as easily as this!

"Not yet."

"Are you going to?"

"Depends what happens. I'm trying to stay with the Germans. They've got the greater chance of picking up a trail."

"It doesn't sound like they did so well with Cologne and Frankfurt," challenged Pavin. He felt drained by the relief.

"Let's talk about the telephone silence," demanded Danilov.

"That's just it. There's nothing to talk about, because we're not hearing anything."

"They know we're listening, just as Cherny knows the Americans picked him up," insisted Danilov.

"Which means they're leading us by the nose." And at that moment I couldn't be happier, thought Pavin.

"As they've been leading us since the beginning!"

"Dimitri! We've got the name. There'll be another time if we don't get him on this occasion."

"I want him *now*!"

But God determined against it to save you, decided Pavin. "What are you going to do?"

"There's nothing I can do except wait, without having any proper idea what I'm waiting *for!* If Parker's ruined this, I'll make sure everyone knows: make sure he's a laughingstock!"

"You told me," said Pavin. He didn't like Danilov talking irrationally, ridiculously, like this.

"So what's the answer, about Melton?"

"We speak—meet, in fact—most days. I don't get the impression he's holding back. But then, as I've said, there doesn't seem to be anything to *hold* back. They're our taps on the landlines into Varvarka and the restaurant. We'd have picked up something."

"What about Bill, in Washington?"

Pavin hesitated. "I've kept in touch."

"Nothing on legal extradition?"

"Nothing that he told me," avoided Pavin.

"Get on to the federal prosecutor," instructed Danilov. "I want to know if there's been any direct official communication between Moscow and Berlin."

Pavin was disappointed by the other man's desperation. "I don't believe things will be moving that quickly."

"Do it!" demanded Danilov. At once, more quietly, he said: "Sorry! Please, just do it. Try to get some guidance on how the authorities here are going to react."

"I'll do what I can."

"I'm sorry at the way I spoke," repeated Danilov.

"If you force things too hard, you're going to make mistakes, Dimitri Ivanovich. On this case, more than any other, you can't afford to make mistakes."

"I won't, insisted Danilov.

Perhaps there wasn't after all so much to be relieved about, thought Pavin.

"Tell me about Berlin. And Moscow," demanded Leonard Ross.

Cowley wished he could. Apart from the congressional budget rearrangement, his meetings with the director had settled into a regular morning and afternoon schedule but today he'd been peremptorily summoned earlier. The director was wearing a freshly pressed dark blue suit and a fresh, unwrinkled shirt that portended a visit farther along Pennsylvania Avenue to the White House. Cowley said, "I'm sorry, sir. Nothing's come in overnight to add to the fact that Sam Campinali is known to be in Berlin."

"Nothing on anyone associated with Brigoli?"

If there had been, I would have told you, thought Cowley. "No."

"I've just spoken to State—to the secretary himself. There's something going on in Berlin that doesn't square. No one's giving straight answers or replies to anyone about anything, and we're not talking diplomatic bullshit. State says they don't understand the stalling."

"Neither do I," said Cowley, experiencing the same surge of relief that Yuri Pavin had known an hour before, five thousand miles away. "Nothing's come in overnight from Germany or from Russia to explain any stalling or obstruction."

"You haven't spoken to Jed yet?"

They were back to Christian names, Cowley noted. "I was waiting to talk to you first, to *hear* if there had been anything back from the State Department or the attorney general."

"Get on to Jed right away. See if he can give us a steer. And maybe get on to your guy, Dimitri."

Whom he had been specifically ordered not to go behind Parker's back to contact, remembered Cowley. The political tendrils were getting thicker and more difficult to cut his way through. Determined against becoming totally entangled, Cowley said, "With or without Jed's knowledge?"

There was one of the silences with which Cowley was becoming increasingly familiar before the director said, "Just find out. I need to know if there's a glitch over there on the ground. A lot of people have become involved, ambassadors among them. I don't want any embarrassments."

Despising himself for even thinking of his need for a Teflon deodorant, Cowley said: "Do you want a written explanation—if indeed there is one—from Jed?"

There was another reflective silence before Ross said, "Yes, I think I do. But see what you think, when you talk to him. If you don't think it's necessary, don't bother."

It wasn't a Teflon deodorant he needed, Cowley accepted; it was a Teflon-lined, blast-proof bunker. "We're working on impressions, right?"

"Impressions of people whose business and expertise is using impressions to guide them to decisions."

It was degenerating into farce, thought Cowley, irritably. "I'll get back to you."

"With something that makes sense."

"Yeah," agreed Cowley, sardonically. "That would be a great leap forward, wouldn't it!"

He reached Jed Parker at the American embassy, consciously resisting the temptation to gauge attitudes or situations from voice tones, leaving that expertise to impression-gleaning experts. Cowley said, "There wasn't anything overnight?"

"That's exactly right. There wasn't anything overnight," Parker responded with B-movie glibness.

"So there's nothing on Campinali? Or Brigoli, not even if he's in Germany?"

"If there had been, there *would* have been an overnight report."

"Something wrong, Jed?"

"Like what?"

"Like my every question being answered with a question."

"Nothing's wrong. We've still got our Russian hobbled."

"But leading us nowhere because hobbled horses can't lead: they stay where they are?"

"He's not here on vacation," insisted Parker.

"Just enjoying one," retorted Cowley. Parker definitely wasn't sounding right, talking right.

"What's happening elsewhere?"

"Nothing," replied Cowley. "Which is worrying. Everything's gone quiet, the lull before the storm."

"That's obvious. There're still four days to go."

"I got called in by the director this morning. We're getting diplomatic obstruction to the extradition idea. You any idea why that might be?"

"Who have you been talking to?" demanded Parker.

"I just told you, the director. Who wants to know, in a memo, if there's a problem."

"Bruised feelings," said Parker, obscurely. "The Germans were pissed off we didn't tell them right away we had Orlov's man under wraps."

"Was that a good idea, not telling them?"

There was a snort from the Berlin end. "You forgetting what the director told me personally, that this had to be an American-led—and successful—investigation!"

It was true, Cowley remembered: Parker wasn't in any trouble. "Maybe a point to make in your memorandum."

"You really want me to write a report!"

It actually was save-your-ass bullshit, thought Cowley. "I don't. The director does. He's caught up in a lot of politics. I don't know what the agenda is."

"Talk to you later," dismissed Parker and put down the phone. Which he picked up immediately to redial and which, in the U.S. embassy in Moscow, John Melton answered just as quickly.

Brightly Melton said, "So what's going down?"

"Shit's going down," responded Parker, keeping to his B-movie dialogue. "Still nothing from the telephone intercepts?"

"Zilch."

"You think the Russians are fucking us? What about that big ox, Pavin?"

"We're talking, all the time. Lunching today, as a matter of fact. I think he's being honest with us. Why?"

"I've got an operational problem here in Berlin. We could be closed out by the Germans."

"What the hell for!"

"That's not important: doesn't affect your end of the operation. But there's a lot that does. Keep your lunch date. Hook Pavin with our identification of Cherny to make him think we're still passing the plates around the table. But suck him dry as you do so. We're not going to lose the lead on this. We still got Sheremet'yevo covered?"

In Moscow Melton frowned into the receiver. "Of course. A mouse farts in the mansion or the restaurant, we hear it. So, because they've got the landlines, do the Russians."

"Not if it's a cell phone," said Parker.

"We're not sharing?" asked Melton, pedantically, determined against misunderstanding.

"We're not sharing diddly-squat with no one. We're going to get Tinelli all to ourselves and bring him home in a bag: body bag if necessary."

Melton's frown deepened. "Jed, what are you telling me?"

"Just that. That Tinelli's ours. No one else's. No help from anyone, no discussion or liaison from anyone. That clear?"

It was and it worried Melton. And then he thought of Parker's family connections and decided there were things going on that he didn't know about and most probably didn't *need* to know about. "It's clear. You sure there's nothing more I should do?"

"Just what I've told you."

The cell phone rang precisely at the prearranged time in the Ulitza Varvarka mansion and Igor Gavrilovich Orlov let it ring until the moment it would have switched to the message service before snatching it up, wanting the listeners to be listening.

From Brighton Beach a well-rehearsed Veniamin Yasev said, "Have you heard how it's going?"

"Well," said Orlov. "Everything exactly as planned."

"How about the Italians?"

"Again, exactly as planned."

"You must be feeling very happy?"

"I will be, after the sixteenth."

"When are you off?"

"Shortly."

"The others?" asked Yasev, literally reading from the Zhiken-dictated script.

"On their way to the airport now."

The alert from the scanner listeners mobilized the American watch squad at Sheremet'yevo Airport, and three FBI agents easily managed to get ticketed aboard the Berlin flight in pursuit of the photographically identified Russians who had featured in Orlov's sting. John Melton was warning Jed Parker of their Berlin arrival before the aircraft cleared Russian airspace.

An hour later a completely unnoticed Igor Gavrilovich Orlov caught a flight from Sheremet'yevo, an airport so much more under his control than that of official authorities that he could at all times have kept his name from any passenger list or reservation record. Everything he planned might have been different had Orlov known that aircraft manifests had linked him with Mittel and Lapinsh.

But he didn't know. And on this second expedition into the West he intended very much to leave a trail for the idiots to follow.

23

The nine A.M. meeting for what was to be the most strictly timed and complicated day in the life of Feliks Romanovich Zhikin so far was at the Wannsee villa, for which Zhikin arrived necessarily separately and early, apprehension bubbling within him at this very moment, when he would initiate Orlov's demands. Campinali and Brigoli were precisely on time, in a legitimately purchased and officially registered, Russian-supplied Mercedes. Campinali came blank-faced into the entrance hall where Zhikin waited. Brigoli was smiling. Zhikin greeted them solemn-featured. It was Campinali who detected the seriousness it wasn't difficult for Zhikin to enact.

"Something wrong?" the American asked at once.

"It's off," Zhikin announced. "Everything's canceled." The uneven voice wasn't difficult either. It actually fitted.

"What?" said Campinali, sharply but totally controlled.

Zhikin took his lead from the other man's calm, pulling back. "The FBI is here, looking."

"What!" Brigoli wanted to suck in the panicked response, swallow the word, the moment it emerged.

Zhikin held back.

"How?" demanded Campinali, still calm.

"I don't know," said Zhikin, relaxing into his role, enjoying it even. "We've obviously got sources within the Bundeskriminalamt. All I know at this moment is that an FBI task force have arrived here, in Berlin." He paused. "So obviously there can't be a meeting. Everything needs to be rescheduled, relocated. I'll fix it; be in touch."

"How!" repeated Campinali, relentlessly.

Any preparation had been impossible, and it wasn't planned for Zhikin instinctively to look toward Brigoli, but having done so—improvising in a way he'd mentally criticized Orlov for doing—Zhikin said, "It came from Europe . . . the information, from Europe . . . that's virtually all I know—"

"Not from Italy!" Brigoli blurted out, so quickly and so automatically that the intended denial sounded like a positive admission. Appearing to realize it himself, the Italian said, "There's no way it could have come from us. There was commission discussion, of course. Each of you knew that there was going to be. But there was nothing of the planning, where our meeting was going to be. My father, myself. Just the two of us knew. No one else."

It would have been impossible for Zhikin to have anticipated Brigoli's reaction but had he done so, he would never have believed the opportunities open before him. "I'm not making accusations, Paolo. Of course, not against you or your father. All I am telling you is that the Americans are here because of what they've been told from *Europe*." Fully assessing his opportunity now, anxious to turn away as much suspicion and responsibility as he could, Zhikin went on, "I hope to get more later.

"It won't come back to Italy," insisted Paolo again, too anxiously.

Zhikin shrugged and said, "Then I don't know from whom—or from where—the information came. Our source insists Europe."

"It's essential that we find out!" said Campinali. "And not just how? It's just as important to establish what—how much—they know."

"Which we will," promised Zhikin. "But the information is not our immediate concern. You both have to leave Germany at once. There needs to be substantial replanning . . . reassessment . . ."

"It shouldn't have occurred," declared Campinali. "I know precisely how many people —who those people are—who knew of my coming here."

"As we do," said Brigoli, still sounding defensive.

Campinali said, forever calm, "Let's examine the situation . . . the dangers."

"Minimal," asserted Zhikin, confident now, sure he was controlling the encounter. "There's a direct flight to Rome for you, Paolo, from Cologne at three this afternoon. For you, Sam, there's a London-routed plane from Frankfurt at five. I've got cars on the way here, with drivers. All you need to do is pack. You can be moving"—

Zhikin looked at his watch—"thirty minutes back to the hotel, not more than three hours on the road." From the time check Zhikin calculated that the car he'd sent overnight to pick up Igor Orlov would have long ago reached Switzerland.

Before Zhikin could continue, Campinali said, "We need to think it through. What's there to find out here?"

"Nothing," asserted the Russian, at once. "There's no record, no evidence, of either of you having been here. It's fortunate we used pseudonyms. This place, the other places, are in the name of a nonexistent Swiss company cutout. We just walk away—abandoning the money which came entirely from our side—and rearrange when we've learned more about how it came to be discovered we were meeting here."

"The fact that it *is* known is what's important," persisted the American. "It could affect everything."

The possibility of America—or Italy—withdrawing entirely was glaringly obvious, but it hadn't occurred to either Orlov or Zhikin. Hurriedly Zhikin said, "Until I find out the extent of the FBI's—and presumably the Bundeskriminalamt's—knowledge we can't anticipate how it will affect our future plans. If indeed it affects them at all."

"I do not think Mr. Tinelli will want to explore this further until we know the answers to these uncertainties," declared Campinali.

As he spoke he looked accusingly at Brigoli, who at once said, "I don't imagine we will, either."

"I don't think these are decisions that can be reached now," said Zhikin.

"I'm not announcing a decision, simply an expectation," said Campinali.

"As I am," dutifully followed Brigoli. He spoke actually looking out of the hallway window, as if expecting the arrival of siren-wailing vehicles. At that moment, quite coincidentally, cars did arrive, although silently, and at once the Italian shouted, "What the hell!"

"It's OK!" interjected Zhikin. "My people. I told you I've arranged transport, with drivers. You don't need the car we'd given you any longer. I think it's time to go."

"Yes," agreed Brigoli, anxiously.

"Mr. Tinelli will want the answers to all the questions," repeated Campinali, unhurriedly.

"Which we all will," agreed Zhikin, an idea forming from the movement of the cars outside. To Campinali he said, "Perhaps you'd give me a ride back into the city?"

"Of course," the American said at once.

Brigoli looked between the other two men, remembering his father's warning against alliances but unable to think of a way to prevent the other two men being alone. Inadequately, he said, "We'll hear from you?"

"Or from Mr. Orlov himself, to your father." Zhikin hadn't intended the dismissal to be apparent as it sounded. He said, "We'll obviously be in touch very soon, within the week," which didn't do anything to make it better, but about which Zhikin decided he wasn't particularly concerned. He had far greater concerns about other, more important things than salving the younger man's feelings.

"Let's go," urged Campinali at last, his attitude changed.

Zhikin rearranged the pickup by the waiting, driver-accompanied cars under the pretense of arm-waving indications that the lakeside villa be locked and totally secured behind them. He was aware of Brigoli's concerted attention as he got in beside the American.

As the car moved off, Campinali said at once, directly. "You think it was the Italians?"

Zhikin shrugged, aware he was edging out into an unknown wilderness. "I'm not accusing anyone. I know you wouldn't have invited the FBI. We certainly didn't."

Campinali jerked his head back to the following car. "Why'd the Italians send a kid?"

"He's Brigoli's son."

"Still a kid, for something as important as this!"

"I'm not sure our sources here will know how the FBI got involved," encouraged Zhikin. "You got anyone inside the Bureau."

"Police level, not the Bureau itself," said Campinali. "What about your source here?"

"Police level, irritated at the foreign intrusion." Zhikin was sure he was layering the necessary personal protection.

"You think it could have anything to do with Brighton Beach?"

"How could it?"

"No," agreed the American. "I guess it couldn't, although it was your guy, Yasev, who passed the travel details on to me at Kennedy Airport."

"This is an irritation, nothing more," insisted Zhikin. "It shouldn't be allowed to affect the formation."

"It won't, if we can get the Bureau out of the way."

He had to stop what Orlov intended, Zhikin decided. He'd been against it from the beginning but now it went beyond being ridiculous to being potentially wrecking, despite what he was trying to achieve now. "We don't have any eyes or ears in Italy."

"We do," promised Campinali. "And we'll use them."

"I think you and I should keep in close touch."

"So do I," agreed Campinali. He took a prepared card from his pocket. "These are special numbers. Unlisted. Can't be intercepted."

"We'd like to know if there's anything from Italy."

"You'll be the second to hear," said Campinali. "The first will be those who spoke when they shouldn't have, if indeed they can be found."

"An arrest warrant!" exclaimed Danilov, smiling alone in his hotel room, glad now that he'd registered at the Russian embassy.

"The possibility of German police exercising one against Orlov if he is located there," qualified Pavin, guardedly. He was smiling, too, in his Petrovka office, not viewing the development as a setback to his determination to protect Dimitri Danilov. "The advice from the federal prosecutor's office is that they've asked our legal attaché in Berlin to explore with the German Justice Ministry their acting upon a warrant, if one is issued here." The Russian hesitated, baiting his lure. "Sounds like everything's going to be mired in a diplomatic bog."

"Not with my actually being here, able to talk personally to the attaché."

It was the response Pavin had expected. Warningly he said, "The prosecutor's office didn't say anything about your doing that—becoming involved at this stage. What they do want from you to formulate a charge is the more detailed information you apparently offered." He paused again. "You didn't tell me what that was, so I couldn't help them."

Danilov's smile vanished. "What have you told them?"

"That I'd make this call and come back to them. Where's the file?"

"You know there isn't one, as such," said Danilov, irritably.

"Then it can't go forward," judged the deputy, satisfied.

"You told me it had!"

"Nothing more than a general inquiry, through the embassy," said Pavin. He hated having to have these two-tiered exchanges, in his anxiety to gauge what Danilov would do.

It was enough, Danilov decided. Enough for him to speak to the attaché and enough hopefully to reestablish a working relationship with Horst Mann and make whatever use he could of the Bundeskriminalamt. Danilov said, "Let it lie. If they come back to you, tell them it's a working file that I've got with me, that I'll send the details direct from here, through the attaché."

Pavin's silence lasted so long that Danilov suddenly said, "Yuri Maksimovich! You still there?"

Danilov would definitely invent sufficient evidence for a charge and send it direct to the prosecutor, Pavin knew. Forcing the words, he said, "You told me in the beginning you didn't want to compromise me. You're asking me to lie, to the federal prosecutor . . . to lawyers . . ."

Now it was Danilov who remained silent. Then he said, "I'm asking you to tell lawyers what I am in turn telling you. Nothing more, nothing less. You'll not be compromised."

"Dimitri Ivanovich—" his deputy, began but Danilov didn't allow the man to continue.

"There's nothing to say. If you want it to be an order, then I'll make it one."

"What I want is for you to pull back, not throw everything away," said Pavin. "And not bring our friendship to a point I never ever imagined it could reach . . . never wanted it to reach."

There was more silence from Berlin before Danilov said, "I've made my choice, Yuri Maksimovich. You must make yours."

Pavin already had, although not about everything. His next call after breaking off from Danilov had to be to Cowley, in Washington, although he didn't know what the American could do to stop Danilov either.

The legal attaché at Russia's Berlin embassy was a fussily agitated, bespectacled man named Vladimir Nemptsov, whom Danilov instantly recognized as the sort of man who anxiously bent to the current prevailing wind. He wondered how easy it was going to be blowing him in the direction he wanted. He sat patiently through Nemptsov's charade of apparently needing a reminder of Moscow's message, followed by a fumbling search for the actual cable—which turned out to be the uppermost in a disordered pile on his disordered desk—and dutifully made sympathetic noises to the protests of being overwhelmed by work. "But criminal law is not at all what I am accustomed to."

Which was precisely what Danilov had hoped to find. He said: "You appreciate, of course, that it's hugely important. An international investigation into an international crime conference."

"Of course I recognize that," said Nemptsov. "It's something on which I am going to need a lot of guidance."

Danilov said, "Which is why I came, immediately after I heard from Moscow."

"They've spoken to you?" demanded Nemptsov, misunderstanding as Danilov had intended him to.

"In detail. You know there's a stipulated date for this conference?"

"Yes."

"Have you raised the question with the German Justice Ministry?"

"It was discussed at this morning's conference with the head of chancellery."

"And?" pressed Danilov, consciously bullying as he'd bullied the cleaner who'd discovered the bodies of Mittel and Lapinsh.

The attaché fingered the Moscow message. "There is nothing here authorizing me to discuss this with you."

"You know from the head of chancellery who I am and what I am investigating," said Danilov, whose first insistence had been that the lawyer check his official and now Moscow-confirmed registration. "You also know, *from* that cable, what we're trying to do, seize Igor Gavrilovich Orlov. If, as the result of my being misled—worse, if something goes positively wrong from your refusal to discuss everything with me—I shall make it quite clear in an official complaint who is responsible."

"I am not refusing to discuss things fully with you!" the man protested weakly. "I was just making the point."

Which Danilov accepted Nemptsov would do with Moscow the moment this encounter ended. Formally he said, "Has the request been communicated to the German Justice Ministry?"

"Yes," said the lawyer meekly.

"As an official note? Or orally."

"Both." The man less than an hour earlier had claimed to have forgotten the existence of the Moscow instructions.

It was better than he'd hoped, thought Danilov. "What impression have you got, having actually talked to German lawyers?"

"It's too early even to contemplate a decision—" tried the other man.

Danilov blocked him, impatiently. "I didn't ask—obviously don't expect—a decision in hours. I asked for your *impression*. Now I'm asking you again. Having spoken in a very preliminary way to German government lawyers, is it your impression that it will be considered favorably? Or dismissed out of hand? Which?" Was this man receptive enough to have inferred a German eagerness to rid itself of any involvement, as he'd inferred from Horst Mann's attitude?

"As I said, it's too early—" Nemptsov tried again, and again Danilov refused him.

"How long did your conversation last?"

The man shrugged. "A few minutes."

"One minute? Five? Ten? How long?"

"Maybe five," allowed Nemptsov.

"That's long enough. You must have got a feeling in five minutes whether or not they're going to cooperate?"

"They said they'd consider it seriously."

"What about quickly? We're operating to a time limit."

"I made that point," assured Nemptsov. Unnecessarily, he added, "The date's stressed in the cable."

He had sufficient to confront Horst Mann, Danilov decided. "I expect you to discuss this meeting with Moscow. As I certainly will, if called upon to do so. And I am going to make sure it is quite clear, as the chief investigator of the Organized Crime Bureau, that I expect full local cooperation."

Nemptsov again waved the cable, like a flag of surrender. "I had no authority . . . You weren't mentioned. This is not the sort of thing I'm familiar with."

"Then you're having to learn in a hurry, from me," said Danilov, unsympathetically, guessing the other man would have very much liked the whole thing to have been swallowed up by what Pavin had probably accurately called a diplomatic bog. "I'm at the Hilton, where the Americans are staying. The moment you hear from the Justice Ministry, I want you to call me there. And in between times you and I are going to keep very closely in touch, so that nothing gets forgotten or overlooked. And if anything comes up that you're unsure about, I want you to discuss it with me. Don't you think that would be a good idea?"

"Probably," capitulated the man.

"Not probably," insisted Danilov. "Definitely." It wouldn't take him long to fabricate a file sufficiently detailed to convince Moscow, but he needed to speak to Horst Mann first. From an empty beginning it was becoming a crowded day and it was a long way from being over.

"Has there been a playback from Berlin?" queried John Melton, immediately Pavin stopped speaking.

"Not yet. I've asked to be told, the moment there is," exaggerated Pavin. It was irritating, time-consuming, when there wasn't time to consume, to have to pass news of the Russian decision through the FBI station chief but at the same time necessary to conceal that Cowley was maintaining their unofficial back-channel contact.

"There's not enough time," complained the American. "We've only got two more full days, after today."

"That's what I'm afraid of," agreed Pavin. Not afraid, he mentally corrected himself: hoping for. Just as he was hopeful that Cowley's idea of getting the Russian application stalled by linking it with a repeated American approach and by doing so convince Berlin that Washington and Moscow were combined in an independent, German-ignored investigation. He wished he—and Cowley—could have thought of something better guaranteed to block any serious German consideration.

Melton was uncomfortable following Jed Parker's insistence upon holding back from a Russian whom he liked and trusted. Admired even. "You think this is going well, as well as we might have expected with all the breaks there seem to have been?"

"No," said Pavin at once, a more encompassing reply than to the immediate question "I don't think it's going at all well or as we might have expected."

"What's wrong?"

"Too much top-heavy pressure, too many conflicting interests." Dimitri Danilov's being the most conflicting of all, Pavin thought.

"We've got leads in Berlin," allowed Melton, deciding he could make the concession.

Pavin instantly recognized the plural. "I know about Cherny."

Melton looked at him for several moments without speaking. Then he said, "I didn't say anything."

Could there be something that the overambitious Parker was even keeping from Cowley but needed Melton to back him up on? "You think there's a chance of getting Orlov?"

"I didn't say anything."

Pavin was as sure as he ever could be that Parker was most definitely saying nothing to Danilov in Berlin, either. "Should I do anything?"

Melton shook his head.

Pavin said, "Thank you, for not saying anything."

Melton smiled.

Cowley's back still had to be covered. "You'll tell Washington about our legal moves, of course."

"Of course."

But it wasn't William Cowley whom Melton decided initially to telephone, the moment his conversation with Pavin ended. First he'd telephone Jed Parker, in Berlin.

Everything was a bluff, so Danilov set out by bluffing, expecting Horst Mann to refuse his calls—which the German did—and refusing to talk through intermediaries, insisting there was an unspecified development that he could only discuss personally with the Bundeskriminalamt officer under their agreed arrangements.

Mann returned the call in twenty minutes, at once demanding, "What is it?"

"I'm in the same hotel as the Americans. I don't want to talk on an open line." The Hilton was, in fact, remarkable for the absence of those whom Danilov had positively identified as FBI: remarkable and worrying, but something that might be utilized in the coming hour.

"It's important?"

"That's why I insisted upon speaking to you."

"All right. Come now."

Danilov detected no hostility from the other man when he entered the German's office. Searching for an attitude, Danilov decided it was a wary neutrality that could tilt either way at a misspoken word. He also decided Horst Mann would be a difficult person to bluff and that the wrong tilt might not even need a misplaced word. As he sat, uninvited, Danilov said, "Has there been any decision over withholding?"

"You're here to tell me something," refused the German.

"Moscow has officially asked your Justice Ministry to institute any arrest warrant issued against Igor Gavrilovich Orlov," announced Danilov.

"Which I would have been informed about," said Mann, immediately giving Danilov his opening from the phrasing and which he just as quickly took.

"But of which you haven't yet *been* informed. Until now. I am not interested—involved—in anything America is doing. Which I hope my coming here now, telling you what I am telling you, will convince you. I simply want to return a wanted professional criminal—a murderer—under arrest to my country. But to do that, I need your cooperation and your manpower. I am asking, again, that we work together. Everything I have, you have. I will operate entirely under your jurisdiction." There was a visible easing in the stiffness with which the other man was holding himself, and Danilov decided the tilt was in his favor.

"Do you know what the Americans are doing?"

"No," admitted Danilov. It was an oversight not to have spoken to Cowley before coming here. A snippet to have further insinuated himself with Mann's confidence would be abusing his friendship with Cowley. But anything that got him to Orlov was justified. Quickly he added, "The hotel's deserted."

Mann hesitated at the moment of decision. "There is a hotel in the eastern suburb of Weissensee, the Adler. Five Russians, all men, booked in the day before yesterday."

"The Americans led you to them?" anticipated Danilov.

"It wasn't a particularly difficult surveillance."

"Do you have identities?"

There was another deciding hesitation before Mann took a sheet of paper and slid in across his desk. "They're the registration names. They're the five in the photographs who tricked the FBI in Moscow. I'd like crime file checks."

"Of course," said Danilov, suppressing the satisfaction. He'd have even less to fabricate in his arrest-supporting dossier. "What about the first man the Americans kept from us, Stefan Cherny?"

"Flew back to Moscow yesterday. Two FBI agents were on the same plane."

"He knew he was under surveillance," insisted Danilov, for the second time.

"And if he knew, then the others—and presumably Orlov—know. So there won't be any international crime conference. It would be insane to contemplate holding it."

"So what is the group at the Adler doing?"

Mann shook his head in uncertainty. "Ridiculing those watching them?"

"What's the point?"

Mann gave another head shake. "I don't know."

"Are we working together again?"

"I certainly need some help, some understanding of the Russian mind, to work out what's happening," conceded Mann.

"They're difficult minds to read," said Dimitri Danilov. Perhaps mine most of all, he thought.

The meeting place was outside Berlin, in a restaurant near Falkensee overlooking the Spree whose menu boasted their fish were caught daily. Feliks Zhikin arrived early, expecting to have to wait, but the travel-stained Mercedes was already in the parking lot. Orlov was at a window table, with the Switzerland-collecting driver from the Berlin brigade, their wine bottle already half empty.

Zhikin said, "I didn't think you would be here yet."

"The German autobahns are fantastic," enthused Orlov. "It's all going to work perfectly."

Zhikin recognized Orlov's mood, a close to sexual excitement at the nearness of physical violence. "There's a lot for us to talk about."

"I know, I know. But order lunch first. The trout is the speciality."

24

Zhikin ordered the recommended trout—and a second bottle of wine—for the first in a very long time unresentful of Orlov's automatically demanded acquiescence to something as inconsequential as what food he should eat, a necessary concession for the later persuasion Zhikin hoped to achieve. During the feigned menu consultation, Orlov's driver was dismissively relegated, with Zhikin's chauffeur, to an adjoining although strategically protective table nearer the door.

"So!" further demanded Orlov. "How did it all go? In detail."

Zhikin decided detail was essential and went into it, to Orlov's nodded approval. The man laughed outright at Zhikin's account of that morning's confrontation at Wannsee and the unrehearsed allusion that the leak of the intended conference could have come from Italy. "Excellent!" enthused the gang leader. "What do you think of the Brigoli kid?"

"That's what Campinali called him, a kid. I agreed."

"It was a mistake for Brigoli to have used his son," insisted Orlov.

For once the paranoiac was right, reflected Zhikin. Encouragingly, he said: "Disrespectful."

"That's exactly what it was, disrespect!" acknowledged Orlov, his mouth automatically tightening in anger at what he instantly saw as a calculated slur. Was Zhikin showing him sufficient respect? Orlov asked himself, the reflection continuing. Incredible though it seemed in such a short time, Zhikin's attitude toward him appeared changed, a definite lessening of deference.

"Campinali said there would be inquiries in Italy. It'll become known, embarrassingly to Brigoli."

Orlov hesitated, wine glass half raised. Suspiciously he said, "You've thought it all through, haven't you?"

Zhikin shrugged, apparently casual despite a stomach blip of concern. "It's obvious, scarcely needs any working out."

After a further pause, covered by his finally sipping his wine, Orlov said: "No problem in their leaving?"

Zhikin shook his head. "Brigoli will be in Cologne in time for a late lunch."

"What about Irena and Ivan?"

"Checked out of the hotel precisely on time this morning. By now they'll be on board the plane." He look at his watch. "Takeoff's in fifteen minutes. It's on time."

"Someone making sure, at the airport?"

"Of course."

"Of course," echoed Orlov, an edge to the mockery.

"Isn't that what you want—what you expect?" Zhikin didn't like the underlying distrust in Orlov's attitude.

Their fish arrived, sparing Orlov a reply. Instead he said, "And what of our irritating Americans?"

"Everywhere our newly arrived bait goes, they go. So everything they do, we know. And *they* think they are monitoring *us*!"

Orlov nodded, smiling. "They're hooked."

"Definitely," said Zhikin, avoiding any facial reaction to what he was sure was the unintended analogy to the meal in front of them.

"But we've only moved so far singly or in pairs?"

Zhikin suppressed the sigh. "Only singly or in pairs."

"And the Germans?"

For the first time Zhikin was glad of a useful question from the other man. "That's one of the uncertainties. We've isolated nothing that looks like a joint operation. It's always been the Americans by themselves."

"Working *by* themselves?"

"That's what it looks like."

"We need more wine," announced Orlov. As Zhikin gestured for it, Orlov pointedly picked up: "*One* of the uncertainties?"

"Sam Campinali was very concerned," embarked Zhikin, carefully.

"Said that until a source was located for the leak, Tinelli might decide against continuing."

"You've covered it—covered it well—by hinting at the Italians. I need to think about it, but I might suggest to Tinelli that we go ahead without Brigoli. I don't like him. Don't trust him."

Zhikin breathed in, preparing himself. "He also said none of us should do anything to attract attention to ourselves."

This time Orlov heavily put down his half-raised glass, coming forward across the table. "Explain that."

"I'm telling you what he said. What's planned does the opposite. And it involves American law enforcement officers."

Color suffused Orlov's face and an abruptly dilated vein in his temple began pulsing. "You want to call it off?" Orlov's question was initially more incredulity than anger at anyone opposing him.

"I am repeating exactly what Campinali told me," insisted Zhikin, doggedly. "You asked for everything in detail. That's what I'm giving you, everything in detail."

The color began to subside. The vein stopped pumping. Orlov said, "So the answer's yes, you do think we should cancel everything?"

The apprehension was a solid lump, deep in Zhikin's stomach. "I am suggesting the answer is to avoid attracting any more attention to Berlin. If we walk away, we leave the FBI looking as stupid as we made them look in Moscow."

"That's not enough, not enough publicly."

There was no going back, Zhikin decided, although at that moment he wished that there were. "It's surely enough to avoid the collapse of months of negotiation?"

Orlov picked up his wine. "It was Tinelli who asked for the example to be made in Brighton Beach."

"This is different."

Why, wondered Orlov, did people get overconfident, imagine they could question him the moment he allowed them a little responsibility? But Feliks Romanovich was right, the difference being that for the moment he was too necessary to be disposed of, as everyone was disposable. "I haven't told you about Switzerland!"

Zhikin stared across the table, baffled at the tangent. "No, you haven't . . ." he stumbled.

"I like it. I really think I might buy something. I've looked at three chalets in St. Moritz and two in Gstaad. I'm looking at another tomorrow afternoon."

Zhikin had the first flicker of understanding. "I see," he said, disappointed that he did.

"Everything in place?"

"Yes."

"How many?"

"Two cars. They're very careless at night. Totally unguarded."

"Ours?"

Zhikin hesitated. "Is it necessary?"

"Of course it is." Orlov smiled at the sudden idea. "Something else to blame on the Italians . . ." The smile went. "You haven't answered my question."

"Yes, ours, too."

"Letting them think the sixteenth was the date served its purpose. We'll bring everything forward."

"To tonight?" guessed Zhikin.

"You've told me everything's ready?"

"Yes."

"Who've you put in charge, now Cherny's back in Moscow?"

"I've been working through Nikolai Fedorovich Raina."

"And you're absolutely sure the Americans follow us everywhere."

Zhikin didn't try to cover the sigh. "Everywhere."

"So we simply continue baiting the hook." He finished his win. "I can be back in Switzerland in good time for tomorrow's meeting in Gstaad."

"What's happening to our approach?" demanded Jed Parker.

"Nothing," conceded Cowley. "What about the Bundeskriminalamt?"

Parker hesitated. "Won't take my calls. Any reaction from the director to my explanation?"

It had been very cleverly worded, reminding Leonard Ross of his America-must-lead guidance. "If there had been, you'd have had it. What about Danilov?"

"Son of a bitch sided with Mann, trying to cut us out."

Professionally the most obvious thing to have done, despite Danilov's private agenda, thought Cowley. "So we're still stalled?"

"Working on a couple of things," said Parker.

"Like what?"

"Ideas from watching Cherny before he went back," avoided Parker, further convinced how he was going to recover. The official Russian request bolstered Washington's separate approach, in his judgment lessening the jurisdiction problem. Which would become academic now, with two countries demanding access, when Tinelli and Orlov were in the bag. Which they were going to be, in a tightly sealed American bag, the very personal property of Jed W. Parker.

"What sort of ideas?"

With just two days to go Parker realized it was time to cover his ass against later accusations of keeping back from Washington the identification of the Russians Orlov had used in the Moscow sting. "Maybe a lead to some more of Orlov's people."

"How strong a lead?" pressed Cowley.

"Still checking. I'll let you know the moment we confirm it."

"Do that," insisted Cowley.

In my time, not yours, thought Parker. "I'll be in touch."

"So there's cooperation between Dimitri and the Germans?"

"Which worries me," said Pavin.

"We're still excluded, according to Parker," said Cowley.

There was no immediate response from the other end. "Parker's problem from the way he's behaving after the Cherny business?"

What? thought Cowley desperately. Wincing at the cliché, he said, "You tell me."

Intuitively Pavin said, "You know Cherny flew back to Moscow, yesterday?"

"Yes."

"And?" pressed Pavin.

"Tell me. I'm fed up fucking around."

"All the others we know to be Orlov's people have flown into Berlin. I'm running the manifest listed names through records at the moment. There's one so far, for aggravated assault: blinded someone who wouldn't pay protection. They're all staying together in the same hotel, in the East. The Germans who told Dimitri—gave him the names—simply followed your guys."

"How do you know?"

"Dimitri, three hours ago." Pavin considered the question, then decided to ask it because so much—professionally as well as personally as far as Danilov was concerned—depended upon it. "Parker hasn't told you?"

"He talked about leads that needed confirming."

"The sting photographs confirmed it, after the German's followed your guys from the airport yesterday. It's been positive for more than twenty-four hours. What's going on, Bill?"

"Ambition's what's going on." He couldn't prove—even if he'd wanted to—that Parker had positively lied to him about the identification of Orlov's group.

"A professional international investigation is what's supposed to be going on. But isn't." Which Cowley and he had known—conspired together not to happen in their concern for Dimitri Danilov—for too long, thought Pavin. He said, "This is becoming ridiculous."

Cowley said, "You're right. Everything's gone off track."

"How do we get it back *on* track?"

"Dimitri knows how the Russians were located?"

"Yes."

Frustration burned through Cowley. "But Parker doesn't know the Germans are tracking him and his task force?"

Pavin's sigh was audible. "Not unless he's told you. John Melton hasn't told me, here. So either Parker's holding out on him, too, or he's told Melton to hold out on me. Either way, what we've got is a mess with every potential for ending up a disaster—and there's been too much of that already, don't you think?"

"I can't believe our guys don't *know* they're under surveillance! They're supposed to be trained, for Christ's sake!"

"Too focused," suggested Pavin.

"Too arrogant," said Cowley.

"Maybe they *do* know."

"We speculate any more we're going to disappear up our own ass." Cowley felt dizzied by the revolving conversation.

"The Germans are happy to let the Bureau lead," theorized Pavin.

"You get it wrong, it's the Bureau's mistake. You get it right, it's the Bureau's seizure."

"You're forgetting legal jurisdiction."

"No," denied Pavin. "Jurisdiction's imposed the moment they're seized."

"That's too much speculation," protested Cowley.

"No," refused the Russian, again. "We know the German reluctance, right?"

"Right," reluctantly accepted Cowley.

"So it makes sense for them to let your guys make all the dangerous moves, ready to step in the moment it's convenient and safe to do so."

Into Cowley's mind suddenly came the memory of his confrontation with Leonard Ross and the enigmatic references to diplomacy and interested parties and finally, literally, an echo of his own protest. *For me not to know something could easily result in my making a wrong decision, one that might easily jeopardize—wreck even—what we're trying to achieve.* Was it possible that it wasn't the potential mess he and Yuri Pavin believed it to be but rather some political decision for it to unfold this way? There was certainly a convoluted logic. "Did you get this indication from Dimitri?"

"I'd have told you earlier if I had."

"There's still two days before the sixteenth."

"I scarcely need reminding of that," said Pavin."

"Time for me hopefully to get some steer from here," accepted Cowley

"That's what we need," agreed Pavin, sincerely, "a steer in the right direction from somewhere, wherever that is."

"Raina understands?" demanded Orlov.

"Perfectly," said Zhikin. He felt trapped, an insect pinned to a display board. Or rather someone nailed to a cross, unable to prevent what was going to happen to him. He didn't enjoy either sensation.

"It's clever to use the Potsdamer Platz," insisted Orlov, whose idea it had been. "It's symbolic."

And insane, thought Zhikin. Everything was insane, like Orlov himself. Zhikin looked through the car windows in the direction of the white cross memorials to those killed by East German mines trying to escape over the Berlin Wall and said: "There're a lot of people about."

Orlov shrugged, disinterested. "You told Raina eight o'clock?"

"Yes," said Zhikin, wearily. He'd already confirmed the timing twice before. Orlov wasn't nervous, Zhikin knew. It was excitement.

"He understands it's a trap, as it was in Moscow?" The deference definitely wasn't there anymore.

"Yes."

"And that he's only got to say what he's been told?"

"Yes."

"It's time!" announced Orlov. There was an immediate reply to the cell phone call. "Nikolai Fedorovich? It's me."

"Yes?"

"It's definitely tonight. You know where to come?"

"Yes."

"How long will it take you?"

"Thirty minutes, to leave here."

"No longer. I want you all here when everyone else arrives."

"We'll be there."

Dimitri Danilov was in the bar, for its strategic view of the hotel lobby, and was immediately aware of the sudden flurry of activity among those he knew to be FBI. Danilov reached the foyer as Jed Parker hurriedly emerged from the elevator, two other agents close behind.

Danilov said, "You going to tell me what's happening?"

Parker snorted. "Arrests are what's happening."

"Let me come with you."

"Go fuck yourself."

From the lobby telephone Danilov could see the Americans' cars burst too fast out of the parking area, nose to tail. The telephone clicked and reclicked in Danilov's ear as he was patched from extension to extension in the Bundeskriminalamt search for Horst Mann.

"Yes!" came a demanding voice at last. There was a babble of noise in the background.

"They're moving!" declared Danilov. There was the numbness, the unreality, he'd felt at confirming that Igor Gavrilovich Orlov was Larissa's murderer.

"We picked up the call on our scanner," said Mann. "It looks like it could be the beginning. Something. I'll send a car with a radio link, to get you to wherever—whatever—we're going. So you'll be involved."

Despite the tingling numbness—what he knew to be the closeness, at last!—Danilov remained sufficiently objective to recognize why the German was including him so closely. "I'll be waiting at the door."

Which was where Igor Orlov was—at the door of their car—impatient for the first sight of the follow-the-leader cavalcade from the east into the west of the city. To Zhikin, motionless inside the Mercedes, he said, "I should be seeing them by now!"

"Igor Gavrilovich!" protested Zhikin. "If you don't come back inside the car, you'll miss the opportunity. They couldn't have made it this quickly."

"Thirty minutes, he said!"

"And then they've got to get here, be led here. Ten more minutes at least, depending on traffic."

As he got back into the car Orlov said, suspicious again, "How did you get on with Campinali?"

"Professionally," said Zhikin at once, pleased with his reply. "I thought I'd made that clear?"

Definitely a changed attitude, Orlov decided: a *wrongly* changed attitude. "How'd you leave things?"

"That we'd be in touch," said Zhikin. Then, at once, "Here they come!"

Which they were, the Mercedes limousine with all five known Russians in the lead with three American-tagged rental cars following like ducks in a line. Orlov giggled and said, "Perfect! It couldn't be more perfect!"

The electronically activated bombs in the Mercedes and two of the following three cars were detonated simultaneously by the same control box button beneath Orlov's impatient finger, but the impression from inside their safely distanced vehicle was that the Mercedes erupted seconds before the others, jackknifing into the air as it broke in half and disintegrated further before being swallowed in the yellow and red flames that engulfed its pursuers. The second of those following cars was not bombed, but so violent were the explosions that the bursting fuel created an expanding, all-engulfing fireball—and so close were all three traveling that the intervening vehicle was totally destroyed as well. Still the fireball was not spent. It rolled along the street expanding as it went, and the car in which Orlov and Zhikin sat was rocked by the force and felt the heat.

"Fantastic," giggled Orlov, sexually flushed. "It's never been so good."

Zhikin already had the engine running. "We've got to get away from here. Get you to the car to take you back."

"Yes," agreed Orlov. "I don't want to be late for Gstaad. The chalet there could be the best so far." As they drove away, to the distant sound of the approaching emergency vehicles, Orlov strained through the rear window, not wanting to lose sight of the devastation until the last possible minute. "Fantastic," he said again.

Orlov was still flushed when they reached the waiting Mercedes to take him back to Switzerland. As he got out, to transfer from one car to the other, Orlov tossed the detonator onto his seat and said, "Get rid of that."

Zhikin sat, watching the Mercedes disappear, and then looked down at the device, shaking his head in disbelief. When he reached the Grand Hotel on the Friedrichkstrasse he very carefully enveloped it in a handkerchief before, still gently, putting it into his pocket.

25

The final death toll was twenty-eight, with seventeen more horrifically and permanently scarred by burns. There were a further ten whose injuries, over the course of several years, were minimized although not totally concealed by plastic surgery. The immediate dead included Jed Parker and eleven other FBI agents as well as all the sacrificial Russians. The three man Bundeskriminalamt Adler Hotel surveillance team also died when their car was overwhelmed by the rolling fireball, as did a totally uninvolved driver and observer in a police patrol car parked in a Potsdamer Platz side street adjacent to the explosions. The other dead and injured were innocent bystanders and pedestrians, which included four children, nine teenagers, and three American and two English tourists. Some of the burn victims were trapped in the four shops and a restaurant that were set alight and completely burned out.

Dimitri Danilov didn't understand the first alert that came over the police car radio but guessed at the seriousness from the urgency of the dispatcher's voice. His police car driver said "Scheisskopf" and swung across a swerving, horn-protesting traffic line to cut down a side street, switching on a howling siren as he did so. He waved a word-searching hand toward Danilov in the rear seat and in English managed: "Bomb . . . bad . . ." He turned the radio volume up and kept repeating "Scheisskopf" and occasionally, in English, "Bad."

They reached Potsdamer Platz before it was properly sealed off, but it was already blocked by cars, several of which had collided, forcing them to complete the last hundred meters on foot. Danilov hurried close to his uniformed driver, needing the man's authority to get past initially uncoordinated police cordons being set up. Before they finally negotiated the barrier of stranded and crashed cars Danilov could see against the night sky the flickering reflection of the still burning but unseen vehicles and then, when they rounded a slewed van, the actual flames from the blazing buildings. Danilov's driver had to intervene twice to get him through police blocks. At the last Danilov picked out the reference to Horst Mann's name and followed the gesture of the permissive policeman to see the diminutive detective superintendent, with two uniformed officers, in the lee of an unmarked police car partially shielding them from the scorching heat. All three had their backs to him, concentrating upon a side street where a police squad were clearing a path for fire trucks and ambulances by manhandling abandoned and damaged cars out of the way. There were bodies—and body parts—strewn in the road and in the gutter. Blood was already baked brown by the heat. In one of the still blazing cars there was the clearly identifiable shape of an atrophied man at the still intact steering wheel. A lot of people, bystanders as well as injured, were screaming.

Mann turned at Danilov's approach and said in a voice dulled by shock: "It's a massacre . . . a total massacre."

Danilov said, "How many?" He tried to get closer to the half-protecting car, out of the near inferno. There were popping sounds of the paint on its far side bubbling and exploding.

"Still counting," said Mann. "A lot who aren't already dead will be, over the coming days."

Danilov squinted against the glare at the twisted metal. "Any of your people among them?"

"The car that alerted us to the American surveillance leaving the Adler Hotel after the telephone call saying the meeting had been brought forward. A patrol car that was here, by coincidence."

"How many Americans left the hotel?"

"Twelve."

"Parker?"

"It looks like it. I couldn't reach Samuelson at the embassy when I tried, though they said he was there. Everything's gridlocked, but I'm surprised he's not already here." Peter Samuelson was the FBI station chief in Berlin.

"It's Orlov," Danilov declared. "This is how he kills . . . likes to kill."

Five fire engines and three ambulances finally got through to Potsdamer Platz. As hoses began playing water over the wrecked cars and the already gutted buildings, Mann said, "You think he's here?"

"Of course he is. Certainly was."

"Bastard!" said the German, his voice dull, speaking to no one. "Murderous fucking bastard!"

"The man, Cherny, identified the Americans that followed him," insisted Danilov. "It's obvious." There was no I-told-you-so satisfaction.

An unmarked van came out of the cleared side street and pulled up beside their sheltering vehicle. Men, some already in white scene-of-crime protective overalls, emerged from the rear of the van, instantly took in the scene, and lost their impetus, shuffling into its lee to spare themselves from the paint-blistering heat. Those wearing them began to shed their overalls. There was a quick, shoulder-shrugging exchange between one of the newcomers and the Bundeskriminalamt detective chief, after which Mann said, "Forensic. It'll be hours before they'll be able to get near anything. Find anything."

"Find anything in this!" echoed Danilov, disbelievingly.

Mann shrugged again. "It's their job to try."

"Unfortunate we didn't do ours," said Danilov. He realized at once it sounded like an accusation against the initial German reluctance to the investigation, but he didn't care. Igor Gavrilovich Orlov, the man who killed Larissa, was—or had been—somewhere here in the city and they didn't have him where he should have been, in a cell or, better still, at the point of a gun. His gun, cocked and ready.

Horst Mann didn't appear to pick up the inference. He said, "We're not contributing anything standing around here, either. It'll be a long time before everything's cooled down enough for us to get closer. You seen enough for the moment?"

"For the moment," said Danilov.

"Then let's get out of this damned heat. I'll leave word for the FBI."

The Potsdamer Platz was properly sealed now, blocking cars being turned by their drivers or pulled away by tow trucks, their passengers and gawking onlookers pushed farther and farther back by a shoulder-to-shoulder police phalanx and bullhorn demands to clear the road for more emergency vehicles. It was only when the perspiration began to chill upon him, his clothes soaked, that Danilov fully realized how incredibly hot it had been at the scene. His face and hands stung, as if he, too, had been burned. When he saw them approaching, Mann's driver broke away from one of the police lines to open the car doors.

Beside Danilov in the rear of the vehicle Mann said, "We're trying to seal the city—even the main roads as well as the airport and railway stations—but it's pointless, not knowing by sight, by sufficient description even, who or what we're looking for."

"We know Campinali came in through Frankfurt," Danilov reminded him. "And there's an identifiable photograph of him from Kennedy airport. What about hotel checks here in Berlin?"

Mann shifted on his seat, discomfited. "The checks were suspended after the disagreement with the Americans."

Danilov stared incredulously across the car. "There was information that a Russian organized crime leader—*the* leader, even—was hosting a meeting here in Berlin at least with a lawyer for the Mafia boss of America, if not someone from Italy as well!"

"It's old ground that there was nothing illegal in that," said the German, defensively.

Danilov jerked his head back toward the Potsdamer Platz. "You going to have any problem calling the carnage back there illegal!"

"It was a mistake, in hindsight," admitted Mann. "The decision was reached by people in higher authority, which I'm not using as an excuse. I went along with it."

For the first thirty minutes in Mann's office Dimitri Danilov sat uninvolved and uncomprehending amid the avalanche of telephone conversations, all the lights on Mann's desk console blinking with held calls as he responded to them in order. Mann was fully recovered and in control now, his voice never raised or animated, his face impassive. He was still talking, the console glowing, when Peter Samuelson arrived. Mann held up a splayed hand, indicating five minutes, to which Samuelson nodded, coming over to where Danilov was sitting.

"You seen it?" asked Samuelson softly, to avoid distracting the German. The blond hair and pale skin betrayed his Nordic immigrant ancestry.

"Yes," said Danilov, softly, too.

"Jesus, what a mess! Those guys got wives. Kids."

"Was Parker among them?"

Samuelson nodded. "I need to tell Washington, but I decided to come here first, get an update. You think it's your guy?"

"I'm certain of it," said Danilov. From the way Samuelson was holding his head, Danilov guessed the Berlin-based, German-speaking man was trying to overhear as much of the telephone conversations as he could.

"I think . . ." began Samuelson but stopped as Mann finished his last call.

Gesturing toward the telephone, Mann said: "Mostly political, wanting answers I don't have. Nothing from the scene."

Samuelson said, "I haven't spoken to Washington yet—I need to talk to you before I do—but I want to say even before I do that we can't afford any more problems between us. We're all of us going to need as much help as we can get from each other. There's got to be complete cooperation. I need to know everything I can before I get on to Washington."

The man was impressive, acknowledged Danilov.

"Everything has changed now," agreed Mann. "What about Parker?"

"Gone," confirmed Samuelson, for the second time. "There's going to be a hell of a lot of political heat." He came to an awkward stop. "Wrong word, sorry."

"A bomb—bombs—obviously," said Mann. "I know there were twelve of your people, which is our starting figure. It'll take time to get the total. It'll be hours before our forensic scientists get anywhere near the wreckage." He stopped, thinking. Then to Danilov he said, "Have I missed anything?"

Danilov said, "I don't think so." He was aware of Samuelson also looking sideways at him.

The American said, "Orlov's yours. You're the key to our finding the son of a bitch!"

The German crime chief gestured again to the momentarily silent telephone bank. "*Mostly* political. But there was also the Justice Ministry. Moscow's supposed to be issuing an international arrest warrant."

"After *this!*" exclaimed Danilov, the response too quick.

Mann's surprise was in the silence. Then he said, "It's only you telling me that Igor Orlov was responsible. I've no evidence. *We've* got no evidence. We need a lot more than the file you've already supplied. We need what you've promised additionally."

The fabrication was easy now, Danilov knew. Everyone was as desperate as he was to move agianst Igor Orlov. He said, "You'll have everything upon which the warrant will be based." He'd need to speak to Pavin.

The persistent console lighted up again. This time Mann listened, speaking little. From the way Samuelson tensed beside him, Danilov guessed the American followed the gist of the conversation. Mann did not immediately speak when he once again replaced the receiver. At last he said, "There's a registration in the name of I. G. Orlov at the Bristol Kapinski."

"Is he—" Danilov broke in, again too urgently.

"Booked out this morning," anticipated the German.

"The room will have been cleaned by now!" moaned Samuelson, thinking as quickly and as professionally as the other two investigators.

"But not yet reoccupied," said Mann. "It's already been sealed. And I'll have forensic dismantle it brick by brick, fiber by fiber, until they find something."

Luigi Brigoli said, "Accused us by name?"

Paolo shook his head. "He said their police informant told them that the leak came from Europe. Which was virtually the same as accusing us."

"What was Campinali's reaction?"

"I think he believes it's us. He kept saying the source had to be found."

"You think the Russians and Americans are trying to cut us out?"

"Maybe. I don't know. Why invite us in the first place if they didn't want us."

"I didn't like Orlov. He didn't like me. A change of mind."

"I don't know," repeated Paolo.

"All the families expect us to be part of it. We get cut out I lose face."

"What are we going to do?"

"Convince Tinelli that it wasn't us. Which it wasn't. Where's the benefit to us?"

"Zhikin did say it could have been one of our families," remembered Paolo.

Brigoli didn't immediately reply. After a reflective pause he said, "If it was, it's an internal move against me."

"I hadn't thought of it like that," accepted Paolo.

"There was some opposition in the commission to our getting involved with the Russians," remembered Brigoli. "Mine was the casting vote in favor."

"Opposition strong enough to do a thing like this?" questioned Paolo, doubtfully.

"It could be a way to replace me," insisted Brigoli.

"So we start with those who objected to the proposal?" anticipated Paolo.

"But carefully," agreed the father. "If they realize we're making inquiries, it'll be seen as weakness . . . make everything worse."

"What about Tinelli?"

"I'll speak personally with Tinelli."

"You're going to America?"

"I can't risk leaving Italy. It'll have to be by phone."

"I could go," offered Paolo.

Brigoli shook his head. "It has to be Boss of Bosses." Which he had to remain. There was only one way the succession passed to a new *capo di tutti i capi*. By the death of the predecessor.

26

Horst Mann said what Danilov was thinking. "It looks like Berlin just after the war."

Danilov said, "And the Russians did it this time, too."

The Potsdamer Platz was totally sealed off and cleared of people now, eerily quiet and empty except for the white overalled forensic technicians working under light-as-day arc lights, two standby fire trucks and their crews, and a civil maintenance team securing the shattered buildings. There was no longer any heat from the melted wreckage, but there was an overwhelming but varied smell of burning. All the bodies and body parts had been taken away, although one broken-off hand of the atrophied man still clutched the steering wheel of the skeletally burned-out car. A lot of the road and pavement surface was burned away and most of the memorials to the Germans killed escaping over the Wall from the former East Berlin were badly scorched, some even obliterated. Few names or identity symbols were any longer legible. Not needing to squint against an inferno glare, Danilov realized no window for as far as he could see along both sides of the road remained intact. From a lot of the shattered spaces curtains stirred in the slight breeze, like damp flags. Danilov remained close to the German detective chief but was unable to infer anything from the man's hand-gesturing conversation with the forensic supervisor.

"Doesn't seem we're going to get a lot," Mann finally said, turning back to Danilov. "There'll still be surviving DNA from the bodies, despite the burning. Do you have a criminal DNA bank in Moscow?"

Danilov shook his head. "No."

"It might have given us the identities of your Russians. Provided a link to Orlov," said the German. "It'll still be useful identifying people caught up in the explosion." He nodded in the direction of the scientists. "They think the bombs had a phosphorous component. That's what created a fireball and caused the fuel tanks to explode, bombs literally making other bombs. The main component was probably Semtex. So far they haven't found any trace of original detonators. It's all been completely incinerated."

"It's the same trick he used to kill Mittel and Lapinsh, incinerating any evidence," said Danilov. And Larissa, he thought. He'd have to remember to stress that as a connecting modus operandi with this massacre in the case file he still had to compile. At that moment he decided the intended arrest file needed more than one case history. He could remember several to add.

"There could be more from the hotel," suggested Mann.

Or less, thought Danilov, held by the numbing impotence at having been so close to Orlov, which he believed he had. He said, "Let's hope."

They arrived at the Kempinski at the same time as Peter Samuelson, who'd detoured to the American embassy to alert Washington. Samuelson said, "I've lit the fuse."

"You talk to Cowley?" asked Danilov, too preoccupied properly to consider his question.

The American looked surprised. "The watch room, at this time of night." He looked to Mann, lifting a briefcase. "I picked up the case notes, everything we've got. You never know."

The German hefted his own case. "It'll speed things up. I'm having all the hotel's day staff brought back so we can interview them tonight."

At least half the third floor of the hotel was sealed, the barriers at each end controlled by uniformed police, who also monitored the elevators and emergency exit stairs. Too late, decided the frustrated Danilov, again gripped by silent, impotent anger. Where had all these men and barriers been yesterday, the day before yesterday? They could have seized the arrogant motherfucker then, saved God knows how many lives, had Orlov chained and caged if not yet dead. Instinctively Danilov looked directly, fixedly, at Horst Mann.

Conscious of the abrupt attention, the German returned the other man's stare. "What?"

Danilov recovered himself. "Nothing." The word echoed in his head, tauntingly. That was exactly what the Germans had done—or not done—so far, and by their inaction allowed a disaster to happen. Igor Gavrilovich Orlov had been here, walking the same streets, breathing the same air: been here but wouldn't be here any longer. Now he'd be somewhere out of reach, laughing at them, jeering at them, proving himself yet again better than they were, able to do whatever he liked, whenever he liked.

At the last corridor checkpoint, before the final barrier, they were given anticontamination suits that extended to foot and hand cover. It sealed unbroken, at the neck. There was a separate, encompassing, plastic head covering. Everything was too large for Danilov. The suit sagged upon him, concertinaed in folds around his ankles. He knew he looked ridiculous but didn't care. It was easier to scuff along the remaining carpeted corridor than to attempt to walk properly. The suits issued to Horst Mann and Peter Samuelson fitted far better. Passingly, Danilov thought there wouldn't have been a suit large enough for Yuri Pavin. There were still several hours before Moscow awoke for him to contact his deputy. He'd call Pavin at home, hopefully before the man saw the inevitable breakfast television pictures of the Berlin carnage. He needed to speak personally to Cowley in Washington, too. He didn't have a specific reason or point to discuss. He just wanted to talk.

Danilov was surprised, although upon reflection he shouldn't have been, at the pristine neatness of the room—311—booked until earlier that day, or rather now the previous day, against the name of I. G. Orlov. The overalled forensic team, whose noncontamination even included face masks, were dissecting it with surgical precision. Three were sweeping the room with light-sensitive spectro-microscope to register hair, skin, or human fluid debris. Two more were using a similar although smaller machine that Danilov had never seen before.

From their concentration upon the hard surfaces of tables, ledges, and furniture he guessed it to be some sort of sophisticated fingerprint apparatus. Another group, supported by a spectromicroscope examining operator, were using long-handled tools meticulously to strip and fold the bed covering item by item until they finally reached the mattress cover and then the mattress itself. Two men were maneuvering a transparent-cased vacuum device to sweep the bedroom carpet, furniture, and the inside floors of the closets. Through an open door Danilov saw two more repeating the process in the bathroom. A third had already dismantled the basin piping and was scraping for debris inside with a spatula.

"They're getting stuff," translated Samuelson softly, overhearing the exchange in German between Mann and a forensic leader. "Several sets of fingerprints. Some cloth fibers."

There was a shouted report from the bathroom, and Samuelson said, "The guy at the basin says there's enough shaving bristle detritus for a DNA sample."

"It's getting better," said Mann, leading the way back out into the corridor. "Let's hope there's something positive after elimination."

There were seven people, four men and three young women, waiting in what Danilov presumed to be a small conference room on the ground floor of the hotel, on the side of the foyer farthest from the expansive bar. It was while he was crossing the foyer that Danilov saw the possibility, but he decided to wait until Horst Mann opened the interviews, maybe even let it run a while.

The atmosphere inside the room was a mixture of curiosity and irritation at their being literally brought from their beds at what was now fifteen minutes before four in the morning. Predominantly, though, it was irritation. Everyone was haphazardly, hurriedly dressed, mostly in jeans and sweaters. None of the women wore makeup. All agreed, when Mann asked, that they had no difficulty with English. All had heard about the Potsdamer Platz disaster. All but one had seen television pictures. The irritation seeped away.

"You had a man here until yesterday, a Russian named Orlov. We want to know everything you can remember about him, starting with a description."

"He did it?" demanded one of the girls, a receptionist. "He was such a nice man. Polite."

"And he tipped," said a male porter. "Most of them don't."

"We need to know about him," intruded Danilov. "Talk to him."

"You're Russian?" identified the daytime doorman.

"So's Igor Orlov," agreed Danilov. "That's why I'm here. There are other things, in Moscow. We need your help resolving them."

The descriptions came piecemeal, one recollection prompting another from someone else, a verbally disjointed jigsaw that meant nothing to the now eagerly cooperating hotel staff. But to Danilov's easy satisfaction, as well as to that of Mann and Samuelson, it increasingly matched the verbal image they already had of Igor Gavrilovich Orlov.

Choosing his moment, Danilov jerked his head back in the direction of the foyer. "I saw a closed-circuit television camera. How often's the loop changed?"

"Every day," said one of the day managers.

"When?" demanded Mann, urgently.

"Six," said the man.

"Get it," ordered Mann, at the same time nodding approvingly to Danilov.

As the manager left the room, Samuelson said, "Let's look at other photographs while we wait. He took their existing file pictures from his briefcase, prompting Mann to do the same. They spread them out in a mini gallery on the conference table.

Mann said, "Was Orlov visited by anyone you recognize from these pictures. Do you recognize *anyone* from these pictures?"

The hotel staff stood in line against the table edge and took their time as they were told, the girls whispering to each other. The eldest, to whom the other two girls deferred, passed a hand over one of the prints and stopped uncertainly until the other, so far unspeaking, chambermaid, said, "That's Mr. Harrison. I don't know if he met Mr. Orlov. I certainly didn't see them together. But that's definitely Mr. Harrison. He left early yesterday, too."

Samuelson reached across the table, reversing the Kennedy Airport photograph of Sam Campinali and Veniamin Yasev, smiling alternatively sideways first to Mann, then to Danilov. "Bingo!" said the American.

He said it again, fifteen minutes later, when they were all crowded into the CCTV viewing room and the doorman said: "There! There he is. That's Mr. Orlov."

At Mann's instructions the technician rewound the loop and freeze-framed to the doorman's instructions to stop at a tall, stoop-shouldered man coming through the main door.

"At last!" said the German. "We can enhance that sufficiently to get a workable photograph of Igor Gavrilovich Orlov!"

For a moment Danilov was unable to move at the first positive visual impression of the man he had hunted for so long, disappointed that there wasn't a physical feeling of hatred. The paralysis ended when, at Mann's urging, the loop was rerun four more times in a failed attempt to isolate Sam Campinali.

"Brigoli isn't there," complained Samuelson. "And no one picked him out from the Italian criminal records photograph."

"Two out of three is a good enough start," said Mann.

It wasn't, thought Danilov. It was a start too late.

William Cowley drove through a still dark, deserted D.C. to the night-staffed J. Edgar Hoover Building immediately after the Watch Room awakening and at first remained in the FBI's twenty-four-hour communication center to look at the CNN television coverage of the Berlin atrocity. It was in the Watch Room that the separately alerted director reached him, at once demanding, "What more is there?"

"Nothing beyond what I know you've already been told," said Cowley. "Samuelson's log is that he's out, at the scene."

"There's no doubt about Parker?"

"Samuelson was coordinating from the embassy, knew where everyone was, what everyone was doing. Jed's definitely among the dead. Samuelson's already given us a full list of names."

"Holy shit!"

"And more," agreed Cowley, emptily

"I'm coming in," declared Leonard Ross. "I need to be fully up to speed before the calls start."

"I'll have everything ready," promised Cowley.

"This is a mess, Bill. One hell of a great big mess."

Back on first name terms, accepted Cowley. It didn't seem important any more.

27

By the time the director reached FBI headquarters from his Maryland home Peter Samuelson had completely briefed Cowley on the overnight investigation in Berlin, fully preparing him for the encounter on the seventh floor. Even before Cowley sat, Ross announced: "I spoke from home to the speaker and the chief of staff. I'm due at the White House in an hour."

Cowley said, "The death toll is eleven FBI and three CIA, in addition to Parker. I've got all the names. I've told Langley about their guys. Individual identification is only going to be possible from DNA. Samuelson has arranged German forensic to go through the hotel rooms they occupied to get comparisons if they can. Hair's the most obvious. I'm going to have people here check with their physicians in the hope there might be surviving blood samples."

"I caught the pictures on CNN," said Ross. "There's going to be a media circus when it emerges that twelve American agents—one of them Parker, with his family connections—are victims. We've got to work out a statement."

Not my problem, thought Cowley. "There's a provable connection between Tinelli and Orlov. We've got positive witness's identification of Orlov on a hotel CCTV loop. And we've got four hotel staff identifying Campinali from the Kennedy Airport photograph. He was at the hotel under a pseudonym, Harrison."

"Brigoli?"

Cowley shook his head. "The Germans have seized every CCTV loop from every camera in the hotel. Samuelson says they intend to identify every single person against every single-loop image from the register and hotel staff recognition."

"So what's the statement?" insisted the director.

"Ongoing international criminal investigation?" suggested Cowley, irritated by what he considered a side issue, although conceding that there would be a media sensation.

"Media won't be satisfied with that," refused Ross. "I'm not satisfied with that."

"I'm trying to run an investigation that has quite literally blown up in our faces," protested Cowley. "Media statements are for public affairs. They should be involved." He had political weight on his back now, he acknowledged.

"*After* the White House," decided Ross. "They—and George Warren—will want to be part of any discussion about public statements."

Then why the hell ask me, thought Cowley. "Samuelson says German forensic has picked up a lot of stuff from the room Orlov occupied. Fingerprints as well as enough physical evidence for DNA traces. They also think the loop pictures of Orlov can be enhanced into a very positive image. At last we're going to know definitely what he looks like!"

"At last!" echoed Ross, although bitterly. "What do we do about Campinali?"

The former judge was silent for several moments. "Nothing, not yet. Campinali being in the same hotel as Orlov, even using a pseudonym, is contributory, not prima facie evidence. I don't want Campinali—or Tinelli—to know we've got a connection until we've got more, a lot more."

"Isn't it sufficient to get a judge's order for a wire tap?"

Ross again considered the question. "Not on Tinelli. We could make application for Campinali. Talk to counsel about it. And bring Jimmy Pearce up to speed in Chicago."

"I think we should lay on an FBI plane to bring the bodies back from Germany."

"That will makes it a media event," Ross pointed out.

"That makes it the proper mark of respect the Bureau should show to agents dying in the line of duty. We've got a commemorative wall downstairs. And there's nothing we can do to prevent it *being* a media event."

Ross frowned at the implied rebuke. "We'll talk about it after the White House. How the hell did it happen! I mean what were they *doing*, to be there!"

"Following some Moscow-identified Russians. They thought they were going to where the formation conference was being held and get all three *capo di tutti i capi* at the same time."

"Parker tell you he was in pursuit?"

"No time, according to Samuelson," said Cowley.

"What about your Russian?"

Cowley frowned at the reference to Danilov. "I haven't spoken directly with him. He's been with Samuelson during the night."

"What's happening about the Russian arrest warrant?"

Cowley shifted uncomfortably. "That's something I need to talk to him about."

"Why the hell wasn't Orlov, who was registered under his own name, picked up before!"

He wasn't going to provide any escape routes for the older man, Cowley decided. "You know why. Parker screwed the cooperation. The Germans were more interested in looking at us than looking for Mafia leaders."

"What about this time!" demanded Ross. "Did Parker tell the Germans before taking off?"

"No," stated Cowley.

"Samuelson was left as coordinator. He tell Samuelson to warn the Germans?"

"No," repeated Cowley, glad he'd already posed these questions to Samuelson in Berlin. "The Germans were keeping surveillance on our guys."

"Stupid son of a bitch saw it as personal recovery time," said Ross.

"It wouldn't have prevented it happening," reminded Cowley. "The cars were wired before they took off."

"They should have been checked. It's elementary."

"Yes," agreed Cowley. He wasn't sure he would have established an inspection routine.

"Jed was sloppy. Arrogant and sloppy," decided Ross.

They weren't the words Leonard Ross would use to describe the House Speaker's nephew at the forthcoming White House meeting,

Cowley decided. Remembering Danilov's assessment, he said: "He wasn't a good field operator. He should have stayed a headquarters man." And then, too late, he remembered it was the director who had personally appointed Jed Parker the field leader. Hurriedly he said, "I didn't . . ." but the older man talked over him.

"You're right. It was a mistake. Like a lot of others—too many others—it shouldn't have been allowed to happen. There's a lot of catch ing up to do. Do we need to replace agents in Berlin?"

"They won't risk a meeting there now," Cowley decided at once. "Samuelson says the Bundeskriminalamt is going through the city like an invasion force."

"I want you there," abruptly declared Ross. "I want you heading everything up, wherever that means you have to go. Call in whatever support you want. Just sort this goddamned mess out, Bill, before it pulls us all down."

"Yes, sir," accepted Cowley.

"And Bill?"

"Yes, sir?"

"I want it to be our international arrest warrant that gets Orlov. And I want him in an American court."

The director was rehearsing for the White House meeting, Cowley knew.

"Anything we haven't anticipated?"

"Not that I can think of," said Cowley.

But there was.

"You still have doubts?" demanded Danilov. It had taken him what remained of the night and well into the morning to compile a twenty-page dossier providing the basis for any Russian arrest warrant, but he had no thought of sleep.

"You know that wasn't what I was arguing against," said Pavin, who had assembled in the Moscow office in which he was sitting the four additional case histories of car bomb murders that Danilov chose to itemize. "What have you done with the stuff from here?"

"Given it to our legal attaché at the embassy, for formal submission to Moscow. I've included everything we know so far about Potsdamer Platz, too. And I've given our file to the Germans for guidance."

"It's been overtaken by what happened last night, surely?" The Potsdamer Platz massacre took precedence over whatever fabrication Danilov had created, so it was unlikely ever to be challenged or exposed in a court. And even more unlikely that Danilov would ever get close enough to the Mafia leader to do what Pavin was sure he had intended.

"They still wanted it."

"Why would Orlov have registered under his own name while Campinali used an alias?"

"Orlov is absurdly and totally arrogant, believes he's untouchable. Campinali isn't."

"And why Campinali, the consigliere, not Tinelli, if it was to be a Boss of Bosses summit?" persisted Pavin.

"We still don't know he wasn't here, using a pseudonym," said Danilov. "We're going to back to the hotel staff with an FBI photograph of Tinelli. And forensic are using it for comparison against all the CCTV loops. As soon as they can lift the best possible image of Orlov from the loop I'll have it wired to you, to be issued to the airport watch on incoming German flights."

"He's had almost fifteen hours to get back. And there've already been three incoming flights. No one fitting the description was on any of them, and his name wasn't on any passenger list." Pavin paused. "Which presumably it would have been if he's arrogant enough to register himself in the hotel?"

"You've got a problem with that, haven't you?"

"It doesn't feel right."

"It happened," insisted Danilov, physically shrugging in his hotel room. "I want Stefan Sergeevich Cherny brought in. He had to be the one who somehow identified the FBI people, so he's complicit. He's the one who can tell us what the plot was, from the beginning."

"You think he's likely to do that!"

"I think it's essential—and obvious—for the investigation."

Pavin smiled to himself, alone in his office. It was good to have Danilov thinking—behaving—like the proper detective he was and not like an avenging vigilante. "Of course it is."

"You had any contact from Bill yet?"

"Not yet. He's got other concerns."

"Orlov *is* arrogant," insisted Danilov. "This time he's made a hell of a mistake. America and Germany are going to hunt him down like the mad dog he is."

"They're still going to need legally acceptable proof," reminded Pavin.

"Maybe," said Danilov.

"What's that mean?" frowned Pavin.

"I'll be there when he's caught," Danilov promised himself, and Pavin's earlier relief faltered.

"Are you sure this conversation is safe?" queried Joe Tinelli. There had been no named identification.

"Most definitely from my end," assured Luigi Brigoli.

"I am sure from mine," said the American *capo di tutti i capi.*

"Have you seen television?"

"Yes."

"It's being said here that there were German police among the victims. Do you think he planned it?"

"I don't know."

"There is an unpredictability about the man that worries me."

"I had not reached that decision."

"It will not have been a wise thing to have done, if it was him."

"No."

"Do you know how they knew about Berlin?"

"Not yet."

"An inference was made."

"Was there?"

"I give you my word it is totally unfounded: nothing came from here."

"If that is your word, then I accept it."

"We must find out how it happened," insisted Brigoli.

"I intend to."

"Let's work together on this."

"I'd welcome any help you can give."

"As I would, from you. I will keep in touch."

"So will I." Tinelli replaced the telephone and said: "He's insisting the Berlin leak didn't come from Italy."

"He would, wouldn't he?" said Campinali. "What's he think of the bombing?"

"That it's a mistake if Orlov organized it."

"It would be," agreed Campinali. "What are we going to do?"

"Nothing," said the older man, at once. "We wait. There's too many things about which I am uncertain. There's a lot I need to know more about. Starting with the leak. Make the inquiries in Italy. Find out if Luigi Brigoli is a man of honor whose word can be trusted."

"I should have bought something there a long time ago," said Igor Orlov.

"It'll be convenient for meeting the Swiss lawyers," agreed Feliks Zhikin. He'd caught an earlier return flight to Moscow, doglegging through Prague, and had been waiting in the Ulitza Varvarka mansion when Orlov arrived, two hours earlier. Orlov had already replayed twice the recorded television footage of the Berlin bomb scene.

"Gstaad's very fashionable. A great social scene."

In which Orlov would be as acceptable as a leper in a maternity hospital, thought Zhikin. He said: "Irena called."

"Stupid bitch! I told her not to use an open line!"

"She didn't. It was cell phone, hers to mine. And not here. I was at my place."

Orlov settled back in his chair from which he'd actually started forward in instant fury. "What did she want?"

"To know when you'd be back."

"What did you tell her?"

"That I didn't know. But that I'd call her when I knew. But I warned her not to call here, even on a cell phone."

"I need somewhere secure to speak to Tinelli, so I'll go back up to the dacha," said Orlov. "I'll see her there."

"I'll tell her."

"We don't need Stefan Sergeevich Cherny any more," decided Orlov. "Fix it, OK?"

"OK," accepted Zhikin.

"Anything from Italy or America?"

"It's too soon," said Zhikin. Like too much else had been too soon, too badly thought out. Madness.

As if aware of the other man's thoughts, Orlov said, "I'm going to insist our supposed Berlin police source is adamant the information came from Europe."

Zhikin hesitated, knowing from the man's reaction to Irena's approach that irrational anger bubbled constantly just beneath the surface. "What's our strategy there?"

"Divide and rule," smiled Orlov, at once. "I want Tinelli's trust in me, his distrust in Brigoli. To play one off against the other until Brigoli becomes dispensable, like his cocky little bastard of a son."

Zhikin thought that if Orlov revolved in any more tightly drawn circles he'd disappear up his own ass. Continuing the reflection, Zhikin decided it would be a disappearance he would like to see. How soon could he risk a direct approach to Campinali, to begin his move against Orlov? Not yet, he warned himself, remembering his earlier doubt about things happening too soon, without proper thought. But there could be a lot of personal advantage in whatever scheme Orlov intended to embark upon. "It'll need careful planning."

"Of course it will," said Orlov. "And you can help me." There was another smile. "Now I want to watch that Berlin video again."

"He's back," announced Yuri Pavin, flatly, all his fears crowded back upon him. "And it wouldn't have helped if we'd had the enhanced loop images."

"Why not!" demanded Danilov.

"Igor Gavrilovich Orlov didn't return from Berlin. His flight was from Geneva. And his name's on an outgoing Swiss flight, five days ago."

"The bastard thinks he can play with us again!"

"Our alert was for an I. G. Orlov on an incoming flight from Berlin. I decided to spread it. An I. G. Orlov came in on the Swiss flight three hours ago. I checked back to find his outgoing flight."

"We missed him?"

"We were concentrating upon Berlin flights."

There was a pause before Danilov said, "He's back in our jurisdiction!"

"If it's the Orlov we're looking for," qualified Pavin.

"It's him," determined Danilov, with his usual insistence. "I can *feel* it's him."

No longer the properly investigating, objective policeman, thought Pavin. He said, "I've had a message from Washington. Bill Cowley's coming to Berlin."

"He's already on his way, in an USAF plane to take the American bodies back," said Danilov. "He called me direct."

Thank God the American would have a curb on Danilov, thought Pavin, who never carelessly invoked the Lord's name.

28

What they initially judged to be quick progress brought more confusion than breakthrough, irritatingly repeated throughout that day in separate parts of the investigation.

It was Dimitri Danilov who argued, prior to Horst Mann's summons to the Justice Ministry, that despite the Kempinski registration and the presence there of Sam Campinali, albeit under an assumed name, it was unlikely that the organized crime leaders of America, Italy, and Russia would meet anywhere as public as a hotel unless it was Mafia owned, which, Mann insisted, none were in Berlin. And which spread the inquiry to private rental properties. By midday the concerted search located Otto Müller and his three Wannsee mansions. They postponed their intended reinterviews at the Kempinski, going instead to Müller's Kandertaler Weg office, where there would be records.

On the way the German police chief outlined the press statement agreed at his Justice Ministry meeting, his satisfaction obvious that he had successfully argued against any personal publicity as head of the German investigation. Danilov said at once that he would refuse any personal identification as well. Peter Samuelson wished he'd had time to consult with Washington but until he had the opportunity decided to follow the lead of the other two and remain anonymous, although he'd always fantazised about becoming famous from a high-profile investigation like this.

The plump, self-satisfied Berlin real estate broker tried to talk about client confidentiality until Mann cut him off, voicing their combined irritation. "Have you seen what happened yesterday evening on the Potsdamer Platz?"

Müller's pomposity leaked like air from a deflating balloon. "They were . . . knew . . . were part of it?" His voice was so strained, little more than a whisper, that he repeated the question a second time, although no more coherently.

"Tell us all about it," said Danilov, ignoring the groping question. This man would have been in Orlov's presence, Danilov thought, maybe even physically touched him, shaking his hand, been close enough to kill him.

"And we mean *all*," insisted Samuelson. "We want every word: everything that was said, all your impressions, every single impression, each and every arrangement that was made."

Müller talked haltingly, stumbling, and had constantly to be prompted to bring any coherence into the account, and even then there were gaps.

"Did any of the three appear to be in charge?" opened Danilov, determinedly.

Müller shrugged. "Not really. Maybe the Russian."

"How do you know he was Russian?"

There was frowned hesitation. "The name, Antipov. That's how he introduced himself when he came here, to the office. By himself at first. Antipov's a Russian name, isn't it? And the accent was right."

"What about the other two, when you met them?" demanded Samuelson. "What names did they give?"

"They didn't," said Müller.

"What about between themselves?" persisted the American. "Did any of them call each other by name?"

Müller appeared to consider the question. "I don't think so. Not that I can remember."

"We're going to show you some photographs," said Mann, opening his briefcase. "Take your time."

Müller stared down at the prints set out before him and at once jabbed a nail-bitten finger at the Kennedy Airport picture of Sam Campinali. "That's him, the American. He was one of them."

"What about this man," urged Danilov, pushing forward the enhanced image of the man the hotel staff identified as Orlov. It was of a sharp-featured, thin-faced man, receding hair giving him a high forehead.

"No," said Müller, at once. "He wasn't one of them."

"You've got to be sure about this," warned Danilov.

"I am. Antipov was much fuller faced and he had a mustache. His hair was waved. This is nothing like him."

"What about this man?" asked Samuelson, offering the FBI's criminal records picture of Joseph Tinelli.

"No," said Müller, positively again. "The third one was the youngest."

"Him?" questioned Mann, pointing to the Italian-supplied picture of Luigi Brigoli.

Müller shook his head. "I told you, the third man was younger . . . although I can see a similarity."

There was a momentary silence of disappointment among the three investigators. Then Mann said, "All they wanted were the houses? No staff, no outside intrusion whatsoever?"

"That's right."

"What about rental contracts, insurance, inventory deposits, all those sort of things?"

Müller shifted, too obviously discomfited. "Of course."

"Of course what!" demanded Danilov, the most frustrated of them all at the failure to get an identification of Igor Orlov.

"They're the usual formalities," said the rotund man.

"Which we haven't spoken about so far," said Mann. "We want all the contracts . . . want to know in far more detail what they did and didn't want."

"I'm not sure exactly where they—"

"Stop!" insisted Mann. "Cash, right?"

Müller swallowed heavily and then nodded.

The German detective superintendant said, "Otto Müller, take this as an official caution. I do not have the slightest interest or concern at your intending to withhold from the tax authorities what you were paid in cash. But if you withhold anything, anything at all, from us— most particularly any written, signed documentation—I shall officially charge you with impeding and obstructing a multiple murder inquiry and have you disgraced in a public court and have your license revoked. And I will also inform the tax authorities of your avoidance and evasion and ensure that a separate prosecution is brought against you. He held out his hand. "The documentation. Now!"

The man retreated behind a desk that was too large for him, scrambling into a cavernous drawer and silently offering what he retrieved to the other German. Horst Mann accepted the double-sheeted contract delicately, by one corner, and said, "I'll have an officer fingerprint you, for elimination. And I want the money that was handed over in cash, for fingerprint comparison. . . . It'll be marked as an exhibit and returned after the investigation is completed, and I'm sorry that'll mean the tax authorities will know about it. Life just isn't fair, is it, Otto?"

Straightening the paper by holding its lower edge, Mann read aloud, "Instac, 232 Rue de Rive—"

"Geneva," finished Danilov.

Samuelson said, "You know it!"

"Guessed it," said Danilov. "Geneva's where Orlov had his PF Holdings company, remember?" He came close to Mann, to read the contract over the man's shoulder. "I can't decipher the signature as Antipov but I'd say the handwriting is that of a Russian. It isn't labored, like someone copying Russian letters."

"The youngest of the three," said Samuelson, going back to the realtor. "You heard him talk?"

"Yes?"

"What was the accent?"

There was an uncertain shrug. "Italian maybe. I couldn't be sure."

"They talked about holding a conference?" prompted Samuelson, recalling part of Müller's earlier account.

The German nodded. "An important and sensitive one was what the American called it. I supposed that was why they were bringing in their own staff . . . looking after themselves."

"But there were only the three of them?" said Samuelson. "They didn't have drivers . . . people around them . . . a gang, as it were?"

"Antipov by himself, to begin with," repeated the plump man. "Then the other two for the viewings. But that's all there ever was, just the three, no one else."

"No one's been in any of the three villas since their inspection?" questioned Mann.

"No."

"I'm sealing them, for forensic examination."

"For how long!" demanded the man.

"For as long as it takes."

"That's outrageous!"

"So's cheating on your tax."

"Nothing fits," protested Samuelson, on their way back to police headquarters.

"It might," said Danilov. "They *are* Boss of Bosses. They don't make their own bookings. Others do. And Campinali is listed on your FBI files as Tinelli's consigliere."

"Orlov was the convening host, according to what we know from the phone intercepts," recalled Mann. "That could account for his being here ahead of the other two."

"We're not seeing the right picture," persisted Samuelson.

It was Mann's decision to extend the hotel staff interviews beyond those they had questioned the previous night, for which he assigned a squad that included three forensic specialists and needed a larger conference room than before for the enhanced photographs to be displayed on a series of easel-mounted foam boards.

By the time they reached the hotel there were three more positive identifications of Orlov and four of Campinali, all from chambermaids who'd worked on their respective floors. After reporting that the squad leader triumphantly announced, "And there's a woman."

"What?" demanded Mann.

"The three chambermaids each independently say there was a woman with Orlov while he was here."

"Does she show up on the loops?" asked Danilov.

The man shook his head. "We've taken them past every print at least twice. And we're doing it a third time now. They can't find her. And that's another problem. We're still working on it, obviously, but so far there are fifteen people we can't connect with names and room numbers. And ten of the loop images are too poor to enhance."

"You going to be offended if I suggest we have a go at loop enhancement in Washington?" Samuelson asked Horst Mann. "We've got some pretty impressive image-intensifying stuff back there."

Mann at once shook his head. "If my people have finished with them, you can ship them out tonight on your funeral plane."

"That's what I'd like to do. With whatever DNA material has been retrieved from the rooms at the Hilton."

"That, too," promised Mann.

Three of the staff they'd interviewed the previous night—two receptionists and a floor manager—remembered Orlov with a woman. Their varied descriptions distilled down to someone between thirty-five and forty-five, comparatively sharp-featured, blonde, with a full figure she emphasized with tight-fitting clothes. They—and the chambermaids—all insisted that the blonde photographed on Orlov's FBI sting in Moscow was not the woman who'd shared the room booked in Orlov's name. Both receptionists said there didn't appear to be a lot of communication between the couple.

The photographic display had been duplicated, the loops printed in the continuous sequences in which they had been recorded before the individual prints were lifted. Having concentrated for much of the day upon the separate image of Igor Orlov, Danilov switched to the continuous, enhanced run, and was at once caught not by what he could but what couldn't see on a partial frame of Orlov. As he turned, questioningly, the forensic supervisor was waiting.

"That's one of the ones we can't bring up."

"Probably her?" said Danilov. "It looks as if she's right behind him."

"It's a good bet," agreed the scientist. "It's not all bad news, though. There were some bad photographs from the Moscow restaurant?"

Taken by the FBI couple, who were among the dead, Danilov remembered. "What about them?"

"There's a very good forensic match now to the man being identified at Igor Orlov."

Samuelson approached at Danilov's gesture with the mobile phone to his ear. As he reached the display, the American said, "Bill Cowley's at the embassy. Looking forward to seeing you."

For the first time ever, Danilov was not looking forward to seeing the American. He and Yuri Pavin would have had a lot of conversations about him, Danilov guessed.

Each consciously tried to avoid making wariness obvious, and each failed, was overeffusive in his greeting, each trying to say too much too quickly. It was Danilov who recovered first, despite his having snatched maybe three hours sleep in the last forty-eight. His quiet manner encouraged the jet-lagged Cowley, although the uncertainty between them was only just subdued. The arrival of Peter Samuelson, with the promised original loops footage and the hotel room DNA, helped, properly giving them a professional rather than a personal focus. Danilov was impressed by Samuelson's updating debrief, only feeling it necessary twice to intrude.

"At least the DNA will enable us to put names to bodies," said Cowley. It had been obvious for him to get to Berlin on the body recovery plane but everyone else on the flight had been morticians or pathologists, neither being his choice of ideal traveling companions.

"I wish everything else were straightforward," said the pessimistic Samuelson.

"We're less than twenty-four hours into the investigation and we've got a definite make on Igor Orlov," said Cowley. "We're doing good."

"And we know he's back in Moscow," reminded Danilov.

"All we need—" Samuelson stopped at the abrupt entry of an FBI communication's officer.

"The German Justice minister is making a statement, live on television," said the man. "He's talking about joint cooperation and international criminal conspiracies. And he's listed twelve Americans among the dead."

"Shit!" said Cowley. "We should have liaised, made sure public statements were coordinated." And despite it not being his function, Leonard Ross would have expected him to anticipate it.

The telephone rang in the FBI office, and Cowley said, "That'll be Washington."

It wasn't. It was Horst Mann. "The Justice Ministry have received the arrest warrant from Moscow," he said.

29

The focus continued to be scientific, which in turn continued to be frustrating. After the easy elimination of Otto Müller's fingerprints on the rental contract, and those of Horst Mann at either stretching corner, there remained two sets. But there was no match to any of the prints lifted from the Kempinski hotel room occupied in the name of Igor Orlov nor that in which Sam Campinali stayed, under the false identity of Harrison. On the money that Müller reluctantly surrendered, the predominant fingerprints were those of Müller and whoever else had handled the contract. Again there was no comparison from the hotel rooms. Only Müller's prints showed on the forensic scouring of the three Wannsee villas.

"How the hell could three men examine three villas in the sort of detail Müller described without leaving a single dab!" protested Mann, in a rare loss of control.

"Because they're professionals and because your eager Herr Müller was always rushing ahead of them, opening and closing doors," guessed Cowley. "There wasn't a *need* for them to touch anything. The money and the contract were all that had to be handled." In the diverting, commanding presence of the German detective the underlying uncertainty between Cowley and Danilov was lessening, and at that moment Cowley's greater preoccupation was getting Washington's guidance—for which Peter Samuelson had remained at the U.S.

embassy—to the official German announcement. And try to learn whether blame was being personally loaded onto him within the J. Edgar Hoover Building.

"*Very* professional," accepted Mann. "We've already heard back from Switzerland, because it was such an easy check. There's no such company as Instac at 232 Rue de Rive, Geneva. It's a women's lingerie shop. Instac isn't on any company's register, either."

"So they gave a phony company name and address but that in itself isn't an offense, anymore than it's an offense for Sam Campinali to have used the name Harrison at the hotel," Cowley pointed out. "Everything at Wannsee was paid for. Everything at the Kempinski was paid for. No one was cheated. There's no criminal offense."

"That's what our lawyers are arguing," agreed Mann. He looked to Danilov. "The only legal evidence is yours, from Moscow. You've got your warrant. And that's your prosecution, not ours. At the moment, our thinking is that that's exactly what it's got to be, a Russian prosecution."

The dominant echo through all Cowley's other conflicting thoughts was Leonard Ross's parting words: *I want it to be our arrest warrant that gets Orlov. And I want him in an American court.* Immediately regretting the loudness the moment he began to speak, but not lowering his voice, Cowley said : "Twenty-eight people were incinerated! Dozens more maimed! And the investigation is scarcely up and running!"

"Of course we're not going to give up!" the German insisted, regaining his composure as Cowley lost his. "I'm trying to introduce some objective practicality into the investigation. I believe, from what Dimitri has provided, that Igor Gavrilovich Orlov was involved in the massacre. Just as I believe, from the proven presence here in Berlin of Sam Campinali—as well as that of another unknown man, most likely Italian—that some international consortium was to be established. You already know that under German law, that is not an offense. And I do not have—none of us have—a single piece of producible, incriminating evidence to link Orlov to the bombing. Without it, there's no case to be prosecuted here in Germany." He went back to Danilov. "If we'd found him here, we'd have arrested Orlov on your warrant. But he's not here, not any longer. According to your most recent information, he's back in Moscow. So arrest him. Get him off the streets while we go on looking for something that will tie him in with what happened here. Then we can make a claim for extradition."

"It's what I was going to suggest," Danilov said quietly, and smiled.

Cowley detected the satisfaction in the Russian's voice and expression. "When are you going back to Moscow?"

"Today, if there's a flight."

"I'll come with you," Cowley decided.

"Determined to be in on the kill?" said Danilov, heavily.

"No," said Cowley. "That's the last thing I'm determined to be in on."

Danilov accepted that there had been a lot of conversations between William Cowley and Yuri Pavin. They wouldn't stop him, though. Nothing was going to stop him.

"Hello," said Irena tentatively, from the doorway of the Zagorsk dacha.

"Come on in," said Orlov, gesturing invitingly to a chair on the other side of the low table at which he was sitting. He didn't stand to greet her. "You want some vodka, help yourself." There were glasses and a bottle on the table.

The woman hesitated and then sat where he'd indicated without coming around the table to kiss him, reminding herself that theirs wasn't that sort of relationship. Not yet, at least. She poured herself a drink, jerking her head back toward the grounds around the villa. "Still expecting a war?"

"Being cautious," said Orlov, who'd installed barricading cars and men along the approach road resembling the protection of her first visit.

Irena smiled at him again, knowing this time. "That was a hell of a thing in Berlin."

Orlov shrugged. "Lessons had to be taught."

"Difficult for them not to be learned after that," flattered the woman. The hesitation was longer this time, the uncertainty greater. "I was part of it, wasn't I?" The dismissal of her husband was intentional.

"Another precaution," allowed Orlov. He supposed he had to expect the questioning, but it irritated him. Irena irritated him.

"I don't understand."

"You don't need to understand. You had your trip, and that's it."

"You should tell me, Igor Gavrilovich."

"I will, if it's necessary. Until it is, we'll leave it."

Irena at once recognized another barricade. "I did everything you asked."

"I'm grateful. We'll go out to celebrate when I come back to Moscow."

"You promised I could move in, if I persuaded Ivan to do what you wanted. Which I did."

"Yes?"

"I did it. Everything you asked," stressed Irena.

"What have you told Ivan?"

"Nothing. Not until I spoke to you."

Now Orlov waved his hand generally toward the guards outside of the dacha. "What do you think all that's for, out there?"

Irena frowned. "Protection, obviously."

"Which I might need, more than ever, after Berlin," said Orlov, who'd put the cars and the armed men in place for Irena's benefit. "I'm not going to put you at risk until I'm sure."

"Sure of what?" Irena's frown remained.

"That everyone's got the message."

"The television reports talked of police being involved? American as well as German?"

"It's the unknowns that are the danger," insisted Orlov. This charade was necessary because Irena might be necessary, but it still bored him.

"I don't care what the dangers are! I want to be with you!"

"You'd be a weakness. Someone to go for."

"I'd never betray you to the police!" protested Irena.

Orlov couldn't suppress the impatient sigh, careless how she interpreted it. "It's not them I'm concerned about. I've got opposition. I'm not going to make you a target, to get to me. That's what happened with Georgi, remember? I don't want to have to correct it again, like I had to correct it before—" he staged the hesitation—"because then you'd be dead."

This time the smile was of shy uncertainty, at her groping hope that he was at least talking of affection. She was too much of a realist to ever imagine it was possible for him to love her. Irena didn't love Orlov: she was in constant aphrodisiac awe of him—need of him—which she again realistically acknowledged, and that was enough. "You're worried about me?"

Very worried, thought Igor Orlov. The moment she and her limp-dicked husband had served their purpose—if indeed they were called upon to serve his intended purpose—she'd have to be disposed of. She was, Orlov accepted, the weakest link in the protective chain with which he had enclosed himself. "Don't you want me to be worried about you?"

"Of course. It's just that . . . I didn't think . . ."

"You don't have to. I'll think for both of us."

The feeling that engulfed Irena was close to being sexual, which tempered her question. "What do you want me to do?"

"What does Ivan think about Berlin?"

"That I organized a surprise break, needing one after what happened to Georgi. Which incidentally, he didn't enjoy. We spent a lot of time apart, by ourselves, like we do here."

"You didn't say anything about leaving him?"

"Of course not. That's what you and I arranged, didn't we? That we'd meet like this."

"Go on as before, until I'm sure. Until I know it's safe," ordered Orlov.

"Then we'll be together?" she demanded, urgently.

"That's what I promised, didn't I?"

"Take me to bed, before I go back."

The time difference between Moscow and Chicago was in his favor, calculated Orlov. And he had nothing else—or nothing better—to do. "You didn't think I was going to let you go that easily, did you?"

"I'd hoped not."

"Berlin's a mess," declared Orlov. "One of the dead was even related to a politician of yours." Which made it a mistake and which worried him, although the avoidance was in place, as securely as his alibi was established. His shoulder hurt, where Irena had bitten him when she'd orgasmed. He hadn't.

"Not just an ordinary politician. Which takes it beyond being a mistake," said Tinelli. They'd gone through the ritual of assuring each other of the security of the telephone conversation. In his Chicago mansion Tinelli had the receiver on its conference call hookup so that Campinali could hear the entire conversation.

"Have you heard from Don Brigoli?" asked Orlov, grimacing at the need for the respectful title.

"No," the American lied. "Have you?"

"No. And I'm not surprised."

"Why aren't you surprised."

"Our informant, in the Bundeskriminalamt. It's being kept at the highest level, but the word continues to be that the leak came from Europe. And that means only one place, as far as I am concerned."

"Where's Brigoli's advantage in leaking it?"

"Who knows?" responded Orlov easily, everything rehearsed in his mind. "Maybe the idea of a global association is too rich for his blood. But he's determined against it going ahead without him?"

"He could have simply said no."

"And lost respect? This way he's wrecked everything: ensured—more by luck than judgment perhaps, but still ensured—that there's going to be a huge investigation."

"What's that likely to produce?" demanded Tinelli.

"Who knows?" repeated Orlov, intentionally tossing every ball back into the American's court. "I tried to guarantee as much security as possible. Got Sam out before the massacre. But because of all the law enforcement victims, this isn't going to be an ordinary investigation."

"We're already agreed on that," reminded Tinelli.

It was time, Orlov decided. "I don't want to continue if Brigoli's involved. It's not safe."

"Everything's off then?"

Orlov smiled at a response better than he had hoped for. "I wish it weren't. I wish we could combine together, just the two of us. That would still be an unimaginable empire."

"Maybe we should consider that," suggested Tinelli. "Watch what happens in Berlin but at the same time think about a link between America and Russia."

"I will, for my part and on behalf of the brigades I represent," said Orlov.

"As I will, for America," assured Tinelli.

The American *capo di tutti i capi* and his consigliere remained unspeaking for several moments after Tinelli concluded the conversation with Moscow and even then all that Tinelli peremptorily managed was, "Well?"

"He sounded all right," Campinali said guardedly. "It was he who thought the whole thing was over."

"What lead are you getting out of Italy?"

"New York's Genovese family have the best connections there. What they're telling me is that things are unsettled. Seems the commission weren't keen on the linkup. Brigoli's was the casting vote."

"So he's not in control?"

"He might have opposition."

"Which Orlov doesn't have."

"You going to go ahead with it?"

"Like I told Orlov, everything's on hold until we see what comes out of Berlin. Too many law enforcement people died . . . one in particular."

"Why was he allowed to do it!" yelled the FBI director into the phone.

"Because Hitler doesn't run the country anymore," snapped the jet-lagged, exasperated Cowley. The Washington edict had been that no public statement whatsoever was to come from the Berlin embassy, which there hadn't been, but Otto Müller had destroyed any element of American surprise in the still undecided confrontation of Sam Campinali. They later learned, because Leonard Ross pointlessly insisted upon finding out, that the real estate broker had made his own approaches to the state television studios, after which he was swept up by every media outlet—print, radio, and TV—with offices in the German capital and the day after by others who flew in to join the media frenzy. Müller's every interview became more exaggerated in the telling. He began talking of all three men with whom he negotiated visibly carrying guns and of his ignoring death threats by speaking as he was but basically he was remarkably close to the truth. There was to have been an international crime conference involving America, Russia, and Italy, and it had been discovered by the police, who had been slaughtered in the Potsdamer Platz bombing to save the ringleaders from capture. He had identified the American leader from a photograph the police had shown him, and he was sure he could identify the other two when they were caught. It would be the trial of the century. That later inquiry also discovered that Müller had signed four separate media contracts for his exclusive account to earn himself in excess of $1 million.

"He was a material witness."

"Not yet associated with the crime, according to the Germans."

"They're wrong."

"Maybe," agreed Cowley. "There's nothing we can do about it now."

"It's the major story in every newspaper and on every TV channel here," said Leonard Ross, his voice calmer. "And that includes the *Chicago Sun-Times*."

"So Campinali's warned," accepted Cowley. There was every reason for Ross's fury. It was a total fuckup, like virtually everything else in the investigation.

"We got a judge's order for a tap. Campinali hasn't made or received a single call," said Ross.

"You going to bring him in?"

"For what it's worth," said the director. "There's no alternative now."

"There could be something," suggested Cowley hopefully.

"Or nothing," said Ross. "What time's your flight?"

"Eight."

"We got twelve Americans dead. We got every right to take part in Orlov's interrogation."

Cowley frowned at the lapse from the former judge. "The arrest warrant isn't for the Berlin bombing."

"I want you there, Bill. I want you there every minute."

"Yes, sir," said Cowley. He was still the duty scapegoat, he accepted.

30

Jimmy Pearce recognized it was the most important interrogation of his entire career and the artificial civility of it all unsettled him even further. He desperately hoped it didn't show. He'd spent three hours the previous night preparing with an FBI lawyer, Wendall Correy, who had flown in from Washington. Sam Campinali was accompanied by Walter Sweetman, the senior partner of the law firm that carried Campinali's name as a partner. Campinali had shown no surprise at their eight A.M. arrival at his Lincolnwood mansion, invoking his legal right to telephone Sweetman before agreeing to go with them to the Bureau's Chicago office. There had been no conversation whatsoever during the journey, nor in the already prepared interview room prior to Sweetman's arrival. Only then did Pearce switch on the recording apparatus, identifying everyone in the room.

"My client has the legal right to be told why he has been asked to come here," Sweetman said. He was a large and loud, but he conveyed an avuncular air.

Pearce didn't need Correy's warning pressure on his leg beneath the table, pedantically reciting the Miranda warning against self-incrimination before replying to the lawyer's question. "We are seeking Mr. Campinali's help in connection with ongoing inquiries under RICO legislation. And I wish to place on record at once our appreciation of Mr. Campinali's cooperation in agreeing to this interview." He was sure there was nothing in his voice to betray his inner uncertainty.

Sweetman looked at Campinali, who nodded. Sweetman said, "This is entirely voluntary."

"That has already been made clear, on the tape," said Correy.

"The interview will proceed under advisement," insisted Sweetman. "I also wish it to be made clear on the tape that Mr. Campinali has absolutely no knowledge or awareness of any activities that could be construed as racketeering or corruption."

Pearce cleared his throat. "Do you know Mr. Joseph Tinelli?"

"I decline to answer that question, on the ground of lawyer-client confidentiality," said Campinali at once.

"Do you legally represent Mr. Joseph Tinelli?"

"I decline to answer that question, on the ground of lawyer-client confidentiality."

"Have you, in the past, legally represented in court associates of Mr. Joseph Tinelli?"

"I decline to answer that question, on the ground of lawyer-client confidentiality."

"Do you know Igor Gavrilovich Orlov?"

"No, I do not." There had been no hesitation.

"Have you ever met Igor Gavrilovich Orlov?"

"Mr. Campinali has already answered that in his response to the previous question," intruded Sweetman.

"Do you know or have you met Luigi Brigoli?"

"I do not know and therefore have never met anyone named Luigi Brigoli."

From beside him Pearce detected the almost inaudible sigh of frustration from Wendall Correy. Turning slightly toward the tape recording apparatus, Pearce said, "I am showing Mr. Campinali a photograph taken at John F Kennedy Airport, New York, at 11:30 A.M. on May 12 of this year." He slid the print across the table and went on. "Is that a photograph of yourself, Mr. Campinali?"

For the first time there was the slightest hesitation before Campinali said, "Yes."

"Who is the man you are with?"

"I decline to answer that question, on the ground of lawyer-client confidentiality."

"The photograph of the man with you is that of Veniamin Kirilovich Yasev, is it not?"

"I decline to answer that question, on the ground of lawyer-client confidentiality."

"Do you acknowledge Veniamin Yasev to be an associate of Igor Gavrilovich Orlov?"

"My client has already made clear he does not know an Igor Gavrilovich Orlov," refused Sweetman.

"Can you tell me what you did on the eleventh of this month?"

There was another hesitation. "I did not bring my appointments diary with me."

"It was just seven days ago, Mr. Campinali. Surely you can remember what you were doing seven days ago?"

"Of course!" said Campinali, in apparent abrupt recollection. "Germany!"

The son of a bitch was playing with them, Pearce accepted. It would be a cardinal error to give way to the anger that churned through him, overwhelming the uncertainty. "Can you tell us the reason for your visit?"

"Why?" intruded Sweetman, again.

"Because it's relevant to our inquiries," said Pearce.

"Why?" repeated the accompanying lawyer.

"We are making inquiries into the mass murder in Berlin of twenty-eight people, twelve of them FBI and CIA personnel," said Pearce.

"You told us at the beginning of this interview that it was in connection with racketeering and corruption legislation," said Sweetman.

"Of which the mass murder of twenty-eight people forms part," said Pearce. "There are also inquiries into the holding of a conference in Berlin of organized crime figures." He wasn't nervous anymore. He knew that the interview wasn't going well—that it was legally too easy for them to hide—but he was getting everything necessary for a first interrogation and, totally controlled though the man appeared to be, Pearce was sure he'd shaken Campinali by the extent of their knowledge. "What did you go to Germany for, Mr. Campinali?"

"A brief vacation."

"Which you could not remember when I first asked you?"

"I've been extremely busy since I got back. Time flies."

"Now you have remembered?"

"Yes."

"Where did you go, what did you visit, on your brief vacation?"

"Berlin. I had not been there since the Wall came down.

"Did you meet Igor Gavrilovich Orlov there?"

There was the third hesitation. "I have already told you, I do not know anyone named Igor Gavrilovich Orlov."

"Did you meet Luigi Brigoli there?"

"I have already told you, I do not know anyone named Luigi Brigoli."

"If Berlin was your destination, why did you fly into Frankfurt?"

"There was not a direct flight that suited me."

"How did you reach Berlin from Frankfurt?"

"Train."

"Where did you stay in Berlin?"

There was a groping arm gesture, for recollection. "The Kempinski."

"Under the name of Harrison?" seized Pearce.

This hesitation was the longest yet. "Apart from in Italy mine is a difficult name in Europe." There was a shrug, a smile. "It's a harmless convenience, using a name hotel staff find easier."

Their awareness of the pseudonym had unbalanced the man more than anything else so far, gauged Pearce. "You do not know, nor have you ever met, a Russian named Igor Gavrilovich Orlov?"

"Mr. Campinali has already answered that question several times!" protested Sweetman.

Pearce ignored the interjection, his concentration totally upon Campinali. "Were you unaware that Igor Gavrilovich Orlov was also staying at the Kempinski Hotel, at the same time as you?"

Briefly, for a fleeting second, the surprise showed on Campinali's face. "I have already given my answers to all your questions about Igor Gavrilovich Orlov. But for the benefit of the tape I will repeat, for the last time, I do not know such a person, have never met such a person, and was unaware of any such person being in the same hotel as myself during my stay in Berlin."

"What did you do in Berlin?"

"Visited tourist sites. Went back and forth between East and West, where the Wall used to separate them."

"Did you look at villas, at Wannsee?"

"No," said Campinali, at once.

Damn Otto Müller to hell, Pearce thought. "A witness has sworn a lengthy affidavit positively identifying you, from the Kennedy Airport photograph, as one of three men who negotiated the rental of three villas in the Wannsee area on the fourteenth of this month."

"He's mistaken. I have—I had—no interest in rental villas at Wannsee. By the fourteenth my vacation was at an end. I flew home the following day."

"From Frankfurt?"

"From Frankfurt," echoed Campinali.

"In the hope of concealing the fact that you had been in Berlin?"

"Mr. Campinali does not recognize that as a question to be answered," Sweetman interjected. "I believe, in fact, that we have cooperated to the fullest of our ability and that there is little more help we can give you in what is clearly a wrongly initiated inquiry into circumstances and events of which Mr. Campinali knows nothing."

Pearce looked sideways to the FBI lawyer, eager for prompts now, but Correy gave no reaction to the attention. Pearce said, "We thank you for your time."

"I have heard—I have inferred—nothing from this interview to connect Mr. Campinali with an investigation under the RICO statute," said Sweetman.

"We have a full record of Mr. Campinali's assistance," said Pearce, nodding toward the recording machine. "As I believe I made clear at the beginning, it's an ongoing inquiry."

"With which I very much doubt Mr. Campinali will be able to help you any further."

"We'd very much appreciate Mr. Campinali's continuing cooperation if anything arises from the ongoing inquiries," insisted Pearce, sufficiently confident now not to be intimidated.

"Mr. Campinali will not be subjected to harassment."

"Quite so," agreed Pearce, throwing the threat back at the man. "Mr. Campinali will not be subjected to harassment."

Pearce and Wendall Correy didn't bother to move from the interview room after the departure of Sam Campinali and his lawyer. Pearce said, "I hated that . . . The son of a bitch jerking me off, thinking he's fireproof."

Correy shook his head. "He doesn't think he's fireproof. You did good. You rattled his cage with what we knew."

"But now he knows," protested Pearce. "He can cover his ass. Sing in the choir on Sunday and do nothing further to incriminate himself."

"He'll have to make some moves, to cover that ass. What about Yasev?"

"We're leaving him for a day or two. He's hopefully wired every which way, although he keeps switching cell phones. If Campinali gets into contact, we should get it."

"I think there's enough to go back to a judge for a wire on Tinelli."

"Do it then," urged Pearce. "I want to nail Campinali. And Tinelli with him. All we need is one incriminating reference to the Berlin massacre."

William Cowley had read the Russian arrest warrant on the previous evening's flight and was at America's Moscow embassy early for the scheduled meetings he'd arranged before leaving Berlin. Cowley shook his head against John Melton's offer to surrender his office, as he had to Samuelson in Berlin, saying he was sure they could share without getting in each other's way. Cowley had dropped the arrest warrant off at the legal attaché's rooms on his way to the FBI suite.

Melton said the CIA's Al Needham had positively confirmed that the enhanced CCTV photograph wired from Berlin was that of the tall, stooped man he'd seen at the Brooklyn Bite. They'd had agents eat there every night, even those nights when, as they now knew, Orlov hadn't been in Moscow, but the man hadn't shown. Neither had he been seen going in or out of the mansion on Ulitza Varvarka. There had been no telephone conversations picked up on the landline tap or by the cell phone scanners. A briefing was scheduled for early afternoon for the additional agents who had flown in overnight direct from Washington. He'd already advised Pavin.

"And the director wants an update call," the FBI station chief concluded. "The moment we get Orlov, they're going to arrest Yasev at Brighton Beach."

"Why didn't they get Yasev at the same time as Campinali?" frowned Cowley.

"Director's idea," said Melton. "Wants to see which way Yasev will jump."

"That's dangerous," said Cowley at once.

Melton indicated the American newspapers neatly stacked on a side table. "The media are going ape shit, led by George Warren, who seems to be giving daily press briefings. Ross needs to be seen to be doing something."

"I think we all need to be seen to be doing something," said Cowley.

The legal attaché was a lugubrious, heavy-jowled New Englander named Allan Plowright whose dolefulness was offset by a purple shirt, yellow tie, and red suspenders supporting the trousers of his brown and fawn checked suit. The five-page arrest warrant was strewn across his desk, Danilov's supporting material in a separate disorder to one side.

Plowright waved a large hand toward it and said, "Reads OK, but has Danilov got the evidence to base it all on?"

"He says so," said Cowley, cautiously.

"So why didn't they bust Orlov before?"

"They didn't have a connection."

"I still don't see one with Berlin, apart from the modus operandi. And any first-time court attorney would get that dismissed as coincidence on day one. The fact that Orlov was apparently in Berlin just before the explosion isn't enough, either. I sure as hell wouldn't like to put it to a grand jury."

"The director wants Orlov before an American court," said Cowley.

Plowright theatrically exaggerated the surprise. "I'm sure he does. The Speaker's openly demanding an American trial. They're not going to get it from anything I've read or from what you've told me." There was another gesture over the haphazard papers. "Quite apart from about a hundred legal questions, nothing here has anything to do with America or American law. It's strictly Russian."

"I know," accepted Cowley. "I just wanted an opinion."

"Sorry it wasn't what you wanted to hear."

"It was what I expected to hear," further conceded Cowley. "There could be something from the Campinali interview."

Plowright staged another exaggerated surprise. "The guy's a professional mob lawyer. Being brought in for questioning is an occupational hazard."

Despite the clown outfit the lawyer's pessimism matched his attitude. "It'll stir the dust. All we need is to intercept one call from him to Orlov, here, and we've got the connection you can't find so far."

Any more than they'd so far found Orlov, Cowley mentally qualified.

"Best of luck," said Plowright, doubtfully.

The need for which emerged as the consensus at the briefing meeting. Ten agents were maintaining surveillance on their two target addresses, but with the Washington additions a total of thirty agents—as well as Danilov and Pavin—assembled in the incident room established by Jed Parker. It was dominated now by a corkboard upon which there was a solitary, enlarged photograph of Orlov. Cowley led the discussion, but let Melton give an account of the so far failed observation.

"From what you've told us he's kept ahead all the time so far," said one of the newcomers. "He'll have a safe house somewhere. Probably several."

"He's guessed a lot right, to stay ahead," said Danilov. "But he won't know there's a warrant out."

"So where is he?" questioned the first man. "We're pretty sure he's back in Moscow, aren't we?"

"OK, he's got another house somewhere," agreed Danilov. "What I'm saying is that he won't hide in it. They're his world headlines. He'll want to be on show, proving how untouchable he is. Which makes the restaurant, a place with an audience, our best chance. And where it'll probably be the easiest to get him."

The Russian believed he had everything worked out, even to the best assassination spot, Cowley decided. "According to Parker's surveillance—which fits your scenario—Orlov always surrounds himself there with a lot of his own guys. We've got to anticipate some resistance. If there's shooting, innocent people could get killed . . . maimed. And there's already been enough killing and maiming of innocent people."

Too many, Yuri Pavin at once agreed, making up his already and increasingly uncertain mind. "I think I know how he's getting in and out of Ulitza Varvarka without our knowing. I've kept looking for plans of the building. And finally found some. There's a servants' walkway to and from Ulizta Varvarka to what used to be their quarters in a separate house on Rybnyj Lane. Now that we do have his photograph, we can watch the second house . . . see him going in there."

"Why didn't we talk about this before!" demanded Melton.

"I only got it confirmed this morning, just before you called," said

Pavin. He'd apologize for the lie in his prayers. He knew from the other man's frown that Melton didn't believe him.

Danilov shook his head, doubtfully. "We know there are two rear entrances from the main Ulitza Varvarka house. And the front door. Now this. From the servants' house there'll be what, at least three exits? The restaurant has to be the place."

"The house in less risky," objected Cowley, sure now that Danilov's plan was to kill Orlov in the confusion of a shoot-out.

"All we need is a sighting to hit the bastard," said Danilov, too eagerly.

"No," qualified Cowley. "All we need is a sighting to arrest the bastard."

It took the rest of the day for Sam Campinali securely to arrange emergency contact with Tinelli, even though provisions were permanently in place for such an eventuality because the American *capo di tutti i capi* was a cautious man. Automatically—and logically—assuming he would be under twenty-four-hour surveillance and that his home telephone would be monitored, Campinali went directly from the FBI building to his professionally protective partnership law offices, the legitimate divisions of which occupied three floors of a skyscraper building on Balbo Drive, with a panoramic view of the lake. The building housed fifteen other businesses, with total staff close to a thousand, which made total observation virtually impossible. It also made it impossible successfully to attach listening devices to every telephone, facsimile machine, and computer e-mail.

Joe Tinelli was alerted by Campinali's telephone call from one of those untraceable law office telephones to an equally untraceable cell phone connection at the Evanston house. There was no exchange of names and no location was mentioned when the appointment was fixed for that early evening. Tinelli didn't ask what the crisis was. After one more call from the secure telephone, Campinali and Sweetman spent an hour legally dissecting the FBI interview, concluding that the Bureau had been panicked by the Otto Müller media coverage and had insufficient evidence for any formal charge.

"What we can't anticipate is any linking factor we couldn't satisfactorily answer," warned Sweetman. "The Bureau isn't going to give up on this: they can't. You're going to have to examine the toilet bowl every morning before you sit down. And afterward."

"They're not fully on track," argued Campinali, in attempted reassurance.

"Going close enough in the right direction," the other lawyer retorted.

"There's still a lot of assumptions—mistakes—in the questioning," insisted Campinali, deciding Tinelli's input would be better at that moment than Sweetman's.

Sweetman said, "We lunching?"

"Wrong to appear to be frightened," said Campinali, who was.

"What time will the car come?"

"Three-thirty's early enough."

They ate very publicly at the Empire Room—briefly, at first, trying unsuccessfully to isolate Campinali's watchers—and just as publicly reentered the Baldo Drive building, Campinali tensed now for the evasion. It was essential they were the last into a crowded elevator, from which Campinali disembarked at the first floor, hurriedly descending by the fire escape to bypass the ground floor for the basement garage. Dutifully waiting for him was a chauffeured, smoke-windowed, unmarked courtesy limousine from a legitimately operating but completely Mafia-owned hotel on Monroe Drive.

When Campinali stretched out across the rear floor, the driver said over his shoulder: "That probably isn't necessary."

"Let's not take any chances." It was the first time Campinali had been personally involved in the prepared emergency system, and he felt embarrassed.

The driver drove in the opposite direction from Monroe Drive when he emerged from the ramp and was silent for ten minutes before saying: "We're clear. No one's with us."

Campinali got gratefully up from the floor, still feeling ridiculous and wondering how difficult it was going to be to adjust to the precautions he would be forced into taking in the coming weeks and maybe even months.

The driver said, "Everything's ready."

"I expected it to be," said Campinali.

The hotel garage was underground, too, but at its far end there was a close-meshed, electronically gated separation. The driver depressed the remote control sensor several yards from the gate and scarcely reduced speed to pass through, triggering its closure behind him.

"Home free," said the man.

For how long, thought Campinali. He said. "Thank you."

It was a dedicated elevator, only serving the never-let penthouse into which it directly opened. Joseph Tinelli was totally alone in the lounge, watching golf on the sports channel. He saw a putt being sunk before turning to his consigliere. He left the picture on but turned down the sound.

He said, "So?"

Campinali recounted the FBI encounter with a lawyer's recall, rehearsed by his earlier reexamination with Walter Sweetman. Tinelli listened, head sunk, with his chin against his chest. He still didn't speak for several moments after Campinali finished.

"I don't understand their saying Orlov was at the hotel," said Tinelli.

"Neither do I."

"You think he was, just letting Zhikin front for him?"

"It's possible, although I would have expected to see him."

"But you didn't?"

"No."

"And the Bureau thought we were all there, Orlov, Brigoli, and me?"

"Yes."

"They specifically talked about an international association?"

"Yes."

"No mention of the Brigoli boy?"

"No."

"That wouldn't happen, would it, if Brigoli's the source? He's known as the Italian *capo di tutti i capi*, so there's no risk in his name being included: it even gives him an alibi, as far as we're concerned. But the kid's kept out of it."

"There's an argument there," agreed Campinali.

"For the moment you're legally safe?"

Campinali stirred at the time qualification. "There's no proof of anything."

"It's still not good, Sam. Not good at all."

"I know."

"The kraut real estate broker is your weakness. Get a contract organized. A freelance who doesn't know it's coming from us."

"Right."

"What about Yasev? He could be another problem, being on that photograph."

"I warned him from the office. Gave him a cover story."

"What about intercepts?"

"He's changing cell phones every week, with preordered numbers."

"He heard from Orlov?"

"No."

"You tell him to warn Orlov."

"I specifically told him not to, in case it's a setup with a wire on Orlov."

"It has to be," decided Tinelli. "They should have picked him up the same time as you. That's the only way it makes sense to have left him. Don't have the Bureau waste their time here," said Tinelli. "Be seen about, although stay away from Evanston."

"I understand."

Tinelli lapsed into silence. Campinali knew he wasn't expected to prompt the discussion. At last the older man said, "Has the Genovese family got enough muscle in Italy to take out Brigoli?"

"Yes," said Campinali at once.

"You think we should?"

"It'll attract attention."

"It could deflect it, away from us," countered Tinelli. "Brigoli's an uncertainty."

"Yes," agreed Campinali. Would Tinelli come to regard him the same way, he wondered.

"Get back to the Genovese family. Tell them I want to know definitely whether we've got a problem with Brigoli. They say we have, they organize the contract, OK?"

"What about the Russian linkup?"

"I don't want to lose it," said Tinelli, reflectively. "It's too good to lose. It would be my legacy to be the *capo di tutti i capi* of two countries."

Campinali hoped the older man wasn't letting ambition cloud his judgment.

Their copy of the Chicago interview with Sam Campinali had been relayed to Moscow during the afternoon to be played to the reassembled squad and had obviously been the main subject of conversation at dinner, which Cowley insisted on hosting at the Savoy Hotel, his favorite in the very center of Moscow. It had not been an intentional maneuver for Danilov to be flanked on either side by Cowley and Pavin, as if they were protectively watching his every move, but that's how they were positioned. Cowley wondered if Yuri Pavin saw the ironic significance. So far there had not been an opportunity for Cowley and Pavin to talk alone.

"Forced into it as we were, I think Jimmy Pearce did pretty well," judged Cowley.

"All it needs is the panicked contact call," agreed Pavin, unknowingly repeating Cowley's hope to the embassy lawyer that morning.

"And for us to pick it up," cautioned Danilov. John Melton's supervision of the electronic and now increased visual surveillance of the restaurant and the prerevolutionary mansion had kept him from joining them in the Savoy's baroque dining room.

"Let's drink to it," urged Cowley. He'd kept himself to one scotch before dinner, and there was still wine left in their second bottle. He'd already spoken to Pamela that afternoon and knew he was sufficiently in control to call again that evening. He might, he decided, if nothing came up, which by now seemed unlikely.

"It's got—" began Pavin before thrusting his hand into his jacket pocket for the vibrating cell phone a second before it switched to ring. He listened, said, "Right!" and then to the other two men, "Igor Orlov just walked into the restaurant. John's getting everyone together at the embassy."

Dimitri Danilov's smile was of anticipation at the long-sought chance to get Orlov at gunpoint. And pressing the trigger.

31

Diverting all their forces upon the positive restaurant sighting, Melton reduced the house surveillance to a five-man skeleton crew, three of them upon the newly disclosed Rybnyj Lane servants' quarters. Everyone else except that night's FBI diner who'd initiated the alert from a muttered washroom identification—and then returned to his table, waiting with reordered coffee and brandy, for the mass entry—was already in the incident room when Cowley, Danilov, and Pavin reached the U.S. embassy. They were greeted throughout the room by a foot-shuffling, murmured impatience, stilled more in surprise than acceptance when Cowley announced that everyone, including himself, was subservient to Dimitri Danilov, who was serving a Russian arrest warrant under Russian legal jurisdiction and was therefore officially the commander of the operation.

As Danilov switched with Cowley on the incident room dais, an unidentified voice from the body of the room said, too loudly, "Asswiping a Bureau too corrupt to trust its own officers for the job."

Seizing upon the remark, Danilov said, "You're right. And it's not something I'm proud of, any more than any of you can be proud that your Bureau hasn't beaten the Mafia corruption of your own country in almost a century. Which is why we're here, to stop their control from spreading. And why twelve of your guys—guys I guess some of you knew, were friends with—were burned to a crisp, because of some who's-in-charge territorial bullshit. It's not important who's technically in command. What's important is that we nail the bastard. So now I'm going to stop to give everyone their chance with the *Die Hard* one-liners."

There was less foot-shuffling than before and what there was now was of awkwardness, not embarrassment. Cowley thought that if he hadn't known—or thought he knew—of Danilov's secret agenda, he would have been impressed by the put-down.

Danilov came within a hair's breadth of extending the challenge too long before abruptly declaring, "Good! Everyone listen up and listen good to how it's going to be done."

The single photograph of Orlov had been moved aside for an enlarged plan of the Brooklyn Bite on Skornjaznkyj Lane to be displayed on its own individual corkboard. Its rear door and two emergency side exits, as well as the front entrance, were marked out in red. Also in red was the metal door over the basement delivery chute in the rear alley. Danilov said Yuri Pavin would be in charge of the rear, as the necessary other Russian arresting officer if Orlov tried to escape from the back of the building. There would be three Americans on each of the three potential rear exits, with another three on both side doors. Additionally, two more agents would, at the precisely timed and radio-coordinated moment of entry from the front, go in through the rear and side jackhammered doors. John Melton would remain at the embassy, ready to trigger the simultaneous arrest of Veniamin Yasev in America. Pavin would go direct from the restaurant to Petrovka to detain Alexandr Ognev.

Danilov went on. "I will head the group entering from the front—"

"With me," Cowley broke in determinedly. "It's essential we anticipate any possible legal maneuver, particularly that of jurisdiction and wrongful arrest. My being with Dimitri at all times will establish the seizure as a government-to-government agreed joint operation."

Once more Danilov extended the pause, looking accusingly between Cowley and Pavin. Turning back into the room, Danilov said, "As I was about to say, Bill will be with me. We do have to anticipate every legal maneuver, but effectively Bill is joint coordinator in fact if not by title." There was a preparatory pause. "Everyone will be armed and must be ready to defend themselves. Unless we can achieve the element of complete surprise, there'll be the resistance we spoke about this morning. We don't, obviously, initiate it. But we've got to be ready for it and react to it in the proper professional manner. I don't want any innocents killed or injured. I don't want any more of you guys killed or injured."

Cowley suddenly realized that Danilov was not only—or even purposely—setting out necessary legal or safety precautions. With such a pedantic, observing-the-legalities briefing he was guaranteeing in advance, in front of dozens of witnesses, that in any subsequent inquiry he would be proven to have specifically warned *against* what he intended to do

"What about logistics?" demanded a voice. "Medivac backup. SWAT teams?"

"I thought we understood that, without needing to talk about it. There won't be any, to avoid Orlov being tipped off. We can—and will—summon medical backup immediately after we go in, if it's necessary. I'm hoping it won't be."

"Jesus!" said the original complaining voice.

"You feel like praying, pray," said Danilov. He affected to check the time. "Orlov's held court for an hour and half. Let's go spoil his day."

The first opportunity for Cowley and Pavin to speak out of Danilov's hearing came with the quick assigning of agents to the positions Danilov specified.

"How clever was that?" demanded Cowley.

"Too clever," agreed the Russian. "He's going to kill Orlov."

"I know that."

"We've got to stop him."

"I know that, too. What I don't know is how."

"You'll be with him. It's up to you to prevent it. I'll get in as quickly as I can."

"Let's not forget what we're really supposed to be doing," said Cowley. "You watch your back. There's a lot of it to hit."

"You, too," said the Russian.

Danilov's impromptu planning was for the swoop to be made at eleven, each assigned unit liaising sotto voce over American-supplied radios between each other and separately with John Melton in the embassy incident room. There was no forced, wisecracking bravado in any of the approaching cars. Cowley wondered if there had been in Jed Parker's cavalcade just a few short days ago among the squad believing they were on the point of seizing all three Mafia leaders. Melton had been the incident room coordinator then: he would know. It would have been a macabre, ghoulish question to ask the man. Danilov was rigidly beside him in the rear of their car, staring fixedly ahead, moving only to respond or relay their position as they got closer to Skornjaznyzi Lane. Once Melton relayed an all-listeners alert from the agent already inside the restaurant that more people had come in to join the partying Orlov, which prompted Danilov to repeat the incident room warning for everyone to be ready to protect themselves. He added that where it was feasible—particularly with those at the rear—they should park away from the building and not approach it en masse but singly or in pairs, only coming together a few moments before the intended strike time. Danilov's incident room remark abruptly came into Cowley's mind, and he wondered how many in the squad were saying a silent prayer. Yuri Pavin certainly would be, although knowing the man as well as he did, Cowley didn't think it would be for himself. Washington had obviously been alerted that the operation had begun, and Cowley guessed word would be percolating through the J. Edgar Hoover Building. It was inevitable that Pamela would pick it up. She was the most adept of headquarters manipulators and would now be tuned into every gossip wavelength because of his personal involvement. He was curious if she would be saying a prayer for him. He doubted it. Like him, she wasn't a believer.

Cowley's attention came back inside the car with Danilov's radioed announcement that they'd reached Skornjaznyj Lane. At the driver's indication Danilov added that they were stopping about forty meters short of the entrance. Two of the other cars, one of those assigned to the rear, the other to a side door, quickly reported they were still minutes away. Just as quickly, Melton came on with another all-listeners reminder that it was only 10:50, which kept everything perfectly on schedule. "Which can be adjusted, if necessary."

"The front looks quiet," said Danilov. There was an uneven timbre to his voice.

"Let's hope it stays that way," said Cowley. He felt the first surge of apprehension but wasn't ashamed or worried by it. This was probably the most direct and certainly the most dangerous confrontation he'd ever knowingly faced. It was natural—necessary—that he felt worried: he *needed* the feeling, to have the adrenaline moving through him, to be quick enough to react to whatever he was going to encounter. He said, "Everyone OK?"

There were grunts from the two Americans in the front. Danilov didn't make a sound or give a gesture. First the delayed side door squad and then the lagging rear entry team reported they were in position.

"Ten-fifty-four," said Danilov. "Keep to the schedule. We go in at eleven."

Danilov was out of the car first, hurrying forward. Cowley, following, was immediately caught by the stiff-armed awkwardness of the Russian in front. In the abrupt light of a passing car he saw that Danilov already had his Makarov out from its holster and was carrying it in readiness. Cowley unclipped the restraining strap on his own Smith and Wesson, hurrying to catch up. Two other squads that were to make up the frontal assault were approaching from the opposite direction, strung out in an unconnected line according to Danilov's instructions.

They came together as a group precisely on time and place outside the main restaurant entrance. Danilov thrust in without changing stride, Cowley tight behind him. Danilov's gun was up now, ready to fire with the safety off, professionally clasped, his left supporting hand against the 9-mm kickback over his right wrist. Momentarily, the front-of-house man froze, then went for some alarm button, but Danilov intervened, the muzzle jerked under the man's chin to ensure that if he fired, it would take off the top of his head. Having prevented that initial warning Danilov jerked the gun barrel fiercely, breaking the man's larynx before casting him aside in an onward, door-bursting rush.

There were screams and shouts from inside now, at the rear entry, and at least two pistol shots, and Cowley thought, Shit, another massacre, and as if in confirmation there were maybe three more shots and the screams got louder.

They hadn't properly anticipated the panicked rush of innocent people directly against their entry from the front, and there was a surreal hiatus as the incoming and outgoing pressures against the inner double doors equalled each other, making it impossible for either to move. Danilov broke the jam, firing the Makarov into the air, bringing down a snowstorm of plaster. It divided the pressure against them, though, and by concerted, unified weight, the doors were forced inward upon another headless-chicken melee of people surging for escape in each and every different direction. Almost at once Cowley was carried away from Danilov. Cowley saw two bodies lying motionless toward the rear of the restaurant and a man he thought he recognized as an FBI agent slumped at a table, blood from a wounded shoulder seeping through his fingers. And then, abruptly, he saw Orlov, unmoving, untroubled, actually smirking in the bodyguarded eye of the storm. That belatedly brought him back on professional course, and he thrust people aside to get to the Russian Mafia leader.

The impression of calm was even greater when Cowley got past those fighting to escape. He saw Danilov, too far away to intervene or jostle from position, and Orlov even farther away, impotently distanced at the far end. Danilov was crouched in a trained firing stance, too close to miss. Orlov saw him, too, saw the determination and the smirk drained away, and he came urgently forward and said something and the protectors around him began to grope inside their jackets. Cowley was never sure in which language, Russian or English, he shouted to stop them drawing their weapons, but they did stop, and there was a suspended, slow-motion moment when Cowley and Pavin and the phalanx around Orlov stared at Danilov, waiting for the explosion of the first shot. The Makarov, momentarily steady, wavered, streadied, then shook again. The white knuckles remained white but the quivering finger didn't tighten around the trigger and the moment went—was lost—with Cowley and Pavin continuing on. Cowley physically intervened between Danilov and his victim seconds before Pavin reached them, his more controled gun directed at the no longer posturing man.

Orlov said, weakly, "He was going to kill me! The motherfucker was going to kill me!"

Behind Cowley's intervening shoulder, too faint for anyone except Cowley to hear, Danilov moaned, "I couldn't do it. I tried to press the trigger but I couldn't. I couldn't kill him. And I promised Larissa."

By the time Yuri Pavin made the formal arrest, Orlov's smirk was pasted back in place. When Pavin finished the carefully observed formalities, Igor Gavrilovich Orlov said: "You're all going to look so stupid. I want you to write that down now, for everyone to hear what I said when you arrested me."

Which was how Feliks Zhikin saw Orlov being led away, in manacles. Zhikin was standing among the throng of escaping diners who had alerted him to the raid and now lingered outside the restaurant, eager to see what was happening. Zhikin was late arriving. He had been told by those assigned to finding him that Stefan Cherny still hadn't been located. Zhikin was relieved not having to face Orlov's fury when he told Orlov this. He had to get on to their Petrovka source, to find out what was happening.

"Your boss has been arrested in Moscow," announced Jimmy Pearce. It had been Leonard Ross's idea to have the Chicago station chief maintain the continuity of the interrogations, although Hank Slowen was with him in the Manhattan interview room. So was the lawyer Wendall Correy, again for continuity.

"Who's my boss?" demanded Veniamin Yasev, who'd given no response to the carefully read Miranda warning and hadn't yet asked for an attorney, although he had just as carefully, on tape, been offered legal representation.

"You tell me!" demanded Pearce, giving way to impatience. At once there was the FBI lawyer's warning pressure beneath the table dominated by the recording equipment.

"I don't have a boss. I run my own restaurant."

"Marat Zubov was murdered in that restaurant, wasn't he?" said Slowen. "Along with Nikolai Nyunin and Lev Gusev."

"No," denied Yasev. "No one was murdered in the Odessa."

"We found forensic evidence," said Slowen.

"I don't know anything about any forensic evidence." The sports shirt Yasev had been wearing, with chino pants, when he was arrested at Brighton Beach was strained across broad, bull-like shoulders. The accent was more Brooklyn than Ukraine.

"We'll see about that, in time," said Slowen.

Yasev shrugged but didn't respond.

Pearce slid the print across the table and said, "Who is this man?" Toward the recording apparatus he said, "I am showing Veniamin Kirilovich Yasev a photograph in which he is shown and which was taken at John F. Kennedy Airport, New York, at 11:30 A.M. on May 12 of this year."

Yasev said, "A lawyer."

"What's his name?" asked Pearce.

"Mr. Campinali."

"How do you know Mr. Campinali?"

"I don't know him. I was given his name. As a good lawyer."

"Why do you need a good Chicago lawyer?" took up Slowen.

"I'm thinking of opening another restaurant. In Chicago. I need premises."

Pearce kept his tightly clasped hands beneath the table to conceal his frustration. "How, out of all the lawyers in Chicago, did you come to approach Samuel Campinali about the opening of a restaurant?"

"I told you, I was given his name."

"Who by?" said Slowen.

"A customer in the Odessa. He said he was from Chicago. He knew Mr. Campinali."

"What was the name of this man?" sighed Pearce.

"I never knew. He just gave me Mr. Campinali's name and said he was a good lawyer."

"You really think—" Pearce started impatiently but was stopped by Wendall Correy's under-the-table pressure and Hank Slowen talking over him.

"A good lawyer for what?" Slowen said.

"What?" echoed the Ukrainian.

"What branch of law?"

"The guy didn't say."

"Do you know who Joseph Tinelli is?"

"No."

"You've never heard of Joseph Tinelli?"

"No."

"Samuel Campinali is the legal counsel for Joseph Tinelli, a court lawyer. And Tinelli is the Mafia Boss of Bosses in America."

Yasev shrugged again. "I don't understand what you're telling me . . . what the point is."

"The point is that Campinali doesn't do property deals. He does criminal law."

"I didn't know that." There was a growing wariness about the Ukrainian.

"You had this recommendation, from an unknown man who came to the Odessa and to whom you spoke of opening a restaurant in Chicago?" persisted the New York station chief.

"That's right," said Yasev, cautiously.

"And you called Campinali?"

"Yes."

"Where from?" said Pearce, seizing the opening.

"What?"

"Where did you call him from?"

Another shrug. "The restaurant, I guess. Yes, the restaurant."

"And spoke with him personally?"

"Yes."

"And said what?"

Yasev made another uncertain gesture, almost too obviously seeking an escape. "I don't remember the exact words."

"Of course you don't," cajoled Slowen. "What did you tell him generally?"

"Just that I wanted to open a restaurant, I guess."

"And what did he say?" asked Pearce, all anger gone now, as alert as Yasev was uncomfortable with the direction of the questioning. "Not the exact words. Just what you understood from his reply."

"I don't remember," blurted Yasev, floundering.

"He didn't say he was a trial lawyer . . . that he couldn't help you?" pressed Pearce.

"He may have done . . . I don't remember."

"He may have done . . . I don't remember," mocked Slowen. "Look at the photograph again, Mr. Yasev. Where was it taken?"

"I don't—" Yasev started, but stopped. "Kennedy."

"Kennedy Airport, New York," pedantically recorded Slowen. "Into which, in a private jet, Samuel Campinali, who is not a property lawyer, flew in to talk to you about buying or leasing a restaurant. Is that what you're telling us, Mr. Yasev?"

"No. I mean, we met." Yasev improvised. "But he didn't come specifically to see me. He had a business meeting. It was convenient to see me."

"Where was his business meeting?"

"I don't know."

"We've got the flight details of airport arrivals and departures," said Slowen. "Campinali's jet arrived at 10:58 A.M. You and he met on an outside airport balcony for a total of twenty-eight minutes. Campinali's plane left at 12:10 P.M. Campinali couldn't have made any business meeting, anywhere, during a time spread of one hour and twelve minutes . . . unless, that is, the meeting was actually at the airport where you and Campinali met?"

"His meeting was canceled," tried Yasev, desperately.

"So he carried on anyway to see you?"

"I guess."

This time Wendall Correy's pressure beneath the table was encouraging. Responding to it, Pearce said, almost dismissively: "What did you talk about?"

"The restaurant."

"What restaurant?"

"The restaurant I want to open in Chicago."

"Tell us about it," came in Slowen. "You got plans drawn up? Architects and designers? That sort of stuff?"

"Not yet," said Yasev, carelessly.

"So what did you talk about?" repeated Pearce, lapsing into a hard cop, soft cop routine.

"What I had in mind, a bistro or a big place."

"Campinali still didn't say he didn't do property?"

"He may have. I'm not sure."

"What sort of place do you plan for Chicago?"

"Big place, maybe."

"How big?"

"Fifty, a hundred covers."

"That's what Campinali is looking out for you, a big place of a hundred covers?"

Yasev realized his mistake too late. "Something like that."

"But he knows what you want."

"I made it pretty clear."

"You haven't made anything clear to us, Mr. Yasev. Except that you're lying," said Pearce. "We'd like you to listen to this."

The first of Yasev's intercepted telephone conversations echoed in the room. Pearce turned off the replay after a few minutes and said, "We've got several more."

"Why don't we go back over a few points, starting with what we found at the Odessa Bar and Grill at Brighton Beach?" said Slowen. "We got all the time in the world and you're not going anywhere, so—"

"I want a lawyer!" the man suddenly demanded. "It's my right. You can't refuse me."

"Nothing's inadmissible?" asked Pearce, anxiously.

Wendall Correy shook his head. "There'll be application to have it struck out, but you covered it. Everything he's said so far can be presented before a grand jury or a court."

"And he's lied and we can show that he's lied," insisted Pearce. "He said he called Campinali from the restaurant. We know from the wiretap that he didn't, and we can prove it by getting the phone records before the tap was in place."

"It's something to put to Campinali, too," said Slowen. "I thought the director was wrong, leaving Yasev until now in the hope of us intercepting a call between him and Campinali, which we didn't get. But now I'm not so sure. We didn't get the clincher, but we've got more questions to ask both of them."

"Is the provable DNA from Marat Zubov enough to hold him on?" asked Pearce. "We want Yasev off the streets now, where Campinali can't get directly to him."

"In my legal opinion, yes," replied Correy, at once. "His lawyers will challenge it, of course. But we can contest the challenge, and I think we'll win. Whatever, he'll be in custody for a few days."

"Good," smiled Pearce. "I'm calling in a few favors among crime reporters in Chicago, getting them to carry the press release of Yasev's arrest. See if that and the Moscow arrest sweats Campinali into making any indiscreet calls."

"He hasn't so far," reminded Slowen.

"Things have moved forward since we brought Campinali in," insisted Pearce. "Things are too spread out for them to be sure of anything. It's got to turn our way."

"Got to," echoed Slowen.

That echo didn't reverberate for anyone else.

"You can't prove anything," sneered Alexandr Ognev. The detective sergeant was a fat, disheveled man only just managing to maintain his bravado. He'd been on the phone to Feliks Zhikin, protesting ignorance of the arrest, when Pavin had come into the squad room to arrest him.

"We can," said Pavin. "You're going to be charged with corruption and you're going to go to jail, and you know what happens to former police officers when they go to jail, don't you."

"Go fuck yourself!"

"That's what's going to happen to you, a lot, in prison," said Pavin. "I'm going to lock you in a cell on the same corridor as Igor Orlov. Maybe you'll be able to shout to each other, try to get your stories straight." He hoped there was some attempt at contact. Pavin was posting a detective whom he believed he could trust in the corridor, just in case.

The three who died in the Brooklyn Bite incursion were all in the rear of the building, all of them supposed Orlov protectors. There were twenty gunshot injuries within the main restaurant, none of them life threatening, including seven FBI agents.

Cowley said, "It was good. Better than I thought it would be."

They were in Pavin's office in the Ulitza Petrovka, the arrest formalities completed, the drama draining from everyone except Dimitri Danilov, who'd taken no part in those formalities but remained—still protectively between Cowley and Pavin—near comatose. Which was how, and where, he sat now seemingly unaware of anything happening around him.

Pavin said, "We were lucky."

Cowley said, "Whatever. It worked." He deserved a drink later, he decided. By himself, reflectively. There was a lot to reflect upon.

"You seen the warrant?" asked Pavin.

"And the supporting evidence," confirmed Cowley.

"It won't stand up, even in a Russian court."

"I didn't think it would."

"So where are we going from here?"

"I don't know," said Cowley, who couldn't remember ever feeling so impotent, in any situation.

Danilov roused himself and repeated what had become a mantra. "I couldn't kill him. I had him but I couldn't kill him."

"It might have been easier if you had," said Cowley. Where the hell, he wondered, *were* they going from here?

They all turned at the entry of the communications room clerk, who wordlessly handed Melton a torn-off news agency wire story. The Moscow station chief spoke while looking down at it, his voice uneven in disbelief. "Mr. Speaker Warren has just announced, from the floor of the House, the simultaneous arrests in Moscow and New York of prime suspects in the Berlin massacre of American law enforcement agents." He looked up, smiling wanly. "The time difference, between us and Washington, means it'll hit all the main news channels. All hell's going to break loose."

Otto Müller was alone in his Kandertaler Weg office, in the process of locking up after the last member of staff had left, when the outer door opened. He turned to the man, smiling, and said, "We're just closing, but if there's anything—"

"I know you are." The man shot Müller fully in the chest. The force threw Müller back into his chair, which overturned. The noise was almost greater than the sound from the silenced Smith and Wesson. Unhurriedly, the assassin went around the desk and professionally fired once more, a coup de grâce shot to the head. He left just as unhurriedly, knowing from his patient observation of the office that by the time the body was found by the cleaner next morning, he would have already landed back in New York.

32

All hell did break loose and continued to reverberate for several days, like the aftershocks of an earthquake. Stirred from his self-recriminating torpor, Danilov that night urged the federal prosecutor's office to limit the Russian statement to confirming an arrest, during which three people died and a number of others were injured, as part of an earlier and continuing investigation but to refuse to affirm any connection with Berlin. Danilov also took the telephone call that came within minutes of the Washington news agency flash and assured Horst Mann that nothing had emerged in Moscow to take the Berlin investigation forward, although Orlov was definitely in custody. Cowley was calling Washington for guidance from another room in the FBI suite: they'd get back to him if there had been anything they were unaware of from the seizure of Veniamin Yasev.

Suspiciously, Mann said: "Are we back where we were, people working independently?"

"No!" denied Danilov at once. "We don't know what the hell's going on, any more than you do. Any progress at your end?"

"Müller's been killed. I was on my way when I heard about Washington," announced the German police chief. "Professional job, a body shot and one to the head."

"There goes our best identifying witness," said Danilov.

"We'll go through the motions, but that's all it'll be, pointless motions. And far too much publicity," said Mann.

"Which mob did it?" wondered Danilov

"It's academic," said the German, resigned. "We might get an indication from the bullet of what sort of gun it came from, but that's not going to help us."

"What about the massacre?"

"We know the explosive was Semtex, obviously detonated by remote control," said Mann. "Forensic are still trying to establish if there was a phosphorous component. Orlov's clever, torching everything."

Horst Mann didn't yet know how the arrest warrant could be exposed as being fabricated, Danilov suddenly remembered. Was it too much—too desperate—to hope that Veniamin Yasev had instantly collapsed, admitting all the connections they needed? But one confession wouldn't be enough. There needed to be independent corroboration, supporting scientific evidence. "We'll be in touch, as soon as there's anything."

"Any of our people among the dead there? Or badly hurt?"

"No. No innocents killed, either."

"What did Orlov do?"

Danilov hesitated, confronting what, he guessed, would be one of many uncertainties still to come. "He laughed at us . . . at me."

"He did what!"

"Laughed. Didn't let any of his immediately surrounding people intervene. They didn't draw the weapons we later found on them."

Now the hesitation was from the German. "I don't understand that."

"Neither do we, not yet." Would they—more importantly, would he—*ever* understand?

"He tricked you before, in Moscow," heavily reminded the German.

"I know," acknowledged Danilov. What the fuck was the trick this time? It was a fleeting, prompting question. He'd failed the first opportunity, creating incalculable difficulties. What about a second chance, the hesitating demons suppressed. Even though he hadn't talked it through—thought it through—Cowley had been right. It would have been better,—it would have solved most if not all their problems—if he had forced himself, been brave enough and loved Larissa enough, to pull the trigger.

"Don't let him do it again," warned Mann.

This was terrible: unthinkably, unacceptably terrible. "I won't," undertook Danilov, unsure what he was promising. There were no self-pitying recriminations any more. Just scourging professional guilt, not just at what he'd done but at what the unknown, incalculable outcome might be.

"If there's something I need to know, I want to know it right away," persisted Mann. "This whole damned thing is getting out of control . . . has always been out of control."

"We'll speak tomorrow," said Danilov.

William Cowley stumped back into Melton's office and said, "You got a drink here? Scotch would be good." Then he said, "Politics! Fucking politics."

Everyone apart from Yuri Pavin accepted the drinks produced from the bottom drawer of Melton's desk, Pavin's concern now switching to the American. Cowley caught the attention and shook his head in reassurance.

Danilov said, "What?"

"Veniamin Yasev didn't break. He was close, but pulled back. The director thinks his job's on the line, tells Warren too much about what's happening. Including the simultaneous arrests. Warren goes for the headlines and sure as hell gets them. Leaving us double-fucked."

"What's your official line?" asked Danilov. "Horst's been on. Needs guidance."

"The same recycled crap about ongoing inquiries, which the media isn't buying any more. Christ knows how—on what it's based—but we're now getting cover-up conspiracy theories."

"There's something you don't know," said Danilov. "Otto Müller's dead. Shot. Professional hit, according to Horst."

"Oh, Jesus H. Christ!" said Cowley. He offer his glass to Melton, took a sip, and said, "I needed that."

"What did you tell Ross?" asked Pavin.

"I told him that because of what Warren's done, at this stage, it's likely that the whole investigation will collapse. And I asked him to tell George Warren that, in the hope of keeping the self-publicizing son of a bitch away from the media." He took another deep swallow. "Ross won't, of course. Which is why I'm putting it in writing."

"Igor Orlov could go free, get away with it all, because of what I've done, couldn't he?" fully realized Danilov. "I could have actually protected— saved—him!"

"No," refused Cowley. "That can't happen."

"It's happening," said Pavin.

"Then we've got to make sure it doesn't," insisted Cowley. He looked directly at Danilov. "But properly. No more vigilante shit."

Could he do it if he got a second chance? Danilov asked himself.

There was a triple irony in Gennardi Renko being Orlov's totally unexpected and surprising defense attorney. The first was that the young, intense and so far believed-to-be incorruptible lawyer was the foremost publicly acknowledged advocate for the reform of Russia's traditionally easy state-manipulated Criminal Procedure Code. The second was that he'd agreed to represent the Russian Mafia leader, although they conceded that there was no previous conviction against the man. And the third was that with their personal dedication to legal justice—albeit briefly endangered—both Danilov and Pavin admired the man for charting a legal course they were striving to observe themselves.

Before they could begin the following morning's initial interview the blond, stone-faced Renko insisted, for the first time ever, on the installation in the interview room of recording equipment, upon which he immediately challenged William Cowley's presence. And just as quickly—upon Danilov's assertion that the joint investigation had been accepted by both Russian and American governments—established his intention formally to have a pretrial ruling of inadmissibility upon any part of the interrogation involving a foreign national with no legal authority or jurisdiction within the Russian Federation. Throughout the exchanges Igor Orlov maintained the perpetual smirk of his previous night's arrest, overtheatrically lounging in his chair, arms folded, sometimes gazing at the ceiling.

Having apparently satisfied himself with the interview arrangements, Renko said: "Upon what alleged charge or charges is my client being held?"

"Involvement in organized crime," tested Danilov. He felt hollowed out, knowing before he started that he was going to lose.

"There is no such offense in the Russian criminal code," countered Renko, at once.

"Murder," stated Yuri Pavin. "Bribery and corruption of a serving officer in the headquarters of the Moscow Militia."

"Specifically," demanded the man, impatiently, as if he were already late for another appointment.

Instead of speaking—because he didn't want to—Danilov pushed across to the lawyer the list of accusations that had been put to Orlov within an hour of his arrest and to which he had declined any response, apart from demanding his right to appoint Renko as his defender.

Renko's response was to behave as if Danilov, Cowley, and Pavin were not in the room. He read and reread every word on the charge sheets before going through them for the third time with Orlov at his elbow, muttering replies to equally muttered questions.

Prompted, Danilov said, "The accused and his lawyer are engaged in discussion unable to be registered, as insisted upon by that lawyer, Gennardi Renko, which it is the prosecution's wish be placed on official record."

Renko ignored the intervention, continuing, inaudibly, to mumble through the charge sheets. Finally he said, "These are the questions put to my client, Igor Gavrilovich Orlov, after his arrest last night?"

"Yes," said Danilov, aware he was being made to perform like one of the dancing dogs at the Moscow State Circus.

"To which he said what?"

"Nothing, apart from asking that you be contacted."

"What time was this?"

"One-thirty-five."

"Precisely?"

"Precisely."

"I was not contacted from these headquarters until six-thirty this morning."

How many more misjudgments were there to be laid at his door, wondered Danilov. "One-thirty-five was thought inappropriately early."

"By whom?"

"Me."

To the recording machine, the lawyer said: "Dimitri Ivanovich Danilov?"

"Yes," confirmed Danilov.

"Denying Igor Gavrilovich Orlov legal representation throughout the night?"

"Igor Gavrilovich Orlov was denied nothing!" retorted Danilov. "He was not interrogated without legal representation, which is the official requirement under the newly introduced Criminal Procedure Code of the Russian Federation, clause two, subparagraph one."

"Having requested legal representation, that legal representation shall be immediately provided and available, clause three, subparagraph one," quoted back Renko. "I officially reserve the right to lodge a protest at the denial at a later stage and date, if indeed that becomes necessary."

"Noted," acknowledged Danilov, tightly. "We now seek, under the code, an official response to the accusations."

Orlov's smirk widened into a fuller smile as Renko said, "Complete and total denial. I intend to take out, on behalf of my client, a writ of habeas corpus ad subjiciendum as provided for under clause five, sub-paragraph four, of the Criminal Procedure Code. I shall also consider a separate writ for wrongful arrest."

In the never-before-mourned old days of the Communist interpretation of justice, he could have secretly recorded the earlier private, hour-long cell meeting between Orlov and his lawyer to learn the basis for this belligerence, Danilov thought, nostalgically. Wearily, he said, "Can we proceed with this interview."

"Most definitely not!" exclaimed Renko. "You have, through me and on record, my client's response to the accusations laid against him. That is all he is legally required to provide, and all he chooses to provide, prior to a habeas corpus examination before a judge. There is no legal requirement for him to answer any questions or make any statement. This interview is terminated"—he made a show of examining his watch—"at ten-thirty-two. We'll meet again in court."

No one spoke until the three of them regained Danilov's Petrovka office. The moment they did, Cowley exploded, "That was fucking unbelievable! He made *us* the accused!"

"Everything's covered by the code," accepted the more controlled Yuri Pavin. "For more than seventy years, under the Communist regime, the legal system could be bent whichever way suited the government or the prosecution, usually both: retrials, show trials, whatever was needed to get whatever predetermined verdict was necessary. It still applies, in some regions of the Federation. But it won't be here, not with this case. This is going to be Gennardi Renko's international stage, and he knows it."

"And why he's taken the case," accepted Cowley. "He's all set to become the international defense lawyer of this or any year, and even he doesn't fully realize it yet."

"It'll be difficult to resist a habeas corpus application," predicted Danilov, once again almost in conversation with himself. "It wasn't supposed to get this far."

"But it has," said Cowley, continuing the cynicism. "And I don't even want to guess how much farther it's going to go."

Dimitri Danilov's summons to the federal prosecutor's office came an hour later.

"They're detention charges," insisted Danilov. "Subservient to Berlin."

"They're not, not unless I have supportive, sworn evidence of every accusation," disputed the federal prosecutor. His name was Boris Fedorovich Ivanov. He was a spare, almost skeletal figure, a man who had so far successfully bridged the old and new ways of Russian justice but was uncomfortable with the international attention.

"We've got producible evidence of the bribery and corruption of Sergeant Aleksandr Ognev, a Petrovka officer, supported by a scientifically established voiceprint referring to a Colonel Alexei Kosov, who was murdered along with his wife in a car-bomb explosion. That is the first charge against Orlov."

"I've read the files," said Ivanov, impatiently, anticipating the defense. "Is Kosov specifically named? According to the file—which doesn't legally apply to the atrocity but is part of the Berlin inquiry— the reference is to a given name and patronym which Kosov could have shared with a hundred, a thousand, other men!"

"Just the given name and the patronym," conceded Danilov. How could he have failed Larissa so miserably?

"Ognev's under arrest?"

"Yes."

"Has there been an admission? A sworn statement?"

"No."

"What's the evidence?"

"Intercepted telephone conversations," conceded Danilov. Anticipating the rejection he added, "Given names and patronyms again."

"What about corroborative evidence of the other accusations?" said Ivanov.

"We don't have it," admitted Danilov.

"What do you mean, you don't have it!"

"The files have been tampered with, the proof removed," said Danilov, despising himself for the oiled evasion, although until comparatively recently it was an explanation with which the man would have been familiar and untroubled.

"I authorized the arrest warrants on the basis of what you presented as supportive evidence!" protested Ivanov.

Another performer with a self-chosen role upon the international stage, acknowledged Danilov. "I was not aware until I got back from Berlin of the interference with the records. Neither was my deputy."

Ivanov stared down unseeingly at the fabricated paperwork before him on the desk. Abruptly he said, "What's the progress in Berlin?"

"Otto Müller was assassinated, sometime during the evening or night."

"So you're going backward?"

"They've identified the explosive."

"Which proves what?" demanded Ivanov.

"Nothing," said Danilov.

"But we're sure Orlov was there?"

"There's positive identification."

"And of Campinali?"

"Yes."

"Luckily the habeas corpus application will be a private hearing," said the lawyer. "I don't want to be humiliated."

"None of us do," said Danilov. "What's Savin like?" Viktor Aleksandrovich Savin was the judge who'd agreed to hear the release-from-custody appeal.

Ivanov made a to-and-fro, rocking motion of uncertainty with his hand. "Old-time traditionalist."

"Renko won't like that."

"I do," said the federal prosecutor. "It's to our advantage to have someone who knows the way of things. I'm hoping he won't reject us, not at least on the first application."

"Yes," accepted Danilov. A judge who had administered Russian law by its previously understood but unwritten code would be far more sympathetic than a younger one influenced by the legal reforms. Danilov was surprised at the indication that the federal prosecutor still intended personally to contest the application instead of assigning a subordinate to argue it.

"I want an American lawyer with me at the hearing," demanded Ivanov. "It's admissible, as an observer."

"I'm sure the Americans will agree: they want to be involved. But Renko challenged Cowley's presence at this morning's interview. He's guaranteed to object to an American lawyer being in court."

"Let him," said Ivanov, dismissively. He tapped the charge sheets. "Any possibility of recovering what's missing?"

Danilov hesitated at the old ways of referring to falsifying material to support the accusations. Replying by implication, he said, "Not sufficient to be unchallenged by Renko."

"No," accepted Ivanov, at once. "Everything depends on Berlin. If there isn't something from there—and quickly—Orlov's going to walk free and we're all going to end up looking fools." He hesitated, looking down at his notes. "And if Orlov walks, you've got to release Alexandr Ognev."

"No!" protested Danilov. "Renko isn't representing him!"

"He might, on a combined charge. I'm not taking that risk."

Would he be able to kill Igor Orlov if there was a second chance, Danilov asked himself yet again, wishing he could answer his own question.

"Al Fieldgate's OK. One of ours," guaranteed Sam Campinali. That day he'd gratefully trusted the driver's guidance that he didn't need to prostrate himself in the smoke-glassed escape car beneath the skyscraper office block. His evasion of the oppressive FBI surveillance went as smoothly as before. And, as before, Joe Tinelli had been watching golf when Campinali arrived at the penthouse on Monroe Drive.

"Who's Fieldgate responsible to?"

"The DeCavalcante family."

"Has it been made clear to him there can't be any fuckups?"

"Absolutely."

"Why the fuck did this Yasev guy go solo in the beginning?"

"Arrogant," said Campinali. "All these Russian guys are arrogant, too used to there being no law in their own country."

"Good you gave Yasev the number, as a precaution. He say anything he shouldn't have done before Fieldgate got to him?"

"Not according to Al. Some bullshit about casually getting my name and approaching me for help about a restaurant lease. Weak as cat's piss but not a problem, He's buttoned now."

"Any chance of getting to him in jail? Removing the uncertainty?"

"We're trying, obviously. But the Bureau isn't taking chances. We're being told he's got personal prison guards, around the clock. None of them ours."

"Make it a good contract. I want him whacked."

"It's a quarter mill."

"Go higher, if necessary," ordered Tinelli. "I don't like not knowing about Moscow, either."

"Orlov will be OK."

"It all settles down, we need to talk to him. Set some guidelines we all follow."

Campinali nodded. "The word from Italy is that there's a lot of unrest but nothing positive to put against Brigoli."

Tinelli remained silent for several moments, watching a putt for a birdie on his mute television screen. Nodding toward it, the wizened man said, "Guy's good." Then: "We cut Brigoli out, whatever happens. Just us and Russia. We decide to include Italy, we do it after we're established."

"Brigoli could resent that," warned Campinali.

"I resent his sending a kid to do a man's job. It didn't show proper respect. You tell the Genovese to prepare a contract?"

Campinali recognized that in his own mind Tinelli had already decreed himself architect of the combined association and elected himself its *capo di tutti i capi*. "The day you ordered it."

"Issue it," instructed Tinelli. "If Italy comes in at all, it'll be on our terms, knowing who's in charge from the beginning."

Once again Sam Campinali felt a sweep of unease at the readiness—and the way—that Tinelli chose to remove what he considered weaknesses or obstacles.

Boris Fedorovich Renko set out from the start to dominate the court, objecting to the presence of U.S. embassy legal attaché Allan Plowright as an observer and, when that was overruled by the judge, protesting the presence in the court of William Cowley. When Viktor Savin rejected that submission, Renko openly attempted to intimidate the white-haired, physically ill judge by insisting upon being recorded his objection in law to both refusal for production at any subsequent appeal or legal challenge. He prodded an increasingly frustrated and exposed Dimitri Danilov through each of the specified murder charges, leaving all four threadbare and holed. It was an act of obvious desperation—once more against renewed but unsuccessful protests from Renko—for Federal Prosecutor Ivanov to call a well-briefed Allan Plowright to testify to an American legal request for Igor Orlov to be held in connection with an ongoing murder investigation in Berlin, under the terms of an extradition treaty between Russia and the United States.

Renko held the American legal attaché in the witness box longer than he had Danilov, questioning him just as relentlessly, eventually extracting the disclosure of positive, witness-supported proof of Orlov being in the German capital at the same time as a known American organized-crime figure.

At that disclosure Renko suddenly ceased his questioning, although finally getting from the judge the concession to renew it after successfully arguing that the habeas corpus hearing be postponed to the following day to give him the opportunity to be properly briefed upon further accusations against his clients about which he'd had no prior warning and for which it had obviously been impossible for him to prepare.

"I also reserve the right to call witnesses of my own," concluded the lawyer.

"Witnesses to what!" demanded the federal prosecutor, in their after-court review.

"It's another trick," anticipated Danilov, his conversation with Horst Mann in Berlin fresh in his mind. "Orlov thinks he can make us look stupid again."

"So far he's doing a hell of a good job," accepted Cowley.

33

There were audible sounds of surprise at the entry into the closed court of the couple Gennardi Renko called as witnesses.

"So this is the trick," said Cowley. It came out as a groan, although in despair rather than at the hangover pain banded around his head. He didn't regret the binge. Maybe this would justify another.

"Bastard!" Danilov hissed back, as the man affirmed his intention to tell the truth. Renko's smile was as triumphant as Orlov's as he rose, pointedly surveying where the prosecution was grouped before going back to the man. "Please give the court your full name."

"Ivan Gavrilovich Orlov."

"Your profession?"

"I am a doctor."

"At the Burdenko Hospital?"

"Yes."

"What's your relationship to Igor Gavrilovich Orlov?"

"He is my brother." He did not look at his sibling.

"Your twin brother?"

"Yes."

"Your *identical* twin?"

"Yes."

"Where were you on the tenth, eleventh, and twelfth of this month?"

"Berlin."

"On vacation?"

"Yes."

"With your wife?"

"Yes."

"Was your identical twin brother with you?"

"No."

"Where did you and your wife stay?"

"The Kempinski."

"For how long?"

"A week."

"Did you see your identical twin brother at any time during that week?"

"No."

"Did you tell your identical twin brother that you were going to Berlin on vacation?"

"No."

"So he would not have known you were there?"

There was an almost imperceptible hesitation. "I don't think so."

"You've been extremely helpful," said the lawyer, briskly. "Please remain in the box."

But to the surprise of both Danilov and Cowley the federal prosecutor declined any cross-examination. He didn't question Irena, either, when she corroborated her husband's statement and identified herself as the person who told her brother-in-law of the German trip. Neither did Ivanov challenge Renko's claim that he had clearly established a case of mistaken identity, further to support which he had legally sworn affidavits from four Swiss real estate agents with whom Igor Orlov had discussed chalet purchasing during the time the prosecution were claiming he was in Berlin. Neither did the prosecutor present a counterargument to Renko's insistence that there were no grounds whatsoever to associate his client with any ongoing investigation, either in Moscow or Berlin. His only intervention came when Renko was demanding Orlov's immediate release on bail on a charge-by-charge denial. On the accusation of the car-bomb murder of Colonel Yevgennie Andreevich Kosov and his wife, Ivanov argued the linking allegation of corruption against Alexandr Mikhailovich Ognev clearly established a case for Orlov to answer, but he was outargued—as he'd feared during his precourt meeting with Danilov—that the given and patronymic names were insufficient proof that Kosov was the person referred to. Renko also insisted he was disputing the voice print upon which the corruption charge was laid to be that of Igor Orlov. The judge ruled on Orlov's immediate release without bothering with any adjournment to consider the supposed written evidence.

"There's something wrong with that alibi," protested Danilov, the moment they got into the federal prosecutor's anteroom. "It might have come out if you'd cross-examined the brother."

"The only thing to come out would have been how much invention had gone into the charges," rejected Ivanov. "I had nothing to argue with and you know it. Just as you know, because I warned you, that I was going to limit how foolish I was being made to look. Apart from the corruption—and that's flimsy without a confession from Ognev, which we don't have—you don't have any cases to take to trial. You tricked me, Dimitri Ivanovich. I'm going to lodge an official protest with the Justice Ministry and recommend that without further evidence—further *corroborated* evidence—none of these charges be proceeded with." He jerked his head back in the direction of the courtroom. "The bail's renewable in a fortnight. That's your maximum: how long you've got to produce something I'm prepared to take before a judge and a jury. And release Ognev, who's clearly more frightened of Orlov than he is of any authority in Petrovka." He turned to Cowley. "I want you to tell Washington everything I've told you. My ministry will obviously be in contact with yours. It was from them that the pressure came to issue the arrest warrants."

"Covering his back every which way," complained Danilov, on their way back to the American embassy.

"And exposing ours," said Cowley. He'd definitely have a few drinks later tonight.

"The wife, Irena," said Pavin. "She was in the restaurant when we arrested Orlov. I remember her."

"She admitted in court telling him of the Berlin trip," reminded Cowley.

"Like Dimitri, I've got a feeling about the alibi," said Pavin. "When we get to the embassy, I'd like to talk to the agent you had inside, before we went in."

"Let's all talk to him," said Danilov, who respected his deputy's instinct.

They hadn't spoken on their way back from court, but as soon as they got into their apartment, Ivan Orlov said, "It was all a charade, to protect him!"

"You weren't asked to lie. Your precious integrity is safe."

"I won't go into court for him again!" insisted the man.

"Independence at last," mocked the woman. "You won't be asked. You served your purpose."

"Why!"

"You know why. He got the people who killed and mutilated Georgi. We had a debt."

"Georgi died because of him!" said the father. "You know that!"

"It's over," dismissed Irena.

"I didn't realize you despised me so much."

"Now you're no longer in any doubt."

"What else do you do for him?" blurted the man.

Irena smiled. "Anything he asks. And he asks me to do a lot."

"Whore!"

"Something else you're not in any doubt about."

"Why stay?"

"I don't intend to, not any longer."

"You going to him?"

"Of course."

"You disgust me."

"It's a mutual feeling."

"Tell him what I said, about not going into court for him again."

"If it's necessary, you'll do what you're told. You always do. And always will, Ivan Gavrilovich."

"Go away. Please just go away."

Luigi Brigoli didn't headquarter himself in a backroom of red-checked table-clothed restaurants, which he despised American family heads for doing, as if performing to some Hollywood soap opera script. He always alternated the guarded villas to which he summoned the family-ruling dons for commission meetings, but he did have a careful selection of favorite eating places, always in Rome, at which he hosted individual encounters with chosen family individuals, protectively never identifying the location until the day of the meeting.

The luncheon choice that day was a newly discovered and preferred trattoria close to the Sisto Bridge with a terraced view of the

Tiber. The reservation included three adjoining tables to accommodate not only his own bodyguards but those of Don Silvio Caselli, who headed the most powerful of the three families in the Italian capital and who had been Brigoli's proposer in his successful election to *capo di tutti i capi* eight years earlier.

As cautious as he now felt it necessary to be, Brigoli had his own guards around the restaurant before the reservation was made, to ensure no sudden, suspicious arrival of more people than should have been there to protect Don Caselli.

Caselli was one of the new-style mafiosi whom Brigoli wanted and encouraged, like Paolo, a university graduate who, with an economics degree, had established five successful—and legitimate—operating companies to front the traditional family businesses. He was younger than Brigoli by twenty years, a discreetly suited and barbered man who greeted Brigoli with the fitting deference although obviously not in public with the kiss of respect.

Over pasta and veal and Chianti they talked of the ruling Italian Mafia commission's opposition to the worldwide linkup and the Berlin bombing, Caselli insisting that he had heard no rumors to suggest the mass killing had been instigated from Italy as a challenge to Brigoli's leadership. Caselli's convincing argument was that no Italian don had known the precise location or date of the intended formation meeting, and so could not have carried out such an ambush. Caselli suggested that in the all-too-bright international light cast by the Berlin killings another commission summit be convened to discuss their further involvement. At the previous convention he had voted in favor of the amalgamation, but now he was doubtful.

"There's too much attention, political as well as criminal."

"I intend to organize the meeting," promised Brigoli. "And this time to recommend our staying out."

"Soon," urged Caselli.

"Next week," promised Brigoli. "Certainly the week after, if that's too soon."

"You're the *capo di tutti i capi*," reminded Caselli. "People come when you tell them to, whether it's convenient for them or not."

"Next week," said Brigoli, irritated at himself for what would appear weakness in the other man's eyes.

Brigoli's arrival route had been through the old town, which decreed it be changed for his return to Ostia. His car, with its front and back escort vehicles, swung immediately across the Sisto Bridge, clotted with the customary Rome traffic. At the river-bordering junction with the Lungotevere della Farnesina there was a truck-breakdown gridlock, to make the assassination easy. Luigi Brigoli's car was sprayed from the front as well as from both sides by Uzi submachine-gun fire—as were the escort vehicles—and grenades were tossed in through the shattered windows to ensure no one survived. Two passing pedestrians died.

There was a similar vehicle-obstructing ambush where the private road from Brigoli's villa on the outskirts of Ostia joined the main Via del Mare highway an hour later, when the panic-alerted cavalcade of Paolo Brigoli descended in an identifying plume of dust on their way to the assassination scene. Brigoli's guards realized the danger too late, needing to slow to turn on the single-lane strip, which was sufficient for the two cars to be riddled with submachine-gun fire before, again, being grenaded.

"How friendly?" demanded Cowley of the FBI agent who had been in the Brooklyn Bite on the night of the raid.

"Hand-in-the-lap friendly," said the man.

"More than sister-in-law to brother-in-law?"

"I'd like my sister-in-law to be that friendly if she didn't weigh 250 pounds and suffer from halitosis."

At that moment Irena was photographed by the FBI surveillance team entering Orlov's Varvarka mansion through the second property on Rybnyj Lane. She was carrying a suitcase.

34

The tension in the Varvarka lounge was palpable. Igor Orlov was sprawled in an easy chair, momentarily ignored celebratory glass in hand. Feliks Zhikin was standing, but awkwardly, as if as a punishment, which in fact was the intended humiliation.

Irena said, "I did what you told me always to do, called Feliks Romanovich. Not here direct."

"It's not your fault," said Orlov. Dismissively, he waved both toward chairs.

Zhikin nodded toward the suitcase, forlornly sitting near the door, and said, "You didn't tell me you'd left Ivan."

"We made an arrangement," said Irena, talking to Orlov.

"Not for you to come this quickly. They're still watching the house, could have identified you. You've compromised yourself—compromised me!—if you and Ivan are recalled to another hearing." The lawyer had talked about it being a possibility, although he'd thought the stronger likelihood was the abandonment of the prosecution after the courtroom humiliation.

"I'm sorry . . . I didn't think."

"Ivan knows you're coming here?"

Irena nodded, deciding not to tell Orlov of her husband's weak threat not to testify again. He *would* do what he was told; he always did.

"What did he say?"

"Told me to get out."

Which was what Orlov planned to tell her, although not yet, not while he might still have a need for her. He should talk everything through with Gennardi Renko.

Defensively, Zhikin said: "She came in through the other house. We haven't spotted any surveillance there."

"It still shouldn't have happened." The fault *was* Irena's, for not telling Feliks Romanovich she'd walked out on Ivan.

"What do you want me to do?" asked Irena meekly.

Until the lawyer told him Irena wasn't any longer necessary she had to go on believing he'd eventually take her in, acknowledged Orlov. "You'll have to go to a hotel. Maybe to the dacha later."

"By myself!" protested the woman.

"You shouldn't have told Ivan! Or walked out without talking to me first!"

Irena bit her lips tightly together for several moments before saying: "You are going to let me stay when it's all settled, aren't you?"

Shit! thought Orlov. "We made a deal, right?"

"I meant what I said, about not being jealous . . . not complaining about anybody else?"

The pleading irritated Orlov: everything about her irritated him. "We'll sort it all out in good time. It'll be good. For the moment we've got to put this right. We'll have a few drinks, something to eat, while Feliks Romanovich arranges a hotel . . . the Metropole. You'd like the Metropole, wouldn't you?"

"No one can get close to you at the dacha, can they? We could be together at the dacha."

"I can't leave Moscow, not with everything that's going on. Surely you understand that!"

"I suppose so."

"Talk things through with Feliks Romanovich in future, OK? I don't want any more mistakes like this."

"I'm sorry if I've fucked things up."

You certainly will be if you have, thought Orlov. "Everything's going to be fine. Trust me."

Her problem was that she didn't trust him, Irena realized. There was another quick realization. It didn't matter. She knew too much for Igor Gavrilovich Orlov to dump her. He could fuck as many other woman as he like, but she would still be the queen.

The director ordered Jimmy Pearce's dogleg journey from Chicago for the New York bail hearing of Veniamin Yasev, insisting upon a personal overnight review from the most hands-on agent readily available in an investigation leaking into the sands of too many faraway international deserts. In any other circumstance Pearce would have regarded his passing through heaven-annexed portals to the seventh floor of the J. Edgar Hoover Building as the career opportunity of a lifetime. But Pearce did know the vanishing circumstances—enough of them, at least—cynically to accept that there was little that was going to endear him to the politically endangered Leonard Ross. And that he, like so many others, was going to be associated with failure in the former judge's mind. And not just in the director's mind. In that of Henry Warren, the House Speaker, as well.

It was Pearce's first personal encounter with the director, and the Chicago agent-in-charge was genuinely shocked by Ross's haystack dishevelment, worsened by the visible mental distraction evident from the first question.

Which was: "What do you think?"

"About what, sir?"

"You've picked up on the Brigoli assassinations?"

"Yes."

"Car bombing again. Orlov's style."

"They were shot first, finished off by grenades, according to the reports I've heard. I don't see the pattern."

"Orlov's walked. The lead from Moscow is that we need better evidence. Which they don't have. That puts you top of the list, with Yasev."

Pearce shifted in his chair, discomfited. "Yasev's gone into a legal shell. What he said before he got a lawyer doesn't amount to a hill of beans. Wendall Correy, our counsel, is going to oppose the bail application, as a matter of principle, but we're going to lose. Because we chose to go public with Yasev's arrest, to spook Campinali, the hearing's going to *be* public. Counsel's frightened, as I am, what Al Fieldgate is going to let out. He's a mob lawyer, by the way. Yasev knew to call him the moment he claimed his rights."

"How, for Christ's sake!"

Pearce shrugged. "Fieldgate's closed him down for any more interviews. We can't ask him. Not that he'd tell us anyway."

"Campinali?"

This time Pearce spread his hands in helplessness. "I'm using every agent in the Chicago field office, plus eight more seconded from here. Campinali goes every day to his office, never close to Joe Tinelli, at Evanston. From there he vanishes. We're following every car, van, and delivery truck from his house and from the office building and failed to pick him up. We try phony client contact calls; a spokesperson promises to call us back. And always does, offering to put us through to Campinali. We've accepted, five times. Five times he's apologized for not being able to take the case through pressure of prior business. He's jerking us off, enjoying himself. And Correy has forbidden us doing it any more. Says it amounts to entrapment: harassment certainly."

"It does," ruled Ross, professionally. "And you're not making me feel comfortable."

"I'm not comfortable myself. As far as I can see, we've only got one shot."

"What?" demanded the director, eagerly.

"Offer Yasev witness protection, a whole new identity, location and pension deal, in return for full cooperation."

"Do it!" said Leonard Ross at once. "Offer Fieldgate the complete package. He's client-bound to pass it on to Yasev. Good thinking, Jimmy! Damned good thinking!"

"Only if Fieldgate *does* pass it on. *And* Yasev catches the ball."

"It's the first positive idea I've heard for days. Do it."

Maybe it hadn't been such a bad personal encounter after all, thought Pearce.

The FBI tail was too quick picking up the hotel courtesy car as it emerged from the basement parking lot of the Balbo building.

The driver said, "Company."

Campinali swiveled in his seat. "You sure?"

"FBI trademark Ford. Took off—in too much of a hurry—right behind me. I can see the observer on the cell phone now. It's not a problem."

"How do we shake them?" demanded Campinali.

"We don't," said the driver. "You can't have been seen. The windows are too dark. The phone call will be to check the license, which will show the hotel ownership. We don't make the usual detour, just enough to make sure."

"Then what?"

"We go on to the hotel. We got the hideaway there, so it doesn't matter if they follow us into the garage there. They hang around, I simply make a lot of journeys for them to waste their time on."

The confirming detour was two blocks off what would have been the direct and obvious route to Monroe Drive, to a gas station. Before he pulled up in front of the pumps, the driver suggested Campinali go down on the floor. "The windshield's clear. They could see in from the front. And they're parking where they could do that."

Campinali didn't feel any of his initial self-consciousness lowering himself between the seats. The driver's performance was that of the professional chauffeur, checking the oil after filling up with fuel. As he eased out into the traffic, he said, "It's all right to get up now."

Campinali said, "You've done this before"

The driver said, "You got your job, I got mine."

The concealing inner door of the hotel basement lot was closing behind them before the following FBI car got down the ramp.

Campinali said, "You do yours very well."

For the first time Joe Tinelli wasn't watching golf on television. Instead he was tuned to CNN, with film coverage and commentary on the assassination of Luigi Brigoli and his son. Tinelli said, "It was a good hit."

"Silvio Caselli is going for the leadership. You want any indication relayed?"

Tinelli shook his head. "Let it stay internal. Let them sort themselves out. What's Fieldgate saying?"

"He's confident he'll get Yasev bail."

"We ready?"

"All set up."

"It'll leave us without an easy link to Orlov."

"Zhikin, the guy I dealt with in Berlin, called me on one of the unlisted office numbers I gave him. The Russian police fucked up big time. The charges against Orlov don't stand up."

"It safe to deal like that, direct on the telephone?"

"He thinks so. He's got a place in the country nobody knows about, he says. It's clean at my end. It's swept daily."

"It would keep things simple. I'd like that."

"You and I are going to have to talk on one of the numbers, too. We had a Bureau tail today. We can't use any traceable hotel vehicles again for a while."

The American Boss of Bosses nodded. "Afterward, tell Zhikin we're sorry about Yasev. Tell him it was for the best."

"He'll understand. The Bureau pressure might get heavier for me, after Yasev."

"I guess," accepted Tinelli. "But without him what can the Bureau do?"

"Nothing," accepted Campinali.

"The German hit was good. We'll use that guy again."

"With us keeping in touch on one of the safe phones, I'm going to move around more openly. Identify and record the surveillance. Then claim harassment."

"It'll piss them off, but there's nothing to lose, I guess," said Tinelli.

"Only for them," said Campinali. "And they must be getting used to that by now."

John Melton at once recognized the head-bowed, suitcase-carrying woman the Rybnyj Lane surveillance picture showed entering the mansion through the secondary entrance. The photograph of her emerging, two hours later, was even clearer. This time the suitcase was being carried by a man whom Melton, whose job as incident room supervisor was to maintain the photographic evidence collection, was sure he also recognized.

It took him two hours to isolate the matching image of one of the unidentified men on two of the enhanced stills lifted from the CCTV cameras at Berlin's Kempinski Hotel at the same time as Samuel Campinali.

35

"Absolutely no doubt whatsoever," agreed William Cowley, comparing that evening's photograph to the hotel CCTV shot already mounted on the foamboard.

"A positive connection between someone in Orlov's organization, Berlin, and the consigliere of America's boss of bosses!" enumerated Danilov, at Cowley's shoulder. He and Cowley had been in the Savoy bar less than an hour before Melton's excited recall to the embassy, only enough time for Cowley to have two scotches. Danilov had stayed with one, his mind locked on the thought—and his doubt—of trying once more to kill Orlov. Now that wasn't a pressing decision.

"So who is he?" wondered Melton. "He doesn't show on any of the photographs taken at the restaurant arrest."

"Important, to have been in Berlin," suggested Danilov. "Same level as Sam Campinali perhaps?"

"Orlov's consigliere?" said Cowley. "The two of them setting up the formation meeting for their respective *capo di tutti i capi?*"

"It's the most obvious interpretation," agreed Melton. "Doesn't give us the bosses, does it? These guys are replaceable."

"Depends on how they feel about being sacrificed," argued Cowley.

"We've got Ognev in custody," reminded Melton. "He'll know who this guy is."

"No!" said Danilov at once. "I don't know how much longer Ognev will be in custody after today. If he gets bail, he'll warn Orlov and whoever this man is."

Cowley gestured toward that night's print. "Was there a tail?"

Melton nodded. "Irena booked into the Metropole by herself. The guy went back to Orlov's place, again through the back way."

"They still there?" asked Cowley.

"Haven't heard different," said the Moscow agent-in-charge. "I've called in backup, ready to follow if and when they leave. And when they do, we could simply lift the guy."

"No," refused Danilov again. "This *is* a breakthrough. And this time it's got to be one hundred percent tight. No loopholes for Gennardi Renko to guide them through. At the moment there's not enough to pick him up *for*."

"What's the other story here, Irena going to her brother-in-law with a packed suitcase? And then, by the look of it, being turned away?" invited Cowley.

"Cuckolded husband?" offered Melton. "They were hugger-mugger in the restaurant, remember?

"The prosecutor could have done a hell of a lot more about that alibi if we'd had this in court," said Danilov.

"If he'd wanted to," said Melton, cynically.

"I'll take it to him tomorrow," said Danilov. "Maybe he'll change his mind about withdrawing the charges."

"Not on this alone," disputed Cowley. "So Irena's fucking her brother-in-law. Happens all the time. You start questioning her about that, you blow the only piece of linking Berlin evidence we've got. Sure, Irena's important, but for later, not now. Like you said, Dimitri, now we've got it, we can't risk losing it." It *was* the only worthwhile evidence, and Cowley was exhilarated by it, glad he'd only had two drinks and now not wanting any more.

"While we're talking about what we should and shouldn't do, let's be careful with the surveillance on Mr. Mystery Man," said Danilov. "Let's not make the mistake we did with Orlov, get spotted, and be given another runaround."

Both Americans took it as the objective remark it was, without offense. Cowley said, "There's another long shot way we might get an identification. We know the guy didn't stay at the Kempinski. So where did he stay? We give Horst Mann the photograph overnight, he could start the Berlin hotel checks all over again. We get lucky, he might have used his own name."

"We get even luckier, the other hotel might have CCTV of him with Campinali and whoever the Italians had there," said Melton. "Wouldn't that be a bag of squirrels?"

"We're running too fast," Danilov cautioned. "Of course, Horst has to be told, with everything done as you suggest. But here's where the man is whom we now know to have been in Berlin with Campinali. Here's where the name is, on some property register or in a telephone book."

"And then maybe in some criminal record file," said Melton.

That, too, was an objective, not a snide remark, but Danilov said, "I don't think our luck's going to hold that much. Let's just hope for an address from which we can work."

Cowley said, "Let's not forget Irena arrived and left with her suitcase, the possibly rejected lady. We need to know all the time what she does and where she goes. We got enough people for all we've now got to do?"

"I think so," said Melton. "Depends how long it takes."

"Shout early if we need more," said Cowley.

"You going to tell Washington?" asked Danilov.

The big, big question, Cowley acknowledged. After a moment's reflection he shook his head. "Nothing to tell them that makes any sense at the moment."

So engrossed were they that all three jumped when the telephone rang. While Melton was listening, the second light on his console lit up, and he switched between the two calls before ending both. He said, "They're on the move. Orlov from the front of the mansion, surrounded by his guys. Our man from the second house, by himself."

"For Christ's sake, let's not lose him," muttered Cowley.

It was Igor Orlov's decision to reestablish direct contact with America, which Zhikin seized on to justify his driving from the center of Moscow to the guaranteed security of his Zagorsk dacha, an excuse he'd been seeking to speak without the risk of official interception—or Orlov's suspicion—to Campinali about so much more than Orlov's release from custody. Zhikin felt endangered by too many things. Irena's misunderstood arrival had ignited Orlov's initial anger, which had worsened with his having to tell Orlov after taking her to the hotel that Stefan Cherny still hadn't been located. Orlov's fury had swiftly swung to a paranoiac conviction that Cherny, having guessed he was at risk, had sought protection from either the Militia or the FSB, the successor to the KGB for which he'd once worked. In hindsight, it had been a rare mistake to argue against Orlov that Cherny would never do either, but the vein-pumping, manic apoplexy the opposition caused convinced Zhikin that despite the so far protective family connection he risked elimination, as dismissively as anyone else who offended Orlov. Before setting out from the city that night, he'd actually had one of the Rybnyj Lane house guards start his car and bring it to him, while he tensed behind a protective wall for a possible explosion.

As he turned off the main highway into the forest in which his dacha was hidden, Zhikin confronted another fear, the most important—and potentially fatal—of all. How could he, over a telephone link of thousands of miles, communicate without actually saying it was his now determined intention to overthrow Igor Gavrilovich Orlov as *capo di tutti i capi* while continuing with the conglomerate negotiations? Accorded a place at the top table alongside Joseph Tinelli and whoever succeeded Luigi Brigoli, there would be no cause nor need for the bloodletting with which Orlov had ascended his slippery, gore-splattered throne.

Zhikin was prepared for a delay, not knowing, in fact, if the connection would work at all, which was a further uncertainty, but he recognized the voice the moment Campinali answered, as Campinali recognized his without the need for identification.

"I was about to try to reach you," said Campinali. "There's a lot to talk about."

"Almost too much, without meeting personally."

"That wouldn't be practical for me, at the moment," said Campinali. "Later, certainly."

"Why?" demanded Zhikin, immediately alert but at the same time thinking Campinali's response was the sort he'd hoped to hear. He listened, his mind jumping, to Campinali's terse account of his FBI arrest after the Berlin hotel identification and of his being associated with Veniamin Yasev by the Kennedy Airport picture.

"I'd given Yasev a lawyer's name, if anything ever went wrong. He thought at first he could handle it by himself," continued Campinali.

"What did he tell them!"

"Nothing that mattered, fortunately, not before he got the legal protection. But we decided he was a weakness that had to be rectified."

"Has it been?"

"Today, as he left court."

"How?" Please, not another bombing, Zhikin thought.

"Shot, on the steps. Long-range sniper. The guy was good."

"That going to create more difficulties for you?" How could he use what he was being told for what he wanted to achieve? Wondered Zhikin.

"At the moment Yasev was shot in Manhattan, I was under FBI surveillance lunching in an open-air cafe overlooking the lake," replied Campinali. There was a pause. "It had to be done."

"Of course."

"I hope Igor Gavrilovich will be as understanding."

"I'm sure he will be," said Zhikin, seeing his opening. "This will work well in the future, between the two of us. We can put someone else into Brighton Beach to maintain the money laundering, but I don't think we need an intermediary any more. It was, as you say, a weakness." He hesitated, momentarily unsure whether to continue. Then he said, "Maybe it was a mistake from the beginning."

Now the pause was from Chicago. Then Campinali said, "It's resolved now. What's happened at your end?"

Zhikin had his recital prepared and delivered it inserting what he judged to be just the right amount of dubious inferences. "I wondered, even, if Mr. Tinelli would want to continue after so much publicity, particularly in your country. And after what's happened to you."

I wondered, noted Campinali. Not Igor Gavrilovich wondered. "Perhaps it would have been better had there been more discretion." He offered a lure.

A dangerous jump, but it allowed him room to step back, decided Zhikin. "There was no way it could have been anticipated, but too many Americans were killed in Berlin. Too many people altogether."

"Luigi Brigoli is no longer a factor," reminded Campinali.

So they believed the Italian was responsible for the massacre, acknowledged Zhikin. He needed time to work out how that could be used to his advantage. "I wasn't aware how uncertain the situation was in Italy."

I again, isolated Campinali. "None of us were."

"Have you heard who the successor will be?"

"Not yet," Campinali lied.

"It's a complication, having to begin all over again with Italy."

"Maybe, initially, Italy shouldn't be included, not until things have settled down there."

The most important remark of the conversation so far, identified Zhikin. Joe Tinelli—the Americans—already saw themselves dominating the amalgamation. Zhikin decided he would be quite comfortable with that. "I think that's probably wise."

"Will Igor Gavrilovich?" asked the American.

Something else he had to think through to find all the personal advantages, Zhikin acknowledged. "I'll point out the benefits to him."

"That would be good," said Campinali, who decided he was learning far more from this conversation than he'd expected. "What about the case against Igor Gavrilovich?"

"It's too obviously a setup. The lawyer doubts it will ever get to court."

"So Igor Gavrilovich was right," suggested Campinali, setting a fresh snare. "He is above and beyond the law—untouchable?"

Zhikin at once recognized the invitation, worried and pleased in equal measure. He was damned by whichever answer he gave. "I hope what's happened now doesn't lead to overconfidence," was the best he could manage.

"*Is* overconfidence a risk?" persisted Campinali.

Zhikin realized he was inexorably being drawn into a commitment. "It might be."

"That should be guarded against."

Zhikin saw that he'd gone far enough, maybe even too far. "It could result in problems."

"There are too many already."

"I agree." Your commitment, Zhikin determined. He wasn't going to edge his toe one inch farther across the demarcation line of personal survival until he got a firmer response from America.

Campinali said, "We need to establish a more positive communications channel between us two."

"Me to you," chose Zhikin, at once. "We know Igor Gavrilovich is under concentrated electronic and visual surveillance. It'll increase, after the court fiasco. It's best I decide the safest times, from the safest place this end."

"When things quiet down, I think it's essential we meet again."

It had all gone his way, Zhikin decided. "I think so, too. There are a lot of things best talked about face to face. Not like this."

"Mr. Tinelli wants his best regards passed on to Igor Gavrilovich."

"And Igor Gavrilovich's, to Mr. Tinelli."

"Take care."

"That's essential," agreed Zhikin. "Taking care."

"You sure?" demanded Tinelli.

"As sure as I can be, without personally meeting him and getting the definitive approach," said Campinali. He preferred their talking this way, by telephone, he able to look out over the sail-speckled lake instead of crouched on the dusty floor of a street-dodging hotel limousine.

"Interesting," allowed Tinelli. "What do you think of him?"

Campinali could hear the muttered golf commentary in the background at the other end. "Good."

"Good enough to be a successor?"

"Possibly," said the lawyer, always unwilling to offer a positive assessment that could later be thrown back at him.

"It would make it easier for me," said Tinelli.

"That's the way I am thinking."

"Encourage him," ordered Tinelli. "It would be a useful possibility for us to have available."

"I've already prepared the ground," said Campinali.

"Was it your idea to whack Fieldgate as well as Yasev?"

"It cleans everything up."

"Good thinking," praised Tinelli. "What about the Bureau?"

"They bring me in about Yasev or Fieldgate, we're ready to file for harassment. They got nothing, and they know it if their counsel have got half a brain between them."

"I'd like to get them off our backs," said Tinelli. "Get back to something like normal. All this is wasting time."

"It'll take time, with so much political attention. We've just got to be patient." Out on the lake a small-boat sailor who hadn't been patient tacked too sharply, shipped water, and began to wallow. Campinali, who wasn't a superstitious person, thought that anyone who was, would have regarded that as a bad omen.

"They're actually making the accusation that it's like Chicago in the twenties," complained Leonard Ross. "Warren's threatening to convene a special Intelligence Committee hearing!"

"You bringing Campinali in again?" questioned Cowley.

"No point," dismissed Ross. "He's got a five-man FBI stakeout as an alibi for where he was in Chicago when the assassinations took place! We couldn't prove in a million years that he had anything to do with them; perhaps he didn't. It could have been ordered by Tinelli or a hundred other people, without Campinali knowing, although I doubt it." There was a snorted laugh over the line from Washington. "You know the irony? Yasev was offered witness protection that would have kept him alive. He turned it down!"

"What about something in Fieldgate's records?"

"Nothing," said the director. "If we're going to get out of this mess, something's got to come from you."

If Ross had known, he would have been gambling with his career by holding back, Cowley accepted. But there *wasn't* enough to talk about at that moment. "It's not looking good."

"Nothing's looking good," moaned the director.

The forest-sheltered, two-car FBI surveillance teams had only taken over from the all-night squad an hour before Zhikin left the Zagorsk dacha, his departure timed to miss the Moscow morning rush hour. Observers in both vehicles, alternating positions in pursuit in order to avoid being detected, maintained a continuous radio commentary of their descent into the city, so that two more vehicles, with a third in reserve, were in position to take over the moment they reached the built-up suburbs.

An unaware Zhikin drove directly to his house at Ulitza Kuznechij 36. By midday Yuri Pavin had located the name Feliks Romanovich Zhikin in the central Moscow city directory.

It was around midday that the secretarial aide from the Burdenko Hospital arrived at the apartment of Dr. Ivan Grigorovich Orlov.

36

Several more pieces were found for the empty mosaic in that short time, while others didn't fit or initially went unrecognized. Provided overnight with the photograph of the then unidentified Feliks Zhikin, an equally pressured Horst Mann committed all the officers under his command—and seconded in another twenty—to check every hotel in Berlin, from five-star to doss-house, and before noon had a positive identification from the Grand Hotel on the Friedrichstrasse, on the former eastern side of the Wall. Zhikin's cover name there had been Vaslav Settin, not Antipov. The recorded address was central Prague, close to the Charles Bridge. It was basic police procedure to check the name against every recovered item and document from the office of the assassinated Otto Müller, which threw up diary appointment entries over three days prior to the Potsdamer Platz massacre for a Vaslav Settin. Against the name, on the second entry, was additionally scribbled Wannsee. The receptionist at Müller's offices, as well as his personal secretary, provided sworn affidavits that the photograph was that of a man they'd known as Vaslav Settin, with whom their murdered employer believed he had concluded the best deal of his life and later became famous for being the only person to have confronted international terrorists and gangsters and briefly survived.

In Moscow the federal prosecutor at first refused Danilov's request for a personal interview, only agreeing when Danilov exaggerated the important new evidence. But Boris Ivanov's reaction was almost immediately as Cowley predicted, that the identification of Zhikin in Berlin had no bearing upon the existing charges against Orlov.

"Nor is it sufficient to charge Orlov additionally in connection with the Berlin bombing, which in any case is not within Russian jurisdiction," ruled Ivanov. "What can you bring before a court? That Zhikin was in Berlin at the same time as a known American gangster associate. And that Zhikin is an associate of a suspected—but unproven and unconvicted—gang leader here in Moscow. Corroboration to go with other evidence, perhaps. By itself, proof of nothing. I personally don't doubt their involvement in the Berlin outrage and in some international crime gathering, Dimitri Ivanovich. But I'm not being asked to prosecute that, because I can't. Nor could any other prosecutor, without more."

"The woman," argued Danilov. "The photograph surely shows collusion. Isn't it sufficient to recall her and her husband for questioning?"

"They're defense witnesses, not mine. I could only recall them with Gennardi Renko's consent. Which he might even give, to ridicule us further. Why shouldn't a sister-in-law visit her brother-in-law? Bring a suitcase to stay for a few days? Again, I don't doubt it's far from innocent. But again, it's proof of nothing."

"They could break, under cross-examination," said Danilov.

"I told you after the hearing, I'm not going to be made to look a bigger fool than you've already made me appear." Ivanov paused. Then, heavily, he added, "I'm not sure you can risk much more, either."

"I don't understand?" frowned Danilov.

"Renko has filed an official complaint with the Justice Ministry. The claim is that at the moment of arrest you came close to shooting Igor Orlov. That others had to intervene to prevent it."

"That's nonsense," refused Danilov. "I was prepared for resistance. We all were. If I'd wanted to shoot him, I could have done it."

"It's an official complaint you'll be called upon to answer," insisted Ivanov. "Renko is also threatening a suit for wrongful arrest and has separately filed for the return of the fingerprints and the DNA samples taken immediately after his arrest. Part of that complaint alleges technical physical assault in the obtaining of hair for DNA comparison. They're out to bury you, Dimitri Ivanovich."

"It certainly looks like it." Did the warning indicate that Ivanov wasn't going to make his threatened official complaint?

"Is there something personal between you and Orlov?" abruptly demanded the lawyer.

"No."

"Be careful, Dimitri Ivanovich," warned the prosecutor. "You created a mess. Don't make it any messier."

"I don't—" started Danilov, but was stopped by the telephone.

It was a brief call. As Ivanov replaced the receiver, he said: "I certainly can't question Ivan Grigorovich Orlov any further. He's dead."

Ivan Orlov had fallen sideways from his desk chair, but surprisingly the needle hadn't broken, so the hypodermic was still embedded in his left forearm, although little of the cylinder appeared to have been injected. There were five empty morphine ampoules strewn across the disordered desk, alongside the official witness summons for the habeas corpus hearing that had prompted the Militia call to the federal prosecutor.

The medical examiner said: "He didn't need the last injection. He collapsed before he could administer it. He'd already had enough to kill an elephant."

"No doubt that it's suicide. There's a note," said the uniformed Militia sergeant who led the response unit after the panicked alert of the Burdenko Hospital secretary. Deferring to authority, he offered the single sheet of paper to Danilov. The handwriting was uneven and haphazard, misspelled words uncorrected, a disjointed listing of thoughts rather than a composed letter.

"*Irena a whore,*" Danilov read aloud. "*In it together with the bastard. Mad man. Berlin a trick. Laughing at me. Always laughing. Georgi violated and killed, because of him. Boasting the sacrifice revenge. Won't be tricked, to save him. Laughed at. Let him rot. Irena rot. Whore. Boasted knowing. Whore . . .*" Danilov looked up. "And it's not signed."

Cowley said, "Boasted about knowing what?"

"A question to ask her," said Danilov. He'd driven direct from the prosecutor's office to the Orlov apartment, collecting Cowley from the embassy on the way, giving them time to talk.

"Maybe it should be me who asks her," said Cowley, Danilov's account of his confrontation with the state lawyer and Renko's legal moves in the forefront of his mind.

Danilov shook his head. "I'm not being frightened off. I've nothing to be frightened *about*. It's gamesmanship. Which we shouldn't ignore. Why does Renko feel the need to cover everything, as he's doing?" They were talking in English, to prevent the conversation being understood by anyone else in the room.

"You told me why! Because he's a good lawyer who *does* cover everything."

There was another head shake. "Renko's uncomfortable, defending a cunt like Orlov: he knows he's made an integrity error in the eyes of the new judiciary."

Cowley shrugged. "It's academic. He's filed the complaint, you've got to respond to it, you're distracted, diverted."

"That's the point I'm making! Renko went for the justice-for-all shit—and the money, I guess—but now regrets it. He's arguing against it coming to court as much for his own reputation as he is to get the charges against Orlov dismissed, before they can ever be determined in court."

"You're snatching for straws, and I don't see any," rejected Cowley.

Danilov straightened from the shoulder-slouch into which he'd descended. "Ivan Gavrilovich Orlov was a material witness, and he has died in suspicious circumstances. I've got every legal justification to search this apartment thoroughly. You want to help me?"

It was midafternoon before Zhikin left his Ulitza Kuzneckij house, the unsuspected, rotating surveillance tight behind him. By then they'd had scanners in position for three hours but picked up no mobile telephone traffic. They didn't themselves risk any transmission when they handed him over, silently, to the team in place at the secondary entrance to the Varvarka mansion.

Igor Orlov was waiting inside, familiarly impatient, which Zhikin hoped he would be and why he had delayed his arrival until the afternoon. Orlov said at once, "Where the hell have you been?"

"I slept at the dacha. Didn't come down until this morning."

"Why not?"

"Took me a long time. Turned four o'clock, I guess, before I got hold of Campinali," said Zhikin, everything prepared. There hadn't been an indication to sit, so he accepted he was yet again being childishly rebuked.

"What's he say?" demanded Orlov.

Zhikin didn't hurry. Instead he sat, uninvited, and took his time recalling his conversation with Tinelli's consigliere, trying to see a discernible reaction on Orlov's unmoving face. It was several moments before Orlov spoke, after Zhikin finished.

Then he said, "Veniamin Kirilovich Yasev was ours. I should have been consulted first."

"The Americans thought it was necessary."

"I should have been consulted," repeated Orlov, his voice rising.

"They hoped you wouldn't be offended."

"I am! It was my decision, not theirs."

"They want to go ahead with the association," said Zhikin.

"Why shouldn't they?"

"Campinali has been identified as having been in Berlin. He'd been brought in for questioning by the FBI."

"Your mistake!" accused Orlov, at once, his need to avoid responsibility greater than any concern about possible harm to their linkup between their two organizations.

"There was CCTV at the Kempinski. He flew into Frankfurt under his own name. It *wasn't* my mistake." He hesitated, uncertain how to return the accusation. "We haven't sufficiently anticipated the depth of the investigation."

"You were responsible for the Berlin organization. You should have known the hotel had security cameras!"

He should, reluctantly conceded Zhikin. "Campinali says it's not a problem, not now Veniamin Kirilovich isn't any longer a risk."

Orlov sat regarding him for several moments, unspeaking. "What else?"

"The Americans have made a proposal," exaggerated Zhikin.

"What?"

"That with Veniamin Kirilovich gone, the liaison from now on should be direct, between Campinali and me. We keep the Odessa just for laundering."

Orlov suppressed the fury, although with difficulty, managing even to smile in anticipation of the punishment he would personally exact. This stupid, overambitious man had just signed his own agonizing death warrant. Without Yasev, without an established and accepted channel of communication, there was, frustratingly, nothing that he could do. But the moment it was set up, Zhikin became disposable. He didn't need a consigliere. Others might, but not him, not Igor

Gavrilovich Orlov. Who was, after all, the only person he could truly trust. "I need to meet personally again with Tinelli."

"That's not a good idea, not this soon. Campinali says there's too much FBI attention to them at the moment. That you should wait. And be careful. I should go first, to set everything up. Make sure it's safe."

Now the pigfucker was actually telling him what he could and could not do! Imagining he was being clever. He'd make him beg forgiveness when the time came: plead and scream and be denied. Make a spectacle, as a warning to others made to watch. "That sounds like a good idea."

"Irena's called me twice. Wants to know when she can come. What shall I tell her."

"That she can come when I tell her, not before."

"When will that be?"

"It won't. She's a problem that'll have to be solved the moment the court thing's settled."

John Melton looked up curiously as Yuri Pavin's shuffled into the embassy incident room and said: "They've already gone to the hotel. I'm joining them as soon as I've annotated Ivan Orlov's suicide. You coming?"

"I don't think so," said the huge man, lowering himself uncomfortably on a chair that was too small for him.

"What?" asked the FBI station chief, concentrating fully upon the Russian.

Pavin stared at the photographs that now occupied virtually all of one wall, the evidence folders on tables beneath them. "It's here somewhere. I don't know what it is, but somewhere here there's something we've missed or haven't realized."

"What are you going to do?"

"Start again from the very beginning."

37

Feliks Romanovich Zhikin was a day-into-night, night-into-day person, as they all were, so he came out of a deep, alcohol-blurred unawareness of the bedside telephone just after ten, a time he could rarely remember ever consciously being a part of in the morning, although he supposed he must have been, at least for school, which he could scarcely remember either. He had no recollection at all—not even of her name or what they had or had not done sexually—of the naked, large breasted woman snuffling even more deeply asleep beside him. He managed "Yes?" into the receiver and at once began to drift back into a welcome unconsciousness, only fleetingly—at first not hearing—the shouted insistences from the other end. But the occasional word penetrated and connected with another and at last, still befogged, he said, "Who? What?" and had more unthreaded words strewn at him before there was anything like comprehension.

"Irena?" he groped.

"Wake up!"

"I'm awake."

"Listen to me!"

"I'm listening."

"Ivan's dead."

Zhikin awoke fully. "How?"

"Killed himself. Morphine. I need help. I need Igor."

"Where are you?" Zhikin swung himself onto the edge of the bed, his back to whoever it was he'd unknowingly and unpleasurably spent the night with, his concentration entirely upon what he was being disjointedly told, anxious to isolate any personal advantages and pitfalls.

"I didn't know where to go from the apartment. The hotel. That's where I am now, at the hotel. There's a lot to sort out . . . Stupid bastard, that's what he always was, a stupid bastard . . . shouldn't have done this . . . doesn't make sense . . ."

"I'm coming . . . just stay there . . . don't do anything until I get there." He elbowed the woman behind him, to rouse her. "Don't talk to anyone. Have you talked to anyone?"

"There was a Militia guard, at the apartment. Wouldn't let me in to get more of my stuff. That's what I went there for, to get more of my stuff."

"Do the Militia know where you are?" Zhikin cut her off.

"I told them the hotel. I didn't know what to do."

"I'm coming," repeated Zhikin. "Just stay there . . . Wait for me. Don't say anything to anyone if anyone gets there before me . . . wants to talk to you."

"What shall I say, if anyone does come . . . the Militia . . ."

"You're a witness in a court case. You can't speak to anyone without your lawyer, not about anything. You understand? You don't speak to anyone apart from me without your lawyer being there."

"Ivan committed suicide. That's what the Militia officer said. I didn't know . . . wasn't there . . . you know I wasn't there."

"I know you weren't there. That you know nothing about it," said Zhikin. "But they'll twist things. That's why you've got to say nothing until I get there. OK?"

"OK. Tell Igor. I want Igor to know."

"I will," lied Zhikin.

"What is it?" groaned the woman behind him. She broke wind.

"Nothing," said Zhikin. "Get out." He took another fifty dollars from the bundle on his bedside table, deciding she was an amateur for not staying sober enough during the night to wake up and rob him while he drunkenly slept. Which, he accepted, made him an even greater amateur. "Take this."

"You want to see me again?"

"I want you to go. I got business. I'll see you again. Now get out." Zhikin was already moving toward the bathroom, the money now safely in his hand.

"You were terrific," she called after him. "The best ever."

Zhikin closed the bathroom door without replying.

The telephone exchange was picked up—and simultaneously relayed to the U.S. embassy incident room—from the cell phone scanners now permanently positioned around Zhikin's house on Ulitza Kuzneckij.

It had been Danilov's idea to post a uniformed guard on the dead Ivan Orlov's apartment, briefed about what to ask and say, because they could not have approached the woman at the known Metropole Hotel without disclosing that she was under surveillance. At the end of the relayed recording Danilov said, "Not as good as I'd hoped."

"It'll get better," predicted Cowley. "He's going to her. And we can listen to everything they say."

It had only taken the waiting FBI team thirty minutes to bug Irena Orlov's hotel room and telephone while she'd fruitlessly gone to and from her apartment that morning.

"You've got to remember what the Militia man said," encouraged Zhikin. He was sitting on the edge of the bed, leaning toward her on the only easy chair in the hotel room.

Irena shrugged. "Just that Ivan was dead. That he'd killed himself but that I couldn't go in because there was an investigation that needed the place to be sealed."

"What sort of investigation?" seized Zhikin at once.

There was another shrug. "Into Ivan killing himself, I suppose. He said it was morphine. The guard, I mean. That's what he said. They'd found morphine and things."

"What things!"

"He didn't say."

"Was there anything to find in the apartment?"

"I don't understand," she protested.

"Anything from Berlin?"

"Brochures, maybe. I don't know."

"What did you tell Ivan about going to Berlin?"

"Just that I had tickets. Wanted to go there. He always did what I wanted."

"Did you tell him Igor Gavrilovich gave you the tickets? Paid for everything?"

Irena laughed. "He wouldn't have gone if I had. Would have known it was for something. I know Igor Gavrilovich was there in Berlin. And why we were there."

Zhikin hesitated. "Did you tell Ivan that, when you had the fight?"

"I can't remember. I may have. I guessed he was there when I heard what happened. Then he told me, at the dacha. That he'd killed all those people. That's why Ivan had to be there, in case Igor was seen. So Ivan could say what he had to say in court."

How could he use this woman to undermine Orlov without any risk to himself? "It would have been better for it not to have happened."

"Igor Gavrilovich has got away with it, though, hasn't he? We're going to be all right. Have you told him about Ivan?"

"I wanted to talk to you first."

"Now you have. Can we go now?"

"Ivan killing himself complicates things. That's what the investigation will be about. Igor Gavrilovich will be questioned again. Maybe by the Americans. You can't be with him when they do."

"I don't want to stay in this shitty hotel any longer!"

"You're going to have to, until we see what happens."

"He is going to take me in, isn't he?" demanded Irena, the doubt surfacing.

"Maybe," said Zhikin, carefully choosing the word.

"Maybe!"

"A lot's changed since he asked you to go to Berlin with Ivan."

"Not for me it hasn't. And Ivan being dead makes everything easier. You tell him that!"

Zhikin decided her total amorality made her the perfect partner for Orlov. She'd had every justification—every reason—for revenge but he was sure Irena had enjoyed the slaughter of those responsible for her son's defilement and death. "That's something you should talk to him about yourself."

"You're frightened of him!" she accused.

Zhikin thought he saw an avenue. "Igor Gavrilovich is not a man to be confronted."

"I'm not frightened of him!" lied Irena, the bravado too obvious.

"Perhaps you should be."

The remark quieted her. "He's not going to take me in, is he?" Her voice was thick with final acceptance.

"That's something else you should talk to him about yourself."

"I know what the answer will be. Help me, Feliks Romanovich! Please help me."

Begging humility didn't suit her. Zhikin said, "I don't know what I can do."

"Tell him how much he needs me!"

"I have to warn him about what's happened," said Zhikin evasively. "You're sure Ivan had nothing in the apartment?"

"There was nothing he could have had to make things difficult for Igor Gavrilovich. You going to him now?"

"Yes."

"Take me with you!"

"I've already told you why I can't."

"I want to see him. Talk to him like you said."

"I'll tell him." Had he sown enough distrust in her mind? wondered Zhikin. And how, now, could he use it?

"It's still not enough." Cowley didn't think he could withhold any longer from the director what was happening but wasn't yet sure how he could introduce it without Leonard Ross knowing he'd been cut out of the loop.

"It's enough to take on Igor Orlov and his smart-assed lawyer better than we were able to do before," refused Danilov, in return.

"Which still *isn't* enough," said Cowley. "I already told you, I'm not blowing this chance. Which is probably the last one we'll get. We've got to have him bagged and trussed, no way out, no miracle escape. And that we don't have."

Yuri Pavin caught the end of the exchange as he came into the incident room. He said, "What don't we have?"

"Sufficient cause—evidence—to rearrest Orlov. We've got a whole bunch of clincher stuff but no smoking gun," replied Cowley, immediately regretting the analogy.

"I have," announced Pavin, quietly. "And it's not a smoking gun. It's a knife."

38

Yuri Pavin was carrying in a glassine evidence bag the odd round-tipped knife they'd recovered from Vitali Mittel's apartment. He held it up in front of them in the overcrowded incident room and said, "Not all the blood was used, for analyses: you can still see some of it on the strange blade. We've already identified it as that of Nikita Yavlovich Volodkin, the gang leader who was mutilated and thrown into the Moskva strapped to a cross."

"Sacrificial revenge!" quoted Danilov, understanding.

Pavin nodded, smiling. "Ivan Gavrilovich Orlov's suicide note. I remembered the way they were all killed, in whatever that turf war was about. And the knife and the fingerprints we thought to be those of Mittel but couldn't verify because the hands were too badly burned. And then I thought of checking the handle again, against the prints we took of Igor Orlov after arresting him. There *are* some we can't match. But three we can, that haven't been obliterated by whoever held it subsequently. They're definitely Orlov's, forefinger and the two adjoining. As they naturally would be as he held the knife to use it."

"We've got him!" said Cowley, almost disbelievingly. "Not for the Berlin bombing, not yet. But we've got him on a positive, evidence-supported holding charge for as long as it takes us to submit the recordings for legal rulings on admissibility . . ."

"And to sweat Orlov and Zhikin and Irena, play one off against the other to see which way and how fast the rats run," finished Danilov.

"But let's be careful," warned Cowley, his earlier caution taking over from the euphoria. "Wouldn't it be wise to check it out with the federal prosecutor *before* we pick up Orlov again? Be sure of official legal backing in advance?"

"He can't refuse this!" insisted Danilov.

"Let's make sure," urged Cowley. "I need to talk a lot through with Washington anyway. I think with proof of Zhikin being in Berlin with

Campinali, we're back on track for a RICO indictment. But I need guidance."

"You're right," conceded Danilov. "Let's make sure."

"Maybe tell Horst Mann. Bring him in even," suggested Pavin, putting the protectively enclosed knife down on the desk.

Cowley said: "That needs to go into a safe. We lose that, we lose everything."

Zhikin's impression was of someone coming to a red-faced, over-heated boil, which was apposite, because when he'd finished telling Orlov of his twin brother's suicide, Orlov almost literally exploded. "The cunt! The total, absolute cunt! He was born a cunt and died a cunt!"

Which is what his judgment is of me, too, thought Zhikin. It was still too early—too fatally dangerous—openly to commit himself. He said, "I don't like the apartment being closed off, not to the wife herself. Or that she hasn't been asked—or hadn't been, until an hour ago—to identify the body as her husband's."

"So what?" Orlov said dismissively. "What I need to know is what the cunt might have left, to be discovered." He was out of his chair, striding jerkily around the Ulitza Varvarka drawing room, momentarily uncaring of his concern being obvious to Zhikin.

"He didn't know anything—have anything—to leave," tempted Zhikin. "At least Irena doesn't think he had."

"*Think!*" Orlov continued to erupt. "Doesn't she fucking well know!"

"It's a complication," said Zhikin, enjoying how easy it was totally to unsettle the other man.

"What do you mean!" Orlov came back to where he had been sitting when Zhikin entered the room.

"She wants to be with you. She told me to tell you. And we can't do anything to remove her as a problem now."

"Why can't we!"

"With her husband dead, our not knowing what might have been recovered from the apartment! Think about it, Igor Gavrilovich."

Orlov slumped down, opposite his consigliere. "He didn't *know* anything, not until he was summoned to court. So there was nothing for him *to* leave." He appeared unaware that he was virtually repeating what he'd been told only minutes before.

"I don't know," said Zhikin. Could this be it? Could there be something here through which—by which—he could make his move against Orlov?

"What?"

Zhikin shrugged. "That's what I mean: I *don't* know. There might have been something we can't guess at. Don't know about."

"What does the bitch say?"

"She doesn't know either. Can't guess. She wants to talk to you."

"Fuck her!"

"If Ivan Gavrilovich had anything—left anything—she'll be the person to know, as next of kin. She's got to be kept sweet, until we know."

He was doing it again: doing it all the time. Telling him what he could and couldn't do. Orlov was overwhelmed by a burning, dizzying frustration. "Maybe the dacha."

"Shall I tell her that?"

"What happens now, the procedure?"

Zhikin shrugged his shoulders, uncertainly. "She'll have to identify the body formally, I suppose."

"Tell her to go along with whatever she's asked to do. To find out anything the cunt might have done. Left behind. When there's something to tell me, we'll go up to the dacha." Orlov slumped farther, head on his chest, looking into his lap. "I want her dead."

"She can't be, not yet."

Maybe you dead first, thought Orlov, looking up at the other man. He'd do it himself, like he always did things himself. Knew it was done properly when he did it himself. Only person he could properly trust, himself. Long time since he'd rafted someone down the river, spread-eagled on a cross. That was the way Feliks Romanovich Zhikin had to go, a disposable, unnecessary person. It would act as a warning to Irena against her doing anything stupid, imagining she could make any demands, until it was time to get rid of her, too. "Tell her what I want . . . what she has to do . . . and about going to the dacha . . .

promise her the dacha . . . but I don't want her at the restaurant, here, until she's got something I want to hear."

"I'll tell her."

"Not like that . . . Make it sound—"

"I'll tell her what she wants to hear," assured Zhikin. But not what Orlov imagined, he thought.

"You're right. It's a complication I didn't need. It was all going well, until now."

"It'll all come good," said Zhikin, a promise to himself.

It won't for you, you overconfident little shit, thought Orlov.

It had been Horst Mann's spur-of-the-moment decision to come immediately to Moscow, encouraged by what he'd further discovered, and by the time he arrived Yuri Pavin had completed the inquiry the German had initiated during their earlier conversation. By then, too, Danilov had returned to the American embassy from his second encounter with Boris Ivanov, and Cowley had spoken personally to the FBI director in Washington, as well as faxing to Leonard Ross all the newly emerging evidence. Everyone was happy.

The German progress was to find from a Czech airline passenger manifest that a Vaslav Settin had flown out of Berlin to Prague six hours after the Potsdamer Platz killings. Working from that earlier relayed information Yuri Pavin had located a Moscow-bound Aeroflot flight within two hours of the Czech arrival. The Russian flight manifest listed a Feliks Romanovich Zhikin as a passenger.

"It's getting better by the minute," said Cowley. "Ross is submitting what I've already given him, before this, for counsel's opinion, but he thinks there's enough to bring Campinali in again and to get a conspiracy indictment against Zhikin. All we need is evidence of Zhikin being part of a criminal organization, which we'll have with proof of his contact with Orlov if Orlov's successfully charged with the gang killing."

"Which Ivanov says he can be," said Danilov. "And Irena isn't out of bounds any more. We don't need to go through the lawyer to talk to her about her husband's suicide." He turned to Melton, the fifth man in the room. "Do we still know where they are?"

"Zhikin's actually with Irena now, according to surveillance. I haven't replayed the tape yet," said the American. "He's been shuttling between her and Orlov all day. And Orlov's at Ulitza Varvarka."

"Let's round them up, hear what they've got to say," suggested Danilov.

39

There was a perceptible hesitation in the seizure planning, understood only by William Cowley and Yuri Pavin, who had caused it when Danilov insisted he lead the squad to rearrest Igor Gavrilovich Orlov. Cowley openly argued the need to be with the Russian at such a moment, if they eventually got Orlov before an American court, and Danilov resolved the hiatus by not opposing the demand. There was no opposition, either, to Horst Mann accompanying them. Yuri Pavin provided the legally necessary Russian presence to initially and officially detain Irena Orlov and Feliks Zhikin. Cowley assigned two female FBI agents for Irena's detention.

"She wants to go to the bathroom, to hide or flush something away, someone goes with her to make sure she doesn't," said the American.

Everything was synchronized to a radio-linked time schedule, to prevent any of the three warning the others of the sweep. Further to ensure that legal jurisdiction was complied with, all three Russians were to be taken to the Organized Crime Bureau on Ulitza Petrovka, not to the nonporous American embassy. Irena and Zhikin were to be immediately separated, Irena to be taken first by Pavin formally to identify her dead husband, Zhikin direct to Petrovka by the finally operationally activated, Russian-speaking, and carefully rehearsed John Melton.

They were leading a twelve-man assault team, all American apart from himself, with the six alerted surveillance officers ahead of them. All had been told that, once again, they were commanded by Danilov, the necessarily Russian detective. Danilov said, "It's different this time."

"This time we get it right," agreed Cowley. He spoke his question tersely into the radio and got confirmation from the front and back surveillance groups that Orlov was still in the Ulitza Varvarka mansion. The schedule was that Orlov's arrest triggered that of Irena and Zhikin. If they didn't, for whatever reason, get Orlov, the seizure of the other two was to be temporarily postponed. Danilov's feeling was quite different from the restaurant assault. Then he'd felt oddly surreal, suspended from himself and what he'd intended to do, watching himself in some out-of-body experience. He was anything but out-of-body this time. This time he was aware of everything he had to do, everything he had to achieve to guarantee Igor Gavrilovich Orlov and a too clever by half lawyer didn't defeat him. Which they couldn't, not on the evidence he had now. That Yuri Pavin had assembled now, he corrected himself: assembled by proper detective logic and deduction, not hate-blinded, easily exposed invention. How seriously would he and his career be damaged by the threatened complaints and protests to the Justice Ministry? Not at all if, this second time, everything worked with the intended precision, Danilov decided. Totally, to possible enforced resignation, if it didn't. Just as he accepted that if it didn't, he would have failed Larissa, who hadn't entered his thinking for what seemed a very long time. Now she did, with Danilov's renewed determination not to fail her or her memory. He was lucky, luckier than he deserved to be, to get this second chance.

Beside him Danilov was conscious of Cowley murmuring into his radio and of their turning off the inner ring road on to Ulitza Varvarka. The second car took the turn on to Rybnyj Lane, to reinforce the agents at the rear. Cowley ordered, "Everything sealed, front and back," and then turned away from the radio. "Everyone ready?"

"Ready," assured Danilov. Which he was.

"Let's get on with it," said the German, with nervous impatience.

The formidable-appearing, metaled front door gave way at once to the FBI jackhammer, crashing inward. Danilov and Cowley led, stumbling over it and yelling in Russian, "Militia! Militia!" One of the two guards sitting in the vestibule had the Makarov in his lap and managed two shots before Danilov hit him fully in the chest, killing him instantly and sending him and the chair crashing backward.

"Don't!" Cowley ordered the second man, who didn't, stopping with his hand just inside his jacket.

More men—five or six, Danilov wasn't sure—came running from the back of the house and there was more firing and shouting, and two of the Russians went down, and someone—one of the two FBI agents appeared to be wounded, although only superficially—fell behind, to Danilov's left, crashing into him and sending him sideways into Cowley, who still managed to keep his weapon level on the frozen guard.

There was firing now from the rear of the house, from the squad coming in from Rybnyj Lane, and abruptly the bodyguards who'd run in from the back of the vestibule stopped shooting, realizing they were trapped.

Danilov said, "Let's find him!"

They did, in a side room fitted out as a study. Orlov was crouched in the knee well of a desk, his hands before his face like a child hiding its eyes from something it didn't want to see. Danilov kicked the desk chair aside. Orlov whimpered, "Don't hurt me. Don't hurt me."

Cowley moved to shoulder his way between the two Russians, but Danilov said, "I've got a better idea," and believed he had to achieve everything he wanted.

Into the radio he still carried Cowley said, "Go! Pick up the others."

Feliks Zhikin actually emerged from the Metropole Hotel onto Prospekt Marksa as Pavin and John Melton's FBI group were establishing contact with the already emplaced Bureau surveillance. Pavin saw him before Zhikin realized what was happening and simply put himself in the man's path, blocking him, and announced his arrest.

"This is a mistake," tried Zhikin.

"Not anymore," said Pavin. "We've through making mistakes. Now it's your turn."

"What am I accused of?"

"We're still counting," said Melton. "It'll be quite a list by the time we've finished."

Irena mistook their knock to be Zhikin's return, actually calling out the man's name when she shouted for them to enter her hotel room. She was still sitting in the chair in which he must have left her, stiff-faced, as if tensing herself against some emotion. When Pavin showed her his identification, she said, "About Ivan Gavrilovich?"

"Your husband's death. And other things," said one of the two female agents.

"Why are you here, an American?" asked Irena at once, detecting the accent.

"The other things," replied the second woman.

There was an unheard bugging tape of Irena and Zhikin, Pavin remembered from Melton's remark back at the embassy. They had to hear that before any detailed interrogation. "Let's get through what has to be done about your husband."

"What did he leave in the apartment?" Irena demanded at once.

"All in good time," said Pavin.

"I want to know!"

"There's a lot we all want to know."

Irena shrugged, picking up a discarded jacket as she passed the bed. The more positive reaction came as she emerged from the hotel to see a handcuffed Feliks Zhikin in the back of an FBI car specifically parked for him to be seen. She stopped, abruptly, looking between the car and Pavin.

She said, "What's happened to Igor Gavrilovich?"

"He's in custody, too," said Pavin. The seizure couldn't have worked better to unsettle them, he thought.

"What for?"

"We're not discussing it here, on the sidewalk," said Pavin. "I've already told you, there's a lot we need to talk about later."

The previously unheard tape began with Irena's voice, then the sound of the hotel room door closing. *"What did he say!"*

"He wants to know if Ivan left anything in the apartment before he killed himself," replied Zhikin.

"I meant about us! Him and me!"

"He can't decide anything until he knows."

"We talked about it earlier. Ivan had nothing to leave."

"He might have left something written down."

"What? He didn't know what Igor Gavrilovich did in Berlin."

"He could have guessed, like you did."

"So what? He's dead now. It wouldn't mean anything."

"That's what they're trying to get him for, what happened in Berlin. That's why he has to know. When you find out, he says you could go up to the dacha."

There was a pause on the tape. Then Irena's voice again. *"That's my reward, is it? I'm allowed up to the dacha—allowed to see him—when I find out if he's in any danger from what Ivan might have done or said before he killed himself!"*

"You asked me what he said. I'm telling you."

"He is dumping me, isn't he! The moment the bastard knows he's OK, he's dumping me!"

"Perhaps it won't be like that."

"You know it will, Feliks Romanovich! Don't tell his lies for him."

"Do as he asks, Irena."

"Like you always do."

"For as long as it suits me."

Another pause. Then Irena again. *"What's that mean?"*

"Nothing. It means nothing."

"Is there any proof that he was in Berlin?"

The hesitation was from Zhikin before he said, *"No, of course not. Ivan had to be there in case he was seen, but he wasn't. He was only there a few hours."*

"Tell him I'll do what he wants."

"Good. He'll be pleased."

"As long as everyone pleases Igor Gavrilovich!"

"You'll be able to talk to him, up at the dacha."

"Should I call the Militia about Ivan?"

"Do that. Say you want to get back into the apartment. That you can't understand why it's sealed."

"I'll call you in the usual way."

"I'll be waiting."

John Melton, who'd heard the tape at the U.S. embassy before bringing it to Danilov's Petrovka office, snapped off the replay button and said, "That's it! All of it."

"It's enough," said the German. "More than enough. We've got the bastard."

"She worked hard to keep her promise," said Pavin. "She scarcely looked at her husband, to identify him. Just kept on and on about the apartment and what was in it. Insisted she had a right to know! It was more important to her than realizing she was being arrested when I brought her here."

"I think she's got to be first," decided Danilov.

"And then Zhikin," suggested Cowley. "Let Orlov stew until last."

"He's already doing that," said Danilov, who'd spent the time it had taken Melton to fetch the tape confronting an increasingly subdued Gennardi Renko. "His lawyer told him they couldn't challenge his being kept in custody. Orlov's behind bars and nothing's going to get him out now."

"Only the walk to the death house," said Cowley.

"We don't have the death penalty in Germany," said Horst Mann."

"We do in America," said Cowley.

There was no guarantee that Orlov would be successfully extradited, thought Danilov. And even then, with the American appeals process, an execution could take years.

40

The rats ran in every which way—and back again—in their fervent determination to avoid or evade charges against them, accusations refuted by counteraccusations, denials by counterdenials, lies—some disproved, others not—by lies.

Irena Orlov broke—although with initially imagined cleverness—that first day, after listening stone-faced to the two bugged hotel conversations between herself and Feliks Zikhin and after that being shown her dead husband's suicide note. With the predictable vindictiveness of a woman scorned, she claimed she was unaware, until his admission to her upon their return, why the gang leader paid for her and her husband to holiday in Berlin. Pressed about the suicide note's reference to boasted revenge, she also insisted it was only then that he also told her how he'd avenged the kidnap and killing of her son. Professionally curious at his not picking up earlier on the association with the child murder, Yuri Pavin discovered that the case had been concealed in the Unsolved Crime files by Alexandr Mikhailovich Ognev, who was later rearrested and charged with conspiracy to commit murder.

Often against legal advice, Feliks Zhikin made several conflicting and contradictory statements, in each trying to minimize his importance in the Orlov organization, desperate to avoid any charge that carried the death penalty in Russia. Zhikin's final collapse came when the fingerprints on the Wannsee rental agreement—and some of the payment dollars—were proven to be his. Ironically, and quite inadvertently, Zhikin's twists and turns supported Irena's protests of innocence in the mutilation and slaughter of the Volodkin family hierarchy: to have admitted being in the warehouse and organizing the sacrificial disposal of the bodies would have resulted in just such an indictment. By the time Zhikin's questioning became concentrated upon Berlin, the Russian knew there was no death penalty in Germany but by then, too, Igor Gavrilovich Orlov had invoked the earlier Swiss defense witnesses to his having been chalet buying in Gstaad and accused Zhikin of triggering the Potsdamer Platz bomb. Confronted with that anticipated accusation, Zhikin risked—he hoped minimally—incriminating himself by disclosing the carefully retained electronic detonator that bore Orlov's fingerprints and which had already been identified by German forensic scientists as the type necessary to set off the Berlin explosion. Zhikin denied being present. He only knew afterward, when he was told to dispose of the detonator. He denied knowing or meeting a Sam Campinali. He did not know of any intended Mafia conference. He did not know a Joseph Tinelli. Most definitely he was not the consigliere of the ruling Mafia family in the Russian Federation.

To seal any escape, Boris Ivanov insisted from the first encounter with Irena Orlov that his advising Federation lawyers as well as defense attorneys were present at each prosecution interview, every one of which was, with defense agreement, electronically as well as stenographically recorded, which was a sensible precaution because as well as Zhikin some of the evidence-denying statements were made against individual lawyer's advice, particularly Gennardi Renko's to Igor Gavrilovich Orlov.

The cross-referencing questioning took two weeks, which for Dimitri Danilov, William Cowley, and Horst Mann later seemed to have had no separation between night and day, day and night. As well as there being—by official Russian invitation—consulting American and German lawyers in Moscow, every shred of evidence and confessionally incriminating or denying word was daily transmitted to Washington, D.C., and Berlin for independent legal analysis, assessment, or query.

It was five days into his court-ordered detention that Feliks Zhinin, faced with the CCTV evidence, withdrew his initial denial and admitted to having met Sam Campinali in Berlin and to the presence there at the same time of the later assassinated Paolo Brigoli. That ill-considered admission at last officially brought Italian legal observers into the investigation. And it was enough for Washington lawyers to decide there was sufficient evidence to detain Joseph Tinelli and Sam Campinali under the provisions of the RICO act. Once more it was the House Speaker, George Warren, who grabbed headlines by disclosing the global extent of the conspiracy and connecting it to the murder of his nephew—"a true American hero who died in the service and defense of his country." There were photographs of Tinelli and Campinali in handcuffs. Reluctant to lose the credit to American law enforcement for preventing the creation of an international crime consortium, the Russian federal prosecutor released arrest photographs of Igor Gavrilovich Orlov, Feliks Zhikin, and Irena and in an accompanying statement confirmed the link to the Berlin massacre. Cowley said the renewed media assault must be like the siege of Stalingrad. Danilov thought it was worse.

That exchange came at the end of a frantic fortnight, in the familiar, although latterly little used, bar of the Savoy Hotel. It was the eve of Danilov's departure, with Cowley and Horst Mann and teams of Russian, German, and American lawyers, for a legal conference in Berlin to be attended also by diplomats from the American and Russian embassies, as well as from the German Foreign Ministry.

Cowley, who insisted on being host, raised his glass of Macallan, and said: "We made it, eventually."

"Largely thanks to Yuri Pavin," acknowledged Danilov, gesturing with his own glass toward his towering deputy.

"We all made it," said Pavin, modestly.

"Not quite, not yet," qualified Danilov.

The detective chiefs' combined presence in Berlin was advisory. They were to be instantly available if a query or uncertainty about the investigation arose, but from its commencement—and the unexpectedly vocal participation upon every point by the assembled diplomats—it was obvious that jurisdiction—where the three Russians would face trial—depended as much, if not more, on political pressure as on legal precedent. The charges pending in Moscow were of conspiracy and complicity in the Berlin murders and singly of murder against Igor Orlov for the killing of Nikita Volodkin. Before that first day was over, the Russian delegation signaled its willingness to extradite the three on the greater and more serious conspiracy indictments and leave the Volodkin charge on file, to be brought before a Russian court at an unspecified later date.

It took two more days, sometimes of heated argument and, clearly, intervention by the American State Department in Washington, to reach a satisfactory compromise. The three would be charged under German law with conspiracy in the massacre and arraigned before a Berlin court, the accusations would be registered on the public record and remain outstanding. Based upon a preliminary prosecution outline of the case, the United States—from which the greatest number of victims came—would apply for extradition. As well as murder conspiracy under American law, from Moscow interrogation statements, there would also be indictments under the RICO statute, for which Joseph Tinelli and Sam Campinali would be arraigned.

"Something close to a Solomonic judgment," assessed Cowley. "Everyone gets a court hearing—reassuring the public they're safe in their beds—and if anywhere along the line a prosecution fails, there're backup charges in another country where they can be tried without a defense of double jeopardy. And the damage we've inflicted on the Mafia structure on two, maybe three, continents will take them a long time to recover from. So we're all happy."

"My case file isn't complete," announced Danilov. "Both Orlov and Zhikin eventually named your two guys. I need to put their accusations to Tinelli and Campinali."

"It would need an official Justice Ministry application," said Cowley. "You could fix it."

"We're not giving anyone any chances of a loophole, remember?"

"You're tired."

"Are you surprised, after what you just made me do!"

"I didn't make you do anything," said Pamela Darnley. "You wanted to do all of it!"

Cowley sat with his back supported by the headboard, Pamela nestled in the crook of his arm. "In the end we kept telling each other it seems to have taken forever."

"That's how it seemed here, too." She hesitated, comfortable with their naked bodies interlocked. "It wasn't because of—?"

"No," he denied, stopping her. "All I can ask you to do is believe me. And I do ask you to do just that. There was one bad night, that's all. I could lie to you now, but I'm not going to. That was it. Just one night, and it didn't affect the investigation. It was Dimitri who fucked everything up."

"Because of Larissa?" asked Pamela. When they'd first started living together, Cowley had told her of Danilov's consuming obsession with finding Larissa's killers.

"It was obviously Igor Orlov, but there wasn't proof. Dimitri invented it, went over the top."

"Stupid son of a bitch!"

"He'll be the first to tell you."

"So what's wanting to get statements from Tinelli and Campinali all about?"

"I don't know," conceded Cowley. "He's got the legal right under shared-country legal prosecutions, which this will be. But Tinelli and Campinali are surrounded by lawyers, and unlike what happened in Moscow, they are refusing to say anything about anything."

"So what's Dimitri hope to achieve?"

"I don't know," repeated Cowley. "If I did, I'd try to prevent it, because he's still under investigation in Moscow, although it'll be dismissed—even if it's pursued—after what's happened."

"Could anything go wrong with the prosecution?"

"I'm worried that there's something more I've missed. Or am missing. That's why I'm talking to you about it."

"So we'll keep talking about it."

"We don't have much time. Moscow's request was approved today. He'll be here the day after tomorrow."

Dimitri Danilov brought a bucket and brushes and scourers to the Novodevisky Cemetery and was glad he did, because the fallen leaves had been soaked by rain and the marble surround and headstone were badly stained and needed several washings before he was satisfied.

As usual, unashamedly, he talked to Larissa as he scrubbed and polished. "I'm sorry, darling, but I couldn't pull the trigger when I had the chance. Now I've got another. I won't fail, this time. I promise I won't fail again."

41

The diminutive American *capo di tutti i capi* appeared even more wizened in his outsized pale-blue prison scrubs, although there was a darting intensity in the eyes that followed every word and gesture. By comparison, an hour earlier, Sam Campinali's prison uniform could have been tailored for him. The constantly protesting Walter Sweetman had again represented Campinali, and it was during that seemingly unproductive interview that Cowley, the jurisdiction-required American presence during Dimitri Danilov's questioning, believed he understood why lawyers for both detained Mafia figures had agreed to Russian examination; appeals—based on the bias of pretrial publicity—had been lodged against the refusal of bail and Cowley guessed both legal teams hoped for some inadvertent misstep by Danilov to provide further supportive grounds. Which hadn't come, in Cowley's judgment, during Danilov's first confrontation. That had degenerated into a recital of questions formulated from the already available twist-and-turn statements of Orlov, Zhikin, and Irena, virtually all of which had been legally blocked or guided into banality. Cowley's greater worry remained his suspected hidden reason for Danilov's insistence upon confronting Tinelli and his consigliere.

For the benefit of the inevitable recording apparatus, Jerome Hitchen, Tinelli's trial lawyer, formally identified by name everyone in the prison interview room, concluding that the defense agreement to such officially logged interrogation illustrated his client's eagerness to prove his total innocence of any involvement or knowledge of organized crime activities, either in the United States of America or elsewhere in the world.

"Mr. Tinelli," Danilov began, "do you know a Russian named Igor Gavrilovich Orlov?"

"My client has no knowledge of a man of that name," interjected Hitchen at once.

"Did you not meet Igor Garilovich Orlov on April 19 at your house in the Chicago suburb of Evanston?"

"If my client does not know such a person, there could not have been such a meeting," said the lawyer.

"Igor Gavrilovich Orlov has described in detail the interior of your Evanston mansion. What comment do you have about his being able to do that?"

"My client has no comment upon that."

"There is documented proof of Igor Gavrilovich Orlov arriving at O'Hare Airport on April 19 and of his having stayed at the Hyatt Regency Hotel with two companions."

"My client has no knowledge of airline arrival, departures, or hotel reservations of someone he does not know."

"Igor Gavrilovich Orlov has made a statement claiming that you, Mr. Tinelli, told him you were organizing the killing of Russians in Brighton Beach, Brooklyn, who were affecting your operations there. And named three people who were subsequently murdered."

The recitation was virtually the same as it had been with Campinali, and he'd warned Danilov to expect it before he'd even left

Moscow, Cowley recognized. So why? What? Why was Danilov going through this predictably unproductive charade? And what did he hope to achieve? Was he being overly suspicious? Cowley asked himself. Was the simple, unambiguous answer that Danilov, who'd come whisker-close to destroying his career, was now proving himself the regulation-observing policeman and completing a necessary although meaningless formality by talking—or at least trying to talk—to two men eventually to become codefendants with Russians in a sensational international crime trial? Cowley wanted to think so, but still didn't. Danilov had a secret agenda that Cowley at that moment couldn't recognize.

"The idea of connecting organized crime syndicates in Russia, Italy, and America was yours, wasn't it, Mr. Tinelli?" persisted Danilov.

"My client has already denied such a suggestion and continues to do so," said Hitchen.

"It's what Orlov and Zihkin are going to testify."

Cowley stirred, knowing from his verbatim knowledge of every Russian statement that none contained that specific allegation. And it hadn't been put earlier to Campinali.

"My client is a finance-investing businessman and public benefactor with no knowledge whatsoever of organized crime."

"They're going to testify that they were entrapped and that there is no case for them to answer."

That wasn't any part of the Russian evidence, either, and there was no way Danilov could be aware of any defense intention! So what the . . . ? Cowley didn't complete the self-question, sure he didn't have to. Could it endanger the entire investigation as Pamela had wondered? A possibility that would need a lot of consideration, a lot of discussion. Cowley's knee-jerk assessment was that it *was* a possibility. So Dimitri Danilov wasn't a law-observing, law-abiding policeman who had pulled back from crossing a forbidden line. He was someone prepared to risk too much for personal revenge. Did he love Pamela enough—so completely—to do the same? Another uncertainty Cowley didn't want to answer, because Pamela's violent death was included in the speculation. Professionally, he believed he *could* answer it. Morally, he wasn't sure, but didn't think he could sit in absolute judgment upon the Russian.

There was no substantial deviation from the already assembled evidence in any further questions Danilov posed, although he did reveal that both Orlov and Zhikin insisted the intended Berlin gathering had been initiated by Tinelli, which would in any case become part of the necessarily disclosed-in-advance documentation for the RICO trial.

There was no immediate conversation on their way back from the jail. It was Cowley who broke the silence when he got on to the Interstate. "So you had two chances. Why didn't you press the trigger the second time at the Varvarka mansion?"

"Not brave enough, I guess."

"Or stupid enough. That wouldn't have been the way to avenge Larissa."

"No," said Danilov. But she would be avenged, he knew.

"You satisfied with the interviews?"

"They complete the file," said Danilov, staring fixedly ahead.

"But contribute absolutely nothing, just a bunch of legal refusals."

"It had to be done."

"Did it, Dimitri?" asked Cowley, directly. It was important that the Russian knew he understood.

"Yes."

"I know what you've tried to do—are trying to get done," said Cowley accusingly.

"I was completing the files," Danilov insisted.

"You said enough to Tinelli to guarantee there'll be a prison contract to hit Orlov when he's extradited here for trial."

Danilov said, "Why didn't you object to the interviews, get them stopped?"

"I only guessed back there, an hour ago. And there'll still be testimony from Zhikin, maybe Irena, too, to get a conviction."

"You going to warn people?"

"Aren't you under enough official investigation back home? A case like this, there'll be a twenty-four-hour guard anyway."

"You're not incriminated, not in anything."

"I know that."

"Are you contemptuous of me?"

Cowley drove for several minutes without replying. Then he said,

"We'll be back in Washington in plenty of time for dinner. Pamela's doing pot roast."

"I like pot roast," said Danilov.

"Maybe we can stop for a drink on the way. There's time."

"You think that's a good idea?" asked Danilov, his turn to be direct.

"I was thinking club soda."

"You did pretty well this time."

"Well enough," said Cowley.

"You thought of getting help?" asked Danilov.

"Wouldn't look good on the CV. I'll go on coping."

There was a momentary pause. Then Danilov said, "Thanks."

"I haven't done anything."

"That's what I'm thanking you for." Danilov thought, I've kept my promise, Larissa. He'll die. Not by my hand, but the man who killed you is going to die.